THE
SCORCHING

THE SCORCHING

WILLIAM W. JOHNSTONE
AND J. A. JOHNSTONE

PINNACLE BOOKS
Kensington Publishing Corp.

www.kensingtonbooks.com

ISBN: 978-0-7860-4300-2

First printing: September 2021

10 9 8 7 6 5 4 3 2 1

Printed in the United States of America

Electronic edition:

ISBN: 978-0-7860-4301-9 (e-book)

*This work is dedicated to the real-life heroes
who walk through fire
to serve and protect their communities.
Thank you.*

Tillamook State Forest, Oregon

There was an intruder in the woods, and the gray squirrel had never seen its like. From its lofty perch on a pine branch the little rodent's black, almond-shaped eyes fixed on the strange creature, assessing its potential as an enemy. The squirrel had no way of knowing that the invader was a man . . . the most dangerous predator on earth.

He had walked far, the last mile on a badly twisted ankle. The Jeep Wrangler he'd driven was hidden in ferns off a hiking trail. After today, he would have no further need for it. Around him the forest was silent in the afternoon heat, and dusty shafts of light filtered through the tree canopy as hushed and hallowed as sunbeams through a stained-glass window. In the distance a couple of scrub jays disturbed the peace as they fussed and quarreled in the bushes.

The sweet, acrid stench of gasoline suddenly spiked

into the path of a rising south wind as the man sloshed the gas from a five-gallon plastic can, showering as much of the drought-stricken undergrowth as he could. When that was done, he thumbed a Zippo into flame and set the accelerant alight. The fire took, flared and spread rapidly, burning pine needles, leaves, and grass, gorging on fuel and oxygen. The blaze fed hungrily and with mindless ferocity. Now intensely hot, the flames grew in height, the pines became their food source, and within minutes the entire forest around the man was ablaze.

He screamed in delight. He'd played his part well, and from coast to coast soon all of America would burn to ashes. Only now did the man consider himself a martyr.

The south wind fanned the flames around the man, a roaring, red and yellow wall of fire that closed in on him. With terrible intensity, the heat scorched the skin of his face and hands, he found it hard to breathe, and suddenly he was afraid. The fire burned out his throat and lungs, and he could not even scream.

He had hoped to perish like a martyr, but he died hard, and badly, in terrible pain.

CHAPTER 1

Indian Wells, Oregon

Big Mike Norris's smoke jumper crew parachuted onto the Indian Wells fire zone without a detailed map of the area. But they'd been told a crack crew was already in place, local hotshot firefighters who knew the terrain and probably had the blaze well in hand.

"It will be a piece of cake, Mike," Norris's base manager had told him. "A walk in the piney woods."

But when they landed on a windswept clearing on top of a high bluff, there was no one in sight. After he dropped his chute harness and most of his hundred pounds of gear, Norris looked around, cursed under his breath and then said, "What the hell? Where is everybody?"

His was a short crew, only fifteen members instead of the usual twenty, but this was supposed to be a mop-up. The heavy smell of woodsmoke in the air put the lie to that claim.

Cory Cantwell, the only squad leader present, stepped beside his crew superintendent boss. "They must have seen us make the drop, Mike," he said. "You'd think somebody would stop by and say hi."

"Seems like," Norris said. He looked hard at Cantwell. "How's the shoulder?"

"Bad," the younger man said. "But it will stand up just fine."

"What did the doc say?"

"He told me it's arthritis. I said I was only thirty and how the hell could I have arthritis. He said anybody at any age can have arthritis."

"So what did he give you?"

"Nothing. Told me to quit the weight training. I told him that ain't gonna happen. Maybe I'd get flabby after a while. Well, he shook his head and said that every fire-fighter he ever met wants to be Arnold Schwarzenegger, and that includes the women. Finally, since he knew I was making this jump in an hour, he shot cortisone into the shoulder, though he warned me that since medical school he wasn't very good with a needle."

"And was he?"

"No. He was a butcher with a horse needle. It hurt like hell."

Norris smiled and said, "Come over here. What do you make of this?"

He walked to the edge of the plateau and nodded in the direction of a saddle-backed hill that loomed to one side of the rise, the dark evergreens at its base obscured by a gray haze of smoke.

"We got to get down there, Cory," Norris said. "I have no idea where the hell that other crew is. They ain't fighting fires, that's for damn sure."

Cantwell examined the terrain. A dry, steady wind

blew from the heights of the Cascade Mountains to the desert lowlands below. To the east rose the rocky hills of the high desert, covered with bunch grass and cheatgrass with a few ponderosa pines, that descended to sagebrush-covered flatlands. To the west the foothills of the mountains had a dense cover of Douglas fir.

Just before the team had left base, a Red Flag Watch had been issued, which meant high winds, lightning, and no rain. So far, the smoky fire wasn't crowning, but a sudden gust of wind could whip it into flame.

"Cory, the wind is blowing in the opposite direction from what they told us," Mike said. "They should have dropped us on the flat."

"The fire is in the gulch, so how do we get down there?" Cantwell said.

"I'm not happy being on grass above a fire," Norris said. He removed his scarred white helmet, wiped sweat from his brow with the back of his hand. "We have to get down into the gulch somehow."

"We could call it off, make another jump onto the flat," Cantwell said. He knew Norris would nix that idea, but he felt it was his duty to mention it.

"It's a thought, but it would take too long," Norris said. "The fire could spread a considerable distance by then."

"Then we make our way downhill," Cantwell said.

"Damn, it's going to be rough heading down the slope," Norris said. "Broken leg central, huh?"

"Maybe broken neck central," Cantwell said.

"Yeah, why not look on the bright side?" Norris said. "Mike!"

A young dark-haired man with wide shoulders and earnest brown eyes stood at the edge of the rise and pointed down into the gulch, where smoke curled like a great, gray serpent. "Lookee there. I think I found a game trail."

"Going down?" Norris said.

The young man grinned. "It's going both ways, Mike, up and down."

"Smartass," Norris said. "All right, make like Dan'l Boone and go check it out, Wilson. And be careful."

"Sure thing," Bob Wilson said. He disappeared over the rim of the plateau.

"Good kid that," Norris said. "Needs some weight on him though."

"A few years eating National Wildfire Service grub will bulk him up," Cantwell said.

"Meat loaf."

"Beef stew."

"Plenty of protein."

"And cake and Cool Whip for dessert. Plenty of carbs."

"Sounds good," Norris said. "I'm making myself hungry."

When young Wilson returned five tense minutes later, he stepped beside Norris and said, "It's a game trail all right, probably deer, and I think it goes all the way into the gorge."

"Cory, what do you think?" Norris said. "Should we take a shot at it?"

"Where a deer can go, so we can we," Cantwell answered. "Nothing else is presenting itself, so it's sure worth a try."

Norris nodded. "Right, let's get it done. We got a fire to fight." He looked around, and his gaze fell on a man with a goatee beard and overlong hair. "Connors . . .

you're lookout. Stay here until we're safely down and then follow. Okay?"

The man called Connors nodded. "I got it, boss."

"Mike, do you see that?"

This from Cheryl Anderson, at twenty-one the youngest member of his crew. A tall, pretty girl on her first drop, like the rest she'd shucked her heavy jumpsuit and stripped down to boots, a yellow shirt, and olive-green pants. She filled out both shirt and pants beautifully. Her hair was chopped short, a bob that looked like a glossy bronze helmet. The woman pointed to the top of the butte, where stood an abandoned lookout tower, rickety and half-hidden behind a growth of vegetation. Once it had hosted a park ranger, now it was the haunt of owls.

"Yeah, now I see it, Cheryl," Norris said. "That shining example of the National Wildfire Service's folly could be useful as a landmark." He pulled out his cell phone. "Google maps to the rescue."

There was no reception.

Norris cursed under his breath. One more god-damned techno failure. At thirty-five he was old enough to remember when the firefighters relied on human observations, and old enough to be nostalgic about it. If he'd had some good old-fashioned maps, he'd know exactly where he was, the names, the topography, the contours and elevations. Even better, if the lookout tower had been manned, the ranger probably could have put out the aborning fire—which wasn't that big even now.

Instead, a satellite picked up the blaze. A computer produced the weather forecasts given to him. Norris had been handed the printouts before they left the airbase, and it was all supposedly very up-to-date.

And already he could see they were wrong.

For one thing, the satellite had apparently spotted a larger fire than actually existed. Because of that, fifteen volunteers had been drawn from the several crews that were lounging around the Redmond Airport near the end of the season, hoping for some action. It was a far larger team than necessary. Norris thought about sending some of them back but decided whomever he chose would be pissed. By this late in the season, the overtime wages were welcomed.

It was all pretty messed up. At the very least, they should have been dropped farther down, closer to the fire. Well, now Norris had the game trail. While such trails are predominately used by grazing animals, humans have always found them handy. Lost hikers will follow a well-marked game trail to a waterway that could eventually lead to civilization . . . and they provide a stable path through otherwise impassible terrain.

Norris called his people together and ordered them to pick up their gear and head for the trail, except for Joe Connors, who would remain on the butte as lookout and stay in radio contact.

"Cory Cantwell will take the point, and I'll bring up the rear," he said. Norris waited for comments, and when none came, he said. "All right, we got it to do."

"Break a leg, folks," Cantwell said, grinning.

"That," Mike Norris said, "is not funny."

CHAPTER 2

A hot gust of wind blew ash into Mike Norris's face, and he stopped in his tracks, his expression concerned. What the hell? The satellite weather report had said a weak low-pressure system would produce a west wind of four to seven miles per hour. But the wind was blowing from the east, in his direction, and it was stronger, slapping at him a little as a warning. . . . It could be dangerous.

They were only partway down the game trail that had proved to be more difficult than it looked at first glance. If the growing breeze fanned the smoking embers in the gully into life, they'd be trapped like flies on flypaper *above* the flames.

For a brief moment, Norris thought about calling the whole thing off. The possible danger was right there at the center of his inner alarm system. Safety had been drilled into him, but so had the gung-ho, get-'er-done ethos of the hotshots. Ahead of him the crew had stopped again, another damned obstacle in the way.

Norris had to make a decision . . . now.

Then that responsibility was taken away from him. Suddenly the wind battered at him, cartwheeling every which way before it dropped as quickly as it had started. A cloud of gray ash hung in the still air for a few moments and then settled around Norris's feet. He breathed a sigh of relief. It had been a dust devil. That was all . . . just a dust devil.

Wary now, for a few moments Norris stood and tested the wind. The day remained still, the air heavy with smoke, but the breeze had died. He scolded himself for being like the old maid who hears a rustle in every bush, and he stepped back onto the game trail and continued his descent.

Ahead of Norris was Jon Martinson and in front of him brunette Marie Lambeau and blonde Katy Peters giggled at one of their private jokes, probably about Marie's fiancée, an accountant and something of a stuffed shirt. Norris had four women on the team, an unusual number since usually there was only one woman on each jump. He was proud of himself for not taking their gender into consideration when he picked the crew, his experience being that the women were every bit as strong, smart, attentive, and brave as the men

Stumbling a little and just visible in the smoke was a stocky young man with the face of a choirboy who didn't look old enough to be a smoke jumper. But then, they all looked like kids these days. Norris didn't know this firefighter very well. Brad . . . somebody. The kid struggled with the massive chainsaw he carried, and his breathing was labored.

Mike Norris shook his head. Who the hell made this youth a sawyer? He should have been in the digger crew, or at best, a swamper, carrying away the brush. Norris called out, "Hey, Brad, take a rest. I'll carry the saw for a while."

To his surprise, the kid stepped off the trail and turned, frowning. "I've got it, sir," he said. "It ain't heavy."

"Okay, carry on," Mike said. Then, to make the youngster feel better. "You're doing good."

Five minutes later the line of firefighters suddenly came to a dead stop, and Norris brushed past the others and joined Cantwell at the point.

The problem was immediately obvious. The smoke had thickened, and the game trail ahead was lost in a gray and black murk. There was a grass fire in the gulch . . . but how widespread was it?"What do you think, Mike?" Cantwell asked. "Head back up the trail?"

"No," Mike said. "I want to get down to the fire and fight it on the flat."

Then the east wind picked up again, and Norris felt a sudden spike of dread deep in his belly. At that moment, the radio squawked. "Boss," Conner said, trying to sound calm, "are you receiving me?"

Norris unclipped the mike from his shoulder harness. "Loud and clear, Joe."

"What end of the gulley are you on?"

"The wrong end," Norris said.

"I'll come down," Conner said.

"No, you won't. Stay the hell where you're at. Keep us posted."

Norris heard the lookout gasp. And then he saw what Conner saw.

The fire had leapfrogged the gulley and ignited in the thick grass and brush below and to the east of them.

Driven by an out-of-control wind, a towering tsunami of fire hurtled toward the crew at terrifying speed.

Cory Cantwell yelled, "Everybody! Get the hell out of here! Back up the trail!"

Then he turned and stared with remarkable intensity into the gulch.

Norris saw Cantwell standing in the smoke, watching something . . . and then the man was gone, vanished into the inferno.

Oh, my God!

The fire now burned along the entire length of the gully and was rapidly scaling the hill. What had once been a ferny glen where mint-green frogs plopped into dark rock pools was now a blazing annex of hell . . . and people were already dying.

A grass fire is fast. Dreadfully, horrifically fast. It spreads like lightning and often makes a pincer movement. It traps the unwary inside its grasping arms and then scorches them to death, and so far at that dreadful moment in time it had killed most of the jump crew. It had taken only a few minutes.

Norris looked downhill and saw the fire advance on him, roaring now, closing for the kill. His face wild, he turned and ran for the plateau above, fear spiking at his belly. Pyrophobia, the fear of fire, stems from an ancient and primal dread, and few people are immune to it, including firefighters. Norris scrambled up the slope of the game trail and felt heat on his back, as though the devil himself was on his heels. Panicking, he gasped for breath, his mouth wide open in a silent scream. Above the snarl of the fire, he heard shrieks as men and women died in mortal agony. At that moment, Mike Norris, overtaken by a disaster, was not entirely sane.

The sight of Cory Cantwell saved him.

The tall man emerged from the smoke, his face blackened, his fire-retardant shirt tattered and charred on his back and shoulders. He'd escaped the worst of the flames and somehow had managed to regain the game trail.

"Cory!" Norris yelled.

Cantwell turned and looked in his direction.

"Where are they?" Norris said. "Where is my crew?"

Cantwell shook his head. "I don't know. Somewhere in the gulch. I think they're all dead." It was only then Norris saw, hanging by his side, the Glock 19 in Cantwell's hand. The fire was very close, the flames shooting high in the air, the heat blistering. Norris battled to hold on to his shredded nerves. "What happened?" he yelled.

"There were two of them," Cory called back. He continued his trudge toward the plateau. "I killed them both."

"Who? Who did you kill?" Norris almost screamed the words. Then again, "Damn you, where is my crew?"

Cantwell waved the Glock. "I told you, back yonder in the gulch. They're all dead, I could do nothing for them."

"Who did you kill? Damn it, man, answer me."

But Cory Cantwell ignored that and stumbled forward, staring straight ahead of him like a zombie lurching its way through a bad B horror movie.

Norris fought his fear and regained his self-control. Had Cantwell killed two crew members? Had he put them out of their misery? Crazed questions without answers.

He scrambled onto a nearby outcropping of lava rock and scanned the lower slopes, frantically searching through smoke and fire for signs of life as he battled to hold on to his flagging courage. Then he saw them. Barely in sight, Marie Lambeau and Katy Peters were engulfed in fire and smoke. One of the women was kneeling, her head bent as the other tried to lift her to her feet.

Norris cast caution to the wind. He ran to the women, took the burns from the flames without faltering, and, a big man and strong, he grabbed them, one under each arm, and carried them all the way up the hill to the safety of the rock plateau.

Below him the fire burned and ravenously fed on the bodies of the dead.

CHAPTER 3

"Mike, you should get a medal for saving the lives of the two women," Cory Cantwell said. "You're lucky to be alive."

His face and hands heavily bandaged, Mike Norris sat up in his bed in Good Samaritan Hospital in Portland and glanced out the window where a cobalt-blue sky filled the panes. "They don't give medals to screwups, Cory," he said. "I lost twelve of my people." Then, a yelp of pain, but not from his burns . . . from the depths of his tormented soul. "I should've died with my crew. As God is my witness, as long as I live, I'll never lead another."

The room had a hospital smell, iodoform antiseptic and the ethyl alcohol gel dispensers that were everywhere. A cart of some kind rattled past the closed door as though it carried a cargo of cheap tin trays.

"You'll feel differently once you're out of the hospital," Cantwell said. He smiled. "The Forest Service can't do without an old fire-eater like you."

"The service can do without me. It won't even notice that I've gone."

"They'll want you back, I guarantee it," Cantwell said.

"I saw on the TV news that an entire crew was killed in an Austrian forest fire," Norris said. "Did you see that?"

"Yeah, I did," Cantwell said. "Pyroterrorism, and it happened so fast they didn't stand a chance."

Norris shook his head. "Oh my God," he said. "Terrorists in Austria. It doesn't make any sense."

"Terrorist attacks on forests can happen in any country," Cantwell said. "Hell, they can happen in all fifty of our states."

"You're a mine of information, ain't you?" Norris said. "Tell me something I don't already know." Then, looking at the paper sack in Cantwell's arm, "Did you bring it?"

The younger man managed a smile. "Yes, Mike, against my better judgment and against doctor's orders." He took a gallon jug of orange juice from the sack and shook it. "There's a bottle of Smirnoff in there, just as you wanted."

Norris said, "There's a plastic cup on the table. Fill it for me, please. Half and half."

Cantwell did as he was told and passed the brimming cup to Norris, who drained it in a couple of gulps.

"So how was the screwdriver?" Cantwell said. "Now that I'm your bartender, I'm looking for some praise here. Even just an attaboy."

Norris ignored that and said, his voice flat, "Who did you kill?"

"Mike, I didn't . . ."

"Who did you kill, Cory? You said you'd shot two people."

"They were not firefighters."

Wrapped like a mummy, only Norris's surprised blue eyes were visible.

"Then who?" he said. Suddenly he wanted a cigarette.

Cantwell took a long time to answer that question, and when he did his handsome face seemed troubled. "The fire at Indian Wells was started by three men with gasoline. That's why the blaze spread so rapidly. I killed two of them and the third threw himself into the flames and died a martyr."

"A martyr for what cause?" Norris said.

"For the cause of Islamic terrorism." Cantwell said. "Unless they were homegrown, pick any country in the Middle East, and they probably came from there." He nodded to the TV suspended in a corner of the room. "You've seen the news, Mike. California is burning."

"Are you telling me my crew was killed by terrorists?" Norris said.

"Yeah, that's what I'm telling you," Cantwell said. "They call themselves Fire Warriors, and they aim to set the whole country ablaze and kill as many Americans as they can."

"How many of these people have been caught?" Norris said. "In California, I mean."

"California is a people's republic, and it's hard to tell. If any were arrested, chances are they got a slap on the wrist, were told they're the innocent victims of white oppression, and sent to a sanctuary city, where they got a rent-free house, a car, and welfare while they plotted more fires."

"And if you arrest them, Cory. What then?"

"Places like California is why we don't arrest pyro-terrorists, Mike. We kill them"

"For God's sake, who the hell is 'we'?" Norris said.

"I still work for the National Wildfire Service," Cantwell said.

"I know that, but you said, 'We kill them.' You still haven't told me who *we* is?"

"Maybe we should wait until you're out of the hospital before I get into all that," Cantwell said.

"To hell with that. I want to know now. You're such a damned Boy Scout."

"All right, but it will probably bore the ass off you. As far as I know, there's supposed to be a number of us armed volunteers attached to smoke jumper bases around the country," Cantwell said. "But by this time next year that number should increase to at least a hundred, depending on the government's willingness to provide funding. But I don't know if all that's true or not."

Norris sounded incredulous. "And the Wildfire Service okayed this crap?"

"The Department of Homeland Security together with the CIA is said to run the program, so yeah, the new National Wildfire Service must have given it a thumbs-up," Cantwell said. "Probably they weren't given any other choice."

"What the hell do they call you?" Norris said, irritated, "Double-O something, licensed to kill?"

Cantwell smiled and shook his head. "Mike, you'll get a kick out this. Some dude at the CIA with a passion for comic books and a sense of humor christened us the Punishers."

"Comic books . . . I don't get it," Norris said. "And what the hell is a Punisher?"

"There's a comic book about a superhero called the Punisher who metes out pretty violent justice to the bad guys," Cantwell said. "And there were a couple of Punisher movies, as I recall."

"I don't read comic books, and I don't watch movies," Norris said. "So you're a Punisher now? And all this time I took you for a smoke jumper."

"I'm still a smoke jumper, Mike. I just have an extra duty."

"It's a load of crap," Norris said. "Wild West stuff."

"Pyroterrorism is no joke, Mike. It's a real and growing danger to the entire country."

"Yeah, you must tell me about it some time," Norris said with an air of finality, as though he was all through talking.

Cantwell glanced at the clock on the wall. "I got to be going, Mike, let you rest," he said. "I'll stop by tomorrow. Can I bring you anything?"

"Yeah, bring me my crew back," Norris said, closing his eyes.

"I wish I could, Mike," Cantwell said. He moved to the door and stopped and smiled. "I'll see you tomorrow, same time, same place, huh?"

Norris didn't open his eyes. "No, don't visit me tomorrow, or any other day. You might as well know this . . . I got no love for the National Wildfire Service or for two-bit comic book heroes either."

Cantwell tried to come up with a response and could find none. He opened the door and stepped into the hospital corridor. A young Asian woman in a white coat and a name tag on her lapel smiled at him as she passed.

"Cory!" Norris yelled at Cantwell's back. "Losing my crew was none of my doing. The Wildfire Service can't blame me for its own criminal stupidity when they scrapped the lookout towers."

Cantwell stepped back into the room. "Mike, nobody is blaming you for what happened."

"Oh, but they will," the man in the bed said. "Believe me, the sons of bitches will."

CHAPTER 4

Three months after Mike Norris left the hospital, the National Wildfire Service, on the first day in September, retired the last lookout tower in Oregon. The day was unseasonably warm, the noon sky the color of washed-out denim.

The fire season was officially over, but that didn't fool anyone, least of all those firefighters whose responsibility it was to watch over the forests. It was still hot and dry. It was the eighth year of a severe drought, and the El Niño of a few years prior had only made it worse, turning the fresh grasses tinder dry.

The lookout tower was near the town of Bend, on top of a perfectly round cinder cone called Lava Butte. The tower had once been a showcase, state of the art, outfitted with all the new gadgets the Forest Service could provide before that beleaguered agency was wrapped into the larger National Wildfire Service. Unlike most lookouts, located in out-of-the-way places, there was even a gravel road up the butte to reach it.

Mike Norris attended the ceremonial closing as just another tourist. He knew and had worked with most of the people on the speakers' platform. He'd let his hair and beard grow out and wore a Stetson and sunglasses. He couldn't disguise his six-foot-six height, but they wouldn't be expecting him, so he thought he might make it through the day without being recognized. People smelled the booze on him, and he soon became an island in the crowd as others gave him space.

Norris was aware that there was a drone flying overhead, and that it would be transmitting images to some nameless tall building where nameless men and women in cubicles monitored face-recognition software. Ever since last year's Christmas Eve terrorist attack in Washington, DC, there was rarely a public ceremony held without drone protection.

Norris was glad of the beard and the Stetson's wide, face-shielding brim. He wasn't exactly his former employer's favorite person. He'd put up quite a fight trying to save this Oregon tower, blaming the government's reliance on satellite technology for the deaths of his jump crew. A man in a watchtower would have spotted the fire—and the terrorists—and raised the alarm. The satellite had failed, and his people had died horribly, and that was a thing Mike Norris would never forgive or forget

To his surprise, Cory Cantwell was the featured speaker.

Cantwell rarely put himself front and center—no doubt, the brass had twisted his arm. But Norris had to admit that the man was good at public speaking. He was charming and funny, and he had a gravitas that made people listen.

After Cory Cantwell told a few well-worn firefighter jokes, he got serious.

"I started my career on this very lookout, back when I worked for that quaint little organization called the Forest Service," he said. "It was a wonderful summer, and I was both disappointed and gratified that no big fires occurred during my residence. I managed to read all of *Moby-Dick,* that's how isolated I was. It was during those few short months that I learned who I was and what I wanted to do with my life. After all, 360-degree views and total seclusion tend to make any young man think."

Cantwell smiled his genuine smile, and the crowd was instantly won over. If it had been anyone else, Norris probably would have forgotten his vow to remain inconspicuous and heckled the speaker. But Cantwell had once been a friend. "Today marks the end of an era. Much as I wish other young men and women could have the same experience I had, we are only human, and we can't always be vigilant. We sleep, we eat . . . we look at the clouds . . . and inevitably we miss things.

"The cameras and the satellites will see so much more, and at a much lower cost. So as much as I loved the romance of it all, I believe this changeover will be a good thing. For me, it isn't about the cost savings, but because the resources freed up will allow us to broaden our scope, to be in so many more places at the same time.

"We sorely need that, in the light of recent terrorist attacks on our forests.

"So it is with a bittersweet feeling that I say goodbye to this grand old structure and embrace the future of firefighting."

Cantwell sat down to loud and enthusiastic applause.

After that, some of the higher-ups in the National Wildfire Service took the stage, but Norris was uninterested in what they had to say. The bureaucrats had always had their sights set on eliminating the human element in fire-fighting. It was the Cory Cantwells of the world—who knew better—who were the true traitors.

It was nauseating. Norris reached for the flask in his back pocket, then realized he'd left it in the pickup. The flask had been almost drained anyway before he screwed up his courage to join the crowd.

They finished the ceremony by releasing biodegrad-able balloons, because nothing says fighting fires like balloons. Mike Norris snorted and turned away. There were a few half-hearted cheers, mostly from the children in the audience.

What they should have done was set off some fire-works. In fact, Norris was a little put out that he hadn't thought of that. Maybe he could have sparked a few nice fires, engulfed this butte, and burned these idiots to a crisp. Maybe then they'd wake up.

The crowd was thinning out, and Norris began to feel conspicuous. He needed to get out of there before some-one noticed him.

Too late.

Cory Cantwell strode toward him, a big smile on his face, his hand outstretched in friendship. He was dressed in a bomber jacket and jeans and wore a new pair of fire-fighting boots. The collar of his shirt was turned up, so the old burn on his neck he'd taken at Indian Wells was barely noticeable.

"I'm glad you came, Mike," Cantwell said.

Norris hesitated, then put out his own hand and faked a smile in return. "Nice speech . . ."

Cantwell's smile faltered and then died on his lips. He understood Mike well enough to know what was coming.

"Of course, you wouldn't want to tell these people that the whole damned forest could soon be burned down by wildfires and we're doing nothing to stop them. Better to abandon the lookout towers and sell the public on tourism. 'Roll right up, folks, come see the cute teddy bears burn to death.'"

"I didn't come here to scare people," Cantwell said.

"Maybe you should have," Norris said. "A widespread scorching is coming and you know it. The drought is in place, and according to you so are the terrorists, and no one's ready."

"Mike, we're trying to get the Punishers off the ground, but a lack of funding is holding us back. Congress says its new welfare and medical programs for the poorest minorities must take priority. I know how strongly you feel about all this, but I have to work within the system. Hell, even the name 'Punishers' makes the liberals who control the purse strings want to puke," Cantwell smiled. "I think that's why the CIA delights in using it."

Norris really didn't want to mix it up with Cantwell that day. He shrugged. "So there's nothing I can do about it or you can do about it. Let the weather satellites and cameras nailed to tree trunks save our forests, huh?"

The younger man made no answer, and Norris said, "A satellite is a machine, and so is a camera. You know what happens to machines? They break, or they give up the ghost because of a virus or a solar flare, or God knows what else. The only thing you can count on is that mechanical things will fail at some point."

"And people don't?" Cantwell said.

"Maybe they do, but I'd rather trust the judgment of a human being than a machine. You're taking the human element out of fire control, and we're going to pay for it mighty soon."

Cantwell shook his head. "You're talking out of turn and burning a lot of bridges, Mike."

"Go along to get along, huh?" Mike answered.

Cantwell said, "I'd prefer to have both human lookouts and satellite cameras, but that isn't going to happen. I think if the National Wildfire Service wasn't protected by Homeland Security, Congress might just send the available money abroad to Iran or some other dunghill dictatorship and from coast to coast let America go up in smoke."

Mike silently agreed with that. Washington was more focused on cost cutting than they were on protecting the forests or the people that live close to them. At a time when more resources than ever were needed, they were looking for ways to cut corners to spend money on the free-stuff-for-all social programs that attract voters and ensure majorities in the House. When the various jurisdictions that fought fires were placed under the umbrella of the National Wildfire Service, it was supposed to end all the bureaucratic bickering. Instead, the infighting only increased, with each unit struggling for resources.

Then, because he felt Mike should hear it again, "No one blames you for what happened at Indian Wells, Mike. No one."

"You warned me that it was dangerous," Norris said.

"Mike. I say that at every fire. It's in my nature to

worry about the danger, it's in your nature to get the job done. That's why you're a better firefighter than me."

"Sure," Norris said. "I'm a better firefighter than you. Well, tell me what kind of job did I get done at Indian Wells?"

Norris was convinced he knew exactly what other people thought of him. He recalled the horrified look in their eyes when somebody told them, "Yeah, that's Mike Norris. He lost almost his entire smoke jumper crew a few months back. Tough break, huh?"

Yes, it was tough, very tough. Norris tried to blank out the memory, but it came roaring back. It always did.

He remembered the searing heat of the fire, the panic and fear he'd felt as he heard the screams of the dying. And later when he saw the black-cindered bodies of his friends, white bone showing through the burned flesh, he'd puked his guts up.

The disaster had not been his fault, because Norris had one more clear memory of that day, the abandoned lookout tower that had collapsed onto the bluff. In that moment he knew he'd been betrayed. Had the tower been manned, his people would still be alive. They'd depended on space-age technology, and it had failed them . . . not Mike Norris.

"You did your best at Indian Wells," Cantwell said. "No one could have done better."

"A lookout tower would have saved them all," Norris said.

"Maybe that's the case."

"No maybe. That was the case."

"Mike, we'll never know."

"I know."

"There was a freak wind that day," Cantwell said. "No one could've anticipated that."

"A lookout tower . . ."

"Mike, the three terrorists would have killed the lookout ranger. They were armed."

"They started the fire," Norris said.

"You know they did."

"It was fire that killed my people, not terrorists."

"Talk like that and we'll keep going around in circles," Cantwell said.

"I don't want the blame for Indian Wells."

"And no one blames you, Mike. Understand that for God's sake."

A young woman in a ranger uniform hurried up and whispered into Cantwell's ear. Judging by the look on Cantwell's face, Norris decided the news wasn't good.

"Got to go, Mike," Cantwell said and turned away without waiting for a response, nearly running to a green National Wildfire Service SUV that was parked nearby.

"Yeah . . . see you around," Norris said, knowing he couldn't be heard. He walked across the parking lot to his battered Ford F-150, deep in thought. He opened the door, and with hands that shook lit a Marlboro.

"It's been a trying day for you, I think. A most distressing day."

The voice came from behind him. Norris exhaled smoke then turned to find a slender, middle-aged man with dark skin smiling at him. The stranger had probing black eyes and looked vaguely Middle Eastern. He was fiftyish, five-eight, and clean shaven, and he wore a stylish, Italian-style gray suit with a pale blue shirt and red and black striped tie. He had a $10,000 Breitling watch on his left wrist and a diamond ring on the pinkie finger.

"What's it to you?" Norris said, not liking the man on sight.

"Call me an interested party," the man said. "I read your interview in *The New York Times*."

"Then good for you," Norris said.

"The article interested me very much. We're of alike minds, you and I."

"I very much doubt that."

"Please, tell me the real story about Indian Wells."

"All right then, here's the real story in its entirety. I witnessed a tragedy that was none of my doing. Then I fought an uphill battle with the forestry powers that be and lost. End of story. Mister, there is no more, not now, not ever. I'm done."

"Over the next year or so, all the lookout towers will be abandoned," the man said. "You don't approve?"

"It's the worst decision the government ever made. Well, maybe not the worst. There are plenty of other things they've done that are just as stupid."

"Such as?" the man asked politely. "If I may ask?"

"Too many to count," Norris said. He really didn't want to get into a conversation with some stranger, and a foreigner at that.

"Please," the little man said. "I'd very much like to hear it."

The stranger's manner was courtly and polite, and Norris hesitated, on the verge of unloading his entire hobbyhorse of complaints on the man. Then he shook his head. He'd learned that once he got going, he couldn't stop. "Sorry, I have to go," he said, climbing into the truck.

The stranger's voice rose. "Mr. Norris . . . I represent an organization that would very much like to hire you. Do you suppose we could have a talk about that?"

Norris wanted to say get lost. But he'd no woman waiting for him at home, and he really had nowhere else to go or anyone to see. He wasn't getting calls from timber companies anymore, and even the private firefighting outfits were keeping their distance.

As if reading his mind, the black-eyed man said, "I assure you, it will be worth your time." His complexion was good, with few wrinkles, his darker skin able to resist sun damage.

"A job that pays money?" Norris said.

"Big money," the little man said. "You'll be surprised just how big."

He was broke, with no prospects, and Norris made a decision. "Okay," he said. "You've said just enough to interest me. Want to follow me to my place?"

"Do you mind if I ride along? I took a cab out here."

Norris unlocked the passenger door and shoved a couple of empty Budweiser cans off the seat onto the floor. The stranger got in, shuffled the cans aside with his polished shoes, and fastened his seat belt.

A blond woman ran up to the truck, a cameraman following her.

"Wait! Wait! I'm Kimberly Morgan of KTW9 TV news," the woman said, shoving a microphone into the cab. "I wanted to interview four other Middle Eastern gentlemen, probably birdwatchers, but they seem to have left. One of them pointed you out and said you were of Syrian heritage. Is that true?"

"Yes, that is true," the little man said, smiling. "My great-grandfather immigrated to Portland a hundred years ago. What can I do for you?"

"Since you're obviously interested in the Forest Service, I want your opinion on a rumor making the rounds concerning Islamic tourists," Morgan said.

"And that is?"

"That Middle Eastern men suspected of setting arson fires in our nation's forests are being shot on sight by white execution squads. Here in Oregon innocent campers have already been killed, among them two young Palestinian students here on a birdwatching expedition. Have you heard about these terrible murders? And also the rumor that a pregnant Iranian woman who was with them may have been raped?"

Mike Norris cursed under his breath and said, "No, he hasn't, lady, and neither have I."

"The question was hardly directed at you," the woman said. Her Botoxed forehead did not allow her to frown. "My source says the killers who carried out the massacre of these innocents were white men who wore Forest Service uniforms and carried Glock assault pistols. A witness who is scared and wishes to remain anonymous, he said they were probably drunk."

The little man shook his head and again smiled politely. "I have no knowledge of any of those alleged incidents."

"Lady, take a hike," Norris said. He slammed the Ford into drive and hit the accelerator.

The TV reporter, her cameraman in tow, ran into the

retreating truck's dust cloud and yelled, "Wait . . . the killers . . ."

"God, I hate those media whores," Norris said. "What the hell is a Glock assault pistol?"

The little man smiled. "It would seem that she had no love of you as a white man."

"Caucasian males are the root of all evil, as far as the media is concerned," Norris said. He turned his head. "All right, you already know my name, so what's yours?"

"Nasim," the man said, then hesitated. "Nasim Azar."

"Where you from? Let me guess . . . Saudi Arabia."

"Portland," Azar answered. He apparently took no offense.

"Very well, Nasim Azar from Portland," Norris said. "What's your job offer?"

"Since we are soon to be friends, and I sincerely hope that is the case, first let me tell you a little about myself," Azar said. "As I told the TV reporter, my paternal grandparents migrated from Syria around 1900, and my father later started a successful rug and carpet business here in Oregon. At home, we spoke only English, and as a child, the only religious celebration I took part in was Christmas. I lived in a very happy home."

Norris nodded and said, "Good for you."

And Azar told himself, so far, so good.

What he could have added, but did not, was that when he was ten years old, he learned that his family was not of Syrian descent but were Palestinians. Even then, the fact didn't truly register with him until two years later, when his parents sent him to visit his uncle in Lebanon. His uncle was a rabid anti-Semite with a deep and abiding hatred for Israel and the United States. It was on that trip that Nasim Azar first became radicalized. He'd made many trips to Lebanon since and had gorged greedily at the terrorist trough, fed a diet of hate and trained in the ways of violence and, as a Muslim, loyalty to the teachings of Allah.

Mike Norris drove down a winding dirt road too fast, sliding on the corners, throwing up gravel. Azar held tight, trying to ignore the strong odor of beer that suffused the pickup. But Norris negotiated the turns with the sureness of long experience, always correcting in time.

The big man's sloppiness was offensive to the somewhat prissy Azar. Norris was carelessly groomed, flannel shirttail hanging out, dirty blue jeans and mud-encrusted boots, but Azar's research had led him to this . . . what was the word . . . ah, yes, *renegade* . . . and he'd no intention of giving up on him.

Azar was not in the least afraid of Mike Norris. The Beretta .25 he carried in a pocket holster was a puny weapon, but it could be deadly enough in the right hands. And Azar had been trained by experts to use it well.

Norris's eyes were on the road ahead. Without turning, he said, "All right, now we're friends and all that, what can you do for me?"

"I represent a company that supplies firefighters with equipment," Azar said. "We lease gear, mostly. I'm sure you've probably worn or used something we've made."

"I don't work for the Forest Service anymore," Norris said.

"I'm aware of that. In fact, that's why I'm here. We need a third party, someone with no conflict of interest, yet someone who knows the firefighting business inside and out. That's you, Mr. Norris."

"What's the name of your company?"

"Northwest Fire Prevention," Nasim said. "You wouldn't recognize the name. The previous owners weren't serious businessmen, and they almost ran the company into the ground."

Norris said, "And you are a good businessman?"

"Indeed, I am. Very good. I make, how is it Americans say? Yes, big bucks. Oh, and I also buy and sell fine Indian and Persian carpets."

"What do you want from me, Azar? I know nothing about carpets." Norris smiled and said, "You're an Arab. Maybe you sell flying carpets, huh?"

"No, my carpets don't fly, unless they're being carried in an airplane."

"Pity," Norris said. "There are times when a flying carpet could come in handy."

"Let me say first that I'm aware of your quarrel with the National Wildfire Service, and I have to say, I'm in total agreement with you. They are depending too much on technology and not enough on human resources."

"And I'm assuming that most of the gear you sell is to those human resources?"

"Well, that is true. As I said, I'm a businessman. But the point is, we both agree that lookout towers and manpower and training all count for more than satellites and cameras and drones."

"Okay, we agree. So why the hell are we talking?"

"You're a blunt man," Azar said. "I respect that."

"Yes, I am. And you're stalling."

It was true. Azar had expected to lead slowly up to his proposal. He'd envisioned it taking days, giving him time to develop a rapport with Norris, to feel him out, to figure out the best way to approach a very touchy subject.

"Well?" Norris prompted.

"If you don't mind, why don't we talk about it over dinner?" the Muslim suggested, playing for time. "I'll buy, of course. Anywhere you want to go in Portland. Do you like Middle Eastern food? I know a little place in the Alberta Arts District that serves the most delicious mejadra."

Norris grimaced. "Just lay your proposal on me. Right now, I don't have the time nor the inclination for a bunch of crap."

Azar wondered for a moment if he'd chosen the wrong man. But by now, he'd investigated everyone. There were scores of disgruntled former Forest Service and Bureau of Land Management employees, but none of them had the reputation that Mike Norris had. Regardless of how blunt or confrontational the big man was, he had the general respect of his former employers and coworkers, and that could be a major plus.

"If we could show them . . ." Azar said.

"Show them what?" Norris said. His face tightened and wrinkles appeared at the corners of his eyes.

"I mean if we could provide an example of how important human resources are, then maybe they'd be forced to rethink their new firefighting strategy."

"What do you mean?" There was a warning tone in Norris's voice.

Azar plunged ahead. "What if all over the country fires broke out where in previous years lookout towers would have caught them? What if fully trained arsonists . . ."

The Muslim broke off as the pickup decelerated rapidly. Norris pulled off onto the grass verge at the side of the road.

"What are you doing?" Azar said. "Why are we stopping here?"

"Get the hell out of my truck," Norris growled. "Now!"

"I assure you, they would be controlled burns," Azar said. "That's why I came to you, Mr. Norris. So that it would be done right. Think about it. You will train my people to start effective fires, but fires designed to do minimal damage to the forests and cause no loss of life. Please . . ."

"Get out," Norris said. He was staring straight forward, his jaw clenched. "Beat it right now, or I'll break both of your arms."

Azar took a business card from his wallet. "I have a lot of money, Mr. Norris. And I'm trying to help your cause. Think it over." As he got out of the pickup, he laid the card on the passenger seat. "Please call me."

Norris drove out of there, spraying gravel in every direction. A small pebble stung Azar's cheek, drawing a speck of blood. Thunderclouds gathered to the west, the bright day shaded into gloom, and a rising wind whispered among the canopies of the nearby pine trees.

As he waited for one of two cars that had followed them off the bluff, Azar smiled. He knew that he'd planted a seed, and that negotiations were just beginning. Mike Norris would get back to him soon. The man was obsessed, and obsession was a form of madness. Oh yes, the American would call . . . tomorrow . . . or the next day. Very soon.

A black, battered Mercury Grand Marquis pulled up and the passenger door opened. The young Palestinian man inside said, "Peace to you, brother." He wore a white polo shirt and tan slacks, and designer sunglasses were pushed up over his thick black hair. A Khar CM9 lay on his lap in a Kydex holster.

"And to you, peace," Azar said. He slid onto the car seat, and when the driver made to drive away, he stopped him. "Wait. Did we hear yet from Fahim Shalhoub?"

The driver shook his head. "Not yet. He called and said that that he and his holy warriors were about to attack the car of the devil named Cantwell, the murderer of our men at Indian Wells. Since then we have heard nothing."

"Then let us hope that Allah smiled on them and their strike was a success," Azar said. "I assume our intelligence from Washington on the man Sensor has not changed?"

The young Palestinian driver said, "Nothing has changed, master. Sensor will travel to Phoenix, Arizona, the day after tomorrow, and then to a firefighting base camp an hour north of the city."

"Where so many died in a flash flood," Azar said.

"Yes, master, the very place."

"We can rely on this information?"

The younger man nodded. "In Washington the politicians go to dinner and talk, talk, talk. Who among them even notices the silent, brown-skinned waiter who hears their every word? Yes, we can rely on this information."

Azar smiled. "Then praise be to Allah for such good and faithful servants."

He was sure this day would prove to have been a profitable one. He would pass on the Sensor information to his rich client for a good price, but the lack of news from Fahim Shalhoub was worrisome. He should have heard something by now.

CHAPTER 5

As Cory Cantwell left the Black Butte Lookout retirement ceremony, he turned his confrontation with Mike Norris over in his mind. They'd been friends once, but there had been no mistaking the look of anger, almost hatred, on Mike's face when he'd approached him.

A shame. Cantwell had great respect for the man. Mike Norris was the stuff of which legends are made. But something had happened to his mind that day at Indian Wells, something dark, something twisted. He'd quit soon after the disaster, rather than be fired for his outspoken opposition to his bosses and the new satellite fire-spotting technology.

The Indian Wells investigation had exonerated Mike Norris and his crew. They'd been fed the wrong information, dropped in the wrong place, and the topography had led to an entrapment no one could have predicted.

And, more important, the presence of Islamic pyroterrorists had not been foreseen either.

Cantwell's own career advancement was partly because he'd killed two of the terrorists and now led a unit the CIA called the Punishers and others in the National Wildfire Service called the *James Bond Squad*.

No matter what it was called, it was supposed to be top secret . . . meaning that everyone in government and out knew of its existence. The scuttlebutt was that a hostile Congress and media were dead set against the Punishers unit, and only the President and her adviser Jacob Sensor seemed to be in favor . . . and the President was wavering.

Cory Cantwell's driver, a blond, ponytailed NWS administrative assistant with a Maine accent and a Snow White and the Seven Dwarfs charm bracelet on her wrist, suddenly cut into his thoughts. "Mr. Cantwell," she said. "I think we're being followed, a bunch of ragheads in a Jeep Cherokee."

Cantwell turned and looked out the rear window. The car was there, no more than fifty yards away. Two, no three, perhaps four, occupants. He also noticed the massive purple boulders of thunderheads building to the west.

"Let them pass," he said. "Maybe they're in a big hurry to get home before the storm."

"Tried that, sir," the woman said. "They slowed down too. And when I sped up, they sped up. They're tailing us, no doubt about that."

A faint but insistent alarm bell rang in Cantwell's head. He was on a deserted stretch of road, trees on either side, and it was still a few miles to the nearest town. Was he really being followed? A cautious man, he unzipped his ballistic nylon laptop bag and opened the compartment designed to carry a firearm. He drew a Glock 19 from its Velcro-attached holster and said, "Pull into the trees . . . I don't know your name."

"Nancy, sir. Nancy Payne."

"Okay, Nancy Payne, pull into the trees and then get your head down. If shooting starts, stay right there."

"Do you think we're in any danger, sir?" Nancy said.

"I don't know," Cantwell said. "Probably not, but it's better to be safe than sorry."

"Ooh, this is exciting," the woman said.

She swung the Forest Service SUV into the pines . . . and behind him Cantwell saw the Cherokee slow to a stop.

It should be noted here that a week earlier an inter-office CIA memo mentioned that National Wildfire Service supervisor and anti-arsonist chief, Superintendent Cory Cantwell, had spent enough time with the Glock 19 to learn its manual of arms. However, in the last month he'd devoted just one hour and twenty minutes on range practice, asserting that constant firearm recoil pained his arthritic shoulder. The memo claimed to be just an FYI, and ended with, "No conclusions have been drawn from Superintendent Cantwell's behavior."

But later conclusions would be drawn . . . after a couple of minutes of hell-firing gun fury put any doubts to rest about Cantwell's ability with the Glock.

"Down!" Cory Cantwell yelled. Now the Jeep was coming on fast, one man hanging out the rear window with a gun in his hand. Cantwell opened the SUV door, jumped outside, and then hit the dirt, his Glock in a two-handed hold pushed out in front of him.

BOOM! Not a gunshot but a sudden slam of thunder.

"Sir, are you all right?"

This from Nancy inside the truck.

"Stay down!" Cantwell yelled.

A bullet kicked up a startled exclamation point of dirt two inches in front of his face. The swarthy, dark-haired man at the Jeep's rear window was in a cramped shooting position and wanted out of there. He kicked the door open and stepped onto the blacktop, his Smith & Wesson .357 revolver coming up fast. Cantwell fired at the man, rolled, shot again. Hit hard, the swarthy man dropped to his knees and returned fire. A miss, the bullet crashed into the door of the SUV. The front of the gunman's green T-shirt was stained with blood, and his mouth was a scarlet O of pain and shock. Cantwell dismissed him and directed his attention to the driver, who'd just exited the vehicle. Armed with a semiautomatic, the driver yelled something in a language Cantwell didn't understand and cut loose. As bullets whined around him like angry hornets, Cantwell laid the Glock's AmeriGlo front sight on the man and squeezed the trigger. His 9mm bullet hit the steel slide of the driver's pistol, smashed the weapon out of his hand, and then, badly mangled, caromed upward, plowing into the underside of his chin, through the roof of his mouth and into his brain. When the man hit the ground, he was deader than hell in a parson's parlor.

His ears ringing, Cory Cantwell stood, his gaze fixed on the car. Had there been two gunmen in it or three or four? Thunder crashed, and lightning scrawled across the sky like the signature of a demented god. The wind was stronger now, tossing strands of Cantwell's brown hair across his forehead. Behind him, he heard Nancy's cell phone ring, and to his right, chugging toward him, a battered Dodge pickup trailing a blue cloud of smoke straddled the road's centerline.

Slow seconds ticked by. The pickup driver laid on the

horn, an insistent demand to clear the goddamned road, and Cantwell cursed under his breath. A testy motorist was the last thing he needed right now.

Then the Jeep Cherokee moved, a slight rocking of the cab on its springs, and Cantwell tensed. There was still someone inside. He two-handed the Glock to waist level.

"Hey, you!"

The Dodge had stopped, and an older man dressed in denim overalls and a frayed straw hat stomped toward him. And so did his wife, a plump, determined-looking woman in a floral dress who white-knuckled her brown leather purse as though she believed there could be highwaymen about.

Cantwell's heart sank . . . Ma and Pa Kettle, straight from the late, late show, were walking into his gunfight.

Then two things happened very quickly . . .

Nancy Payne, looking official in her olive-green Forest Service uniform and silver badge, ran toward the couple waving her arms. "Back! Back!" she yelled. Then to reinforce her newly acquired authority, "Police!"

At that moment a third gunman burst from the car, a pistol in each hand. Firing both weapons, he charged Cantwell at a run, screaming, *"Allahu Akbar!"*

The man was not directing aimed fire at Cantwell, more a spray and pray that was totally ineffective. Whoever he was, pistols were not his usual weapons of choice.

One of the terrorist's bullets tugged at Cantwell's sleeve as he returned fire at a range of five yards and triggered the Glock dry. It was enough. Hit multiple times, the man staggered and then fell flat on his face. He groaned, tried to rise, and then flopped down again, dying in the blood that spread under his body like spilled red paint.

Footsteps pounded to Cantwell's right, and alarmed, he swung in that direction, the slide back on his empty gun. But it was Pa Kettle, a single-barreled shotgun in his hands. "I'm a lifetime NRA member, and I'll stand with you, Officer!" he yelled. He looked around him. "Bring them on. I'm locked and loaded.

Then, from his alarmed wife, "Oh dear, you're wounded, Officer!"

Now Cantwell felt the pain from the wound in his left upper arm. He'd been burned by a bullet that had drawn blood. It hadn't pained him at the time, but now it hurt like hell.

"I called 911 for the police and an ambulance," Nancy Payne said.

Cantwell nodded. "Good, but I don't think they need an ambulance. They're all dead." Then as the violent reality of the gunfight hit, he shook his head in wonder. "I killed them all. I killed three men in less than two minutes."

The woman's eyes shone with admiration and her lips were moist and slightly parted. "You were very brave, sir." She sounded to Cantwell as though she was speaking from the far end of a long tunnel.

He said nothing. The role of gunfighting hero was not setting well with him.

Then a frown of concern showed on Nancy's face. "Sir, you're bleeding," she said.

"I'm fine, it's only a flesh wound," Cantwell said. He shook his head.

Oh, God, now I sound like John Wayne.

Pa Kettle had been inspecting the bodies, He returned, stood beside Cantwell and said, "Hey, young feller, them boys are all foreigners. Arabs, or the like, if'n you ask me."

Cory Cantwell nodded. "Seems like," he said.

The farmer stared into the younger man's face. "Islamic terrorists. That's what they call 'em on TV."

"Yes, that's what I call them too," Cantwell said.

"Three of them," the older man said.

Cantwell nodded. "Yes. Three of them."

"You did good, Officer, defending yourself an' all," Pa Kettle said. Without taking his eyes from Cantwell's face, he called out to his wife, "Betty, get these officers an apple from the back of the truck." Sirens sounded in the distance. "An Oregon apple will do you good, son, settle your nerves."

"While your wife's at it, have her put your shotgun back in the truck," Cantwell said. "When the sheriff gets here, I don't want him to see a weapon in your hands. Bad things can happen when a cop arrives at a violent crime scene with a gun in his hand and his adrenaline pumping." He passed his Glock to Nancy. "Better put this out of sight for now as well."

Cory Cantwell held the red and green apple, untasted, in his right hand when a couple of sheriff's cars and an ambulance, lights flashing, arrived on the scene. The sheriff, a lean, blue-eyed man with iron-gray hair, looked around at the carnage, placed his hand on his holstered Glock, gave Cantwell the stink eye, and said, "Mister, you got some explaining to do."

Cantwell looked at the sheriff, at his nervous young deputies, and talked fast . . . as though his life depended on it. And it probably did.

* * *

Cory Cantwell described the events following his speech at the lookout tower, identities were checked, calls were made and returned, and Nancy Payne and Ma and Pa Kettle, who turned out to be apple growers named Bob and Betty Potter, were interviewed.

The thunderstorm passed, but a drizzle of rain remained as the state bomb squad checked the Jeep Cherokee but found no suspicious device.

The sheriff, a man named Erickson, stepped beside Cantwell and said, "Mr. Cantwell, until I'm told otherwise, I'm writing this up as you being the victim of an Islamic terrorist attack."

"Sounds about right," Cantwell said. "But how the hell did they know who I was?"

"I'll show you something," Erikson said. He took a folded newspaper from his car and handed it to Cantwell. It was a small publication with an ad for a supermarket on the front. "This shopper is published in Bend," the sheriff said. "Look at the story on page three, alongside Square Deal Henry's used cars ad."

Under the headline "Lava Butte," the single column story about the watchtower closure was only six inches long, but the last sentence did the damage: *Mr. Cory Cantwell, head of the new National Wildfire Service's anti-terrorist unit, will be the keynote speaker.*

"Damn," Cantwell said.

"The Department of Homeland Security and the CIA should know better than to make that kind of information public," Erikson said.

Cantwell was surprised. "You already spoke to them?"

"They just now spoke to me," the sheriff said. "All they said was to leave you the hell alone, and all I said was, 'Yes, sir' . . . 'No, sir' . . . 'Three bags full, sir.' They think I'm a hick."

"Sorry about that," Cantwell said.

"Don't be. It happens all the time."

"Where's your weapon? I was warned not to confiscate it as evidence."

"Glock 19 like yours, Sheriff. It's in the truck. You want to see it?"

"Nope. I want nothing to do with it."

The sheriff stared hard into Cantwell's face. "You've got some powerful friends."

"And with friends like those . . ."

"Who needs enemies?" Erikson said. "Yeah, friends like them can get you killed quicker n' scat."

"Seems like somebody is trying hard to do just that," Cantwell said.

"Watch your back," the sheriff said. "That's all I'm going to say." Sheriff Erikson remained until the bodies and the Jeep were removed, and Cantwell thought it his duty to stay with him. The day was moving into late afternoon when the sheriff got into his car, rolled the window down, and said, "Hey, Cantwell."

Cory Cantwell stepped to the patrol car.

Erikson smiled for the first time that day and said, "You done good."

Nancy Payne waited until Cory Cantwell seated himself in the truck and then she opened the glove box and produced a pint of Jim Beam followed by a pack of

Winstons and a red Bic lighter. "Take a couple of slugs of the bourbon, Mr. Cantwell," she said. "You look like you can use it."

"The farmer gave me an apple," Cantwell said. "He thought it would calm me down."

"And did it?"

"I didn't eat it. I don't know what I did with it. Dropped it probably."

"Bourbon is better," the woman said. She handed over the Beam bottle but held on to the cigarettes. "Do you smoke?"

"I'm trying to quit," Cantwell said.

"Now is not a good time," Nancy said.

Cantwell snatched the Winstons like a drowning man grabbing for a life jacket and said, "Do you give bourbon and cigarettes to all your customers?"

"I always like to supply what a senior manager might want," Nancy said. She fluttered her eyelashes. "Well, within reason."

Cory Cantwell laughed. It felt good.

"One more thing," Nancy said. "The Homeland Security people called while you were . . . ah . . . busy. They've booked a motel room for you in Bend. You're to check in there and await further instructions."

"What do they mean, further instructions?" Cantwell said.

The woman shrugged. "I don't know, I'm just the messenger." Then, "Thirty minutes to Bend, Mr. Cantwell. Enjoy your whiskey and cigarettes."

CHAPTER 6

The Winter Blossom Inn was one step up from a no-tell motel. It probably dated from the 1930s and had an ash parking lot out front. White stucco and windows with water stains underneath that gave them the look of baggy eyes. Camellia plants with red blooms the size of baseballs pushed up against each side of a glass front door that was engraved in the art deco style and was probably as old as the inn.

Inside, the room was small, clean, and slightly musty. A couple of old Civil War battle prints hung on the walls, and the worn, rust-colored carpet on the floor looked as though it had been laid during the Great Depression.

The room came with its own coffeepot, packs of creamer, and three different kinds of sweeteners. And it had cable TV. Cory Cantwell poured a premeasured pack of Folgers into a filter and filled the pot at the bathroom sink. As the coffee dripped, he reloaded the Glock's 15-round magazine from the box of 147-grain Winchesters he kept in his overnight bag and then returned the pistol to his briefcase.

He'd now killed five men with the Glock. Sure, they

were terrorists, but still human beings, and their deaths hung heavy on him. His firearms instructor had fought in Afghanistan and said about that, "Cantwell . . . when the gunsmoke clears, better by far that you are the hero, not the victim. Keep that in mind."

Cantwell poured coffee and accompanied it with Jim Beam and cigarettes. When the pot and the bottle were empty, he showered and went to bed exhausted.

He would always remember that despite the trauma of that day he slept like a baby.

In the morning, at six-thirty sharp, Nancy Payne woke up Cantwell with coffee, orange juice, and a McDonald's bacon, egg, and cheese biscuit. She looked fresh and pretty, and he woke feeling a little rough. He put the blame on last night's coffee. Had to be.

"There's a plane waiting for you in Redmond, Mr. Cantwell," she said. "It seems that some bigwig out of Washington wants you in Arizona as soon as possible."

"Arizona? Cowboy country. Why, for God's sake?"

"I don't know, sir."

"A job for a Punisher?"

"I don't know, sir." Nancy looked genuinely puzzled. Then she said, trying to be helpful, "I saw the movie with John Travolta."

Cantwell managed a smile. "And I'm talking too much." He picked up the Winston pack, found a crumpled cigarette inside, and said, "Hey, it's my lucky day."

* * *

There was a black, unmarked Ford Taurus waiting for Cory Cantwell at the Phoenix Sky Harbor Airport, and its taciturn driver took him to a firefighting base camp in less than an hour.

The camp was like a small town.

All the resources of the firefighting apparatus had been mobilized. Air tankers and helicopters flew overhead, bulldozers and backhoes idled at the edge of camp, spewing diesel fumes. There were parked water trucks and buses, and near them were makeshift shower stalls and dining areas. Stacks of supplies filled most of the empty spaces between . . . cases of sleeping bags and clothing, tools and over-the-counter medications. Radios and piles of batteries, tents, and stakes. The entire National Wildfire Service was represented there. All of it in service of a fire that had already passed, already done its damage.

Cory Cantwell introduced himself to the base manager, a tall, slender man named Stewart Fitch who'd once been a New York cop, and said, "So tell me why I'm here."

Fitch still had buzz-cut hair, and his eyes were guarded and wary, something his experience in the NYPD had taught him. Put him in a lineup of fifty men, and an experienced crook would spot the ex-cop in seconds.

"Damned if I know why you're here," he said. "I wasn't even told you were coming. Maybe it's about the flash flood that killed Steve Bender's team, but I don't think so." He shook his head. "Smoke jumpers drown while tackling a forest fire. Don't that beat all?"

"Hard to believe," Cantwell said.

"I still can't believe it," Fitch said. "But it happened, and it could happen again, I guess. Walk with me." He kicked a loose rock that skittered through pine needles for twenty feet before coming to a halt. "I've heard things," he said. He scratched a mosquito bite on the sun-reddened side of his neck. "Not good things. Well, not bad things either. I should say strange things."

"Tell me about them," Cantwell said.

"I heard some smoke jumpers are to be armed and turned into an anti-terrorism response unit," Fitch said. He turned his head and looked at Cantwell. "Have you heard that?"

"Yeah, I've heard it," Cantwell said.

"Is it true?"

"Yeah, it's true."

"What kind of guys are in the unit? Ex-service?"

"All smoke jumpers are eligible, but they've got to be volunteers."

"It sounds like an interesting job," Fitch said.

"It can also be dangerous," Cantwell said.

Fitch said, "All right, I'll level with you, Superintendent Cantwell, I recognized your name. I heard you're in command of the new unit. Is that true?"

Cantwell saw no point in lying about it. "Yes, I'm the man in charge," he said. "But I have no unit and no idea when one will be formed. It all depends on funding. Police and structural fire departments receive money for the possibility of terrorist attacks, but so far the land management agencies like our shiny new National Wildfire Service get little or nothing to plan for and detect arson threats."

Fitch could have asked more questions, but he saw Cantwell's face tighten and decided to call it quits. He said, "Well, if and when you get the unit formed, count me in."

Cantwell smiled. "You're my first volunteer."

"Better than ten pressed men, huh?" Fitch said.

"So they say. Let's keep in touch."

"Are smokers allowed?"

"Cigarette smokers, you mean?"

"Nah, I just took up smoking a pipe. My wife is pregnant, and she and my two kids hate it."

"There's nothing in the rules that say I can't recruit pipe smokers," Cantwell said. "Or pot smokers, come to that."

Fitch nodded. "Glad to hear it." Then he said, "Walk around if you like. If you're hungry, we've a cafeteria of sorts set up in the tent over there. Fair-to-middling sandwiches and stale donuts mostly. We did have a chocolate cake, but that went fast."

A firefighter standing beside a pile of equipment called Fitch's name, and the man said, "I got to go. Talk to you later, Cantwell."

But for Stewart Fitch there was destined to be no later.

Cory Cantwell walked around the camp, deeply disturbed by what he saw. The flash flood deaths, coming on at the end of a long season of firefighting, had taken a heavy emotional toll on the firefighters, even more so because there was no one to blame. It had been an act of nature, and they knew it.

Cantwell shook his head. The fire was out, the floodwaters had subsided . . . so he asked himself what the hell was he doing there? No doubt time would tell. He got a ham-and-cheese sandwich, a bag of chips, and a bottle of Diet Pepsi from a commissary tent and sat outside on a patch of grass where he'd already dumped his pack. He finished the sandwich and leaned back, intending to rest for a moment. The drowsy day was warm, birds rustled in the surrounding pines, and insects made their small sounds in the brush. Cantwell closed his eyes and drifted into sleep.

"Superintendent Cantwell?"

A woman's voice. For a moment he thought it was Nancy Payne and was fully awake in an instant. Two people looked down at him. One was a short, stocky man with a large mustache and an unruly shock of white hair. Beside him, carrying a black leather briefcase, stood a young woman in a dark business suit over a white silk blouse. At that moment, Cory Cantwell thought her the most beautiful woman he'd ever seen. She was not pretty in the conventional sense, rather she was handsome, with slightly masculine features, especially her strong chin and high, prominent cheekbones. Her eyes, slightly amused, were hazel, green predominating, and her wavy auburn hair cascaded over her shoulders, except for an S-shaped strand that had fallen onto her high forehead. Cantwell's gaze went to her shapely legs and high-heeled shoes, the first he'd ever seen in a base camp.

Cantwell scrambled to his feet as the older man extended his hand to him. He then became suddenly aware that he was still holding the triangular, plastic sandwich wrapper in his right hand. He quickly shoved it into his pants pocket, and it just as promptly fell out again. As the woman smiled, he ignored the damned wrapper, stuck out his hand, and said, "I'm Cantwell."

And where I have seen you before?

"Jacob Sensor," the man said, shaking his hand.

Of course. The famous fixer.

It was widely rumored that Jacob Sensor was the power behind the President, the man who had supposedly urged her to run in the first place. What Sensor wanted, the President wanted, too, or so it was said. The hostile, liberal media called him a lackey masquerading as an honorary senator, but Sensor was nobody's errand boy. He was tough, intelligent, tightly wound, and as ruthless as a Borgia pope.

Cantwell smiled. "What can I do for you, sir?"

"We'll come to that in a moment," Sensor said. "Anyone ever tell you that you look like a young Clint Eastwood?"

"Not recently, sir," Cantwell said.

"Well, you do," Sensor said. He turned to the woman. "Doesn't he?"

"Yes, sir," she said. "I guess so."

To Cantwell's disappointment, she didn't seem too impressed.

Sensor said, "Superintendent Cantwell, you're heading up the new anti-terrorist unit. Am I right?"

"The Punishers? Yes, I am."

"No, Mr. Cantwell . . . a thousand times no," Sensor said. "I don't like that name. It's sensationalist and indicative of how this . . . thing . . . was thrown together by the Homeland Security Administration without any real thought or planning. At this time, how many anti-terrorist firefighting personnel are under your command?"

"I don't know, sir," Cantwell said.

"Where are they?"

"I don't know, sir."

"How many can you contact in an emergency?"

"None, sir."

Sensor shook his head. "Well, that's honest at least." He looked long at Cantwell, studying the younger man's face. Then he said, "Judging by what happened yesterday, terrorists know who you are and what you are, and the media is getting wind of it."

"It would seem that way, sir," Cantwell said. "They say we're killing birdwatchers and innocent tourists instead of people who hate us."

"Yes, it would seem that way," Sensor said. "And they know who I am, so we're very much in the same boat, or should I say, sinking ship. Sinking, that is, until we can get your unit organized. For that I need the President's support, and to get that support, especially funding, I must present her with a coherent plan. Do you understand?"

"Perfectly, sir," Cantwell said. "But at present I am aware of no plan, coherent or otherwise."

"Then it's high time we had one, and that why I'm here," Sensor said. "Every American forest is currently at grave risk of a future pyroterrorist attack. Fire can unleash the latent energy in our woodlands to achieve the effect of mass destruction. We, and by that I mean you, me, and everyone else living in government must make the threat known to the public and have them understand this dire danger to our homeland. Did you know that there are more houses built in the countryside than in our cities? As an example, Montana is a choice terrorist target because of the vast population increase in its forested valleys. Pyroterrorism in the western states is real, and it's no longer a question of if but when."

"States like Montana have first-rate National Guard units," Cantwell said. "Can't the guard be deployed where the danger is greatest?"

"How long does it take to deploy a National Guard unit?" Sensor said. "By the time they arrived, the fire would have run its course, like cops showing up twenty minutes after a bank robbery." He shook his gray head. "No, armed smoke jumpers are the answer. They can get to the attack site while the terrorists are still in the area." Sensor glanced over his shoulder as though fearful that someone may be listening. "Kill enough of the arsonists, and the rest will think twice before they even set foot in a forest. That's my opinion, and I'm trying to get the President to agree with me."

The older man stepped closer. "Superintendent Cantwell, there's one very important point you should be aware of . . . wildfires from terrorism are much more damaging than naturally occurring fires. In other words, strategically placing the ignition points affects how the flames spread over the landscape, and this is a technique that must be taught by experts. Let's hope that we don't have disgruntled traitors in our midst."

Unbidden, Mike Norris sprang into Cory Cantwell's mind, and he instantly dismissed the thought as disloyal and treacherous. For all his faults, Mike was a patriot, and his hatred for the National Wildfire Service would do nothing to alter that. Cantwell felt ashamed of himself, but his moment of self-flagellation passed when Sensor started talking again.

"From now on, you must be discreet, Superintendent Cantwell," the man said. "Yes, by all means go ahead and recruit new members for your team, but do it in the utmost secrecy. The last thing I want is to panic the public and send the media into a feeding frenzy. But the fact remains that pyroterrorists present a serious and present danger to our country, and they must be dealt with and soon . . . if we can find the money. Did you know the liberals in Congress are pushing their OBOA bill, and it could soon pass the House?"

"I've never heard of it." Cantwell said. "What does it mean?"

Sensor said, "OBOA . . . *Open Borders, Open Arms.* Do you believe that crap?"

"I'm sure if the bill passes, terrorists will love it," Cantwell said.

"Damn right. Hell, they love it already. Those who would do our nation harm are well aware that I oppose OBOA and will do everything in my power to see it defeated in the Senate. That's why I'm a marked man, or so the CIA and FBI tell me."

"Then you should have bodyguards, surely?" Cantwell said. He looked around the camp. "Where are they?"

"I've no use for them," Sensor said. "I don't want to be the mark surrounded by a bunch of guys in black suits wearing sunglasses and earpieces that only attract a would-be assassin's attention." He smiled. "Besides, I don't need a bodyguard. I'm a Texas boy born and bred, and I can look after myself."

Cantwell said, "Sir, I've already dealt with five terrorists, and each one of them did his best to kill me. I can't do it all by myself, nor do I want to. The bottom line is that I'm a firefighter, not a paid killer."

"Unfortunately, the only way to fight foreign killers is with killers of our own," Sensor said. "If the President signs off on it, and I see no reason why she won't, by next spring I plan to expand your unit to a hundred men and women, each trained as an arsonist fighter. And that is why I want you to take my young protégé here under your wing." Sensor placed his hand on the woman's arm and urged her forward. "I rescued Sarah Milano from a Department of Homeland Security desk job, and I know you will give her every courtesy."

The woman saw the doubt in Cory Cantwell's face and said, "I graduated from Harvard with a degree in environmental science and engineering, and I passed FBI qualification in the Glock 19M, the Remington 870P shotgun, and both the AR-15 and M-16." She smiled. "And sometimes for recreation I shoot the Colt Python .357 my father gave me as a graduation present. I do love Colt snake guns, Mr. Cantwell."

"You've shot at paper targets. Have you ever killed another human being?" Cantwell said.

Sensor answered that. "No, she has not. But if she ever has to, I'm sure Miss Milano will acquit herself well." For a moment, he watched a backhoe maneuvering around a felled tree trunk and then said, "Cantwell, I want Miss Milano and you to act as a team. You're familiar with Western firefighting, and you'll teach her what you know. What you don't already know, you'll learn together. I want you to discover where we are most vulnerable to terrorist attack. Acting on your recommendations, we'll base our armed smoke jumper teams close to those locations. If anyone, and I mean anyone from the President on down, gives you a hard time, call me. In the meantime, you'll have my complete moral and financial support, but let Miss Milano handle the finances. She's had some accounting training and is very good with budget matters. Now, do you understand all that?"

Cantwell nodded. Sensor looked tough, hard-eyed, and competent, a man of action with no backup in him. Cantwell was sure that hidden under his coat he had an old Texas shootin' iron tucked into his waistband with a dozen notches on the handle. "How long do I have to turn Miss Milano into a Punisher?" he said. He was irritated and used the forbidden word on purpose, a man forced into a job he now wanted no part of, with a woman . . . well, who could prove to be a complication.

"You have as long as it takes," Sensor said. "All I ask is that you give me the basis for an anti-terrorism unit that can stop the arson wildfires." He smiled. "Simple, isn't it? A piece of cake."

Cantwell had nothing more to say. and Sarah Milano seemed to be deep in thought.

"Well, good luck to you both," Sensor said. "Mr. Cantwell, don't underestimate the terrorists. They're well organized and have unlimited funds supplied by several oil-rich nations in the Middle East, and their command and control is simple. I believe one man lies at the heart of the Fire Warrior operation, and if your unit can find him, and kill him, the threat will cease."

"At least until they put a new man in charge," Cantwell said.

"Yes, but by then, God willing, we'll be better prepared," Sensor said.

Cantwell was surprised and more than a little unsettled. When a powerful Washington politician invokes the Deity, things must be really serious.

Base manager Fitch stepped beside Sensor and said, "If you're ready, I can take you to the gully where the flash flood happened, Mr. Sensor. But I warn you, there isn't much to see . . . rocks and water, mud puddles, and then more rocks and water."

"Nevertheless, I told the President I'd visit the place," Sensor said. "She wants to set up a memorial cairn at the spot, and for once both political parties are behind her."

"Near the spot," Fitch said. "The gorge will flood again."

"Then I stand corrected," Sensor said. "On high ground near the spot." He smiled, bearing the blunt firefighter no ill will. "How do we get there?"

"We walk, sir," Fitch said.

"Then lead the way," Sensor said.

But as he followed the fireman, he stopped, turned, and stepped back. He reached in his pocket and produced a cell phone. "I want you to take this phone, Cantwell. It's preprogrammed with two numbers, mine and the head of Homeland Security. You're a smart young man. You'll know if and when you need to use it."

Sensor walked away and again stopped. "One last thing. Do you know a man named Mike Norris?"

Cantwell let his surprise show. "Yes, he was a smoke jumper squad leader, but he's retired now. Why do you ask?"

Sensor shook his head. "No reason. No reason at all. I was just curious."

CHAPTER 7

"Well, where do we go from here?" Sarah Milano said. She had retrieved a small carry-on bag with wheels and a handle from Jacob Sensor's helicopter, and now it stood at her feet along with her briefcase.

"The car that brought me here is gone, so we're lost in the Arizona woods without transportation," Cory Cantwell said.

"It's Hansel and Gretel all over again," Sarah said.

"Let's hope we don't meet up with the wicked witch," Cantwell said.

"You already have," Sarah said.

That last made Cantwell smile. "We sure as hell can't stay here," he said.

"Well, you're the boss. What do we do?"

Cantwell thought for a moment, then said, "We'll hitch a ride to Phoenix and rent a car there."

"And then what?" Sarah said.

"All right, here's how it will go down. We check into a motel . . ."

"Two rooms," Sarah said.

"Of course," Cantwell said.

"Just making things clear, Superintendent Cantwell. I don't sleep with the boss."

"Very wise," Cantwell said. "Anyway, when I'm in *my* room, I'll call Homeland Security and I'll say, 'Hello, this is Superintendent Cory Cantwell here. If it's not too much trouble, can you chaps tell me where my Punishers are at.' They'll all be very polite and helpful and tell me that they can arrange a Punisher meeting. Or maybe just a conference call. I don't know which. And then they'll say, 'Glad we've been of help. Have a nice day, Mr. Cantwell.'"

Sarah smiled. "And if you believe that, I've got a bridge I can sell you."

"You don't think it will happen, huh?"

"I work for Homeland Security, remember. You'll be lucky if they let you talk to a filing clerk."

Suddenly Cantwell was irritated. "Well right now, that's all I've got. Okay, I could get a big map of America's forests and nail it to a wall. Then I could do what Sensor told me to do, stick colored flags into the most to the least vulnerable of them. The thing is, they're all vulnerable to arson attack, every last color-flagged one of them."

"Listen, mister, I don't want to be Little Red Riding Hood and move from state to state, taking long walks in the piney woods following the flags and dodging the big bad wolf," Sarah said, her own irritation showing. "A forest is a forest is a forest . . . and that would be a stupid waste of time."

"Then what do you suggest?" Cantwell said. He wanted to say, "Has anyone ever told you that you look pretty when you're mad?" but decided it could be a bad career move.

Sarah said, "Forget about maps and colored flags.

What we do is concentrate on the Punishers and come up with a way to form them into a well-organized, cohesive, crime-fighting unit."

"Like Eliot Ness did with his Untouchables during Prohibition?" Cantwell said.

"Yes, just like he did. Only instead of Al Capone and the Chicago gangsters we've got pyromaniac Middle Eastern terrorists who hate our guts."

"Exactly," Cantwell said. "So tell me about Eliot Ness."

"Didn't you see the movie with Kevin Costner and Sean Connery?" Sarah said.

"Yes, I saw the movie, who didn't? But I don't remember much about it. I know I got all choked up when Connery got killed. And yeah, and I loved it when Al Capone said, 'You get a lot further with a kind word and a gun than you would with a kind word.'"

"You remember more than you think," Sarah said. "Ness put together a handpicked team of men he could trust, that couldn't be bought, and that's why he called them the Untouchables. And that's what we should do, pick our own crack team of Punishers and present them to Sensor as a fait accompli."

"And where do we find these trusted men . . . and women?"

"Don't worry, we'll find them. Once the word gets out, the best of them will come looking for us."

"I hope that's the case," Cantwell said. "We can set up a tent somewhere and a sign that says, 'Trustworthy Punishers Wanted. Apply Within.'"

"Roll up, roll up," Sarah said. "We offer low pay and lots of danger."

"Umm . . ." Cantwell said. He was distracted, his gaze fixed on the sky. "What the hell? That's not a Forest Service chopper."

Sarah Milano followed his eyes. No more than fifty feet off the ground, a tan-colored, two-seat helicopter raced toward them, its blade-slapping, whop-whop-whop racket shredding the silence. Cantwell caught a glimpse of the pilot and the man sitting next to him before the aircraft passed overhead.

"Sarah, the passenger has a rifle!" he yelled above the clattering din. "Damn it, I think he could be after Sensor!"

Cantwell retrieved his Glock from his pack then ran in the direction of the gully, and Sarah Milano followed after him, unsteady on high heels as she fumbled in her briefcase.

Cory Cantwell sprinted the hundred yards of open ground that led to a rock-walled gorge about forty feet deep, a few inches of water in its bottom and a few splintered tree trunks the only evidence that a killer flash flood had passed that way. Like men on a tightrope, using outstretched arms to steady themselves, two hundred yards away Jacob Sensor and Stewart Fitch walked along the base of the wall, picking their tentative path among sundried boulders and downed pines. Both seemed oblivious to the helicopter that hovered above them like a great, tawny bird of prey.

Cantwell stood on the edge of the gully and, guessing that the younger Fitch would have better hearing, he cupped a hand around his mouth and yelled, "Fitch!"

The firefighter turned, saw Cantwell at the edge of the gorge, and waved.

"Get down!" Cantwell hollered. "Hit the deck!"

Many past dangers had fine-honed Fitch's reactions. If he couldn't make out the words, he heard the spiking alarm in Cantwell's voice and read the tension in the man's body. He looked up at the helicopter . . . and then two events happened very quickly.

Fitch grabbed Sensor and manhandled him to the rocky ground. A moment later, the chopper made a strafing pass, expertly flown, the tips of its spinning blades almost scraping the V-shaped walls of the gorge.

Cantwell heard the flat chatter of a fully automatic rifle but had no time to see the effect of the fire. As the helicopter thundered past him, he got off a shot from the Glock, but the bullet went nowhere. The chopper climbed, then turned, coming in for another strafing run. Behind Cantwell, people were yelling to one another as they dived for cover. He two-handed the pistol into a shooting position as the chopper reentered the gorge. It was like trying to shoot the driver of a speeding NASCAR race car, and again Cantwell's shot missed.

Damn. This was impossible.

He fired again and again as the airborne rifleman cut loose at his targets on the gully floor. Fitch sprawled on the rocks, and it looked like he'd been hit, but he saw no sign of Jacob Sensor, who'd probably taken the first bullets. The chopper hovered, the gunman leaned out of the cab, obviously hunting for signs of life, and the roaring racket of the rotors in the ravine was earsplitting. Cantwell felt a tug on his sleeve, and beside him Sarah Milano held a blue Colt Python with a four-inch barrel.

Cover me.

The woman mouthed the words. And then she was gone, sliding down the wall of the ravine dislodging showers of shingle. Still wearing high heels.

"You get back here!" Cantwell yelled. Like a dad calling after a mischievous toddler.

Cursing, Cantwell went after her . . . the crazy chick was asking to get herself killed.

Sarah's feetfirst descent was arrested by a stunted willow that had rooted itself on the gorge wall. She'd lost a shoe and planted her bare right foot on the base of the tree, her left leg slightly bent as she leaned against the rocky slope. Cantwell skidded to a stop beside her.

"Get out of here!" he yelled. "Hell, too late, he's seen us."

"I think he's got an AK-47," Sarah said. Then, "He's coming after us."

Nose down, the helicopter beat its way along the gully. Sarah yelled. "Shoot at the pilot."

Later a CIA report of the incident mentioned that Sarah Milano "handled her weapon with considerable skill and, according to Superintendent Cory Cantwell, revealed commendable coolness under fire." What Cantwell in fact said was that she'd John Wayne'd it in high heels and mascara.

Sarah Milano opened fire first, a double tap that hit the chopper's windshield. The .357 rounds punched two small spiderwebs into the plexiglass less than an inch apart. The aircraft reared up, roaring like a wounded animal. Cantwell slammed shot after shot into the stricken machine, the flat reports of his 9mm joined by the louder *blam! blam! blam!* of Sarah's bucking Colt.

The chopper's nose came down again, and Cantwell caught a glimpse of the pilot slumped over the controls. The rifleman jumped clear but dropped his rifle. Cantwell didn't watch where the man landed, his attention fixed on the damaged aircraft. With a noise like a spiked iron ball rolling down a marble hallway, the helicopter careened along the gorge until its blades clipped the wall. Its nose suddenly dipped, and it slammed into the rocky bottom and exploded, shooting sheets of yellow and red flame and black smoke high into the air.

Sirens sounded in the distance, and the air was fouled with the smell of burning helicopter. Sarah suddenly pointed down into the gorge. "Cory, look!"

The man who'd jumped out of the helicopter scrambled painfully over the rocks to reach his rifle that lay fifty feet from him. The gunman wore a white T-shirt, black shorts, and a New York Yankees ball cap. His seriously injured right leg was visible. The broken shinbone stuck through the bloody skin, and the man may have been too shocked to feel it.

"Hey, you!" Cantwell yelled. "Leave the gun and stay right there!"

The man turned to the sound and saw Cantwell and Sarah making their way toward him along the wall of the gorge, and his ashen, strained face twisted in malice. He looked away and redoubled his efforts to reach the Kalashnikov.

Cantwell raised his Glock and snapped off a shot. The bullet *spaaang*ed off a boulder in front of the gunman and then . . .

Sensor emerged from a shallow cleft in the rock wall. Cantwell saw him glance at Stewart Fitch's sprawled body before he reached inside his coat and produced a .32 caliber Walther PPK. The gunman shrieked his frustrated anger and increased his efforts to reach his rifle. Sensor raised the pistol to eye level and neatly shot the man in the side of the head an inch above the top of his left ear.

He was already dead when he hit the rocks at his feet.

CHAPTER 8

"Stewart Fitch is dead," Cory Cantwell said. "He leaves a pregnant wife and two kids."

"I'll see to it personally that the Fitch family lacks for nothing," Jacob Sensor said.

Sarah Milano said, "It won't bring the poor woman's husband back."

"No . . . no it won't," Sensor said. "That is why a war like the one we're fighting is such a terrible thing."

Firefighters picked their way into the gully and crowded around Fitch's body, their voices muted, faces tight and pale. Coming on the heels of the flash flood, the death of a respected and well-liked base manager had hit them hard. It was a punch to the gut they didn't need.

Sensor stepped closer to Cantwell, who'd just comforted a female smoke jumper he knew and liked, and whispered, "Come see this. You too, Miss Milano."

Sensor led the others to the dead body of the helicopter gunman and used his foot to roll him onto his back. The dead man had yellow hair, and his open eyes were blue. "He isn't," Sensor said, "a Middle Eastern terrorist. This fool was a homegrown hit man."

Cantwell looked at the dead man and said, "If he wasn't a terrorist, then why the hell did he hold a grudge against you?"

"There's nothing on earth more vicious and dangerous than a snowflake with a cause," Sensor said. "I reckon this man was hired to assassinate me because of my opposition to OBOA, and somebody bankrolled him. Seems like he knew some liberal bigshot with a pile of money."

Cody Cantwell voiced what Sarah Milano was thinking. "That's a stretch, Mr. Sensor."

"Not too much of one," the older man said. "Like our own Mafia, Islamic terrorists do their own killing. They don't hire it done. No, this man had only one target . . . me. Once Homeland Security looks into his background, I'll know who he was and maybe the identity of the man who paid for the helicopter and its pilot."

"The firefighters say the pilot was burned beyond recognition," Sarah said.

"No matter." Sensor toed the dead man. "This one will provide all the information I need." He looked down the gully and frowned. "Here come the cops with their rolls of yellow tape, and I want you two out of here."

"They'll want to talk to us, Mr. Sensor," Sarah said. Her pantyhose were in tatters, and she held her scuffed high heels in her hands. "It was Cory and me who brought down the helicopter."

"Don't worry about that, I'll tell the law who to talk to and when they can talk to them," Sensor said. He looked around and said to an older firefighter, "Please find Superintendent Cantwell and Miss Milano a ride into Phoenix."

"I'll do it myself," the man said. He looked at Cantwell. "I'll let you get your gear, Superintendent. When do you and the lady want to leave?"

"Now. They want to leave now," Sensor said. Then to Sarah, "Keep watching the news."

The driver was a firefighter named John Monahan. He'd served twenty years as a smoke jumper and was due to retire. He told Cantwell and Sarah that he and his wife had already bought a two-bedroom, one-bath, condo in Boca Raton, Florida, with a view of the ocean, a rectangle of blue bookended by two other condos. "The place is big enough for me and Jane," he said. "And the spare bedroom will be nice when the kids visit."

"Happy retirement," Sarah said. "I'm told Boca Raton is lovely year-round."

"Hurricanes can be a problem," Monahan said. He shook his head. "Lot of traffic on this road, huh?" An ambulance with flashing lights and a wailing siren sped past, followed by a sheriff's car and then a posse of media vans with satellite dishes carrying blond female reporters and intent drivers.

"There are some nice motels on the edge of town," Monahan said. "And there's a Budget Car Rental close by and a steakhouse."

"Sounds good to me," Cantwell said.

"Not to me!" Sarah said. "I want a Hilton with a minibar, room service, and a long soak in a big tub. Our expense account can handle it."

Monahan laughed. "Good for you, Miss Milano. Well, Superintendent, is it a Hilton?"

"She's the boss," Cantwell said. "Just stop at a 7-11 or something. I need to buy cigarettes."

"Anyone ever tell you that smoking is bad for your health?" Sarah said.

"Click!" Cantwell said. "According to the adding machine in my brain, that makes the three thousand, seven-hundred and forty-fifth time."

"I've ordered dinner for two, Cory," Sarah Milano said, standing at Cantwell's hotel room door. "At eight o'clock. I hope you'll join me."

"I'd love to," Cantwell said. "Dinner with a beautiful lady. What more could a man ask?"

"I don't know what he could ask. Usually men find that I'm all that they need."

Slightly flustered, Cantwell said, "I'm . . . uh . . . what did you order for me?"

Sarah was dressed in the same white blouse she'd worn earlier but had changed into a pair of faded jeans and wedge-heeled sandals. She'd pulled back her hair and tied it with a pink ribbon. She looked beautiful and cool and poised, like a fashion model. Only a slight paleness and faint shadows under her eyes revealed the toll the events of the day had taken on her.

"Medallions of fillet of beef with au gratin potatoes and vanilla ice cream for dessert," Sarah said. "I kept it simple. Oh, and wine of course. Merlot. But I don't remember the vintage."

"And for you?"

"Same thing. When it comes to food, I like meat and potatoes. I'm not very adventurous."

"I'll knock on your door at eight," Cantwell said. "Black tie, of course."

Sarah smiled slightly and handed him a plastic drinking cup. "Jack Daniel's . . . enjoy." She looked into his eyes. "But no funny business tonight, Cory. I'm too damned tired."

"That makes two of us," Cantwell said. He smiled, then, "I look forward to joining you for dinner."

CHAPTER 9

Nasim Azar got the call he expected at one thirty in the morning as rain rattled on his bedroom window, driven by a boisterous wind. Mike Norris sounded drunk, his words slurred. "We do it my way, you understand?"

"Mr. Norris, how nice to hear from you," Azar said. Then after a moment's hesitation, "Even at this late hour."

"It isn't late, it's early, early morning," Norris said. "Did you hear me? We do it my way, like the Sinatra song."

"Absolutely, Mr. Norris." Azar sat up in bed. "That was always my intention. As far as I'm concerned, you are the boss. From now on, what you say goes."

"Prissy little feller, ain't you? Hey, I've forgotten . . . what the hell are you, some kind of Arab, I think?"

"My grandparents came to this country from Syria a hundred years ago."

"That so? I don't blame them. Syria is a dung heap. And when you go back there you can tell them that."

Azar took no offense. It was the liquor talking with just an edge of repressed anger.

Norris said, "So we want to start a little blaze, right? One where no one gets hurt? Just enough to prove my point that satellites and ground cameras don't work to prevent forest fires. I want to impress on the idiots that all they do is make it more dangerous for the smoke jumper crews on the ground . . . to say nothing of the surrounding residents."

"Exactly," Azar said. "Of course, you must have realized by now, I could easily start such a fire myself. But I'm a humanitarian, and I came to you because I want it to be safe . . . without loss of life. I want the fire to be effective in getting our point across."

"*Our* point across," Norris said. "That *our* puzzles the hell out of me. What do you care, Azar? You're a damned camel jockey from dung-heap Syria."

"No, Mr. Norris, I'm an American, just like you, and I care, but for a different reason."

"That reason being that you want to sell firefighting equipment."

"That's part of it, but I want the watchtowers restored. You could call it a mild obsession with me."

"Hell, apart from me, you must be the only person in the United States who wants the watchtowers restored," Norris said. "These days watchtower is a bad word . . . like shit."

"Yes, I do care, but as a loyal American I need more. Mr. Norris. I want to work to prevent the terrible scorching that is destined to come."

"Scorching? What scorching? You mean more forest fires?" Norris said, drunk, trying to comprehend what the man was telling him.

"I mean forest fires started by Muslim terrorists," Azar said. "I believe hundreds of them, Fire Warriors they're called, are already here and will soon spread across the country. If they are not stopped, this nation will be set ablaze, and only ashes will be left of our great forests and all the many towns in the path of the devouring flames."

"Hey, how do you know all this?" Norris said. He sounded suspicious. "How do you know about them hundreds of fire warriors?"

Azar forced a smile into his voice. "My dear Mr. Norris, Muslims in the community speak to other Muslims. Nothing of this monumental nature can be kept a secret for too long." Then, a careful step onto quicksand. "I understand that a firefighter friend of yours is in charge of an anti-terrorist unit."

Norris didn't hesitate. "Yeah, his name is Cory Cantwell. A good man, but he believes in the new ways of the National Wildfire Service."

"I fully support his anti-terrorism efforts, and I'd like to tell him so," Azar said. "Can you arrange an introduction?"

"The last I heard he's here in Portland. I'll see what I can do," Norris said. He was very drunk. "If we set enough fires, maybe it won't change anyone's mind about restoring the watchtowers, but what the hell . . . it's worth a try."

"I think if we make an effective presentation, it will have more impact than you expect, Mr. Norris," Azar said.

"So, why not?" Norris said. "Where do you want to meet, little Arab man?"

"Why don't we get together tomorrow, say two o'clock? The address of my warehouse is on the card I gave you."

"I looked your company up, Azar. I think maybe I've used some of your pissant equipment. It was all junk, if I remember right."

"Oh dear, I'm sorry to hear that," Azar said.

"Junk . . . it was all junk. Every damn thing was junk, I tell you."

"As I told you, Mr. Norris, the previous owners of the Hestia Corporation were not up to standard. I assure you, at present the company is in fine shape. Now how much money do you want?"

There was a long silence on the other end of the line, and Nasim sensed he'd made a mistake.

"Say that again," Norris said.

"I meant living expenses, Mr. Norris. You'll need something to live on."

"I don't want your money for myself," Norris said, finally. "I need to be sure we have enough cash to buy equipment and . . . and do the job right, understand? You're not . . . you're not bribing me to start wildfires?"

"Of course, not. I meant money for supplies," Azar said. One thing he'd learned selling high-end rugs: when you change your mind, always pretend it was what you meant all along. "Oh, and Mr. Norris, we need accurate maps."

"I've got plenty of those. I got good Forest Service maps. The best there are."

"Then why don't you pick out more than one location for our test," Azar said. "Perhaps one in Washington, one in Oregon, and one in California. We can choose the final locations when we meet."

"See you then," Norris said, his words slurred, barely understandable. "I need to sleep . . ."

Clunk! Silence. Mike Norris had dropped the phone.

* * *

Nasim Azar ended the call smiling. In the morning he'd order a couple of his men to get the warehouse presentable. He'd bought the Hestia company along with its inventory of firefighting equipment, but it was so run-down he'd also purchased some state-of-the-art hoses and other gear. It had to look good for Mike Norris.

Restless, excited by his progress with Norris, Nasim Azar gave up on sleep. He rose from bed, stepped to his bedroom window, and stared out to where the dark sweep of the Willamette River reflected the lights of the tall business blocks on its banks like amber, yellow, and white brushstrokes of paint. Across the street from Azar's apartment, three middle-aged couples, late-night revelers by their laughter and loud talk, hurried home through the rain, scurrying along the Grand Avenue sidewalk like windblown leaves.

Azar's eyes trailed the four walkers until he lost them in darkness. He yielded to his thoughts and pondered the events of the day. The call from Norris had been welcome, though he didn't really need the man. Norris would teach the brethren the best and fastest way to set a dangerous wildfire, and that was all. When he was no longer useful, he could be eliminated. But the news of the deaths of three holy warriors at the hands of Cory Cantwell had deeply troubled him. By Azar's count, the man Cantwell had now murdered five Muslim martyrs, and if the information he'd received from the field was correct, killers from the unit Cantwell commanded had shot another two. That was seven fire warriors dead out of his total strength of fifty, not the hundreds he'd boasted to Norris. Azar's face tightened, its harsh lines visible in his reflection in the window. Cantwell had to die. He would kill the man himself, perhaps after he lured him to the warehouse. Soon, he must make a plan.

He turned and stepped to his desk and retrieved a copy of the manifesto he'd sent out to his operatives across the country . . .

Brothers

As you now know, our new terror weapon is fire, the very thought of which makes the Crusaders tremble in their shoes. No longer must we depend on guns and mass shootings, bombs or speeding vehicles to mow down pedestrians on their filthy sidewalks, but instead we can take up incendiary weapons to cleanse the world of the unbelievers.

Already, such fire attacks, that we have named the Scorching, have destroyed towns, neighborhoods and private, public and government property while claiming hundreds of lives. The jihadi have taught the Crusaders a lesson on just how destructive an operation of such simplicity can be. With some basic and readily available materials, and I speak of inflammables, we can TERRORIZE THE ENTIRE UNITED STATES.

Pyroterrorism, as it applies to the righteous terror mujahid, is to initiate forest fires using flammables to destroy the great woodlands and, in the process, kill thousands of infidels and send them from the inferno of this world to the eternal flames of the next.

All that I require of you, the mujahid, is to acquire the combustibles you wish to use, select your target and determine the best time for execution. Because many flammables are such a part of everyday living, pyroterrorist attacks on forests are very difficult to prevent. A gasoline can bought from any hardware store may be filled at any gas station without raising the slightest suspicion.

Go forth then, soldiers of the Islamic State, and do as God wills. Set this crusader nation ablaze from coast to coast and always remember that Allah does not allow the reward of good doers to be lost. Allahu Akbar!

Azar tossed the memo back in a drawer and nodded to himself. He believed that he'd emphasized to the operatives that pyroterrorism must not be belittled. Even if the forest attacks did not result in hundreds of casualties, harming and enraging the unbelievers would be sufficient reward.

Agitated, his brain now spinning with schemes and plots, Azar stepped back to the window. The view was the same, the river, the rain, and the blustery wind. The street was now empty, uninteresting, and ill-defined, like a splotched watercolor painted by an amateur.

Sleep would elude him tonight. Unless . . .

Hating himself for his weakness and his addiction to female flesh, Azar dialed a number on his cell. When a man picked up at the other end, he said, "It's me." A pause as the other man acknowledged Azar, and then, "I need a white woman for a couple of hours. The usual, a blond with big tits who doesn't mind being slapped around a little." Another pause, then Azar said, "Yes, I know it's late, Darnell. All right, all right, I'm not too fussy, and I'll take what you have. Yes, Corky is fine. She isn't too black. No offense intended, Darnell. Okay, half an hour."

Azar slept naked, but now he slipped on a silk Moroccan sleeping robe and waited.

Corky Jackson, perky and punctual, was always on time.

CHAPTER 10

Mike Norris woke up around eight o'clock in the morning. He'd slept, or fell into a coma, for only a few hours. His head pounded and his belly heaved, and when he tried to drink a cup of coffee, it tasted like black acid.

What the hell did I do last night? Did I call that little Azar creep, or did I imagine it?

He pulled out his cell phone and checked. Yes, he'd called the man at one-thirty . . . when he'd been his drunkest. And yet, now that he considered it, he wasn't really that sorry. Examples needed to be made, small fires, causing little damage, but in places where lookouts would have seen them. The point was, the National Wildfire Service needed people out there on the front line twenty-four-seven, trained and experienced and doing it as an avocation, not a bunch of mercenaries, hired seasonally, minimally trained, who were doing it for the money.

I should talk to Cory Cantwell one last time, he thought. *The guy really might have a point—maybe he can make more progress from the inside. I should give him one last chance. Besides, Azar wanted to meet him. That could be a help. The damned Arab had a glib tongue.*

Norris groaned his way out of bed and stood under the showerhead for as long as the hot water lasted, and when it turned cold, he forced himself to stand there until he yelled in numbed shock. He stumbled out of the shower and grabbed a towel. He finally felt awake.

The last time he'd heard, Cory was working in the 5050 building on Hawthorne Boulevard in downtown Portland. Norris had passed the place a few times, and it was close enough to his dingy apartment block that he could leave his truck and ride his ten-speed.

An hour later, he got on the bike and headed toward the high-rises on the horizon.

"Mr. Cantwell no longer works here," the receptionist at the front desk said.

"What do you mean?" Norris said, annoyed. "I just saw him at an NWS ceremony."

"I didn't mean to imply that Superintendent Cantwell no longer works for the Service, but that he has been transferred to another unit. Mr. Williams is in charge of the Willamette department now. Would you like to speak with him?"

Norris considered it. He'd never met Harvey Williams, but the man had a decent reputation. He was a company man through and through, but apparently, he'd been a smoke jumper who'd spent some time on the front lines.

"If you don't mind talking to him," he said finally.

Surprisingly, Williams made time for him right away.

"Mike Norris!" the man exclaimed, extending his hand. "I'm so glad to meet you in the flesh. You're a damned legend in the Wildfire Service."

"Thank you," Norris said. He ignored the hand and pulled a chair toward him and sat.

Williams had been slighted, and his voice took on an edge. "And you're also an enormous pain in the ass."

The change in tone was so abrupt that it took Norris a minute to react. He thought it was a joke until he looked up into Williams's irritated scowl. The man's skin was a deep mahogany color, and under his shirt he had the shoulders of an NFL linebacker. In fact, he'd played three seasons at left guard for the Detroit Lions until a knee injury sidelined him for good. He wore a Wildfire Service olive green uniform and had a gold wedding band on his left hand.

"I decided to meet you as a professional courtesy, Mike, because I think someone needs to tell you some home truths," Williams said. "Man, you have to back off. You're causing problems for the Service, problems that we don't need. The old days are done and gone. Our funding has been cut to the bone, and observers in watchtowers have given way to on-site cameras and eye-in-the-sky satellites, and that's how it's going to stay from now on." Norris opened his mouth to speak, but Williams held up a silencing hand as big as a baseball glove. "You wanted to see Cory Cantwell, right? Well, Cantwell is off fighting a war, not against forest fires, but the people who deliberately start them. It's a war on terrorism, Mike, and we're all in it. Cory is my boss, and that's why"—he opened his desk drawer and took out a Glock 19—"I carry this thing to work every day. I never know when I'm going to be called upon to use it. Right now, your own little personal war is something we don't need. If you can't be a loyal soldier, then quit. Oh, wait. You did. You have nothing to do with us anymore."

"I resigned," Norris said. "Best thing I ever done."

"I don't know about that," Williams said. "You couldn't get your own way and you walked out in a snit."

"But I still care," Norris said. "I care because I lost almost my entire crew. I care because the satellite had us dropped into the wrong location. I care because a man in a watchtower could have saved us."

Williams shook his head. "No, that's not how it was. Mike, you could've saved your crew, and you know it. I believe you're trying to blame the Service for your own failings. What really happened at Indian Wells, Mike?"

"Damn you, Williams, are you accusing me of cowardice?" Norris said.

"I read your report."

"You didn't read nothing in there about cowardice."

"It was self-serving," Williams said. "To say the least."

"It was the truth."

"Some of it was the truth."

"All of it was true."

"Why did you run for the safety of the plateau while your crew was getting itself killed in the ravine?"

"I saved the lives I could. I saved two women."

"Yes, you did. But they were on the slope, not in the ravine."

"Who says I ran for the plateau?"

"Cory Cantwell told me. He said you were close to the plateau when he saw you."

"Then he's a damned liar," Norris said.

"I doubt if Cory ever told a lie in his life," Williams

said. "He's too much of a Boy Scout for that." The man leaned forward on his desk, his big shoulders pushed forward, as though taking a stance, ready for a tackle. "Here's some advice, Mike," he said. "Even if it's only to yourself, admit the blame for Indian Wells. It wasn't satellites or cameras that failed that day, it was you. You panicked and ran, didn't you? Hell, man, it can happen to anybody, me, Cantwell, whoever you want to name. Now here's more advice . . . from now on learn to live with it . . . and keep your big trap shut."

Norris slammed to his feet. "The hell with you, Williams," he said. "You know nothing. You're only sitting in that chair because you're a black man."

"Mike, everyone thinks you deserve respect and so did I, once," Williams said. "But not any longer. I think you're only one step away from being a traitor to your country. You've become a disgrace, an embarrassment. If I used this Glock to shoot you now, I'd be doing you a favor."

Norris threw an oath at Williams and stormed out of his office. He strode past the secretary, his back stiff, and got as far as the stairwell before reacting. He slammed his fist into the concrete wall and realized he was seething with impotent rage and frustration.

Mike Norris reached his apartment with no clear memory of riding his bike there. His mind tormented by dark, spiking thoughts, he rushed to his bedroom, pulled out an old briefcase from the closet, and started to fill it with maps. He'd only intended to take one, since he'd already marked out what he thought was the most likely spot for a demonstration fire, but now he took them all.

These were the maps that the public didn't have access to, detailed topography for firefighters, wind patterns, water sources, and most important of all, the location of any of the new cameras that could be taken out by drones.

CHAPTER 11

Under a copper-colored sky, Mike Norris drove to Nasim's business located in the city's Pearl District just north of downtown. Most of the old warehouses there had been converted into luxury loft apartments, but Azar's still functioned as a storage and office unit, though he'd converted rooms into a couple of apartments. The corrugated iron front doors had been replaced by wood and led into garage space. To the right, behind glass doors, was an unmanned security desk, then an open stairwell, and beyond that a plain pine door with a sign above it that read in block letters:

HESTIA CORPORATION

Norris knuckled the door, and after a pause a young, dark-haired, dark-eyed man answered. Norris detected a shoulder-holster bulge under the youngster's charcoal gray suitcoat. "Can I help you?" the man said. He had a mid-Atlantic accent, the effete, half-American, half-British, speaking style of the East Coast elite that Norris thought had died with George Plimpton and William F. Buckley.

"Name's Norris," he said. "I'm here to see Nasim Azar."

"Ah yes, he's expecting you. My name is Salman Assad."

The young man let him inside with a slight bow and diffident smile. Then Mike Norris shocked him. With the speed of a striking rattler, Norris turned on the man. His right hand shot out, grabbed Assad by the throat, and slammed him hard against the doorjamb. At the same time Norris's left hand dived into the man's coat, and he retrieved a Smith & Wesson .38 special J-frame from the shoulder holster. He rammed the muzzle of the gun into the man's surprised mouth and said, "Suck on that like it's your mama's teat, boy."

The kid was scared, his dark eyes wide. The crazy man was a finger looking for a trigger.

"What's going on here, Mr. Norris?"

Without turning his head, Norris said, "Is that you, Azar?"

"Yes, of course it's me."

"This is the second time today I've run into a man with a gun," Norris said. "It's starting to irritate me."

"I'm a rich man, and like all rich men, I have enemies," Azar said. His voice was level, calm, unhurried. "The young man is my bodyguard, and he means you no harm."

Norris let Assad go and turned to Azar. "You invited me here and I was greeted by a man with a gun," he said. "I don't call that friendly."

"If I'd known exactly when you were arriving, I assure you Salman would have set his weapon aside," Azar said.

"We agreed on two p.m.," Norris said.

Norris did something tricky with the J-frame. He spun the revolver around his forefinger before it slammed into his palm and he presented it butt-first to Assad. "If I was you, I'd find another line of work, mister," he said. "The bodyguarding business fits you like pantyhose on a pig."

The young man grabbed the Smith, his eyes full of black anger.

Azar recognized potential danger and said, "Salman, return to your post."

Norris had been slick with the .38, but he was not by inclination or practice a gunman. He therefore missed what Assad did next, a move he should've taken as warning. The young Palestinian's eyes never left Norris's face as without looking he slid his revolver into its holster as expertly as a samurai sheathing a sword. Assad had been caught off guard, but a more gun-savvy man than Norris would have recognized him as a trained warrior . . . or assassin. At another time and place, the young man would be a force to be reckoned with.

"I have the maps," Norris said.

"Excellent," Azar said.

"They're Forest Service maps, the best there is."

"I would not expect a man like you to have any other kind," Azar said, smiling.

"Damn right," Norris said.

Azar led Norris to a large room that smelled of carpets and mothballs. Without a word, the big man stalked to a long table at its center and swept a clutter of papers onto the floor. He slammed down his briefcase and spread out his maps.

"We aren't thinking big enough, Azar," he said. "We need to wake up these fools at the National Wildfire Service, and I propose we strike at multiple locations at the same time." He turned to Azar, expecting an objection, but instead, he saw a look of satisfaction on the little man's face.

"Splendid, Mr. Norris, just splendid," Azar said. "That's the way to force them to sit up and take notice. But, before we go any further, did you arrange my meeting with Cory Cantwell?"

"No," Norris said. "He's no longer in Portland."

Azar hid his disappointment. "Ah, is that the case? Well, some other time, perhaps. Now, on as happier note, I've arranged an amusing little demonstration for you." He hesitated. "I trust you don't think me too bold."

"What kind of demonstration?" Norris said, sudden suspicion in his tone.

"A demonstration of our long reach, Mr. Norris," Azar said. "I'll prove to you that even using borrowed untrained . . . ah . . . operatives, nothing is impossible."

It was enough to give Norris pause. But it did not.

"Tell me," he said. "Who the hell are you borrowing?"

Azar said, "Tomorrow morning associates of mine will set a fire in the Hollywood Hills." The man read the question on Norris's face. *I'm borrowing brother jihadists, you ignorant drunk . . .* "Around the famous Hollywood sign to be exact."

It took Norris a few moments to let that last sink in, and when it did, he became angry. "That's damned stupid. No matter what, nobody's going to build a lookout tower in L.A. to spot brush fires."

"I know that," Azar said. "But it will warn the authorities that if we can set a brush fire in downtown

Los Angeles, we can set other fires elsewhere. I can only see it helping our cause, Mr. Norris."

"Cause? I know what my cause is, Azar," Norris said. "What the hell is yours?"

"As loyal Americans we share the same cause," Azar said. "We don't want to see our great forests burned by terrorists and . . . and by criminal negligence."

He told that lie without blinking, and Mike Norris swallowed it hook, line, and sinker.

"Now, let us study the maps and begin to make our plans," Azar said. He took in Norris's hungover appearance and said, "A drink while we work?"

Norris didn't hesitate. "Bourbon . . . neat."

"Coming up," Azar said. He stepped to a heavy oak cabinet bar and opened the doors. "I don't drink alcohol, but many of my friends and carpet-buyer clients do, especially Jews. Jews like to drink."

"I wouldn't know about that," Norris said. "All I know is that I like to drink."

Azar returned and passed the glass to Norris. "Later, for your amusement, I have a woman for you."

"A woman? Here?"

"No, not here. Her name is Corky Jackson, a black girl, and she'll come to your home. I've booked her for the whole weekend, but you can throw her out before then if you tire of her." Azar smiled. "But you'll like Corky. She's a very inventive whore, and she doesn't mind some rough stuff."

Norris was taken aback, stunned into silence.

"Call her a business perk," Azar said. "My little gift to you as my new associate."

Before Indian Wells, Mike Norris would have been

scandalized . . . offended enough to punch Azar on the mouth or at least to tell him to go to hell and take his whore with him. But that was then, this was now. It was a measure of his moral and physical decline that he nodded and said, "Yeah, send her over. I look forward to it. Inventive, you say?"

"Very. You won't be bored."

"Sounds like my kind of gal," Norris said, the bourbon already talking for him.

Azar smiled. He watched Dr. Jekyll slowly transform into Mr. Hyde, and such a man could be used . . . and then, like Corky Jackson, so easily discarded.

CHAPTER 12

It was a small fire, and Merinda Barker's crew contained it relatively quickly, though they'd arrived just in the nick of time. The Santa Ana winds were picking up, and the fire could have whipped up to a dangerous size quickly. The firebreak was nearly complete, and Merinda straightened up and looked down the line. Every one of her people had their backs bent over their shovels, and she nodded her approval.

On the barren hillside, mostly grass and underbrush, the only real damage was to the big letter "D," which was now blackened and listing to one side.

The woman smiled. *So this is Hollywood . . . says it right there. Look at me, Ma, I made it.*

She turned and saw John Aaronson working under the D, and sudden alarm spiked at her. "Get the hell out of there," she called out to the young man. He looked over at her and she waved toward the sign. "It's about to fall over!"

The firefighter's eyes grew big, and he quickly scampered to one side. At that moment, the D gave a screech, toppled over, and then the huge letter tumbled down the hillside, end over end, landing just short of a house at the bottom.

Merinda closed her eyes and said a prayer of thanks to Saint Florian, the patron saint of firefighters, for his tender mercies.

Now the sign read, HOLLYWOO.

When Merinda Barker was a child on a Navajo reservation, she'd been told about her maternal grandfather, who died before she was born. He'd been a stuntman for the same Poverty Row studios where John Wayne had gotten his start. She'd seen Grandpa on screen in a score of shoot-'em-up two-reelers, a short stocky man with the Roman nose her family was afflicted with. Sometimes the nose worked, like with her mother, who was something of a beauty. But a few times it didn't do near so well, as with Merinda.

Well, Ma, big snoot or not, I finally made it to Tinseltown just like grandpa Joe Locklear.

Then . . . suddenly . . .

"Everybody!" A yelp of fear and shock from John Aaronson. Then, "Oh, my God! Oh, my dear God!"

Merinda scrambled through brush to reach to the young man, who stared at what looked like a bundle of clothing at his feet. Aaronson then turned away and violently threw up.

The body had been revealed when the D letter fell and dragged a pile of chaparral with it . . . a man in uniform . . . the dark blue uniform of the Los Angeles Police Department.

Aaronson turned to Merinda, his face ashen, strings of

saliva hanging from his open mouth. "Look at his head!" he said. Then again, "Oh, my God!"

The back of the police officer's skull had been caved in by a blow from a heavy blunt instrument. It looked to Merinda Barker that the cop was very young and that his death had been both violent and quick. Suddenly, she and her eleven firefighters found themselves in the middle of a crime scene.

The Hollywood blaze was the second fire Merinda Barker's wildland crew had contained in the hills above Los Angeles since they'd flown in from Arizona earlier in the day. She and the others had descended into the smoky skies of Los Angeles thinking they were going to get a chance to rest up for a while. But they'd barely debarked from the plane before a National Wildfire Service van pulled up, and grizzled old John Cassidy got out and waved Merinda over.

He shoved out his hand. "Remember me?"

"Of course I do. From the fire in Oregon that time," Merinda said. "It was a bad one."

"A year ago," Cassidy said. "Seems like yesterday."

"And you don't look a day older."

"Maybe not, but the day I'm having is making me feel older."

"I understand we're a backup crew," Merinda said.

Cassidy shook his head. "No, you're not. Hate to do this to you, but you're my troubleshooters, and I need you right away. Everyone else is working on bigger fires, and we've got a little blaze up in the hills that I'd like to put out before the afternoon Santa Ana winds kick in."

Unlike her tired crew, Merinda restrained her groan. "We're ready. If we can change into our fire gear somewhere?"

"Do it right here, no one will notice," Cassidy said.

Merinda looked around. They were in the middle of the tarmac, with the vast windows of the airport lounge a sea of interested faces. She shrugged. This wasn't a time for false modesty. She and her seven men and three women quickly stripped and changed.

"Our equipment hasn't been unloaded yet, Mr. Cassidy," Merinda said.

"No problem, I got the basic stuff you need in the van," the man said. "Like I said, it isn't a big fire. I'll make sure your luggage and gear gets to your dormitory."

They drove through the middle of L.A. with flashing lights and sirens blaring. A fine black dust gathered in the corners of the windshield swirled up from their passage, and it took a few moments for Merinda to realize that it was ash. The air smelled of smoke and had turned as gray as a morning mist. Most cars had headlights on and streetlights flickered on and off, triggered by the gloom.

As it happened, the blaze was small and confined to a few acres of brush, the kind that local fire departments usually took care of with ease. But even a minor fire can be exhausting. For one thing, California was much warmer than it had been in the Arizona mountains, and Merinda Barker's team members were not yet acclimated to the heat. They sweated profusely under the heavy gear, and the one thing Cassidy hadn't thought to bring was enough drinking water.

Once the fire was out, they piled into the van. They

stopped at the first fast-food joint they saw, and all of them ordered the biggest cups of soda or water they could get.

"I'm paying!" Merinda called out, and only then checked to see if her credit card was still in her pocket. Most of her crew then ordered hamburgers and fries while they were at it. They'd barely sat down before Cassidy urged them to hurry.

"We've got another fire," he said. "Around the Hollywood sign, for God's sake. What the hell is happening in this town? I can't remember so many fires in one day."

Merinda frowned and then voiced aloud what everyone else thought. "Arson?' she said.

"I hope to God it's not," Cassidy said. "I'm hearing strange stuff about terrorists and smoke jumpers trained as assassins to kill them." He shook his head. "The world is growing madder with every passing day."

"That stuff can't be true," John Aaronson said, letting his plastic soda straw slip out of his mouth. "I mean, the bit about smoke jumper assassins."

"Why can't it?" Cassidy said. "Where have you been, boy? I'm from Texas, and I've met smoke jumpers there who were mean enough to piss on a widow woman's kindlin'. If one of them boys finds a terrorist with a match in his hand and a fire at his feet, they'll gun him quicker'n scat."

"It's the American way," Merinda said.

Her sarcasm was lost on Cassidy. "Damn right it is," he said. "And if it isn't, it should be."

"It's not for me," one of the female firefighters said, a pretty youngster with her blond hair in a ponytail. "I don't hold with guns."

"The trouble is that terrorists are mighty fond of them," Cassidy said. He smiled. "You know what the gun-toting smoke jumpers are called? Punishers. Heard that with my own two ears. Now, we'd better get going."

"Where are these Punishers based?" Merinda said as she got to her feet.

Cassidy shook his head. "Nobody knows. Maybe they don't even exist, and it's all a big windy."

Cassidy was too old for the front lines, but his job as a supervisor kept him close to the firefighters. "We're putting up you and your crew in the depot annex with some cots," he said as he drove through the rush-hour traffic. "Sorry about that, but we're packed to the rafters."

"How bad has this year been in California?" Merinda asked, as she drank the last of her soda. She leaned back in her seat and sighed. She felt as though she could close her eyes and go right to sleep.

"I think we'll make it just fine through the season if no more big fires start up," Cassidy said. "I don't know about next year. Even if we hire more people now, they won't be trained in time. Sure enough, got all kinds of fancy gear, though."

Merinda shook her head. Cassidy knew as well as she did that it wasn't just the lack of training that caused problems, it was finding the right chemistry in the crews. There were always washouts, and you never knew who they would be. Some burly, strong-looking guy would turn out to be lazy, and some wispy young woman would turn out to be a dynamo. Even in her own crew, John Aaronson was having a difficult time fitting in, but he had ambitions to get on a hotshot crew and was trying hard, and Merinda thought he'd eventually make it.

"I guess the bigwigs upstairs will figure it out," she said.

Cassidy shook his head. "I hope so, Merinda. I sure hope so."

Ahead of them, the chaparral around the world-famous Hollywood sign was burning . . .

CHAPTER 13

"Good morning, and have you seen the news on TV?" Sarah Milano said.

Cory Cantwell stood framed in his hotel room doorway, wearing only his pants. "I haven't seen anything," he said. "You woke me up." Then, scowling, "What time is it?"

"Seven. Jacob Sensor called. He wants us in Los Angeles. Today."

He took the coffee in a plastic cup Sarah handed to him. "Cream and sugar, right?"

"Yeah, that's how I like my coffee, and bring me another gallon."

"What you see is what you get," Sarah said.

"Right now, I prophesy that this is not going to be a good day," Cantwell said.

"Well, here's your starter . . . an arson fire around the Hollywood sign and a police officer murdered. Sensor says it was a pyroterrorist attack."

"He would know, I guess."

"He seemed pretty certain."

"What can you and I do in Los Angeles that the police can't?"

"I have no idea," Sarah said.

Cantwell groaned. "Oh, my head. I knew that second bottle of wine was a bad, bad idea."

"I hate to say I told you so, but I told you so," Sarah said. "Now, jump in a cold shower while I go rent a car."

Cantwell stared at the woman. Despite her limited wardrobe, Sarah looked beautiful in a pink T-shirt, faded blue jeans, and high heels. Her hair was pulled back, and her flawless peaches-and-cream skin was stretched tightly over finely sculpted cheekbones.

Cantwell said, "How come you look so fresh and so pretty . . . and as cool as a glass of ice water?"

Sarah said, "A virtuous life and plenty of makeup, skillfully applied. Now, Mr. Cantwell, suck up the hangover and get your ass in gear. We're burning daylight."

"This is a Kia Limited with the V-6 engine," Sarah Milano said. "Rides well, doesn't it?"

"I feel sick," Cory Cantwell said. "How far to Los Angeles?"

"Well since we've only just got onto the I-10, I'd say another three hundred and seventy miles. We should be in LA by lunchtime."

"When we get near the city, I'll drive to the depot," Cantwell said. "I know where we're going."

"Suits me," Sarah said. "I don't like driving in heavy traffic." She picked up a white paper bag and passed it to Cantwell. "Danish pastries I picked up on my way back from the car rental. Want one?"

"No thanks," Cantwell said.

"Breakfast. Do you good," Sarah said.

"No thanks," Cantwell said.

"Your loss," Sarah said.

She reached inside the bag and retrieved a triangular pastry. "Oh good, raspberry, my favorite," she said.

Cantwell held his head and groaned.

Cory Cantwell and Sarah Milano arrived at the National Wildfire Service depot's office block shortly after two. The air smelled heavily of smoke, as though the whole city was on fire.

Cantwell parked in the employee lot, and then he and Sarah entered the front office, where a number of people recognized him right away.

"Hey, Superintendent Cantwell," a woman in a ranger's uniform called out from one of the connecting offices. "You heading up to Yosemite? I hear you've been posted up that way."

Cantwell figured a small lie was in order. "Hi, Catrina. Yeah, I'm on my way. I just wanted to check in first."

"You heard about the fire at the Hollywood sign?" the woman said. "A police officer killed up there. The LAPD patrols the whole area."

"Yes, I saw it on the TV news this morning," Cantwell said. He saw Sarah standing off a ways, cell phone to her ear, left shoulder raised, protecting her privacy.

"Then you didn't hear?"

"Hear what?"

Catrina Welsh left her office doorway and walked toward Cantwell, eyeing Sarah curiously. She looked to be in her early fifties, attractive, red hair showing no gray, green eyes and a slim, athletic body that spoke of an expensive gym membership she actually used.

"The police found a second body," she said.

"Not another cop?" Cantwell said.

"I don't know. The police are mighty tight-lipped about the whole business."

"Cory, we don't touch it," Sarah said. "We've been ordered to leave it to the law."

"Sensor?"

Sarah's phone hung by her side as her eyes moved to Catrina Welsh and then back to Cantwell. She didn't speak, her quick nod answering his question.

"Then what do we do?" Cantwell said, a scowl signaling his displeasure.

"Stay here overnight and he'll get back to us in the morning," Sarah said. She again glanced at Catrina and moved close to Cantwell. Her voice dropped to a whisper. "He knows who bankrolled the helicopter and paid the hit man to kill him."

"Who?"

"Later."

"Works fast, doesn't he?"

"He has the entire United States intelligence apparatus at his disposal, including the FBI and CIA. Now and again, they get it right."

"Is there something going on here that I'm not supposed to know?" Catrina said.

"Best you don't," Cantwell said. "By the way, you haven't been introduced. Catrina Welsh, this is Sarah Milano. She's . . ."

"She's very beautiful, and that's all I need to know,"

Catrina said. "A woman who lugs a briefcase around with something heavy in it should be allowed to keep her secrets."

Sarah smiled. "At the moment, I'm Cory's assistant."

"Good enough for me," Catrina said. Then, "Are you two planning to spend the night here?"

Cantwell said, "Yes, we are. A couple of dormitory rooms will be fine, if you have them."

Catrina raised an eyebrow, lowered it, and then said, "I can do better than that. Why don't you take my cabin? I have to work tonight anyway. There are a couple of bedrooms . . . much nicer than a dormitory."

"Thanks, Catrina, that sounds just fine," Cantwell said.

The woman turned around and disappeared into her office, then emerged with a set of keys. "Feel free to raid my fridge, anything you want. Except the wine cellar. Touch the vintage wine and I'll never talk to you again."

"Wine is for drinking, isn't it?" Cantwell said, grinning.

"Not those bottles. They're part of my face-lift fund."

"You don't need a face-lift," Cantwell said. "You look even more like a movie star than I remembered."

"I may not need one yet, but I don't want to be taken by surprise." Catrina handed Cantwell the keys. "There's an unopened bottle of good Californian sauvignon in the fridge, if you must. You remember where my cabin is, I assume? You can still find it in the dark?"

Cory flushed a little and shot a glance at Sarah. "Yeah, I remember, thanks. We'll probably be leaving before daylight, so . . ."

"Yes, of course, well, see you next time," Catrina said. She went back into her office.

Cory turned to Sarah and said, "Is a cabin all right with you?"

"Fine. It sounds pretty good, actually. I wasn't looking forward to a dormitory bunk."

They walked out to the car in silence, and Cory navigated his way among the packed buildings. There were people in firefighter and ranger uniforms all over the place. They hadn't gone far when he abruptly pulled to the side of the narrow road.

"Be right back," he said.

He got out of the car and walked over to a group of firefighters. Sarah thought the men and women who surrounded him looked familiar, then she realized she'd seen some of them the day before at the Arizona base camp. They'd been a lot more dirty and tired then, but it was obviously the same crew. They still looked tired, but freshly showered and changed, and she guessed they had probably just returned from yet another fire.

Cantwell introduced himself and received nods of recognition, since most of the wildfire people had heard of him and were aware of his reputation as an experienced smoke jumper. "Did any you work the Hollywood sign fire?" he said.

A tall, athletic woman stepped forward. "All of us did, Mr. Cantwell. My name is Merinda Barker, and I was the squad leader."

Cantwell shook hands with the woman. From her coppery skin, dark hair, and eyes and the cadence of her voice, he pegged her as at least part Native American. She was not conventionally pretty, but her toned, broad-shouldered body and high breasts more than made up for that omission. "Did you discover both bodies at the scene?" he said.

"We uncovered the police officer's body," Merinda said. "The second dead man was found by the LAPD."

"Any kind of identification on him?"

"I don't know," Merinda said. "The police officers didn't share their findings with us. One of their own had been killed, and I don't think they felt like talking to anybody."

"How did the second man die?" Cantwell said.

"That I can tell you. He'd been shot," Merinda said. "Then it seems that the police officer put a bullet into him before he died. But there must have been a third person at the scene."

Cantwell nodded. Then he smiled, tying to lighten the moment. "How long have you been a wildland firefighter, Miss Barker?"

"Six years, but usually on a backup crew."

"Any ambition to be a hotshot?"

Merinda smiled. "It's a big leap from backup wildland firefighter to smoke jumper."

"It's a leap that can be made," Cantwell said. "Have you ever used a gun?"

"I was born and raised on the Navajo Nation Reservation in Arizona," the woman said. "I grew up shooting rifles."

Sarah Milano left the car and stepped beside Cantwell as he said, "Have you heard of pyroterrorism, Miss Barker?"

"No, I've never heard that word used before," Merinda said. "But I'm aware that our forests could be in danger from terrorists, every firefighter knows that . . . and ditto for our Hollywood signs."

"You think today's fire was a terrorist attack?" Cantwell said.

"Yes. I believe an accelerant was used, probably gasoline."

"It could've been a teenage prank that went wrong," Cantwell said.

Merinda shook her head. "Teenage pranksters don't kill police officers."

Cantwell said, "You're right. They don't." Then, "I'd like to talk with you later, Miss Barker. Leave me a contact number."

Merinda gave the number and said, "Can you tell me why, Superintendent?"

"I'd like to offer you a position on my team. The pay is low and the job is dangerous, but you'd be a smoke jumper."

"I'm interested already," Merinda said, smiling.

"Good," Cantwell said. "Then we'll talk later." He thought for a moment and then said, "If for any reason you can't reach me, then talk with Sarah Milano here." After Merinda and Sarah exchanged hellos, Cantwell said, "Miss Milano is a government agent. For now, I'll let it go at that."

The women smiled at each other.

"Please, call me Sarah."

"And I'm Merinda."

"I'm sure you two will get on well together," Cantwell said, grinning, knowing it was a platitude and probably sexist.

"I'm sure we will," Sarah said.

A silence stretched, and then a number of the crew's cell phones all went off at the same time, in a cacophony of ringtones. Merinda extracted her phone, talked briefly with someone at the other end, and then said to her crew, "That was John Cassidy. There's another fire in the Hollywood Hills," she said. "Seems that it's quite extensive. We're backup again."

"I'll let you get ready," Cantwell said. "Good luck, Miss Barker, and we'll talk later."

"I look forward to it," the woman said.

CHAPTER 14

As Sarah and Cantwell walked back to the car, the woman said, "I never knew fires in Los Angeles were this bad."

"They aren't, not like this," Cantwell said. "If the Hollywood sign fire was terrorism, there may be others. No more news from Sensor, huh?"

"I would've told you if he'd called again," Sarah said.

"I know. I was only asking for the sake of asking."

"I guess it means we stay in LA and await further orders," Sarah said. She gave Cantwell a sidelong glance. "You're sizing up Merinda Barker as a Punisher?"

The man nodded. "She's fit and smart and she's a fire-fighter, so she's got sand. And she's comfortable around guns. I think she's got the makings."

"A woman and an American Indian. That's a smart hire."

"Politically correct, you mean?"

"Yes. The people you hire have to look good to the government. Diversity is the big buzzword in Congress these days."

"What do you think of her?"

"I think she'll be an asset."

"She's not pretty."

"What difference does that make?"

"It means no one can say I hired her because she's an attractive woman."

"She is attractive," Sarah said.

"But not overly so," Cantwell said.

Sarah smiled. "A plain-Jane Native American woman. If she takes the job, Jacob Sensor will jump up and down for joy."

"She'll take it," Cantwell said.

"Why are you so sure?"

"Because she's ambitious."

"Well then, Merinda Barker will be your first hire, Cory," Sarah said.

"Depend on it," Cantwell said. Then, "I'm hungry. Let's get some grub at the cafeteria before we look at our lodging for the night."

Sarah said, "I've avoided institutional food since my freshman year in college when I gained ten pounds in two months."

"Forest Service grub is something you need to experience," Cantwell said. "Besides, there's something to be said for a fat woman. She keeps a man warm at night and gives him plenty of shade in summer."

Sarah shook her head. "Cory Cantwell, I'm starting to have serious doubts about your attitude toward the ladies."

"I love them," Cantwell grinned. "All of them, plain or pretty, fat or thin."

"How about cats?" Sarah said. "Do you like kitty cats?"

"Funny you should ask, but I do. When I was a boy, I had a cat named Walker. We went everywhere together that cat and I, even to the local swimming hole."

Sarah smiled. "Then all is not lost. There's a glimmer of hope for you yet."

The dining hall was large but there were few diners. But the food line was fully stocked; nothing fancy, but basic meat-and-potato dishes. Sarah chose meat loaf and a desert of cake with pink frosting and custard filling, and Cantwell ate the same, adding a crusty bread roll.

They sat down in the corner, and both he and Sarah ate with an appetite.

"Surprisingly good, isn't it?" Cantwell said. "If the National Wildfire Service ever starts scrimping on food, they'll have a rebellion on their hands. A firefighter can eat ten thousand calories a day. They'll happily survive on MREs in the field, but when they're in camp, they expect their grub."

"Interesting . . ." Sarah said. But her mind was obviously elsewhere.

"I'm boring you, huh?" Cantwell said. "Sometimes I have that effect on women."

Sarah smiled. "You're not boring me. I was thinking."

"About what?"

"About all those fires today, and those along the coast. Jacob Sensor believes one man is in charge of all the terrorist sleeper cells in the entire country, and that would include those in Los Angeles."

Cantwell nodded. "And your point is?"

"That the terrorist chief . . . boss . . . sheikh . . . whatever . . . might live right here in the city."

"It's possible," Cantwell said. "If he does live in L.A, I guarantee he's lying low, probably some movie star's gardener or a cabdriver or something. So the question is, who is he and how do we get to him?"

"I haven't a clue," Sarah said.

"What about Sensor? Do you think he knows and isn't telling us?"

"I don't know, but I'm going to ask him, Cory. I'm going to ask him tonight."

"And if we find the head honcho and faithful servant of Allah, what then?"

"We kill him," Sarah said.

Cantwell slammed back in his chair in pretend shock. "You don't hold back, do you? Say a thing right out."

"According to Sensor, we're at war, Superintendent Cantwell, at war with terrorism. Our duty is to kill the enemy, is it not?"

"There's no doubt about that. I'm all for killing the enemy before he kills me, and that includes a son of the Prophet. Not politically correct nowadays, but that's how I feel."

"Well, we agree on that subject," Sarah said. "Now it's up to Sensor."

"I don't think Sensor knows who the man is," Cantwell said. "If he did, it stands to reason he'd have taken him out by now."

"Maybe he has clues to his identity that we don't have," Sarah said.

"Maybe . . . or maybe not," Cantwell said. "For all we know, the boss man might be in the Middle East somewhere."

"I guess I'll find out tonight," Sarah said. "Now, shall we go inspect our accommodations?"

On the other side of the parking lot a dirt track wound through pines, passing a large, two-story dormitory and then a few cabins before ending at a wild area where there was another small cabin. Cantwell pulled up in front and parked.

"Home sweet home," he said.

Sarah Milano claimed the bedroom on the ground level, which was obviously Catrina's room, and Cantwell carried his stuff to the loft. Ten minutes later, as the day shaded into evening, they met at the downstairs kitchen table.

"A glass of wine?" Cantwell said.

"Yes, the Sauvignon, not a face-lift vintage," Sarah said.

Cantwell took the wine from the refrigerator and found a couple of wineglasses in a cupboard. "Cheers," he said. They clinked glasses.

"We're going to be very adult tonight, aren't we?" Sarah said.

"About what?"

"The sleeping arrangements."

"I'm upstairs, you're downstairs," Cantwell said. "That's the arrangement, and it's very adult."

"Cory, I just wanted to make it clear that I'm not ready for a relationship. Not yet, at least. I need some time."

Cantwell grinned. "Women always figure every man comes along wants 'em."

Sarah looked surprised. "Is that what you think?"

"That's what John Wayne thought in the movie *Hondo*. He said that to Mrs. Lowe."

"Well, he wanted her in the end, didn't he?"

"Yes, I guess he did. And he got her too."

"Maybe you'll want me in the end," Sarah said.

Cantwell shook his head. "That's a very female question. No comment. More wine?"

Sarah held out her glass, her hand shaking slightly. "Damn, I'm so disappointed. I was pretty sure every man who came along wanted me."

"I used to think the same thing about women," Cantwell said. "After getting slapped down a few times, I changed my mind."

Sarah clinked glasses again. "Well, here's to our disillusionments."

Cantwell grinned. "And let's hope they don't continue."

Cory Cantwell woke with a start.

He lay still in his cot, listening into the night. Nothing moved and there was no sound. He glanced at his watch. Midnight. The hour when fearful thoughts can creep, unbidden, into the darkest crannies of the mind and wake even a strong man from sleep.

What the hell. Cantwell felt his pulse race, and his mouth was dry.

He rose from the cot and walked to the window. A full moon filtered silver light through the tree canopy, and shadows spread like pools of ink on the forest floor. Cantwell found it hard to breathe . . . as though the night reached out to strangle him and he felt its evil.

Something wicked this way comes . . .

Cantwell crossed the floor, took the Glock 19 from his pack . . . black, ugly and reassuring . . . and made his way downstairs on cat feet. He heard Sarah's soft breathing and the plop . . . plop . . . plop of a dripping tap in the kitchen and he felt the thump of his heart in his chest.

Outside the air smelled fresh, of pines, and somewhere close an owl asked its question of the night. The Glock up and ready, Cantwell walked to the end of the dirt track and looked into the moon-splashed gloom. There were cars, trucks, and vans parked everywhere, the detritus left behind by exhausted firefighters. All was still, silent . . . tranquil.

Cory Cantwell lowered the Glock. Now he scolded himself. Like a child he'd wakened from sleep and become afraid of the dark. Just that and nothing more.

Footsteps behind him!

Cantwell turned, bringing up his gun.

It was Sarah Milano, dressed in Catrina Welsh's frayed gray robe. She had her Colt Python in her hand. "Cory, are you all right?" she said.

Feeling embarrassed, Cantwell said, "Yeah, I'm fine. I thought I heard something." Then, "It was probably an animal. Something big, maybe a coyote."

Sarah smiled, the moonlight caressing her. "Hondo, you're sensing Apaches."

Cantwell didn't return her smile. "Yes, that's it, Apaches, out there in the darkness."

"I know. I feel them too," Sarah said. "But it's not Apaches, Cory. It's a much less honorable enemy."

"And a much more dangerous one," Cantwell said.

He looked at his watch. My God, it was twelve-thirty. He thought he'd gotten out of bed just a few minutes ago . . . but he'd been out there alone in the darkness for half an hour.

CHAPTER 15

It was twelve-thirty at night, and Mike Norris was very drunk. As soon as Nasim Azar answered his phone, he yelled, "Azar, you son of a whore, you killed a cop!"

"Please, Mr. Norris, do not shout. It's unbecoming of you," Azar said. "A mistake was made."

"A mistake!" Norris shouted. "Killing an LAPD police officer was just a mistake?"

"The guilty one has already returned to Portland, and he will be punished," Azar said. And then, slightly angry, voice raised, "I lost an operative too. A good man."

"I don't give a damn about who you lost," Norris said. "I told you, Azar, no violence. How the hell did it happen?"

"The police patrol up there around the Hollywood sign," Azar said. "One of my men set the fire and was caught in the act. The police officer shot him."

"Just like that . . . shot him?"

"Yes. There was no warning."

"That's a damned lie," Norris said.

"The man who witnessed the incident knows he will soon die. Why would he lie about it?"

"And it was this man who killed the police officer?" Norris said.

"Yes, with a rock."

"Azar, you're a sorry piece of trash," Norris said. "I hate your guts."

"Harsh words, Mr. Norris. Remember, we're waging a war on the ignorance of the National Wildfire Service. A certain amount of collateral damage can be expected in any conflict. And as I told you, the guilty party will be punished."

"And who the hell is this guy?" Norris said. "Another Arab?"

"His name is Hamed Sarraf, an Iranian. He brought disgrace to me. He's a pig."

Norris said, "Damn you, Azar, you told me you'd set one fire as a demonstration. From what I saw on TV there were fires all over the hills and up and down the coast."

"My people set only one fire," Azar said, "the one at the Hollywood sign."

"Then who's responsible for the others?" Norris said.

"I don't know," Azar said.

Norris wanted to reach through the phone and throttle him. "What do you mean, you don't know?"

"Those other fires were set without my knowledge. I suspect an arsonist terrorist cell is responsible." Then— a nice touch, Azar thought—he added, "Your enemies and mine, Mr. Norris."

"Azar, do you know the danger we're in?" Norris said. "A police officer dead . . . we could be charged with being accessories to murder."

"Our secret is safe, Mr. Norris. Have no concerns on

that score. The lips of the only one who can tie us to the killing of the police officer will soon be sealed forever."

"Handle it, Azar," Norris said. "I don't want to know any more."

"It shall be done," Azar said.

"We have business to discuss. What about the drones to take out the Wildfire Service cameras?"

"That is well in hand. I have purchased three so far and have hired a man, well, a boy really, to operate them and show others how to do the same."

"Who is he? Another damned Iranian?"

"No, a white boy. A computer nerd. He calls himself a gamer."

"I want to talk with him," Norris said.

"I can arrange it," Azar said.

"Maybe this afternoon," Norris said.

"When you're sober," Azar said.

"I'll be sober. What's the kid's name?"

"Randy Collins. He's eighteen. And small for his age."

"I don't give a damn so long as he can fly drones into cameras. Can we trust him?"

"He's being paid more money than he'll ever earn again in his life."

"Then I'll see you around three," Norris said.

"I look forward to it," Azar said, lying through his teeth.

"I beg your mercy, master," Hamed Sarraf said. He was in his late teens, thin and dark, five-foot-six and no more than one hundred twenty pounds. He wore a tan nylon windbreaker, jeans, and white Adidas athletic shoes. He was tightly bound with cord to an upright wooden chair. Earlier he'd been badly beaten, and his bottom lip was split, both his swollen eyes almost closed.

There were four men with him in a disused carpet storage room tucked away on the bottom floor of the warehouse, Azar and his bodyguard, Salman Assad, and two others, all fanatical Muslim jihadists.

"Allah is merciful, Hamed, I am not," Azar said. "You will not die for killing the policeman, but because you have shamed me."

"I had no other recourse, master," Sarraf said. "He would have shot me as he did poor Mohamad."

"Allah be praised, Mohamed Samara died a martyr's death," Azar said. "Even as we speak, he is enjoying the delights of paradise."

"Better if I had joined him," Sarraf said.

"Better for you," Azar said. "You are a pig."

"Then kill me, master," Sarraf said. "Give me the gift of martyrdom."

"Too late for that," Azar said. "Now you cannot die as a martyr." Then, after some thought, "This much I will do. I will let it be known to your loved ones that you died a martyr's death at the hands of the infidels."

Sarraf could not cry tears of joy because of his swollen eyes, both of them a black, yellow, and purple mess, but his voice caught in his throat as he said, "That is indeed a great mercy, Nasim Azar. My father and mother will rejoice."

Azar drew his Beretta .25 from a pocket holster and glanced at his watch. "Hamed Sarraf, you are two minutes away from a paradise so glorious that you have never conceived of it. Yes, you brought shame to me, but die in the knowledge that you struck a blow for Allah, in this, the holiest of all wars and, though not a martyr, you will surely be rewarded."

Sarraf sobbed with joy and gratitude as Azar placed the muzzle of the little pistol between the young man's eyes. He looked at his watch again . . . then pulled the trigger. For all its diminutive size, the .25 round is loud, and its blast racketed around the room, the tinkle of the ejected cartridge case lost in the roar. The single shot was enough to shatter Sarraf's brain and bring instant death.

His ears ringing, Azar raised the Beretta high and yelled, *"Allahu Akbar!"*

And the others cheered, knowing that Hamad Sarraf was at that very moment entering the gates of paradise.

CHAPTER 16

When Cory Cantwell got up and came downstairs, Sarah Milano was sitting at the kitchen table, a cup of coffee in front of her. She'd showered already, and her hair lay over the shoulders of her borrowed robe in damp ringlets. She wore no makeup, but Cantwell thought her beautiful, as though he'd hit the jackpot and woken up beside Angelina Jolie.

"Two calls," Sarah said, bursting his bubble. "Both of them from Jacob Sensor."

"And good morning to you," Cantwell said.

"Good morning," Sarah said. "Coffee's in the pot by the stove."

Cantwell poured himself a cup and sat at the table. He rubbed the stubble on his cheek and said, "No sign of Catrina Welsh?"

"Not yet. But I'm sure she'll want her cabin back soon."

Cantwell glanced at his watch. "Seven o'clock. She must've pulled an all-nighter."

"When I rose at six, the firefighters were already moving out," Sarah said.

"More fires?" Cantwell said.

"I don't think so. They're probably making sure the fires they put out yesterday don't flare up again."

"Sarah, I need a cigarette," Cantwell said. "Want to step outside with me? Catrina doesn't smoke, and I don't want to fog up her kitchen."

"So you'll fog me up instead, huh?" Sarah said. But before Cantwell could answer, she said, "Just joking. There's a bench out there where we can sit. Aren't you interested in what Sensor said?"

"Yes, but not right now. Give me a chance to wake up and drink some coffee. Sensor is hard to take first thing in the morning."

"Sensor is hard to take at any time," Sarah said. "He comes on like a bull in a china shop."

"Nice in the sun, isn't it?" Sarah said, stretching her arms above her head.

Cantwell nodded. "Yeah, it is. Warm."

"Now are you going to ask me about Sensor's phone calls?"

Cantwell drew deep on his cigarette and said, exhaling blue smoke, "Normally, I'd say yes, but . . ." He nodded in the direction of the dirt track. "It looks like we have a visitor."

Merinda Barker walked through dappled sunlight toward them, a tall angular woman dressed in the olive-green shirt and pants of the National Wildfire Service. She looked pressed and crisp, and her thick, black hair was pulled back and tied in a neat bun.

Uncomfortably conscious of an unshaven chin and bare feet shoved into unlaced shoes, Cantwell stood and said, "Miss Barker, nice to see you again."

The woman's smile included Sarah, and so did the knowing, amused look in her eyes. Sarah saw that look and wanted to say, *"Lady, this is not what you think,"* but she thought that would be petty . . . and anyway, who would believe her?

"You wished to speak with me, Superintendent Cantwell," she said.

"Do you have a few minutes?" Cantwell said.

"Yes. My crew is on standby."

Sarah said, "Miss Barker, you can sit here on the bench. There's room for three of us."

"I'll stand, if you don't mind," Merinda said.

"Then I'll get right to the point," Cantwell said. "I've been a placed in command of a specialized unit of smoke jumpers. For want of a better name, we call ourselves Punishers."

Sarah smiled and said, "Cory, sorry to interrupt, but you now have an official name . . . Regulators."

"Huh?"

"Jacob Sensor's idea," Sarah said. "Apparently he's a Wild West history buff. The Regulators were a group of young men who rode with Billy the Kid in the Lincoln County War. They formed a deputized posse that sought revenge for the murder of their boss John Tunstall. This happened in 1879, and when Mr. Sensor called this morning, he explained it all at some length." Sarah read the dismay on Cantwell's face and said, "Sorry."

Cantwell looked at Merinda Barker. "Did you get all that?"

"Billy the Kid . . . I believe I saw a movie about him," the woman said. "I think Bob Dylan was in it and James Coburn."

"Well, anyway, I'm forming the . . . Regulators . . . unit and I thought you'd be a good fit," Cantwell said.

"What does the job entail, Superintendent?" Merinda said.

Cantwell didn't try to dress it up. He laid it out in all its rawness. "We catch pyroterrorists in the act of setting wildfires, and we kill them."

If Cantwell had said, "I raped your grandmother," Merinda Barker couldn't have been more shocked. Her eyes got big, and she stood in a stricken silence, trying to find words that would not come.

"Now, do you want to sit?" Sarah said.

"I think I'd better," Merinda said.

"Sorry to lay it on you like that, Miss Barker," Cantwell said. "But anti-terrorism is a dirty, violent business, and you'd be a part of it."

Merinda retreated into the safety of something she understood. "I'm a firefighter, Mr. Cantwell. I have no training as a smoke jumper."

"The unit won't become fully operational for a year," Cantwell said. "Once we assess your aptitude for the job and you pass muster, we'll have time to train you." He stared hard into the woman's black eyes. "You need to ask yourself if you can handle the task. It's no small thing to kill a person, even a terrorist."

Merinda nodded. "I need time to think it through. It's not an easy decision to make."

"Take all the time you need," Cantwell said. "Miss Milano will give you a phone number where you can reach me."

The young woman looked at Sarah and said, "Are you a . . ."

"Regulator? No, but I've had some experience," Sarah said.

"Have you killed a terrorist?" Merinda said.

"Let's just say that I've recently been involved in such an action," Sarah said. "The job Superintendent Cantwell is offering you is not for everyone. If I were you, I'd think long and hard before I accepted it."

Merinda Barker rose to her feet. "My grandfather is an elder of the Cherokee Nation and a very wise man," she said. "I'll ask his advice."

"Miss Barker, as of now, the National Wildfire Service's anti-terrorism unit is top secret, and the fewer people who know about it, the better," Cantwell said. "This is a decision you must make for yourself, and for now at least, you must speak of it to no one."

Merinda nodded. "I understand."

Cantwell tried to lighten the mood. "Think on the bright side . . . if you accept and you qualify, you can expect a raise in salary, such as it is."

The woman's smile was slight. "More money was always important to me, but right about now it doesn't seem to matter that much."

Cantwell nodded. "Well, Miss Barker, you've got some

thinking to do. And this conversation never happened. You know that, huh?"

"It never happened," Merinda said. "Not a word of it. And I wish that was the truth."

"Well, what do you think?" Cory Cantwell said.

"Did you have to scare the hell out of her?" Sarah Milano said.

"She's in a scary business. She can handle it."

"I think she's iffy at best." Sarah said.

"Really? I think she'll go for it. Her ancestors were warriors."

"All our ancestors were warriors of some kind or another."

"Or at least they carried the warriors' luggage," Cantwell said.

"Speak for your own ancestors," Sarah said. "I'm sure mine were warriors."

"You're probably right," Cantwell said. "Maybe my ancestors carried your ancestors' luggage." Cantwell lit a cigarette and exhaled smoke and words. "What else did Sensor have to say?"

"He says he knows who hired the helicopter and the hit man to kill him," Sarah said.

"He told us that before," Cantwell said.

"I know, and it's a measure of how important it is to him," Sarah said. "He said it's nothing to do with his war on pyroterrorists, but his trade and anti-immigration policies. Those don't sit well with the liberal wing of the Democratic party."

"And someone paid to have him knocked off for that?"

"Apparently there are some radical socialists out there who want him dead. Billionaire socialists, if you can believe that."

"I can believe it," Cantwell said. "In this country socialism is for the rich, and capitalism is for the poor since state policies assure that more resources flow to the rich than to the great unwashed."

Sarah smiled. "Did you think that up all by yourself?"

"Hell no. I read it somewhere," Cantwell said. "What else did Sensor have to say?"

"Only that he's found you a new recruit, a smoke jumper up in Washington State who made quite a hero of himself," Sarah said.

"Smoke jumpers do that every day," Cantwell said. "What did the guy . . . is he a male?"

"Yes, he is."

"What did he do that's different?"

Sarah paused for effect, then said, "He took out four pyroterrorists with the .44 Magnum Ruger revolver he carried for protection against bears and other critters."

"Name?"

"Peter Kennedy. Sensor called him Pete."

"Where did this happen in Washington?"

"Glacier Peak, a still-active volcano in the middle of nowhere. Well, it's seventy miles northeast of Seattle in some mighty rough country."

"How did it happen?" Cantwell said.

"I don't know all the details," Sarah said. "Sensor plans to fax a full report later today. I'll tell Catrina Welsh to look out for it." She pulled her robe over her naked knees. "Exciting, huh?" she said.

"What is?"

"Pete Kennedy."

Cantwell nodded. "Yeah, it is. I'd like to have him."

"There's only one thing, he's forty-two years old," Sarah said. "Getting up there for a smoke jumper."

"He can handle a gun, and he's not afraid of terrorists, so I want him," Cantwell said. He smiled, "Besides, forty-two is not too old."

"I never said it was," Sarah said. "Depending on what you want to do, no age is too old."

Cantwell looked at Sarah, enjoying how she looked in the leaf-dappled sunlight. Aside from her obvious beauty, he'd found much to admire in her. She was intelligent, her courage was not in doubt, and she looked problems in the face and then did something about them.

Sarah Milano, Cantwell decided, would be an easy woman to fall in love with.

"I'm hungry," the woman said. "Are you thinking about breakfast?"

Cantwell blinked, surfacing from his reverie. "Breakfast? Oh, yeah, sounds good."

He rose and followed Sarah into the cabin. Before he made his way to the shower, he said, "The Glacier Peak guy's name again?"

"Peter Kennedy," Sarah said. "I think you can call him Pete."

CHAPTER 17

Squad leader Pete Kennedy couldn't believe he was thinking it . . . but he was ready for fire season to be over. In years past, it would have ended weeks before now, but each year it seemed to extend just a little bit longer. He couldn't wait to get back to his hometown of Leavenworth, Washington, with its Bavarian facades. He knew it was all as phony as hell, but damned if it wasn't charming when the snows fell.

He'd built a house above the town, near Rocky Icicle Creek, and spent most of the winter skiing.

At forty-two, he was the oldest smoke jumper in his crew by far, his chosen career interrupted by three tours in Iraq and Afghanistan. The kids around him on the airport tarmac were tired but still gung-ho, too proud to admit their exhaustion.

"This is going to be a tricky one, not sure what we'll find," Kennedy said, as he finished briefing his crew on their detail. "But I do know that it won't be easy."

The fire smoldered on Glacier Peak, a small volcano that stood lone sentinel on a high ridge. The mountain looked more imposing than it really was because of its sheer, ice-covered upper slopes. It was about halfway between the smoke jumpers' base camp at Winthrop, Washington, and the town of Leavenworth. There weren't any significant structures nearby, but extensive alpine forests and an extreme dryness made the National Wildfire Service higher-ups nervous. There was no easy way to access the burn.

"Sorry about getting this one so late," Kennedy said. "I know some of you are due back in school soon."

"Don't worry, it's overtime!" a pert, brunette girl named Maryann shouted, and the others laughed.

But the laughs were half-hearted. It had been one hell of a season, with very few breaks, and the crew had been moved all over the place. Most of them had already earned more than ever before, and all of them would have given up some of that overtime for some extra help. But despite the ever-increasing size and frequency of the fires, there were fewer firefighters now than five years ago. Normally there'd be four or five crews at the base, but right now it was just Kennedy's people and a few stragglers.

It was clear to all of them that the management didn't know what they were doing, sending them out on little brushfires while serious wildfires burned in the mountains. The National Wildfire Service was penny-pinching, ignoring inaccessible fires and concentrating on fires near housing developments. So this high-mountain operation was a refreshing change, more in line with what Kennedy and his crew were trained for.

But times had changed. He remembered years back when they'd often sat around the base for most of the summer, paperback Westerns and war novels littering the Quonset hut's broken-down chairs and sofas. Bored firefighters needled one another until there were the inevitable fights, and then the drinking sessions thereafter where the battered combatants got sloppily sentimental about what best buddies they were.

But those days were long gone as the number of forest fires grew. In his career, he had seen two different crews wiped out by blowouts. He'd been a rookie when the South Canyon tragedy happened, and he hadn't known any of the fourteen young firefighters killed, but just a few years back at Granite Mountain, he'd known half of the nineteen smoke jumpers who died. Then came the Indian Wells disaster, when Mike Norris, a man he knew and liked, had made himself a hero. But Mike had since quit the service over a disagreement about replacing manned lookout towers with cameras. His going was a big loss.

Kennedy's crew, based in northern Washington, had spent most of this season fighting fires in Colorado. Meanwhile, though there hadn't been any major fires in their home territory, the Western drought continued apace. When they'd returned home from the last trip, Kennedy had been shocked by how primed the forests were for a disaster and how few resources were left to fight them.

The NWS was spread thin, years of budget cuts just when they needed firefighters the most. But when the majority of members of Congress express disbelief in climate change, warnings of continuing droughts fell on deaf ears. To the average legislator, all that was needed was a good rainstorm. Never mind those rainstorms also brought lightning.

It also didn't help that most congresspeople came from districts where wildfire was a minor concern. What happened in the West stayed in the West, and western senators could scream for help all they wanted, but until and unless there was a disaster—when it was too late, in other words—the money wasn't forthcoming.

It wasn't going to be his problem after this season, unless he was crazy enough to stick around and fight the bureaucratic battles. He hadn't told anyone, not even his girlfriend, but he'd been offered a position at a private firefighting company that paid so much he couldn't refuse. It would be a huge step down in prestige, and a huge step up in safety and security.

He looked around at his crew. Maryann Reid and Scott Vern flirted at the front of the plane. They'd be the last duo out. Not a care in the world. Next in line was Dick Mathews, the second-oldest crewmember and probably the next leader. He didn't talk much, but always made the right decision. Long and lanky, which was unusual for a firefighter, most of whom were shorter and muscular.

Jon Carty was next, and he too defied the usual body type, being a big guy, six foot, two inches and over two hundred pounds. His partner was petite Rhonda Evans, short-cropped brunette hair and upturned nose and cute as could be. They were having a secret affair, which everyone in the crew pretended they didn't know about.

Pranda Khan was next, dark haired and sharp featured. Everyone loved her British accent and tried to get her to talk just to listen to her. Her partner was a Mohawk, Jason Coldstream, who was quiet and soft-spoken with eyes as black as obsidian.

And finally, in the middle of the pack was the Ivy

League college kid, Jake Johnson, and the good old boy from Alabama, Jerry Burton, who for some reason got along great, despite having completely different backgrounds.

Pete had decided that ten crew members were enough to start with. It didn't look like a big fire, though it was on tough terrain. If he needed help, he'd call it in.

The crew zipped into padded Kevlar jumpsuits with their high collars and baggy pants. With the parachute harnesses attached, they had to waddle to the aircraft. Below the reserve parachute in front were their personal bags, with food and extra clothing and gear. Topping it off were helmets with their metal faceplates that made them look like somewhat bizarre football players.

After takeoff, inside the plane was hot, humid, and noisy, and the crew sat close to each other yet isolated, each with his or her own thoughts and secret anxieties.

The copilot came out of the cockpit and said to Kennedy, "You see anyplace you want us to try?"

Kennedy had surveyed the terrain below, and it was clear that they'd have to jump very close to the fire, almost on top of it, which made him uncomfortable. But the crosswinds were low, and it seemed safe enough.

He pointed. "How about the hanging meadow there? It's well below the snow line."

The copilot nodded, spoke into his microphone, then made his way to the open rear of the place, where he hooked a line from his flight suit to a secure strut.

"On final!" the copilot shouted.

Kennedy stood. It was too noisy back there to speak. The spotter just tapped him on the shoulder rather than shout. Before he could think, Kennedy jumped, curled into a ball, and counted the four seconds before he felt the parachute unspool. He opened his eyes and shouted, "Hoya!" so that Dick Matthews would know where he was and heard a "Hoya!" in return to his left. He looked up and watched the others safely exit the aircraft.

The ground came up fast. The high meadow clearing, which had looked flat from above, covered with yellow grasses and patches of snow, was littered with sharp rocks, but Kennedy managed to glide his way to an open space.

He turned, gathered up the canopy, and got ready to help anyone who landed badly. They all managed to get down safely, which was a relief because Kennedy wasn't sure about the availability of a backup helicopter.

The crew stowed their gear, shed the bulky jumpsuits, and grabbed their tools.

The flames had already burned through some grassy areas bordered by volcanic rocks and Kennedy relaxed. It was a blackened place they could retreat to if anything went wrong. A thick stand of pines growing below them had not caught fire yet. For now the flames were restricted to some scrub about halfway down the slope. If they could cut a firebreak between the scrub and the trees, the fire would probably burn out.

"Damn," Maryann said. "This looks easy. I was hoping for one last big payday."

"We cut a line downslope of the fire," Kennedy said. "Let it burn upward to the rocks."

The slope was mostly scree, and since the fire didn't seem to be moving fast, they made their way down and around it carefully.

The first tendrils of flames licked at the base of a small scrub fir, and Dick Matthews cut into the grass, throwing dirt on it. The rest of the job was done very quickly. Ten people could clear a large area fast.

"Well, hell," Jason Coldstream said. "This fire would've burned out all by itself."

Kennedy wasn't so sure. The line of trees grew thicker the farther they went down the slope. Beyond was a dense forest that extended all the way to the town of Leavenworth and beyond. A change of wind direction, a little bad luck, and this could have turned into something really ugly. An out-of-control blaze would have spread fast and threatened lives and property.

Kennedy sighed and clicked the radio to call for pickup. At the same moment out of the corner of his eye, he saw a flash.

"What was that?" Dick Matthews said, his voice sounding oddly hollow in the sudden silence.

"Lightning!" Kennedy yelled. "Damn, it's lightning."

Without anyone noticing, a thunderhead had crept up over the mountain behind them. Upslope, a flash of dry lightning struck a wedge-shaped outcropping, and a second later a deafening bang shattered the quiet as though the mountain had been struck with a gigantic sledgehammer.

The hairs stood up on Kennedy's arms, and he sensed they were in a spot the lightning had chosen to strike next.

"Everybody, get down from here!" he shouted.

He scrambled down the slope, he and Matthews herding the others in front of them like a mother hen.

The crew reached the tree line, which all the safety

protocols told them they were supposed to avoid in a lightning storm, but that warning was ignored as lightning struck the slope where they had stood only moments before.

Tense moments passed as the storm passed overhead, and in its wake the sky was blue, without a cloud.

For Pete Kennedy the good news was that they'd escaped the storm unscathed. But the bad news was that an errant lightning strike hit the tallest and deadest tree in the forest, and it burst into flame. Within moments, other pines caught and burned and formed a dancing, scarlet wall.

Kennedy sighed. "Looks like you got your overtime, guys."

He pulled out a roll of red tape to mark where he wanted the fire line.

"I want to see nothing along that line but dirt," he said.

The crew managed to catch the fire quickly enough to keep it from spreading. The finishing touches were made to the fire line, and they all began to breathe a little easier.

By then the day was shading into night and they found a narrow flat ledge on the slope and stretched out where they could. It was going to be a cold night.

At daybreak, Pete Kennedy rose, worked the crick out of his back, and then started the crew in the direction of their previously agreed rendezvous point, a little-used logging road to the south of the peak.

Walking through some sparse hardwoods, Kennedy pulled out his radio and called the North Cascades base for transport home.

"You're going to have to walk at least part of the way," the assistant base manager Ginger Terry said, her deep voice sounding masculine over the radio. "We've had a strange upsurge of fires in the last twenty-four hours."

"Walk out?" Kennedy said. "All the way back to base camp? How many miles is that?"

"No, just stay to the logging road and we'll send a truck for you when one becomes available."

"You're that busy?" Kennedy said.

"Yeah, Pete, something's going on. Wait, we're getting a report." Then after a long pause, "Pete, look to the northwest. Do you see anything?"

The terrain in that direction was a series of wooded foothills below a steep rock bluff. Kennedy saw a column of white smoke, and at a distance it probably looked smaller than it actually was.

"Yeah, I see smoke," Kennedy said. "We're maybe three miles from there."

"It could be nothing, but check it out, Pete," Ginger said. "I'm sorry to do this to you."

"It's all part of the job," Kennedy said. "We're on our way."

"Report back, and good luck," Ginger said.

They started off with the reassuring accompaniment of Pranda Khan's bells. She had sewn a line of small bells down the sides of her backpack and on her hat.

When the woman had joined the crew, the bells had annoyed Pete Kennedy, but he couldn't argue with their purpose. A grizzly in the mountains of Montana had attacked Pranda's previous team, and one man had been severely mauled. Afterward the crew had broken up, with several members quitting altogether.

"Now I want bears to know I'm coming," Pranda said.

Old Ephraim could be a problem in the woods, and Kennedy carried a Ruger Super Blackhawk .44 Magnum as grizzly medicine . . . but that day he was destined to meet an enemy much more dangerous than a bear.

CHAPTER 18

The crew traversed a particularly steep part of the slope when the bells suddenly fell silent. Kennedy turned to ask why Pranda had stopped . . . but she wasn't there.

Then Rhonda Evans shouted in alarm, pointing downslope.

Pranda tumbled head over heels down a talus slope to Rhonda's left, brush sending her first one way then the other. She landed on a flat area of gravel and slid to a stop, sending up a cloud of gray dust.

She lay there unmoving.

Kennedy stepped off the trail and made his way down the incline to Pranda's side. He knelt and felt her neck. Good, there was a pulse, but it was racing and uneven.

Dick Matthews and Maryann Reid reached them a few moments later.

"How is she?" the girl said.

Kennedy shook head. "I don't know. She's alive. But I'm afraid to move her." His crew had gathered around and stared down at him, their faces ashen.

"She must have slipped," Maryann said. "Why did she step onto the steep part of the slope?"

"I don't know why," Kennedy said. "Dick, call for the helicopter. Don't take no or maybe for an answer!"

"What about the fire?" Matthews asked.

"Screw the fire," Kennedy said. "No one living up here anyway."

CRACK! A sound never made by nature split the air.

"What the hell!" Pete Kennedy said.

Just under the armpit, his shirt was glistening with blood. He lifted the shirt and saw a straight line across his chest as though drawn by a scarlet marker pen.

"Pete, that's a bullet wound," Matthews said. "My God, Pranda may have been shot."

Fearing the worst, Kennedy gently turned the woman over. Blood welled from the middle of her stomach, and there was no doubt . . . it was a bullet wound.

Kennedy heard a distant, pulsating thrum, and sudden hope replaced the sense of dread that had overtaken him. He scanned the sky, expecting to see the helicopter in the distance.

But the dark shape didn't get bigger, and he realized the thing in the sky was close, very close.

Kennedy's eyes almost popped out of his head. It was a large, four-motored drone.

The drone flew overhead and dropped a dark object that fell onto the wooded hillside a thousand feet below them. A flash of scarlet fire and a pine exploded into flames, igniting the others around it.

Kennedy heard big Jon Carty gasp and saw the man suddenly stiffen, followed an instant later by the sound of the gunshot. The big man toppled off the trail and rolled down the slope.

Once the others realized what was happening, they threw themselves to the ground.

The hum of the drone returned. It buzzed over Kennedy and Maryann, then darted uphill and hovered over the crew.

"No!" Kennedy yelled.

A cylinder dropped from the drone, and for a moment time seemed to freeze. Then Rhonda Evans jumped to her feet and ran a few steps up the slope. But the blast caught her and lifted her like a ragdoll eight feet in the air before dropping her shattered body on the lava rocks.

But the drone wasn't done killing.

A flashing ball of fire from an incendiary took the others. Horrified, Kennedy watched them die in the flames, their screams such as he'd never heard, not even in combat. The shrieks died to moans, and a silence fell as scattered bodies looked like black cinders against the rocks.

Its work done, the drone hummed away and disappeared into the distance.

Pete Kennedy stood. Of his crew, only Maryann had survived.

"Pete, what the hell's happening?" Maryann said. She took her cell phone away from her ear, shook her head, and said, "Nothing."

"Nobody around to help us anyway." Kennedy said. "Head downhill, Maryann. Stay well to the west of the fire started by the drone. Try to make it to the logging road. I'm going after the people who did this."

"After them?" she repeated, as if the words made no sense.

"Yeah, they shot Pranda and Jon Carty, so they're

within rifle range. I'm going to find them, and then I'll kill them." He glanced at the sky. "I'll catch up to them before dark."

Maryann's face was anxious and very pale. "For God's sake be careful, Pete," she said.

Kennedy nodded. "Go now while you still have daylight. Just stay to the west and head for the logging road like I told you."

He watched the woman until she made her way down the hill, scrambling wide of the burning pines, and then retrieved his backpack. The deaths of his people had transformed easygoing, sometimes gentle Pete Kennedy into a hard, dangerous man whose gun skills had been forged in the heat of battle. He was once again what the Marines had trained him to be . . . a killing machine. The Ruger was warm to the touch as he checked the cylinder. Six rounds of Hornady 240-grain XTP hollow points, enough to slow down a grizzly or take out a man. The revolver was packed with a belt and holster and six spare rounds.

An icy calmness overcame Kennedy. The same calm he'd felt during his entire second tour in Iraq, a calm accompanied by rage so intense that it steadied him.

A fire burned below Kennedy, and to the west there was no vantage point that could've given the shooters a view of the talus slope where Pranda Khan and Jon Carty had been shot. But to the east, the mountainside sloped down into a treed valley before rising again to a high, steep bank crowned by a mix of pine and red cedar. From the top of the bluff, a rifleman would have a view of the entire southeastern slope of the peak.

Kennedy nodded to himself. The killers, whoever they were, had to be there.

He slowly made his way down the incline. There was little cover, and every yard of terrain now represented a danger. Ahead of him pines burned, and moving on cat feet he angled to his east, away from the fire. The smell of smoke was heavy in the air. Suddenly a bird exploded out of the brush, and Kennedy instantly threw himself on his belly and flattened against the ground. Then he slid like a sled on ice, gravel viciously scraping his chest and stomach as he nose-dived down the slope. It seemed that he'd skidded the best part of a hundred yards before he hurtled headfirst over a rock ledge and dropped about eight feet before landing on the top of his head and shoulders.

The impact stunned Kennedy, and he lay still for several minutes hurting all over, fearing the worst. When his head stopped spinning, he moved his arms and then his legs. So far so good, nothing broken. He climbed to his feet. His neck pained him a little, but he was still intact, and the Blackhawk was securely snapped into its field holster. Smoke hung around Kennedy like a gray mist, and he was grateful that it cloaked him from prying eyes, at least until he started to move again.

He was in the narrow valley between the slope of Glacier peak and the adjoining bluff. Fires burned to the west and south, and he feared for Maryann's safety. It was several miles across treed, hilly country to the logging road and a twisted ankle or some other mishap, could spell disaster. But there were faint hiker trails in that direction, and with luck, the woman may have found one of those. Kennedy put Maryann out of his mind. Now he needed all his concentration for the task at hand.

He stepped back, took a look at the height from which he'd fallen, and shook his head. "Pete," he said aloud, "you could've broken your damned fool neck."

Then he saw them.

Not fifty feet higher in the bluff, four men, clustered together on a rock ledge. They faced in the opposite direction, looking into the sky at a returning drone. All four wore olive-green coveralls that gave them the appearance of soldiers, but three of them were bearded, and Kennedy had seen their like before in Afghanistan. They had the look of Islamic terrorists . . . and now the attack on his crew and the vague rumors he'd heard about pyroterrorism began to make sense. Those men were there to light forest fires, and he and his people had gotten in their way.

Kennedy's hatred for a merciless enemy grew to white-hot intensity. He drew the Ruger and stepped into the open, two-handed the big revolver to eye level, thumbed back the hammer, and aimed at one of the terrorists. It was a relatively easy shot, but he took his time, aiming carefully, wanting a sure kill. He squeezed the trigger, the Blackhawk roared and bucked in his hand, and his chosen target screamed and fell. Almost immediately a bullet spattered a boulder near him, and Kennedy ducked back into the cover of the rock face. But he didn't plan to stay there. He would take the fight to the enemy.

Above them he heard the terrorists jabber to one another. They sounded hysterical, screaming their rage, determined to destroy the infidel who'd killed one of their own.

Kennedy shook his head. Those boys were getting too worked up to think straight.

And he was right . . . because fatal mistakes were made.

A shattering shower of gravel skittered down the side of the bluff and rattled onto the ground a few feet from where Kennedy stood. Hammer back, he raised the Blackhawk and stepped into the open. Two men slid down the slope, both with rifles, one of them wearing a pair of bright red Nikes. Both saw Kennedy at the same time, and they dug their heels into the dirt, frantically trying to brake to a halt.

Moments later the terrorists learned that a frontal attack on a trained and angry Marine with right on his side was a bad idea. Kennedy shot fast and accurately, working the Blackhawk like an old-time gunfighter. One of the terrorists dropped, shrieking, with a bullet in his belly that took him out of the fight. But the man in the red Nikes managed to stand and get off a fumbling shot from his AK-47. A miss! But Kennedy's own round crashed into the man's chest, and his rifle went spinning away from him. The terrorist rode a second bullet into hell.

The gut-shot man slid down the hill feetfirst, and he was in a sorry state. His white teeth clenched, he clutched at his belly with scarlet hands, screeching, and his kicking feet chewed up the ground. Kennedy put him out of his misery and then reloaded the Ruger. There was one killer left, and he wanted him . . . wanted him real bad.

* * *

Attacking uphill into the rifle of an entrenched enemy is never a good plan, and Pete Kennedy liked it not. There was little cover, and he'd be an easy target. The daylight was fading, and now the question was: Will the man pull out when darkness falls, or spend the night on the slope, hoping for a clean shot at his unseen enemy come morning?

Damn him, the ball was in the terrorist's court and that rankled.

Throwing caution to the wind, Kennedy darted out from the rock face, snapped off a wild shot, and dived back again, rolling into cover. A rifle cracked, and a bullet thudded into the ground where he'd stood a moment before.

The terrorist hadn't pulled out. He was still there.

Then a man's voice, heavily accented.

"Coward! Show yourself and fight like a warrior!"

Kennedy grinned. "You come and get me, Abdul!"

"Telhas teeze!" the man shouted.

Kennedy had picked up enough Arabic to know what that meant: "Kiss my ass!"

The sun was going down, and smoke smudged the fair face of the still bright sky like dirty thumbprints. Somewhere in the brush a quail called. The forest fire crackled, now driven by a west wind, away, Kennedy noted with some relief, from the settled areas around his hometown of Leavenworth. The wind direction had changed, and he estimated that fire in the valley would spread to his present location in no more than three to four hours. The terrorist up in his high perch on the slope would need to move before then.

Kennedy hunkered down, the Ruger Blackhawk close

at hand. He'd wait until darkness or the flames forced him to move, whatever came first. He had a protein bar in his pocket, and he ate that for energy. It tasted like sawdust.

Night fell, the darkness made lighter by the amber glow of the blazing forest fire.

Pete Kennedy rose to his feet and stepped into the open. He was made invisible by the gloom, and no shots were fired, nor had he expected any. He studied the barren, rugged slope. A man could climb it in the dark and get close to his enemy. And then it would come down to who shot better. The Blackhawk, carried only for bear, was not a familiar weapon to him. A single action's first shot was fast, but follow-up shots, cocking the hammer before pulling the trigger, were relatively slow. He'd seen experts fire single actions with amazing speed, but he was not one of them. Kennedy looked at the slope again. He could only make the best of what he had.

Unless . . .

Kennedy stood at the bottom of the incline, and his eyes searched the darkness. It took several minutes before he spotted halfway up the slope a sudden surge of fire-light glint on blue metal. The dead terrorist's AK-47 had spun away from him when he was shot, and the rifle had landed in a patch of brush. Kennedy holstered the Ruger, and, on all fours, began to climb, at any second expecting to feel the impact of a bullet. But none came. He stood and pulled the rifle from the brush, remembering the familiar kick-ass feel of it in his hands, an unlovely weapon designed to be both lethal and reliable.

Kennedy turned and instinctively dropped to one knee as his gaze moved higher up the slope.

He and the terrorist saw each other at the same instant. Both of them surprised, they faced each other across thirty yards, and there was no doubt in the mind of either that within seconds one of them would be dead.

The terrorist was tall, gaunt, with gray in his hair. He wore a full beard, and his eye sockets and the hollows of his cheeks were deep in shadow, so his face looked like a skull. Kennedy was aware of the crackle of the fire and rustle of the west wind in the pine branches, the tang of smoke.

The man had come hunting for him . . . the moment had arrived.

Kennedy raised the rifle, prepared to fire from the hip. The terrorist did the same.

The margin between them was slight. Kennedy had been a trained as a soldier, the terrorist as an assassin. They fired at the same time.

Flashlight beams angled into the darkness, now and then crossing together like light sabers. "Pete!" a woman's voice called out. "Pete Kennedy, can you hear me?"

"I can hear you, Maryann!" Kennedy yelled. "I'm down here."

"I brought help," the woman said, lowering her voice as she drew closer.

"Too late for him," Kennedy said, pointing the AK-47's muzzle at the man at his feet.

Maryann gasped. "Pete, he's all shot to pieces."

"Five . . . or maybe it was six rounds of full metal jacket will do that to a man," Kennedy said.

Two sheriff's deputies and a firefighter Kennedy didn't know joined Maryann and him on the slope. Kennedy used the rifle as a pointer again. "There and there, two more dead, and another up on the rock ledge."

"What the hell happened?" one of the deputies said. The name tag on his tan windbreaker read CLARK.

"These men are arson terrorists. They killed my crew, and I killed them," Kennedy said.

Clark was trained to react to any given situation, not to think about it too deeply. He took Kennedy's bald statement in stride and said, "That damned fire is getting close."

"Too close," his fellow deputy said, looking over his shoulder at the advancing flames. His name tag said ANDERSSON. He was blond and blue-eyed and looked Swedish.

Kennedy nodded. "If we want to make it back to the road, we'd better leave now."

"What about the bodies?" Andersson said.

"You want to lug them out, Joe?" Clark said.

The deputy shook his head. "Hell no."

"Then let's get the heck out of here," Clark said.

After Pete Kennedy returned to the base at Winthrop, he was interrogated by the local police, and a detective hinted darkly that, as far as he was concerned, murder charges were not out of the question.

The following morning three calls were placed.

One, from the highest reaches of the Justice Department, ordered the cops to lay off Peter Kennedy.

The second was to Kennedy himself from Jacob Sensor.

The third was placed to Nasim Azar, informing him of the martyrdom of four Islamic operatives on Glacier Mountain, Washington.

CHAPTER 19

"The fire warriors were not under my command," Nasim Azar said. "But I deeply grieve their loss."

"They are now with Allah in paradise," Salman Assad said. "That should console you, master."

"It does," Azar said. "Very much so. I'm told that the faithful were killed by a single crusader, a man named Peter Kennedy who has already murdered Mujahideen in Iraq and Afghanistan, curse his name forever."

"Then he is another I will kill for you," Assad said. "He will join the infidel Cory Cantwell in death."

Azar shook his head. "No, Salman, you are my bodyguard and very precious to me. Leave Cantwell to the Ukrainian."

"But we don't know this man," Assad said.

"No, but we know of him," Azar said. "His services are very much in demand, and that tells us much. Twenty-five thousand dollars, Salman. That's what he charges for a kill, and I'm told by the Brothers of the Islamic Jihad in Beirut that he's worth every penny. He is of a mild disposition, a man so soft-spoken that in Tehran they call him the Whispering Death. His most distinguished kill for the Iranians was Adel Shaker El-Tamimi, a close ally of a former Iraqi prime minister." Azar smiled. "He leaves no trail behind him and will serve us well."

"When will I meet this man?" Assad said.

"He flies in from New York tomorrow," Azar said. "I have made arrangements for him to be picked up at the airport and brought here. He may even meet Mike Norris, another of his future targets." He made come-hither motions with his hands. "We must draw them in, Salman, draw our enemies into our web, and then we will kill them all." He touched his tongue to his top lip. "Perhaps destroy them all at the same time. How sweet that would be."

"Pah, I can shoot Norris at any time," Assad said. "The man is a pig."

"Curb your enthusiasm, Salman. Norris can't be killed until he's taught my men the ways of the forest fire," Azar said. "The scorching we set in motion will make this nation whimper for mercy. Think of it, Salman, the American people will demand an end to the jihad and peace at any price . . . and that price will include the utter destruction of Israel and the Jewish people."

"Allahu Akbar!" Assad yelled.

Azar smiled. "Yes, God is great. But in the meantime, we will give Him a little help by using Norris." The man shrugged. "And then you and the Ukrainian can execute him at your leisure."

"That will be a pleasure," Assad said, grinning. "We'll make him know he's dying."

"He comes to the warehouse today to see the drones," Azar said. "Do not provoke him."

"He provokes me by his vile, infidel presence," Assad said.

"Patience, my friend," Azar said. "Your time will come."

* * *

"Did Corky amuse you, Mr. Norris?" Nasim Azar said, smiling. "She always did me."

Mike Norris ignored that, his weekend with the prostitute lost without a trace in a sea of booze. "I'm here to inspect the drones," he said. His stare moved to Salman Assad. "Call off your dog, Azar," he said.

The bodyguard's jaw clenched and his black eyes blazed hatred, but Azar's voice was calm as he said, "Return to your post, Salman. I'll call out if I need you."

The man nodded, glared thunder at Norris, then turned on his heel and left.

"Mr. Norris, be wary of Salman," Azar said. "He's extremely dangerous and at times quite unpredictable."

"It will be a cold day in hell when I let a camel cowboy son of a bitch put the crawl on me," Norris said.

Azar smiled. "Just so. Your courage is not in doubt. Now, shall we inspect the drones?"

"Is that nerd kid here?" Norris said.

"Randy Collins? Yes, he's been working with them since six o'clock this morning."

"Keen, ain't he?"

"As you say, he's a nerd."

The warehouse had a large, open area on the ground floor, but above that was a maze of what had once been cubbyhole offices and storage rooms. Azar led Norris upstairs to one of the larger rooms where an overweight teenager with an untidy shock of straw-colored hair stood at a work bench. In front of him was a large, heavy-lifting drone with six motors.

Azar introduced him to Norris as, "Randy, our expert on all things drone-related."

The kid wore jeans and a *Star Trek* geek T-shirt with food stains on the front. He smiled and stuck out a hand that Norris ignored. "Where did you find him, Azar? In his parents' basement?"

"I don't know where he lives," Azar said. "He answered a help-wanted ad I put in the paper."

"I live with my parents," the youth said. "But I have my own room with my own computer and TV."

"All grown up then, ain't you?" Norris said. He said to Azar, "That thing is way too big. We only need small drones to take out the observation cameras."

Randy Collins was defensive. "This drone can carry a payload, even small incendiary and antipersonnel bombs if you need them."

"What the hell?" Norris said. "Azar, who said anything about bombs?"

"I thought the drone should have that capacity," Azar said.

"Then you thought wrong. For what we plan on doing, a bomb is overkill. We want a small drone, a suicide drone, to fly into the camera and smash it up, that's all. Who the hell came up with the bomb idea?" He glared at Collins and said, "Was that your idea, nerd?"

"No, I came up with it," Azar said. "Perhaps you could make it work, Mr. Norris?"

"I told you, no bombs, not now, not ever," Norris said. He said to Collins, "Where are the small drones?"

"I have four heavy-lifting drones that I adapted for bombs ready to fly," Collins said. He shook his head. "I have no small ones."

Azar jumped in before Norris could speak. "An oversight. I assure you. I'll correct that right away."

Norris nodded in the direction of the drone on the bench. "Get rid of those damned bombers, Azar. That's an order."

"An order I will carry out, I assure you."

Norris stared hard at the other man. "Sometimes I wonder about you, Azar. Sometimes I don't understand your motivations."

"Mr. Norris, you never at any time stipulated the size of the drones. I misunderstood, that is all."

"Just make sure there are no more misunderstandings, or we call the whole thing off," Norris said. "Now do you understand?"

"Perfectly." Azar glanced at his watch. "Now, we must return to my office. There are five young men I want you to meet, men who think as we do."

"Why?" Norris said. "I mean I care about the future of my nation's forests, and you say you care, but why would these young men of yours give a damn?"

"I met them though a college professor of my acquaintance," Azar said. "They are members of a wildlife preservation society and very keen on safeguarding the environment for future generations. The recent spate of wildfires troubles them, and they admire our plan to return the watchtowers and human observers."

"What do they think about a demonstration burn here in Oregon?" Norris said.

"They're very much in favor, so long as no homes are destroyed and no one's life is endangered." Azar smiled. "The young men have heard about you, the hero of Indian Wells, and they've been looking forward to this meeting."

"What are they?" Norris said.

"They're all college graduates."

"I mean what are they ethnically?"

"They're all Americans of Middle Eastern descent, as I am," Azar said. "That's why I've taken such a keen interest in them. As you know, all young men of their age think about is girls and keg parties. It's so refreshing to meet such serious youths."

"They're Arabs," Norris said.

"Of Arab descent, yes. All of them are American citizens."

"Then I'll talk with them, just don't expect me to like them," Norris said.

The five young men were well-dressed in dark business suits and striped ties, and they were clean cut, deferential . . . and, the consequence of many visits with anti-American relatives in the Middle East, thoroughly radicalized. All had been to good colleges, and thanks to lectures from Azar, their knowledge of the nation's forests was extensive. Their spokesman, or at least the one that talked the most, was a twenty-three-year-old named Dilshad Hakimi who had just returned from an extended visit to Yemen, where he'd been given the great honor of executing a suspected Israeli spy. He'd used a *sulthan,* the beheading sword of Saudi Arabia, and had been praised for his skill, decapitating the man with a single stroke.

With the others, Hakimi listened to Norris talk about starting a controlled burn by the use of a drip torch, a handheld canister filled with a mix of gasoline and diesel fuel, which allows a steady stream to be directed to the ground as needed.

Hakimi raised his hand and Norris said, "Speak."

"Do we have any drip torches?" the young man said.

Nasim Azar answered that question. "Yes, I have several in inventory and some fuel."

"Then why don't we get away from the classroom, take a field trip to the nearest national forest, and try them out?" Hakimi said.

Azar spoke again. "Mr. Norris, don't you think that sounds like a good idea while the suicide drones are made ready?"

Norris thought that through. *Why not?* It would feel good to get into the woods again.

"Willamette National Forest is only an hour and a half away," Azar said. "It's the ideal place for a field trip."

Norris nodded. "All right, let's do it. But no big burn, not this trip. I'll show you how the drip torches work and a few other things, but we don't start a blaze."

"When do we go?" Hakimi said. The faces of the men around him were eager.

"Tomorrow," Azar said. "Mr. Norris, does that suit you?"

Norris shrugged. "I don't care. Tomorrow is fine. There will be six of us. Do you have a van?"

"I'll arrange that," Azar said. "You'll enjoy your outing."

"It's not an outing. It's step in the right direction," Norris said.

But for Mike Norris it was a step in the wrong direction . . . a step into madness.

CHAPTER 20

There was a message from Jacob Sensor telling Sarah Milano that the smoke jumper named Pete Kennedy had agreed to become a Regulator. After that, the phone fell silent, and it seemed to Cory Cantwell that he and Sarah would cool their heels around Los Angeles for another twenty-four hours.

Sarah said, "At least another day. I guess Sensor has bigger fish to fry at the moment."

"Seems like," Cantwell said. "I don't think we'll have the cabin tonight. Catrina Welsh has to sleep sometime."

He and Sarah sat in the National Wildfire Service canteen and drank coffee as they half-watched the TV on the far wall. Firefighters came and went, gobbling their food even faster than doctors and nurses, before dashing out again. From what Cantwell heard, fires were still burning along the coast in the hills. That made sense, because he'd seen no sign of Merinda Barker and her backup crew since he'd talked to her earlier.

Cantwell said, "I'm willing to bet Sensor's already forgotten about us. I bet we're stuck here forever and . . ."

He saw Sarah suddenly lean forward in her seat, her eyes fixed on the TV. "What is it?" he said.

"Shh . . ." Sarah said. "Listen."

" . . . the Croatian-born American billionaire philanthropist often came under attack for his liberal views, especially his vocal support for the Open Borders, Open Arms immigration policy favored by many liberals in Congress. Police say an armed man entered Nikola Kraljevic's Hyannis Port compound earlier today while the seventy-two-year-old was in his swimming pool along with two young female house guests. The gunman, described by a member of the domestic staff as a Caucasian male wearing tan pants, a blue polo shirt, and mirrored sunglasses, opened fire and killed all three. He later escaped in a dark gray sedan. Police ask anyone who saw this car or the gunman to immediately contact your local law enforcement agency. Now, for a comment on today's tragedy, we turn to Democratic Congresswoman Jan Cummings . . ."

Sarah looked at Cantwell. "You don't think . . ."

The man shook his head. "Nah. A billionaire like Nikola Kraljevic makes a lot of enemies. It could even be a mafia hit. Didn't he get his start as a union organizer on the New York docks or something?"

"Yes, I think he did," Sarah said. "I remember reading about that when I was working with Homeland Security."

"Well, there you go, a Mafia hit. It has to be," Cantwell said.

"I don't think so. Jacob Sensor told me he'd identified the man who bankrolled the attempt on his life," Sarah said. "And he said to keep watching the news. Too much of a coincidence, don't you think?"

Cantwell thought that through and then said, "Kraljevic had the name of being a rabid liberal and very much in favor of OBOA. As I recall, he was known to be anti-Semitic and fought hard to get the United States to drop its support for Israel."

"And Sensor is very much against both those policies," Sarah said. "So did Kraljevic try to knock off Jacob Sensor only to get knocked off in turn? Makes sense, huh?"

"Maybe too much sense," Cantwell said. "Sarah, who the hell are you working for?"

"I'm beginning to have my doubts that I know the man at all," Sarah said. "There may be more to Jacob Sensor than meets the eye."

"If it was Sensor, his hit on Kraljevic was political, and it's got nothing to do with pyroterrorism or the Regulators," Cantwell said. "In other words, we've no reason to get involved."

"How would we get involved?" Sarah said. "Go to the police and say, 'Hey, we know who killed Nikola Kraljevic'?"

Cantwell smiled. "'It was Jacob Sensor. You know him, lives in Washington, DC, is a government power broker and a personal friend of the President. He's the one what done it.'"

"Would they believe us?" Sarah said.

"Not a chance," Cantwell said.

"So in the meantime . . ."

"He's still our boss."

"The Russian mafia," Sarah said.

"Huh?" Cantwell said.

Sarah had been looking at the TV. Now she turned and

said, "Congresswoman Jan Cummings says without doubt it was a Russian mafia hit."

"Why does she say that?"

"Apparently Kraljevic accused the Russians of attempting to influence the last presidential election."

"Makes sense," Cantwell said.

"But we know better," Sarah said.

"Yeah," Cantwell said. "We certainly do know better."

"Mr. Cantwell, I've decided to take you up on your offer," Merinda Barker said. "I want to be a Regulator."

The woman's face was smudged with smoke, and soot had gathered in the corner of her eyes. Her crew, exhausted, lay on the grass beside the dirt road, but a couple of them followed Merinda's lead and had made their way to the canteen.

Cantwell smiled. "Glad to hear it. What made you make up your mind?"

"I spoke to my grandfather. I didn't tell him what the job was, but he told me I must follow my heart," the woman said. "My heart tells me to accept your offer."

"Then leave it with me, Miss Barker," Cantwell said. "First of all, I'll see about getting you the jump training you need and we'll take it from there."

"Don't I get sworn in or something?" Merinda said.

"I don't think so," Cantwell said. "I've hired you and that's it. We don't stand on ceremony in the Regulators."

Sarah Milano smiled. "All two of you."

"Well, there's Pete Kennedy and a few more," Cantwell said. "Our numbers are growing, albeit slowly."

"Pete Kennedy," Merinda said. "I heard some of the

firefighters talking about him. He made quite a hero of himself up Washington state way."

"And that's why he's now a Regulator," Cantwell said. "You're in exalted company, Miss Barker."

"Aren't you proud?" Sarah said, smiling.

Merinda said, "I'm excited. I really want to do this. Most, if not all, of the fires we've battled for the past week were started by humans."

"Terrorists most likely," Cantwell said. "And it will get worse before it gets better."

"Can we stop it, Mr. Cantwell," Merinda said. "I mean can the Regulators stop it?"

"It will stop when enough terrorists die," Cantwell said. "That's the bottom line."

"I'll do my part," Merinda said. "My grandfather has spoken of terrorists. He says they are cowards who hide behind fire and explosives and never come out to fight in the light of day."

"You grandfather is a wise man," Cantwell said.

"He is a warrior," Merinda said.

"And right now that's what the National Wildfire Service needs . . . warriors," Cantwell said.

"Like me," Merinda said.

CHAPTER 21

Jacob Sensor poured brandy into a couple of crystal snifters, handed one to British MI5 director Sir Anthony Bickford-Scott, and said, "You did well."

As good manners dictated, Bickford-Scott accepted the compliment with no show of emotion. "Thank you," he said. "The Ukrainian is expensive, but he's always reliable and discreet."

"All the same, it's a pity about the two girls," Sensor said. "I was distressed to hear that they'd been eliminated."

The Englishman waved a dismissive hand. "High-class prostitutes. Casualties of war. Put them out of your mind."

"Your prime minister?"

"He knows it happened, but nothing else. He's a blabbermouth and none too bright."

"He was a personal friend of Nikola Kraljevic, or so I'm told," Sensor said.

"They had much in common, both rich men and liberal leftists. A combination I'll never understand."

"And both had an eye for the ladies."

"Russian women, and the younger the better," Bickford-Scott said. "The two dead girls were Russians."

Sensor said, "Initially, there was a great deal of Slavic angst about that, but it was smoothed over. I promised that we'd look the other way when the next Russian assassination on US soil comes along."

"Jolly good show," Bickford-Scott said.

The two men sat in the library of Sensor's palatial home in McLean, outside of Washington, DC, a power center of woodsy parks and quiet, leafy streets where neighbors rooted for one another's kids at Little League games and carpooled to the nearby schools.

"Three shots, three kills," Sensor said.

The Englishman nodded. "It's the Ukrainian's way."

"The police are investigating the incident as a Russian mafia hit."

"Then let them think that."

"Their investigation will go nowhere, and the case will be quietly dropped," Sensor said. "How did it play in London? Or is it too early to know?"

"As far as I can tell, nobody gives a damn. Kraljevic was a naturalized American citizen whose sharp business practices once helped devalue the British pound. He was hardly popular in Whitehall."

"So it's a case of good riddance?" Sensor said.

"Hardly even that. It's a case of, 'Don't bother us with trivia when we're facing another general election.'"

Sensor said, "Now, to change the subject, what is your impression so far of my Regulators plan?"

"My dear chap, it's excellent. Our own force is now in the field, some eighty strong."

"Recruited from firefighters?"

Bickford-Scott shook his elegant, silver-gray head. "That is where we differ. Our operatives are mostly snake-eaters, drawn from the ranks of the Special Air Service and the Royal Navy's Special Boat Service, plus a few intelligence types." The Englishman smiled. "We don't expect them to put out fires, but we do ask them to extinguish those who light them."

"And the Ukrainian?" Sensor said. "Do you use him in that capacity?"

"From time to time, but only to terminate known pyroterrorist leaders. He's too expensive to use for small fry."

"How many Islamic terrorists have you eliminated so far?"

"My dear, Jacob, that number is classified, but I can tell you that in Scotland alone we have erased seven in the past eighteen months."

"I didn't realize that there are that many forests in Scotland," Sensor said.

"Twenty-six that can be called major woodlands," Bickford-Scott said.

Sensor offered the Englishman a cigar, waited until it was lit, and then said, "So, how many operatives can you lend me?"

From behind a cloud of blue smoke, Bickford-Scott said, "This must be kept very hush-hush, Jacob. Remember, the prime minister and parliament have no knowledge of our operations. The British government is made up of wheels within wheels, and it would not do to upset their balance and have the whole setup come to a grinding halt."

"I understand perfectly," Sensor said. His own cigar

glowed crimson in the muted lamplight. The curtains were drawn against the darkness outside.

"Three for starters," the Englishman said. "All SAS and all tiptop chaps, or so I'm told."

"When can you send them?"

"As soon as you need them. As far as I'm aware, they're packed and ready to go."

"I need them now," Sensor said.

"Then I'll arrange it as soon as I return to the embassy."

"They'll fly into LAX, and I'll take it from there. Let me know their time of arrival."

"They're traveling incognito, so if you plan to use them on operations, they'll need to be armed."

Sensor nodded. "It's unlikely they'll go out on operations. I want only their expertise, Bickford-Scott. Your snake-eaters will be in the classroom under the command of Superintendent Cory Cantwell, who's currently here in Los Angeles. I'll let him know they're on their way."

"Does Cantwell have any experience?"

"Yes, he's already deleted terrorists in the field."

"Jolly good," the Englishman said. "That makes a difference."

Then, as his mind came back to the events of earlier in the day, Sensor said, "I can never thank you enough for recommending the Ukrainian."

"No thanks needed, dear chap." He waved a dismissive hand, and the cigar in his fingers trailed blue smoke. "I was only too glad to help."

"Kraljevic needed killing," Sensor said.

Bickford-Scott smiled. "Jacob, do you really need my reassurance?"

"I'm not usually this sensitive, but yeah, I guess I do."

"Then you have it. Kraljevic did his best to have you assassinated, for God's sake."

"Maybe it's the two dead girls that trouble me."

"They were in the wrong place at the wrong time, Jacob," the Englishman said. "Believe me, it could have been much, much worse. The Ukrainian could've taken it into his head to kill the entire household from the scullery maid to the butler."

Sensor smiled. "Would he have done that?"

"Yes, indeed, old chap. He's done it before. A couple of years back in Italy . . ."

"I don't think I want to hear this," Sensor said.

"Wait, it's quite funny in a droll sort of way," Bickford-Scott said. "The Ukrainian put a bomb in the coffin of a deceased millionaire and blew up the entire funeral party gathered around the grave. It was lashing down rain that day, and seventeen people died with umbrellas in their hands."

"Who was the target?" Sensor said, interested in spite of himself.

"The grieving young widow," the Englishman said. "Apparently, she was the heir to the deceased's fortune, but if she died the money would go to the dead man's brother. The brother paid the Ukrainian to solve the little problem of the heiress's continued existence. At least, that's what the police thought, though they could never prove it."

"Where was the brother when the bomb went off?" Sensor said.

"He claimed he got a flat tire and was late for the funeral," Bickford-Scott said. "Now here's the amusing part. Because of the power of the blast, the body of the dead millionaire landed intact on the roof of the St. Marie de Chagrin chapel a quarter-mile away from the cemetery. Poor chap had to be buried all over again."

"With a lot fewer mourners," Sensor said.

"Only his grateful brother," Bickford-Scott said.

"So, even the Ukrainian is not infallible," Sensor said.

"Indeed, it would seem that he's not. He drastically underestimated the power of his own bomb, that's for certain."

Bickford-Scott rose from his chair and moved to the window, where he pulled the curtain aside and looked out on the shadowed front lawn and the white-painted summerhouse.

"We are fighting a war, Jacob," he said. "A war against terrorism we have to win, using fair means or foul. Our good friend Vladimir Putin says that terrorism has no nationality or religion, and he's right. It's a festering wound, an enemy of humanity. Pyroterrorism is just its latest manifestation, and we can't let it beat us."

"Why is the UK a target? Your forests are small, nothing like ours," Sensor said.

"All of Europe is a target, not just the UK," the Englishman said. "But you're correct, the United States is the main focus of this new breed of arson terrorists."

"Then the sooner I get the Regulators up and running, the better," Sensor said.

"Yes, time is of the essence," Bickford-Scott said. "I trust that the men I'll send you will help."

"I'm sure they will," Sensor said.

The Englishman let the curtain fall back into place. "One more word about Nikola Kraljevic, if I may. I wouldn't let him lie too heavily on my conscience. He took a hand in the political game and lost. That's all there is to it."

"You understand that his problem with me had nothing to do with pyroterrorism," Sensor said.

"I know that. But, my dear Jacob, open borders and terrorism go hand in hand. The twisted beliefs of Kraljevic and his kind have everything to do with pyroterrorism and every other kind of terrorism. You do see that, don't you?"

Jacob Sensor nodded. "Yes, I see it. Of course, I see it."

"Good. Now aren't you glad you had the miserable son of a whore shot?" Sir Anthony Bickford-Scott said.

CHAPTER 22

The morning sun rose above the tree line and light reached the forest floor, filtered through the canopies of the gigantic Douglas firs, some of which stood three hundred feet tall.

As Ben Stevens and Bill Baxter walked the tree line, jays quarreled in the branches, and high above a bald eagle quartered the lemon-colored sky. The men had entered the Willamette National Forest just before dawn, but as yet they'd not spotted any deer.

Stevens and Baxter, good ol' boy proprietors of Bill & Ben's Tire and Auto Repair in Portland, were on a pre–hunting season scout, searching for the big bucks they hoped would fall to their rifles in six weeks or so. Their search had so far been disappointing.

But a grassy meadow about a hundred acres in extent, bordered by trees on three sides, revealed plenty of deer sign, and that gave the hunters hope.

"I guess they're keeping to the trees," Stevens said, a gray-haired man who'd hunted all his life. He wore an olive-green L.L.Bean field coat with a corduroy collar, camo hunting pants, and lace-up boots. He had a camo ball cap on his head, and a pair of binoculars hung on his chest.

"Seems like," Baxter, a mirror image of his friend, allowed. "Well, we'll keep looking. Bound to cross trails with some bucks eventually."

The sheer size of the Willamette gave shy deer plenty of options for cover. The forest and wilderness areas covered 1,678,031 acres and included seven mountain peaks and the headwaters of the Willamette River. It was a vast land, breathtakingly beautiful and a haven of rest and relaxation for those who loved and understood it, but it held dangers for the ignorant and unwary.

Like most hunters, Stevens and Baxter were conservationists, and in their minds the Willamette was a piece of paradise that had accidentally fallen to earth in days gone by. And that may indeed have been the case.

The two men scouted the old-growth forest and then trekked into an open area where they crossed a stream and saw ahead of them a thick stand of cedar, hemlock, and white pine. Baxter used his field glasses to scan the trees, and then his gaze lingered on a track that paralleled the tree line.

"What do you see, Bill?" Stevens said. "You see a buck, huh?"

Baxter lowered the glasses. "No, I see people."

"What kind of people?"

"Five, no six, men. What the hell are they doing?"

Stevens used his own binoculars. Then, his eyes still on the men, he said, "They could be hunters on the scout like us."

"Or birdwatchers," Baxter said. "Plenty of those around.

Wait, one of them has a metal canister of some kind. What the heck is he using that for?"

"Beats me," Stevens said. "Let's go ask them if they've seen any big bucks in the area."

Ben Stevens was immediately suspicious. Not a prejudiced man by nature, he did notice that the five young men looked dark and foreign, and the big white man called Norris seemed ill at ease, as though he felt guilty about something, like an overgrown kid with his fingers in the cookie jar.

And Stevens, who'd on several occasions met firefighters in the woods, recognized the cylinder for what it was . . . a drip torch, used to ignite controlled burns. He saw where the undergrowth had been scorched in a dozen different places, and his suspicions grew.

Bill Baxter on the other hand took Mike Norris and his acolytes at face value. "Seen any big bucks, have ye?" he said.

"No," Norris said. "No, we haven't." His eyes were on Stevens. The man, dressed up in field jacket and camo pants, seemed uneasy. Was he armed?

"So, what are you doing with the drip torch?" Stevens said. "Kind of dangerous around the trees, ain't it?"

"These young men are interested in forest conservation, and I'm showing them how firefighters light a controlled burn," Norris said.

"You're not firefighters," Stevens said, and now Baxter stepped beside him, his face troubled.

"They're actually interested in forestry management," Norris said. "I'm teaching them the ropes."

Stevens shook his head. "Not here, you're not. You could set the whole damn forest ablaze."

"Shows how damned ignorant you are," Norris said, his quick anger flaring. "I said a *controlled* burn. Don't you understand plain English?"

"I understand that what you're doing is not legal," Stevens said. "Come with me and you can explain yourself to a ranger."

"Go to hell and mind your own business," Norris said.

Ben Stevens was a tough man and not one to suffer fools gladly . . . and he considered Norris a damned fool. His spine stiffened with a spiking anger, and he stepped to Norris. "Give me that goddamned drip torch," he said. "Hand it over."

It happened very quickly.

One of the young men drew a knife from a sheath at his waist. The blade glittered in the sun for a moment before he plunged it to the hilt into Stevens's chest.

Time stood still . . . a second ticked past . . . then another . . .

"You goddamned . . ." Baxter yelled, his eyes wild. He reached into his pants pocket and drew a Bond Snake Slayer derringer. But before he could level the gun, the other youths were on him, knives flashing, biting deep. Baxter managed to stay on his feet for long moments until he finally fell, the front of his field jacket glistening scarlet with blood.

Mike Norris was horrified. Stunned. He stood rooted to the spot, his eyes seeing but unbelieving. "Oh, my God, what have you done?" he said.

The young men ignored that, and Dilshad Hakimi,

their unofficial leader, said, "Take the bodies into the trees and cover them up. Do it now."

The other four dragged the dead men into the pines, and Norris grabbed by the front of his shirt the man who'd given the orders and yelled, "Damn you! Damn you!"

"They would've given us away," Hakimi said. "They had to be silenced."

"You didn't need to kill them," Norris said. "There was no call for murder."

"There was no other recourse," the man said. "Now, take your hands off me or you'll lose them."

Somewhere in the trees a branch snapped, and a racked buck bounded out of the forest, crossed some open ground, and disappeared into a stand of cedar.

Norris staggered back, sat heavily on the ground and buried his face in his hands. "Oh, my God . . . Oh, my God" . . . saying it over and over again like a prayer.

When the other four returned, brushing off their hands, Hakimi said, "We must get out of here. Bring the drip torch."

One of the men, the youngest of the five, looked at Norris with contempt. "Dilshad, what about the infidel?"

"Bring him."

Norris was hauled to his feet, but he was in a state of complete collapse, and it took two of the young men to hold him upright. "What if we meet up with others?" one of them said.

"He drank too much whiskey too early," Hakimi said. "We're taking him home."

"Our car is a distance away, and he's a heavy man," the youngest said.

"Ismail, that's just one of the sacrifices you must make for the Prophet," Hakimi said. "Do as I told you."

"Pah," one of the youngsters said. "He smells of alcohol."

"He's an infidel," Hakimi said. "He smells of sin and corruption."

CHAPTER 23

"How are you feeling?" Nasim Azar said. He held up an empty syringe. "You were very worked up, and I gave you a mild sedative."

Mike Norris blinked, blinked again, and then said, "Where am I?"

"At the warehouse, in the living room of my apartment. You had a nasty shock."

Norris gradually became aware of his surroundings. He sat in a wooden chair in a simply furnished room, its main feature a large casement window that offered a view of the Willamette River. The murmur of male voices came from somewhere close by, and a man laughed and then fell silent again.

Norris tried to gather his thoughts, then the memory of what had happened hit him with the force of a baseball bat. "The hunters . . ." he said.

"Yes, a great tragedy," Azar said. "I am desolated."

"Your boys murdered them," Norris said. "Stabbed them to death. Both of them."

"The men were eliminated because their deaths were

necessary to our cause, Mr. Norris," Azar said. "I regret the incident as much as you do."

"Damn you, Azar," Norris said. He tried to move but found he was bound to the chair with ropes. He tried to struggle free but could not move, his ankles and wrists tied with cruel tightness.

"The ropes are for your own good," Azar said. "You'd had some kind of fit and were convulsing. I administered midazolam to ensure that you didn't hurt yourself."

"Damn you, Azar, cut me loose," Norris said. "I'm going to the police."

The man shook his head, his black eyes glittering. "No police. You're in too deep, Mr. Norris, deep enough to be charged with an accessory to a double murder, and that means at least fifteen years to life in a federal prison. Do you really want the law to get involved?"

"Damn you, Azar, you're a devil incarnate," Norris said.

"No, Mr. Norris, I'm not a *shaytan*. The two hunters, nobodies, were necessary sacrifices in the war to deliver our nation from the horrors of the Scorching. Keep that thought uppermost in your mind. I will now leave you to think about what I've said."

Nasim Azar stepped out of the door into a dressing area that connected to his bedroom. His five young men stood around yet another casement window, and with them was his bodyguard, Salman Assad, and a small, slender and insignificant-looking man with thinning blond hair and pale blue eyes. He was called the Ukrainian, and if he had any other name, Azar was not aware of it.

"Dilshad Hakimi, this was ill done," Azar said.

"The infidels surprised us," the young man said. "They gave us no choice."

"The man Norris may be of no further use to us," Azar said. "I think his mind is going."

"He does not like the sight of blood," Hakimi said.

"Did he teach you anything?"

"A little. We did not have much time."

"Can you start a forest fire so that it will spread quickly to populated areas?" Azar said.

Without hesitation, Hakimi said, "Yes, I believe we can."

"You believe you can? Answer my question. Can you start a major forest fire and direct its course to populated areas?"

"Yes, master, we can," Hakimi said. "We can use the wind. The man Norris taught us that much."

"He showed you how to harness the wind," Azar said. "That is well. Were there cameras in the Willamette?"

"No, none that we could see," Hakimi said. "Norris has done some research, and he says it could be years yet before a sufficient number of cameras are deployed. At the moment, the cameras are few in number and in any case their range is very short. There is talk of using ground-mounted heat monitors, but that is for the future."

"Then the drones may be unnecessary," Azar said. "That would be a good thing, less to carry into the forest."

"If there are no cameras, we can start fires without the drones," Hakimi said. Then, a plaintive tone in his voice, "Just give us the opportunity to try. Master, let me make something clear, and in this I also speak for the other brothers . . . we desire to be martyrs. We want to die for the holy cause of jihad. That is our fondest wish."

Azar was so moved by this speech he pumped his fist in the air and yelled, *"Allahu Akbar!"* And the others joined in, except for the Ukrainian. He remained silent, and the sphinxlike expression on his face did not change.

"What are you boys celebrating?" Mike Norris said.

Nasim Azar shrugged. "Nothing of any importance. A birthday."

"You're a damned liar," Norris said.

Azar's mouth tightened. He backhanded Norris across the face, the crack of the blow like a pistol shot. He then shoved his face close to the other man's until only an inch of space separated them. Azar's eyes burned with fanaticism.

"You are correct, Mr. Norris, we did not celebrate a birthday. We celebrated the willingness of my young men to strike a blow against the infidels and die bravely as warriors for the coming Caliphate." Azar straightened up and said, "Does not that thrill you, as it does me?"

"I always took you for a damned traitor, Azar," Norris said. "Now I know I was right."

"Because I do not waver in my zeal to serve Allah?"

"The hell with Allah. You damned trash, I hate your guts," Norris said.

"I offer you redemption and in return you offer only blasphemy," Azar said.

"What the hell do you want from all this?" Norris said.

"Want? What my father and his father before me wanted . . . that the American presence, military and corporate, be withdrawn from Islamic soil. All American business interests in Muslim countries must be turned over, not to the governments of those nations, but to the Caliphate. A new Islamic order will soon unite Muslims everywhere and lead them to their God-given place of dominance on earth. If what it takes to accomplish this sacred goal are the deaths of every infidel on the planet, then so be it. Allah wills it. *Allahu Akbar!*"

"You're mad, Azar, stark, raving mad," Norris said.

"Mad because I want to strike at the hearts of the Americans with fire?" Azar said. "Mad because I want them to feel the same pain that untold thousands of my people have felt at the loss of our children, not only to American guns and bombs, but to a satanic culture that seduces them away from the true tenets of Islam." Azar shook his head. "No, my friend, it is you that is mad, not I."

"I'll stop you, Azar," Norris said. "You and your kind."

"Big talk from a man tied to a chair with midazolam in his veins," Azar said. "Listen to reason, Norris, don't fight me, join me. We're teachers, you and I and we can use the Scorching to give our lessons. You can teach yours to the National Wildfire Service, and I will teach mine to the American nation. We must remain allies, not become enemies."

"The National Wildfire Service . . ." Norris said, his face twisted as though the name was bitter gall on his tongue.

"Yes, Norris, teach them a lesson," Azar said. "They abandoned the lookout towers and made you a forgotten pariah. Now the forests are more vulnerable than they've ever been. Teach them the error of their ways. Teach them with fire and flame."

Norris shook his head. "You're a devil, Azar."

"No, my friend, you have your own devils, and now you must deal with them."

"Untie me," Norris said. "I need time to think."

"Then think wisely, Mr. Norris, before it's too late," Azar said. "If you decide to become my bitterest enemy instead of my dark shadow, you won't leave this warehouse alive."

"You're keeping me a prisoner here?"

"Only until you come to your senses."

"Then you'll wait forever."

"I don't want to kill you, Mr. Norris."

"You can't kill me, Azar."

"Why?"

"Because I've become a part of you. I'm a cancer that you can't cut out without dying yourself."

"Foolish talk. To me, you're just another infidel."

Norris smiled. "You're a damned liar, and you know it."

"Enough of this babble. I already have a comfortable room prepared for you." Azar grinned like a cobra. "But bear this in mind . . . my young men are willing to die for the cause, and I really don't need you anymore."

"We believe Cory Cantwell to be in Los Angeles," Nasim Azar said.

"It is a large city," the Ukrainian said. His native accent was barely perceptible, slightly nasal, the words coming from the back of his throat in a whisper.

"And that's why you must find him," Nasim Azar said. He extended a silver box with a cedarwood lining.

"Cigarette?" The Ukrainian took one, and Azar said, "In recent years fatwas have been issued against tobacco. But I ignore them."

The Ukrainian lit his cigarette, inhaled and said, "Turkish tobacco from the Black Sea coast, but blended with Virginia."

Azar smiled. "You know your cigarettes."

"I know many things, but I don't know where to find your man Cantwell."

"He works for the National Wildfire Service, and they have a base complex in Los Angeles," Azar said. "Begin your investigation there."

"I am paid to eradicate targets, not to do detective work," the Ukrainian said. "My price has now gone up considerably."

"And I will pay it," Azar said.

"Fifty thousand dollars. Do you have that kind of money?"

"And more. There is a certain oil-rich sheik who finances my work for the jihad."

"Then book me on the first available flight to Los Angeles," the Ukrainian said. "Half my fee now, the other half when Cantwell is dead."

"It shall be done," Azar said.

CHAPTER 24

Jacob Sensor's voice was even when he spoke to Sarah Milano, but she sensed the tension in the man.

"You've seen the news about the two hunters murdered in Oregon yesterday?" he said.

"Yes, I saw it," Sarah said. "CNN says it was the work of some anti-hunting group."

"That's nonsense we put out to the media," Sensor said. "There was evidence of attempted burning at the site."

"In the Willamette National Forest, according to the TV," Sarah said. She looked at Cory Cantwell and mouthed the name "Jacob Sensor."

"Yes, in the Willamette," Sensor said. "We suspect terrorism, and I want you to leave for Portland immediately. I've booked you and Cantwell on a one-fifteen flight."

"Mr. Sensor, isn't this a job for the FBI?" Sarah said. She'd now caught Cantwell's undivided attention.

"Yes, it is, but I want the Regulators in on it. Pete Kennedy will join you in Portland, and I have three more Regulators arriving soon."

"Sarah, let me have the phone," Cantwell said, frowning.

"Superintendent Cantwell wishes to speak with you, Mr. Sensor," Sarah said, being formal about it. Cantwell took the phone and said, "Mr. Sensor, Cantwell here. I . . ."

"You know about the hunters killed in Willamette?" Sensor said.

"Yes, I saw it on the TV news."

"I want the Regulators to help find the killers. I want a success story to impress the President."

"The news said the hunters were killed by anti-hunting extremists."

"That's bullshit. They were murdered by pyroterrorists. There was grass and tree scorching found at the site."

"I don't think the FBI will welcome us with open arms," Cantwell said.

"I've ordered them to give you complete cooperation," Sensor said. "Superintendent Cantwell, this was a terrorist act, and it can't go unpunished."

"I understand that, sir, but . . ."

"No buts, Superintendent. I need the Regulators to be in on this investigation. This is your big chance to make a name for yourself and finally put the Regulators on the map. Remember, the terrorists tried to burn the forest once, but were interrupted by the hunters. They'll be back."

"How should we proceed? I mean . . ."

"Let the FBI do the legwork, they're used to it," Sensor said. "Just be in at the kill. Superintendent Cantwell, I have every confidence in you. Now, let me talk with Miss Milano again."

Sensor had little to add, except to give details of the

flight and Pete Kennedy's phone number. When he hung up, Sarah said, "Mr. Sensor wishes us luck. We're booked on a Delta flight departing in . . . an hour and fifteen minutes. We'd better hustle, and I'll tell Catrina Welsh that she can have her cabin back."

"Damn it, Sarah, we're going to be as much use in Portland as a sidesaddle on a sow," Cantwell said.

"You know it, I know it, but Jacob Sensor doesn't know it. Throw your gear together, we've got to move," Sarah said. "We'll leave the rental car at the airport."

"I badly wanted to ask him if he'd iced Nikola Kraljevic," Cantwell said.

"If he told you, he'd have to kill you," Sarah said.

Cantwell nodded. "And he would too."

After a stop at San Francisco, the Delta flight landed in a rainstorm at Portland International Airport at seven-thirty with night coming down. Cantwell rented a Toyota RAV4, tossed their bags in the back, and then Sarah insisted they book into the downtown Hilton on Southwest Sixth Avenue. Adjoining rooms.

"I'm not slumming it," she said. "We'll let Jacob Sensor worry about the expenses."

As she'd been ordered, Sarah checked in with Sensor, and an hour later someone knocked on her room door and she opened it to a man in a wet trench coat. Sarah thought he looked like Humphrey Bogart in a 1930s film noir.

"Miss Milano?" the man said. He sounded like Humphrey Bogart too, kind of lispy.

"Yes, can I help you?"

"My name is Tom D'eth." He spelled it out. D-apostrophe-E-T-H. "I'm with the FBI," the man said. He showed his ID. "Can I come in?"

"Of course," Sarah said. Then, louder, and being formal again, "Superintendent Cantwell, the FBI is here."

Cory Cantwell stepped through the open door between the rooms, and the FBI agent stuck out his hand. "Agent Tom D'eth. I was told to check in with you." He smiled. "And I've heard all the jokes."

"Can I take your coat, Agent D'eth?'" Sarah said. "You're dripping all over the rug, I'm afraid."

"Sorry," D'eth said. He took off his coat, then looked around for a place to put it.

"I'll hang it over the bathtub," Sarah said.

"Good idea," D'eth said.

Cantwell waved the man to a chair and then said, "We have a minibar and an expense account. Can I get you something?"

"Nothing for me, thanks," D'eth said.

"Mind if I do?"

"No, go right ahead."

"Sarah?" Cantwell said. "You want a drink?"

"Bourbon on the rocks."

Cantwell poured the drinks and sat on the edge of the bed opposite the agent. "I guess you know why Miss Milano and I are here?" he said.

D'eth nodded. He looked wary, a little ill at ease. "You're here to assist in our investigation into the deaths of the two hunters in the Willamette forest."

"That's what we were told," Cantwell said. "Although how we can help is beyond me. Miss Milano and I are not detectives."

"No, Mr. Cantwell, but you do head up an anti-terrorist unit," D'eth said.

"A unit that exists only on paper," Cantwell said. Then, smiling, "If there is any paper."

D'eth did not return the smile. His lined, slightly weary face grim, he said, "The media is content with the anti-hunting story, since it suits their narrative, but there is no doubt that pyroterrorists were trying to light a forest fire when Ben Stevens and Bill Baxter stumbled across them. That's what we know, but we have a problem."

"And that is?" Cantwell said.

"Our investigation has just begun, but it may already be compromised," D'eth said. "Mr. Cantwell, if that's the case, the lives of you and Miss Milano are in great danger."

Sarah looked shocked. "How? I mean, no one knows we're here."

"No one?" D'eth said, he looked skeptical.

"Our boss," Cantwell said. "Only our boss in Washington, DC."

"And he's got a boss, and that boss has a boss and so on and so forth all the way up to the President," the agent said. "Somebody, somewhere along the line isn't playing a straight game."

Cantwell shook his head. "I refuse to believe that."

"Then believe what you want to believe," D'eth said. "Do you have a gun?"

"Yes, I do," Cantwell said.

"Take my advice, don't leave home without it." He looked at Sarah. "That goes for you too."

The FBI agent got to his feet. "I'll pick you up outside the hotel tomorrow morning at eight," he said. "I'll take you to the murder scene." He saw the perplexed expression on Cantwell's face and added, "You've got to start somewhere, Superintendent."

"I'll get your coat," Sarah said.

D'eth shrugged into his wet coat and stepped to the door. "What kind of firearm do you have, Mr. Cantwell?"

"A Glock 19. And Miss Milano has a Colt Python."

"A Colt Python, really? How quaint. See that you have them with you tomorrow," D'eth said. "We don't want to be outgunned, do we?"

After the agent left, Sarah said, "Is there a mole on Sensor's staff, you think?"

"I don't know. Could be," Cantwell said. "Or on somebody's staff."

Sarah crossed the floor to the minibar. "I need another drink. Do you?"

"Damn right, I do," Cantwell said. Then, "Don't you think that Tom D'eth looks like Humphrey Bogart?"

"Sam Spade in *The Maltese Falcon*," Sarah said.

"No, Rick Blaine in *Casablanca*, I think." Cantwell said. "Standing in the rain."

Sarah raised her glass. "Here's looking at you, kid," she said.

CHAPTER 25

Nasim Azar laid down his cell phone with a thump of frustration. He'd sent the Ukrainian to the wrong city. The assassin was already airborne, and it was too late to call him back. According to his informant, Cory Cantwell had left Los Angeles and flown into Portland that afternoon.

Azar spent the next hour on the phone, ordering, not only his fire warriors, but others in his cell to check every hotel and motel in the city to find out where Cory Cantwell was registered. The story they'd tell the desk clerk was that Mr. Cantwell's sister had been in a car accident and was in the ICU at Cedars-Sinai Medical Center in LA. It was a long shot, Azar knew, but it was worth trying.

Tomorrow he'd recall the Ukrainian, but all he could do now was wait.

He slipped his phone into his pocket and looked out the window at the street outside and beyond that, the river. It was raining hard, and there was no one about. Only the occasional car passed by, its tires hissing.

Adelia Palmer, Azar's part-time cook and cleaning lady, knocked on the door and then stepped inside. "I'll be going now, Mr. Azar," she said. She was an overweight black woman with a round, good-natured face, widowed these fifteen years. She always wore a hat she'd retired from church duties.

"Did you feed Mr. Norris?" Azar said.

"Uh-huh. Cornbread, pinto beans, an' sweet iced tea, just like you said."

Azar smiled. "Thank you, Mrs. Palmer. It's raining, so you take care out there on the drive home."

"I will. Goodnight, Mr. Azar."

"Yes, goodnight, Mrs. Palmer. I'll see you next week."

After the woman left, and without any callbacks as yet, Azar put his .25 in his pocket, left his apartment, and walked downstairs to the ground floor of the warehouse. Mike Norris was held in a room at the back, big enough that Azar had once considered it for his own living quarters. The key to the lock hung by a string from a hook on the wall. His hand in his pocket touching the cool steel of the little Beretta, he unlocked the door and stepped inside.

Mike Norris's ankles were shackled to an iron ring set into a sturdy partition beam, giving him sufficient room to sit on an iron cot and stare without interest at the TV mounted on the wall. The room was spartan, furnished with a dresser and a couple of chairs. A half-opened door revealed the presence of a small bathroom. A pile of carpets lay in one corner.

"You dined well, Mr. Norris?" Azar said.

"It was garbage, and the black woman was terrified of me," Norris said. "What did you tell her?"

"Only that you were a distant relative who'd lost his mind and was locked up for his own safety. Mrs. Palmer is not a questioning woman, that's why I hired her." Azar glanced at the TV screen. "Ah, *The Thin Man Goes Home*. I enjoyed that movie. Did you know that Nick and Nora's drinking was curtailed in the film because of wartime liquor rationing? It was made in 1944, after all."

"What do you want, Azar?" Norris said. "Did you come to gloat?"

"Gloat? Why would I glory in your fall? Mr. Norris, you're a poor, pathetic drunk hated by everybody. Don't you realize that?"

"Yeah. I began to realize it when a man named Harvey Williams called me a disgrace and an embarrassment to the National Wildfire Service."

"Such a cruel thing to say, Mr. Norris. But unfortunately very true."

Norris's anger flared. "Azar, I don't need to hear it from you, so shut your damn trap."

Azar shook his head. "So bitter and so sad."

"I need a drink," Norris said.

Azar smiled. "Ah, just like Nick Charles. No, you're not Nick Charles, you're Mike Norris, a washed-up firefighter with no future." He stepped back a little and took the Beretta from his pocket. "I could leave this with you. It's small, but powerful enough to blow your brains out. Put you out of your misery, as they say."

"I'm not killing myself, Azar," Norris said. "I won't give you the satisfaction."

"Why not? It's a way out your present state of nonexistence. Nobody wants you, Mr. Norris. Nobody even wants to know you. You're a pariah, an outcast, a renegade."

Norris's expression grew crafty. "There is always revenge,

and revenge is sweet. I could wreak my vengeance on all those who wronged me."

Azar studied the man closely. There was little doubt that since Indian Wells Norris's mind was going, teetering along the ragged edge of insanity. Was the man still useful? That would remain to be seen.

"You have two allies in your camp, Mr. Norris," Azar said. "One is me . . . the other is fire. You should think about that."

"You're a damned terrorist, Azar," Norris said. "A lousy terrorist at that."

"And you are not? There are those who would disagree. Have you heard of a man in Washington, DC, called Jacob Sensor? He's a powerful man, a close friend of the President, and a rabid foe of Islam."

"No. I've never heard of him."

"I think he knows you, Mr. Norris. I think he wants you dead." Azar smiled and spread his hands. "That is, if my lowly spies at the Capitol are correct."

"A lot of people want me dead," Norris said.

"Then listen to me," Azar said. "Across the land, the time of the great scorching draws near and you can be a part of it. Turn the tables on those who castigated you and then cast you out. Yes, take your revenge, my friend . . . taste its sweetness."

"Hell, who do you take your orders from, Azar?" Norris said. "Where do you get your money? I saw a Bentley parked at the back of the warehouse. Is that yours?"

"Yes, the Bentley is mine, but I don't use it very often," Azar said. "As for finances, certain interested parties in Iran, a rich sheikh in the Gulf, and many others throughout the Middle East meet my expenses."

"For what?" Norris said. "For playing with fire like an overgrown Boy Scout?"

"No, after the successes of our brothers in California and elsewhere, the Scorching only recently became a major part of the jihad," Azar said. "Before that, I was the acknowledged expert on the C-4 explosive and the proper use of blasting caps, something I learned in Palestine a few years back, and I still keep a supply on hand." Azar smiled. "Mr. Norris, in my time I have taught scores of young men how to blow themselves up with C-4, along with as many as the godless as possible. I have not sat idly by while the jihad raged around me. I've always taken an active part."

"Azar, you're a damned devil," Norris said.

"Perhaps, but I may be the devil that will be your salvation, Mr. Norris."

"Get the hell out of here," Norris said. "Leave me in peace."

"Peace? You poor, pathetic creature, don't you know that only death will bring you peace?"

After Nasim Azar returned to his apartment, his bodyguard Salman Assad knocked on the door and stepped inside. "Well?" he said.

"Not yet," Azar said. "For now, I don't wish to just throw him away."

"Will he join us?" Assad said.

"Perhaps. I don't think he has any other choice in the matter." Azar smiled. "He's quite mad, you know, and I have determined to keep ajar the door that will lead him into total insanity. Then he will do my bidding."

Assad said, "But if you need him killed . . ."

"You'll be the first to know, my faithful Salman."

Five minutes later, Azar got a phone call. Cory Cantwell and Sarah Milano had checked into the Hilton hotel on Southwest Sixth Avenue.

CHAPTER 26

"This is the spot where Stevens and Baxter were murdered," FBI agent Tom D'eth said. "Their bodies were then dragged into the trees, where they were later found by a Willamette park ranger."

Last night's rain had washed the air clean, and the aborning day smelled of fir and damp earth, with an under-note of moss. Birds fluttered in the treetops, and Sarah Milano had caught a fleeting glimpse of a bounding black-tailed doe that thrilled her.

Cory Cantwell examined the patches of scorched undergrowth along the tree line and said, "I believe this was practice, probably with a drip torch. I don't think they were attempting to light a serious fire."

"Whoever they were, they got caught in the act," D'eth said. "They didn't get a chance to light a serious fire."

Cantwell nodded. "Possibly. But it still looks like a practice run to me."

"Why would they do that?" D'eth said. "Any yahoo with a cigarette butt can start a blaze, so why practice?"

"The drip torch has a learning curve, and for a novice it can be dangerous to use," Cantwell said. "Even experienced firefighters can make a mistake with one. About a year ago, my pants leg caught fire while I was burning Gambel oak in New Mexico. And you have to get the mix of diesel and gasoline just right, usually four parts of diesel to one of gasoline, or the torch won't work properly or at all."

"Well, you learn something new every day," D'eth said. He took the McDonald's breakfast sandwich wrappers from Sarah and Cantwell, shoved them in the paper bag they'd come in, and crumpled it in his hands before shoving it in his coat pocket.

"Agent D'eth, did you discover any valuable intel at the crime scene?" Sarah said.

The agent smiled. "Clues? Like Sherlock Holmes does? No, we didn't, apart from establishing the fact the two men died from multiple stab wounds from bladed weapons, probably knives."

"What are we dealing with here, D'eth?" Cantwell said.

"Well, it was either some local anti-hunting nuts or terrorists," the agent said. "My money is on the terrorists."

"So now what? Do you think they'll now target the Willamette and be back?" Sarah said. She wore jeans and a T-shirt, and her hair was pulled back in a thick ponytail. As always, her makeup was perfect.

"Either that or, if Cantwell's practice theory is right, they chose a forest within easy driving distance of Portland," D'eth said. He glanced at the sky. "Looks like it's clouding up again. If there's nothing else you want to see, I guess we should head back to the parking lot."

"I'm done here," Cantwell said. "Sarah?"

"Yes, me too." She looked around. "This is a beautiful spot."

"Yeah, and a hell of a place to die," D'eth said.

* * *

Cory Cantwell and the others took a scenic route back to where they'd parked their car, a hikers' path that led past a stand of mixed fir and ponderosa pine and then into a succession of grassy meadows. Around them in the distance the peaks of the surrounding mountains thrust into a clouded sky, impossibly remote and aloof, their beauty timeless. After thirty minutes of walking, ahead of them rose a shallow green knoll, rocky in places and almost bare of trees. The path faded out for a distance on firmer ground and then started again, curving around the east side of the knoll. As they strolled toward it, Sarah told Agent D'eth about the doe she'd spotted and how beautiful a sight it was. "The first one I'd ever seen in the . . ."

Sarah fell into silence as a startled covey of quail exploded into the air from the crest of the knoll.

Agent Tom D'eth, instinctive and trained to recognize a danger signal when he saw one, yelled, "Down!"

After a moment's hesitation, Cantwell and Sarah hit the deck, one on each side of the FBI agent. "What the hell?" Cantwell said. "It was only a flock of birds."

"Stay where you are," D'eth said, snapping off the words. His dark brown eyes were on the knoll. "Get your guns out."

Sarah had volunteered to carry Cantwell's Glock along with her Colt Python in her briefcase, using its shoulder strap option. She passed Cantwell his pistol, checked the loads in her revolver, and thumbed the cylinder closed.

"We're about to do some quail shooting, huh?" she said.

No one answered. D'eth's slightly asthmatic breathing was loud in the silence.

A minute ticked past and Cantwell said, "It was probably tourists."

"Tourist quail?" Sarah said.

"Maybe a tourist stirred them up," Cantwell said.

"Hunters and hikers maybe, but I don't think tourists ever come this way," D'eth said. His voice had dropped to a whisper. "I'm told they tend to overcrowd into the Three Pools area or Tamolitch Falls."

Cantwell's gaze scanned the knoll. There was no sound and nothing moved. Close by, an insect made its small sound in the grass, and the bright day was made gloomy by cloud.

"D'eth, how long do we stay here?" he said.

"Until I give the all clear."

"When will that be?" Sarah said.

I don't know," the agent said.

He stared at the knoll again, his face thoughtful, and then rose to his feet, his service Glock in his hand. "You two stay here. I'm going to take a look." He smiled, a rare occurrence. "If I come running back screaming like a scalded cat, cut loose and cover me."

Cantwell got up on one knee, his weapon ready. "Maybe I should go with you," he said.

"No, stay right here," D'eth said. "I'll go it alone. This is why you're overtaxed to pay my wages."

Crouching, the agent walked toward the knoll . . . and into gunfire that sounded like a roll of drums.

Three men stood on top of the knoll, one with an AK-47, the others using handguns. They dropped D'eth in the first volley, giving their whole attention to the armed man closest to them. Cantwell triggered the Glock, aiming for the man with the rifle. A clean miss. But Sarah fired and one of the other two threw up his arms, fell on his back, and disappeared over the far side of the rise.

D'eth, though badly wounded, was still in the fight. Lying on his belly, his arms fully extended, he fired rapidly, trying to clear the top of the knoll. As far as Cantwell could see, he scored no hits. "The man with the rifle!" he yelled at Sarah. They both fired at the man and missed.

Then a lucky break.

The AK has generous clearances that will enable it to function even if it's gummed up. But those clearances allow every piece of dirt, grit, and debris easy access to the action. The unlucky rifleman had gotten his hands on a dirty rifle, and he stopped firing as he frantically worked the bolt to clear the jam.

For now, Cantwell and Sarah ignored the rifleman and exchanged shots with the other man. Bullets kicked up dirt at Cantwell's feet, and a round, sounding like an angry hornet, zipped past his ear. Cantwell laid the Glock's sights on the man and pressed the trigger. A hit. The gunman staggered back, hit hard, but still game enough to remain upright and return fire.

Grim and bloody, D'eth rose, weaving on his feet, blood darkening the front of his shirt under his suit coat. He painstakingly sighted his Glock and fired. The man with the AK screamed as the bullet hit him low in the belly, and he dropped to his knees, out of the fight.

The remaining gunman, seeing the destruction of his cohorts, determined to sell his life dearly. He staggered down the slope, a bucking pistol in his extended right hand, ignoring the woman, aiming for Cantwell. Sarah had all the time in the world. She adopted an isosceles stance, thumbed back the Python's hammer, and took careful aim.

Her .357 hollow point crashed into the gunman's forehead, and he dropped, his wobbling legs gone out from under him, like a man very drunk.

After the crashing gunfire, a profound silence fell on the forest. Cantwell was sure the park rangers would soon arrive, and he gave Sarah his gun. "Put that away, and yours," he said. "Just in case we meet up with a badass ranger."

He stepped to Tom D'eth, who was still on his feet, swaying, his face gray and haggard. "How badly are you hurt?"

"I'm shot through and through," the agent said. "Bad enough I guess."

"You'd better sit," Cantwell said. "Let me help you."

Sarah helped lower D'eth to the grass and then she said, "My cell phone won't work. I can't get a signal."

"Sound travels. The rangers will be here soon," Cantwell said. "They'll get an ambulance." Then to D'eth, "Hang in there."

"Not much else I can do," D'eth said. "Cantwell, go check on the men we shot. See if anyone is still alive."

All three were dead, including the gut-shot rifleman, who'd bled out on the grass.

"Pity," D'eth said. "I would like to have talked with one of these men. What do they look like?" He was in considerable pain, fighting desperately to not let it show.

Cantwell said, "Middle Eastern for sure. All three of them young."

"You were the target, Cantwell," D'eth said. "They'd staked out the hotel, and then after I picked you up followed us here." The agent managed a weak smile. "Somebody up there doesn't like you."

"Seems to be the case," Cantwell said.

"I wonder . . . does the somebody include me in his dislike?" Sarah said.

"Lady, if he didn't before, he sure as hell does now," Agent D'eth said.

CHAPTER 27

Jacob Sensor received a phone call at eight o'clock in the evening as a rising wind tossed dry leaves along the sidewalk outside his study and billowed the curtains of an open window.

"Sorry to trouble you, sir, but there's been a development," the voice on the phone said. "A firefight in the Willamette National Forest in which your Regulators were involved."

"How are Cantwell and Sarah Milano?"

"Unhurt. But an FBI agent was badly wounded and isn't expected to live." Then, after a pause, "The three assailants were all killed."

"Jihadists?"

"It seems likely," Daniel Kramer said. He was with Homeland Security's Cybersecurity and Infrastructure Security Agency and a relatively low-level executive, but he was Sensor's eyes and ears. He added, "The investigation into the deaths of the two hunters in the Willamette was compromised from the start."

"But no one but me knew Cantwell and Milano were joining the investigation," Sensor said, his voice sharp.

Kramer was silent for a few moments, carefully choosing his next words. Finally, he said, "That would appear not to be the case, sir."

"Then there's a traitor in our midst," Sensor said.

"Indications point that way," Kramer said.

"Kramer, I want this investigated. Can you get the Secret Service involved?"

"I believe I can, sir. I have several contacts there."

"Start the investigation in Los Angeles. Find out if anyone besides me knew Cantwell and Milano were headed for Portland. I need a name."

"Or names," Kramer said.

"Do it, Kramer. Keep me posted."

Ten minutes after he'd spoken to Kramer, Jacob Sensor answered another call, this one from Sir Anthony Bickford-Scott of MI5, speaking from the British embassy.

"My dear, Jacob," he said, "I've just had a call from the Los Angeles police. Apparently, they've picked up the three Special Air Service men I sent you to join your Regulator team."

"Why were they arrested?" Sensor said.

"As suspicious characters, I'm afraid. Apparently, there's been an outbreak of wildfires in the city environs, and a police officer was killed. Three tough-looking Englishmen claiming to be . . . what's the word . . . armed smoke jumpers raised eyebrows, to say the least."

"There's a large National Wildfire Service depot in

the city. I'll have the police send them there until Cory Cantwell gets back from Oregon."

"Ah, but there's a complication, old chap."

"There always is."

"It seems it's a question of resisting arrest and assaulting a police officer," Bickford-Scott said. "It appears that the LAPD is quite irritated and has chosen to take a rather dim view of the whole situation. Heads will roll, and all that."

"I'll take care of it," Sensor said.

"I wish you would. British nationals in police custody is never a good situation for an embassy."

"Especially when they're on-loan Regulators and our little secret," Sensor said.

"Indeed. Oh dear, it never rains but it pours."

"The whole thing will be smoothed over as a misunderstanding," Sensor said. "But the sooner we get those SAS men out of Los Angeles the better."

"I agree, Jacob. As things stand at the moment, they're a liability. By the way, on a happier note, our Russian friends presented me with a supply of Beluga caviar. May I send some over to you?"

"You know it's against the law to possess Beluga caviar in this country . . . the endangered Black Sea sturgeon and all that rubbish."

"Yes, I know, but the Russians don't seem to give a damn."

"Nor do I. Yes, Anthony, send the stuff over at your convenience."

"You have good Russian vodka?"

"Of course."

"Cuban cigars?"

"I still have a couple of full boxes of Robusto Reservas."

"Jolly good. Now, you won't forget my imprisoned countrymen, will you?"

"I won't. Depend on it," Jacob Sensor said.

CHAPTER 28

The meeting was over, the implications of yesterday's disaster in the Willamette discussed, and the surviving young men of Nasim Azar's terrorist cell filed out of his apartment, their faces grim. One of their natural leaders, Dilshad Hakimi, was numbered among the slain.

When only the bodyguard Salman Assad remained, the man stood at the window, outlined by the morning sun that gilded the panes.

"Three more martyred in the cause of jihad," Azar said. He waved Assad into a chair. "The man Cantwell is a demon incarnate. Perhaps he can't be killed."

Assad shook his head. "He can die like any other man, and the sacrifice of our brethren was not in vain. A great wind blows from the east that will one day scour the earth clean of the American infidels and their corruption. Master, if it is the will of Allah, we will both live to see that day."

"The Willamette must go up in flames," Azar said. "The infidels will know that their vile crimes cannot go unpunished."

Assad jerked forward in his chair. "When will the fires of vengeance be lit?"

"Very soon. I have now decided to exert all my power. I'm in regular contact with Muslim brothers in Los Angeles who call themselves the Jacks of All Trades. If I care to release the man Norris and then have him shot in the back of the head in the street, they will do it. If I want the tourist traps in the Willamette attacked with bombs and bullets, they will do it. And I advise you, brother Assad, to have no further sexual congress with the whore Corky Jackson. Do not bring her here."

Assad was shocked. "Master, I—"

Azar held up a silencing hand. "What do I care what you do with a black whore? But she knows, or suspects, too much. She'll be taken care of tonight by the Jacks, as will the teenager Randy Collins now that he's no longer needed to work on drones. But these are very small matters. Of much more importance I have the assurance of the brothers that when I burn the Willamette, they will also mount an attack on the Three Pools area, where the infidel tourists congregate in their hundreds."

Assad had been chastised, and he knew it. Sometimes when he was with a woman he talked too much, and being reprimanded for it made him peevish. "And what of your Ukrainian?" he said.

"He is still in Los Angeles. I will soon hear from him." Azar smiled. "Don't be offended, Salman. She's only a black whore, and I value you highly."

"Then allow me to prove my worth, master. Let me kill the man Cantwell."

"I fear to risk your life, my friend. I need you at my side."

"I can kill him at his hotel," Assad said.

"And you may get your chance," Azar said. "But wait until I hear from the Ukrainian."

The woman at the reception desk of the National Wildfire Service had a nameplate pinned to her shirt that said, C. WELSH. She gave the Ukrainian her official smile that was totally devoid of humor or interest. "What can I do for you?"

"My name is Dominik Bonkowski." He smiled, explaining the accent. "I'm Polish, you understand?"

"And what can I do for you?" Catrina Welsh said again. A phone rang and she said, "Wait, just a moment. I'm real busy this morning."

As the woman answered the call, the Ukrainian readied the fake ID he used often, that of Poland's National News Agency. Poles scared nobody.

After a few minutes, Catrina returned and said, "Yes?"

The Ukrainian smiled again. "As I said, my name is Dominik Bonkowski, and I'm with the Polish National News Agency. I'm here to speak with one of your firefighters."

"Which one? We have hundreds here."

The Ukrainian pretended to be confused. "Oh, dear," he said. He pulled a piece of paper out of the top pocket of his gray suit jacket and consulted it. "A yes . . . Superintendent Cory Cantwell. Is he available?"

"What do you wish to speak to him about?" Catrina Welsh said. "Oh, there's that damned phone again." She answered the call, said a few curt words, "No. No. All right." And then returned to the Ukrainian. "You were about to tell me why you wish to speak with Mr. Cantwell."

The Ukrainian forged his best disarming smile and said, "Nearly one-third of my beautiful country is forested, and fire is an ever-present danger. I'm preparing an article for my news agency on the latest firefighting methods in Europe and the United States." He smiled again. "The Polish Department of Forestry and Nature Conservation is rather antiquated and set in its ways. I'm hoping that Superintendent Cantwell can help me write an article that will help bring it up to date."

The phone rang again. Catrina Welsh answered, spoke for a couple of minutes and then said into the receiver, "Hold on. I'll be right back."

She returned to the Ukrainian, looking harried, and snapped, "Mr. Cantwell isn't here. He's in Portland, Oregon." She dashed away and picked up the phone again. "Yes, I'm back."

The Ukrainian smiled and spoke into dead air. "Thank you, I'll find him in Portland," he said.

Catrina Welsh hung up the phone, her face pale under her California tan. Why was the Secret Service investigating members of the National Wildfire Service? What did they suspect? Whom did they suspect? She could come up with answers, but they'd be guesses, all of them troubling.

Her face pensive and slightly fearful, she picked up her cell phone and dialed a number.

CHAPTER 29

Fire Chief John Ferguson eyed the three young men standing to attention in front of his desk at the National Wildfire Service depot with considerable distaste. All looked rumpled after a night in the drunk tank, and one of them sported a magnificent black eye. Their battered bugout bags were piled at their feet.

"Identify yourselves," Ferguson said. "And age, please."

The men looked at one another and then the one in the middle spoke up. "Nigel Brown, twenty-five, sir!" He was tall, well-built, and rather handsome in a coarse, ill-bred way.

"Frank West, twenty-three, sir!" Short, stocky, black eye, with the battered features of a bar brawler.

"Daniel Grant, thirty, sir!" Tall, dark and slim, with the pencil mustache of a 1930s matinee idol.

Ferguson, a middle-aged man with close-cropped iron-gray hair, said, "Brown, your Special Air Service rank before you joined the British anti-pyroterrorism unit?"

"Lance Corporal, sir!"

"West?"

"Lance Corporal, sir!"

"Grant?"

"Corporal, sir!"

"Why did you assault the policeman?" Ferguson said, frowning. "That was a damned stupid thing to do. And a major crime in this city."

Grant, belligerent and angry said, "Sir, he was a bloody detective. How was I to know he was a copper? He didn't show us a badge or anything, and when he started asking us a lot of cheeky questions, I clocked him once."

"Did he give you the black eye?" Ferguson said.

"No, sir, his bloody mates did. But they were in uniform. One of them hit me with a stick."

"And me as well," West said. "A big, bloody club. We all got pounded, and then they dragged us into a cage with a lot of drunks and drug addicts and left us there. The place smelled like piss and vomit."

"Were you drunk?"

The men exchanged glances, then West said, "Tipsy."

"Merry," Grant said. "I'd say we were merry."

Ferguson was silent for a few moments, his gaze scalding the three miscreants. Then he said, "For reasons that are beyond my understanding, you men have been assigned to Superintendent Cory Cantwell's anti-terrorism team, called . . . and again I have no idea why . . . the Regulators."

"And we're honored to be a part of it," Grant said. "And honored to be standing in front of you, sir."

"We won't fail your fine fire service again," West said. "Never in a million years."

"You can depend on that, sir," Brown said.

Ferguson shook his head. "Then God help us," he said. "Now, when you leave my office, make a right, and two doors down on your left, you'll find the temporary office of squad leader Pete Kennedy, another Regulator. Introduce yourselves, and he'll fix you up with uniforms and a place to bunk until Superintendent Cantwell gets back. Do you understand?"

"Perfectly, sir," Grant said.

"One last thing," Ferguson said. "Who do you boys know?"

All three Brits seemed puzzled and remained silent.

"Somebody called the LA police on your behalf and made them an offer they couldn't refuse," Ferguson said. "Hell, the cops even drove you here. Any idea who that somebody was?"

"No, sir," Grant said.

"The Queen?" West said, but he sounded doubtful.

"I doubt you'd be released by the LAPD even for the Queen. Then it's a mystery," Ferguson said. He sighed. "That's it, you may leave. You're Pete Kennedy's problem now."

Pete Kennedy was more receptive to the three Brits since he'd been in an action alongside the SAS in Iraq and liked them. "There was one more Regulator here, a firefighter called Merinda Barker, but she's already left for jump training. So I'm afraid you're stuck with me until Superintendent Cantwell gets back from . . . wherever he is."

"The pleasure is all ours, sir," Grant said.

"We're honored, sir," Brown said.

Kennedy smiled. "You don't call me 'sir.' I'm a smoke jumper just like you are."

Grant said, "Begging your pardon, Mr. Kennedy—"

"Call me Pete."

"Begging your pardon, Pete," Dan Grant said, "But we could use a shower and then something to eat. The police didn't feed us."

"Yes, I'll take you to your quarters, and then we'll take care of the rest," Kennedy said. "Later I'll see if I can fix you up with uniforms. Did you bring sidearms?"

"No, we weren't allowed to carry them from Britain," Grant said.

"Browning Hi-Powers?" Kennedy said.

"We used the Hi-Power in the SAS," Grant said. "But for anti-pyroterrorism actions we were equipped with the SIG Sauer P226."

"You're familiar with Glock 19?"

"Yes," the three said in unison.

"Good. That will be your duty pistol in the Regulators," Kennedy said. He rose from his desk. "Now I'll show you to your quarters. They're not very fancy, a bunk and a storage chest."

"A bunk will suit us just fine," Grant said. "We've slept on a lot worse."

"I know all about that," Pete Kennedy said.

CHAPTER 30

That afternoon, Catrina Welsh rang Cory Cantwell and caught him just before he was about to step in the shower. Without preamble, she said, "All right, Cory, Pete Kennedy's left me with quite a problem."

"What kind of problem? And good afternoon to you."

"Yes, yes, good afternoon," the woman said. She sounded annoyed. "I've got three Brits here, one with a black eye, claiming to work for you. Are you aware of this?"

"Yes, I knew they were coming," Cantwell said. "I don't know anything about the black eye, though."

"Who are they? What are they? They won't tell me."

"Who they are, I don't know. At least not yet."

"What are they?"

"They're smoke jumpers on loan from a British anti-pyroterrorism unit. I don't know what it's called."

"What do I do with them?" Catrina said.

"I want them here in Portland," Cantwell said. "And I want Pete Kennedy with them."

"When?"

"On the first available flight out of LAX."

"Cory, who'll pay for all that?"

Cantwell put a smile in his voice. "Spoken like an accountant. Sarah Milano will arrange the financing. Oh, and I want them all armed. Pete Kennedy can organize that, huh?"

"I'm sure he can," Catrina said. "Cory, are you expecting trouble?"

"It's already started and yes, I believe something big is going to go down here soon."

"In Portland?"

"Yeah. In Portland. Call it a gut feeling."

Behind him in the kitchen Cantwell heard Sarah say, "Yes. Yes, I'll tell him." He turned his head. "Tell me what?"

"That was the FBI. Agent Tom D'eth died of his wounds twenty minutes ago," Sarah said.

The news hit Cantwell like a blow. He'd admired the man for his sand. D'eth would be a big loss to the FBI and to law enforcement in general.

"Catrina, I've got to go," Cantwell said. "Keep me posted."

"What was that all about?" Sarah said.

"The three Brits are in L.A. Catrina Welsh didn't know what to do with them, so she's sending them here."

"With Pete Kennedy. Our gang is growing."

"But not fast enough."

"What's going to happen, Cory?" Sarah said.

"I think there will be a major arson attack on the Willamette and the terrorists' aim will be to kill as many people as possible," Cantwell said. "Cause a panicked stampede for the exits, and God alone knows what will happen."

"It would be a good time to coordinate a second suicide attack," Sarah said. "Terrorists with automatic weapons and grenades could kill hundreds."

Cantwell grabbed the towel around his waist as it started to slip. "I don't even want to think about that," he said. "Sarah, fire coupled with bullets and grenades is a nightmare scenario."

"Might it happen?" Sarah said. "What's your gut feeling?"

"My gut feeling is that damn right it might happen," Cantwell said.

After his shower, Cory Cantwell dressed in a T-shirt and jeans and said to Sarah Milano, "Want to take a ride with me?"

"To where?"

"To Mike Norris's place. He's here in Portland, and I still have his address . . . somewhere." Cantwell searched in his bag and found a small notebook where he kept contact information. "Yeah, here it is, 112 Hillock Place."

"Why Mike Norris?" Sarah said.

"He might have heard something."

"About a terrorist plot?"

"Unlikely. But he could have other information. He's out of the fire service, but he still keeps tabs on things." Cantwell made a face. "Mike can be a major pain in the ass, but if there are any rumors going around about a threat to the Willamette, he's probably heard them."

"It's a long shot, Cory," Sarah said.

"I know, but we have to start somewhere. I'm clutching at straws here."

"Not the best of neighborhoods, is it?" Sarah Milano said.

"Quiet though," Cory Cantwell said.

"Poverty Row, if you ask me," Sarah said.

Cantwell smiled. "Snob." He parked the RAV outside number 112, a run-down three-story apartment block, its dust-filmed windows looking out at the street like cataracted eyes. The hallway that led into the building smelled of boiled cabbage and ancient urine and only at the entrance was there a few feet of angled sunlight. The rest lay in shadow.

"Does Mike Norris live here or Edgar Allan Poe?" Sarah said. Her nose was wrinkled against the smell.

"Ah, here's Mike's place," Cantwell said. He used his knuckles to do a rap-rap-rap-rap-rap . . . rap, rap on the door. And waited. And waited.

"He's not at home," Sarah said.

"Seems like," Cantwell said.

The door opposite opened and a gray-haired woman stuck her head out and said, "He ain't there. I haven't seen him in days."

"Did you know him well?" Cantwell said.

"I didn't know him at all," the woman said. "Who'd want to know anyone in this neighborhood?"

"Can you tell me anything about him?" Cantwell said.

"Quiet. Paid his rent, I guess."

"Is he—" Cantwell began, but the slamming door cut him off.

"Friendly neighbors," Sarah said.

"I hope Mike's all right," Cantwell said.

"Why shouldn't he be?" Sarah said.

"He drinks . . . recently a lot."

"You mean he could be lying in there drunk?" Sarah said. "Well, we're not standing out here all day."

She leaned in front of Cantwell and tried the door handle. It turned and she pushed. The door swung open. "Unlocked," she said, stating the obvious.

Cantwell stuck his head inside. "Mike, are you in there?"

No answer. The air inside the apartment smelled stale of booze and cigarette smoke.

"Mike?" Cantwell said.

Silence. Outside a roaring motorcycle racketed along the street. Cantwell stepped inside.

The door opened into a short hallway, a room at the end, another to the left. Both doors hung ajar. Far from reassuring, the profound quiet left in the wake of the motorcycle was menacing, and behind Cantwell, Sarah's breathing came in short little bursts.

Cantwell walked into the room on his left and then stopped in his tracks. It was obviously Norris's living room, and it had been thoroughly ransacked and trashed. Books and papers covered the floor, the bookshelf itself tipped over. Drawers had been opened and their contents flung everywhere, and a couple of prints of forest scenes had been torn from the walls.

"Oh, my," Sarah said.

"Let's try the bedroom," Cantwell said.

It told the same story. Even the mattress was pulled from the bed and tumbled. More poignantly, Norris's smoke jumper gear had been torn from a closet, and his jumpsuit, helmet, boots, Pulaski ax, and firefighter pack were piled on the floor.

"Who did this?" Sarah said, knowing it was a rhetorical question.

"I don't know," Cantwell said. "Somebody who wanted to find . . ."

"What?"

"I have no idea," Cantwell said. Then he remembered that day at the base camp in Arizona when Jacob Sensor casually, perhaps too casually, asked him if he knew a man named Mike Norris. Could this be Sensor's doing, trying to dig up dirt on Norris? He instantly dismissed the idea. Mike was a damned nuisance, a thorn in the side of the new National Wildfire Service, but nothing he said could merit Sensor's attention. But still the thought rankled. "Do you know a man named Mike Norris?" Now, why would Sensor say a thing like that?

"Cory, you're thinking, I can tell," Sarah said. "A penny for them."

"You'll think me crazy."

"Probably. But tell me anyway."

Cantwell waved a hand around the wreckage of Norris's bedroom. "All this . . . could Jacob Sensor be behind it?"

Cantwell expected Sarah to smile, laugh, scoff . . . anything but look pensive, and that surprised him.

"Sensor can do anything he wants," Sarah said. "Could he see Norris as a danger?"

"To what?"

"The Regulators?"

"How, a danger?"

"If he suspects Norris could go over to the other side."

"You mean join up with the Islamic terrorists?"

"Yes. That's what I mean."

Cantwell shook his head. "Mike is a patriot, a red-blooded American. He'd never take the side of Islamic terrorists . . . never, not a chance in hell."

CHAPTER 31

How many times had he watched *High Noon*? Probably at least twenty times over the years, maybe more. Gary Cooper, tall and grim and years too old for the part, filled the screen of the TV on the wall, and Mike Norris thought that for once it would be really great to see Lee Van Cleef shoot him in the back. But that wasn't going to happen.

He turned his attention to the bottle of Wild Turkey that the damned Arab, Nasim Azar, had left him. It was now two-thirds empty. He poured himself a glass, picked up the remote, and thumbed the TV into darkness. It matched his mood. He was a prisoner, and he didn't know how much more of it he could take. Lie to Azar, promise him anything that would get him the hell out of there. That was his only recourse. There was no other option.

Norris forced himself to think. How long had it been since he'd done real, smoke-in-his-lungs firefighting work? It had been a long time, so long he didn't want to think about it. He couldn't do that kind of work now. He was out of shape, probably prediabetic, and he often felt breathless, maybe the booze taking its toll on his ticker. Damn it, he had to get out of here, get fit again, and work for one of the private firefighting companies. Maybe meet a nice woman and get into a steady relationship. Quit the booze . . .

The bourbon a smoky fire in his throat, he turned his head as the door opened and Azar stepped inside, a tray in his hand.

"And how are we this fine afternoon?" the man said.

"Go to hell," Norris said. "I hate the sight of you."

"Scrambled eggs, toast, and coffee," Azar said. "I'll just put the tray on the bed, shall I?"

"A plastic fork?" Norris said.

"A steel one could be a weapon," Azar said. "We can't be too careful, can we?"

"Let me out of here," Norris said. "I need to get the hell out of here."

"You're not ready. You're not ready mentally, Mr. Norris. I think you need therapy, a few sessions with a shrink."

"When will I be ready?"

"Soon, I hope."

"What do you want from me, Azar?"

"It's simple . . . join the jihad. Burn the infidels."

"You're out of your cotton-pickin' mind," Norris said, scowling.

"Then, as I told you, you're not ready."

"How long will you keep me here?"

"As long as it takes."

Norris thought for a few moments, then said. "Not that it's ever likely to happen, but if I joined you what would my payoff be?"

"If the attack on the Willamette . . ."

"So that's what you're planning?"

"Yes. If our attack on the Willamette is a success, and the body count is high enough, you will receive half-a-million American dollars, or the equivalent in euros if that's your preferred currency, and a plane ticket to anywhere in the world." Azar smiled. "We take care of our own."

"What do I do for that kind of heathen money?" Norris said.

"Help us in the Willamette. Ensure the success of the holy firestorm, and your work is done."

"I don't owe anybody a thing," Norris said, his mouth tight and thin. "Do you know that, Azar, you damned Arab?"

"Of course, you don't owe anybody. When was the last time someone did you a favor? When was the last time someone said a kind word to you?" His voice low and soothing, Azar said, "You were a hero, everybody knew that. But they took it away from you, and because of their petty jealousies they cast you out from among them. They treated you like a leper. How can you be loyal to a people like that? Among the brotherhood, you'll be respected and given great honor."

"Given . . . great . . . honor," Norris repeated, savoring the words, his eyes shining. "No more the outcast."

"Honored as a holy warrior," Azar said. "And for the rest of your life, no matter in which part of the globe you dwell, you will be protected from all enemies."

Norris sat in silence for a while, his head bowed. Then suddenly he jerked upright, grabbed the tray of food, and threw it at Azar, who adroitly stepped aside as scrambled eggs flew past him like yellow shrapnel.

"You're the serpent in the garden, Azar!" Norris

screamed. "You're driving me crazy with that smooth tongue of yours. Get out! Leave me be."

"Mr. Norris, you will see things my way or you will starve to death in this room since my food is no longer to your taste," Azar said. "A pity, because I offer you the world, and all you give me in return is your defiance and contempt."

"Let me be," Norris said. "My brain is in turmoil. You're driving me mad."

"One last word, Mr. Norris," Azar said. "Your growing contempt for the human race is misguided. There are more people on this earth than the Americans, who, because of your beliefs, have shunned you. The Willamette will burn with or without you, but I beg you, turn your back on those who have turned their back on you and join us in the great jihad. The Scorching will cleanse with fire the evil from this nation, and men like you, men of great ideas, will again be able to hold their heads high."

"We need the watchtowers back," Norris said. "Why is something so simple so hard for them to accept?"

"Because they are fools," Azar said. "And, because Allah whispered in my ear, my heart has suddenly softened toward you. I'll bring you more food, whiskey, and cigarettes. That is not the way of the infidel, but it is the way of Islam."

After Azar left, Mike Norris stared at the locked door for a long time and then whispered, *"Allahu Akbar."* Then he cried out, bent over and clutched at his belly . . . as though he'd just been stabbed by a bayonet.

* * *

The Ukrainian caught a red-eye flight out of LAX and at five in the morning woke Nasim Azar out of sound sleep.

"I just arrived in Portland," he said.

Azar quickly shook the cobwebs from his brain. "So now you will take care of my little problem," he said.

"A well-aimed bullet takes care of most problems," the Ukrainian said. "Where is the mark?"

"The man Cory Cantwell has a room in the Hilton hotel on Southwest Sixth Avenue. He has a woman with him."

"I'll also take care of that little detail."

"Rent a car and check into the hotel," Azar said. "And then the rest is up to you."

"Yes, up to me. I wish all my assignments were this easy," the Ukrainian said. "It's raining, Azar. Does it always rain in Portland?"

"No, less than half the time."

"But always when I'm around."

Azar smiled. "My friend, it's the heavens weeping for your victims."

CHAPTER 32

Cory Cantwell and Sarah Milano pulled out of the Hilton parking lot at three in the afternoon to pick up Pete Kennedy and the three Brits at the airport. Cantwell drove north on Sixth Avenue a short distance and then turned left onto Southwest Taylor Street. He was vaguely aware of the innocuous Kia compact that pulled in behind him. He turned onto Southwest Broadway and then made another left onto Salmon Street. The Kia was still behind him, the passenger invisible behind the tinted windshield. Cantwell made another left onto Southwest Second Avenue and then took the Morrison Bridge. The Kia stuck to him. Concerned now, he followed the signs for Interstate 85 East. Fifteen minutes later, in heavy traffic, he took Exit 8 for Interstate 205 North toward the airport. The Kia followed.

"Don't look now, but we're being tailed," he said.

Sarah glanced in the passenger side mirror. "The Kia?"

"Yeah, since we pulled out of the Hilton parking lot." He nodded. "My Glock is in the glove box."

"What do you make of him?" Sarah said.

"Hard to tell. He's not very tall, I can see that much."

"Middle Eastern?"

"I don't know. Impossible to say."

"Maybe he's with the FBI," Sarah said.

"Maybe. But I doubt it."

"Me too."

Sarah opened the glove box and laid the Glock in her lap. "A little insurance. If he's not a traveling timeshare salesman from Iowa, he might try a drive-by."

Cantwell smiled. "I love your sense of humor."

"Except I'm not trying to be funny," Sarah said.

"No, you're not," Cantwell said. He glanced in the rearview mirror. "Still there."

Cantwell eased the RAV onto I-205 North and after a mile or so he saw the sign ahead of him for the two-lane merge onto Exit 24A to Airport Way. He stayed on the outside lanes and accelerated.

"Now we mess with his mind," Cantwell said. "Hold on tight."

"What are you doing?" Sarah said, alarm in her voice.

"A kamikaze," Cantwell said. "Banzai!"

The ramp to Airport Way was only a hundred yards ahead. Cantwell suddenly swung the wheel into the outer right lane . . . and into the speeding traffic stream. Behind him a hissing eighteen-wheeler braked hard, and the driver blared on the horn. Cantwell charged into the inner lane, and a panel van screeched as it braked, its rear end fishtailing. Cantwell was aware of Sarah's little yelp of alarm as he hit the ramp fast and merged onto Airport Way, leaving blaring horns and a score of angry drivers in his wake.

But the Kia was no longer filling Cantwell's rearview mirror.

He grinned. "Took him by surprise, didn't I?"

"You took everybody by surprise," Sarah said. Then a frown and, "Don't, ever, ever, do that again."

"There's the airport. Look for Arrivals," Cantwell said. He felt good.

"I'm sorry you gentlemen have to double up," Sarah Milano said. "But the generosity of the National Wildfire Service only goes so far."

"Frank, it seems I'm in with you," Pete Kennedy said.

"Suits me," Frank West said. "Here, you don't snore, do you, gov?"

"No, do you?"

"Only sometimes," West said.

Nigel Brown and Daniel Grant had made themselves at home in Cory Cantwell's room. Brown sprawled in a chair, and Grant studied the contents of the minibar.

"Cory, where do we go from here?" Kennedy said. He was the oldest person in the room and figured that qualified him as spokesperson for the rest.

"The answer to that is, I don't know," Cantwell said. "But I fully expect that future events will dictate our actions. Sorry to sound so stiff and formal, but there it is."

"How far in the future are those events, boss?" West said.

"I don't know that either, but I have a gut feeling it will be soon."

Along with Kennedy, the three Brits were dressed in the olive-green uniform of the NWS, and Cantwell was pleased with them. They were young, and they looked tough and fit and ready for anything.

Cantwell then decided to lay some bad news on them. "According to the FBI, we're all targets," he said. "And I think that's the reason someone followed Miss Milano and me to the airport today. Well, almost to the airport. I managed to lose him."

"Who's got us in their sights, boss?" West said.

"Islamic pyroterrorists are the likely culprits."

West smiled. "Hell, boss, they can't be worse than the IRA. Those boys targeted all three of us for a while when we were in the SAS."

"They're worse," Cantwell said. "And they're right here in Portland."

"Cory is correct, they're much worse," Kennedy said. "I've already faced terrorists, and they're dangerous because they're not afraid to die. In fact, they welcome death as martyrs for Islam."

"And I believe there's a large cell of them in the city," Cantwell said.

"How do you figure that?" Pete Kennedy said.

Cantwell told Kennedy and the others about their gunfight in the Willamette and the shooting and subsequent death of an FBI agent. "His name was Tom D'eth, and he was a brave man," he said, another small elegy for a hero. "I'm convinced the burning we saw in the Willamette was a trial run and that there will be a major arson attack on the forest targeting the crowded recreation areas."

"And we'll stop it," Kennedy said.

Cantwell nodded. "That's the general idea."

"How big is that place?" West said.

"It's 380,805 acres," Cantwell said. "In your metric measure call it 1,541 square kilometers."

West whistled through his teeth. "Bloody hell, that's a lot of ground for a small squad to cover."

Cantwell nodded. "I know. It won't be easy, and it will be dangerous."

"Hey, boss, you mind if I have one of those little bottles of Scotch?" Daniel Grant said.

CHAPTER 33

The Ukrainian had failed in his attempt to kill the infidel Cory Cantwell, and the master was very upset. Salman Assad could see it in the deepening lines of his face as the strain of the jihad and the coming great Scorching weighed on him. It was high time to relieve Nasim Azar of some of his ponderous burden.

A righteous anger spiked at Assad. The Ukrainian said he'd planned to kill Cantwell at the airport. The fool! He'd let himself be tricked so easily. Better he'd crashed into Cantwell's car at high speed and died a martyr's death. But what did a Ukrainian infidel know about holy martyrdom? Nothing.

Assad made up his mind. He would shoot Cantwell down like a dog and gain great favor in the eyes of the master. It would take infinite patience . . . perhaps a long wait for the opportunity to strike. But he would do it. Who would notice a compact black sedan in the busy parking lot of the Hilton? Better that than attack him in the hotel. A six-foot-two man of Middle Eastern heritage would be too conspicuous hanging around the lobby. The parking lot was the only way. The man Cantwell must come out of the hotel sometime, and when he did . . . Assad would be ready.

After a shower, Assad dressed with care in clean clothes and then prepared and ate a dish of *shanklish,* sheep milk cheese rolled in zaatar herbs, chili flakes, and olive oil. It might be a long time before he ate again. He smiled. Perhaps he'd next dine on fruit and honey in paradise.

He swapped shoulder holsters, exchanging the Smith & Wesson revolver for a Glock 48 9mm, preferring it over the 19 because of its slimmer width and greater conceal-ability.

"Know thine enemy, my faithful Salman." The master had once given him a clipping from a small-town news-paper that showed Cantwell talking to a crowd of forestry people and politicians, and now he studied it. Yes, Cantwell was tall, fair and well-built. He'd recognize the crusader on sight.

Dressed in jeans, T-shirt and suede desert boots, Assad wore a light golf vest over his gun, slid a switchblade into his pocket, and donned a pair of dark glasses before he left the warehouse. To his relief, he saw no sign of the master. Perhaps, worn out from all his problems, he was napping.

Fifteen minutes later Salman Assad backed into a park-ing spot at the Hilton where he had a good view of the front entrance. Now his fate was in the hands of Allah, and all he could do was wait.

* * *

Pete Kennedy brought up the subject of ammunition.

"The National Wildfire Service came up with Glocks earmarked for Regulators, but no ammunition was forthcoming," he said. "Hard times and budget constraints, I was told."

"You have none?" Cory Cantwell said.

"Empty guns," Kennedy said. He shrugged, "Not a single round between us."

"Sarah . . ." Cantwell said.

"I'm on it," Sarah said. She consulted her phone. "It would seem that the nearest place to buy ammunition is on Taylor Street, Tiara Gun and Pawn."

"How many do you need, Pete?" Cantwell said.

"I'd settle for a hundred rounds per man," Kennedy said. "Our SAS men know how to shoot, so they don't need any target practice."

"I think our budget can afford four hundred rounds or so," Sarah said. "Cory, I'm the one with the credit card. You want me to take this?"

"After what happened yesterday, I'll come with you," Cantwell said.

"Mind if I tag along?" Kennedy said. He looked around at the Englishman. "Anybody else want to go?"

"Not really," Dan Grant said. "I don't like getting too far from the minibar."

"Go right ahead, Pete," West said.

"And I'll stay here too," Nigel Brown said. "I want to see if there's any football on the telly."

"Mexican or South American, maybe," Kennedy said.

Brown shrugged. "Better than nothing."

"Then let's go," Cantwell said. "A man with no cartridges in his gun is unarmed."

He retrieved his holstered Glock from the bedside table, buckled it around his waist, and pulled his shirt over it.

"Ready?" Sarah said.

"As I'll ever be," Cantwell said.

Great was the rapture of Salam Assad. Allah had blessed him.

After a wait of just an hour, the thrice-cursed Cantwell stepped out of the hotel door with another man and a woman and began to walk across the parking lot, talking to one another.

Allahu Akbar!

Now was the time to strike.

Assad threw open his car door and jumped outside. His gun blazing, face twisted in rage, he ran at Cantwell. A bullet slammed into Cantwell, and he fell heavily against a parked car, sudden blood staining the front of his shirt. After a moment of stunned inaction, Pete Kennedy moved. He sprinted toward Assad, for a vital split second distracting the gunman. It was the break Cantwell needed. He drew his Glock and fired, fired again. Two hits at a range of just five yards. Assad knew he'd been hit hard and he screamed his frustrated rage. Kennedy slammed into the Muslim, hit him at hip level, and took him down. Cantwell slid to the ground, his back against the front bumper of the car, slipping into unconsciousness. Assad lost his gun when Kennedy tackled him. Leaving a snail trail of blood behind him, he crawled on his belly toward the Glock, but Kennedy kicked it away from him toward Sarah. Shrieking in a language no one understood, Assad staggered to his feet. Lurching toward the now-unconscious Cantwell, he pulled the switchblade from his pocket and thumbed it open. "I'll kill you!" he screeched.

BLAM! BLAM! BLAM!

Sarah Milano pumped three shots into the Muslim from his own Glock and dropped him in his tracks. The man crumpled like a puppet whose strings had just been cut, dead when he hit the asphalt.

In the ringing silence that followed, as hotel staff rushed into the parking lot and police sirens wailed in the distance, Sarah kneeled beside Cantwell. "Cory, talk to me," she said.

There was no answer.

"Cory, hang in there," Sarah said. "For God's sake, don't leave us."

CHAPTER 34

"The bullet entered his left shoulder and exited just above the scapula," the St. Vincent Medical Center emergency room doctor said. He was young and grave. "The wound is serious, but not fatal."

"Can I see him?" Sarah Milano said.

"Yes, for a little while. He's regained consciousness but is very weak."

The young police officer posted outside the recovery room gave Sarah an appreciative glance as he opened the door and let her inside. She stepped to the bed and smiled. "How are you feeling, Cory?" she said.

"Just great," Cantwell said. He was very pale, and his voice was little more than a whisper.

"I didn't have time to pick up black grapes," Sarah said.

"A pint of bourbon will do," Cantwell said. "If you have one about your person."

She sat on the bed and took her hand in his. "I've been so worried about you," she said. "It seemed that you were in surgery forever."

"The doc says the bullet didn't hit anything vital,"

Cantwell said. "Apart from the fact that I'm shot through and through, and it's my arthritic shoulder. A 9mm hollow point can put a hurting on a man." He smiled slightly. "There I go sounding like John Wayne again."

"The terrorist is dead," Sarah said.

"Who was he? Anybody find out?"

"The police are still trying to ID him. He's young and looks to be Middle Eastern, and so far, that's all they know."

Cantwell fell silent and Sarah said, "Jacob Sensor is very concerned about you."

"That's nice of him," Cantwell said. "You look real pretty today."

"Thank you," Sarah said. Then, "Sensor says Pete Kennedy will take over the Regulators while you're convalescing."

"Does he have a task for us yet?"

"He didn't say."

"I'm not convalescing."

"Yes, you are."

"You can sit me in a chair in my hotel room and prop me up with pillows, but I'm not convalescing. I still think something big is coming, and I want to be in on it."

"We'll see how you feel when you get out of the hospital," Sarah said.

"I'll feel the same way," Cantwell said.

Sarah stood. "I'll let you rest now. The doctor said I could only stay for a little while."

"Where are the others?" Cantwell said. "My merry band of Regulators."

"In the waiting room."

"Chasing nurses, I bet."

"Only the Brits. Pete Kennedy is way too dignified for that, and besides, he has a girlfriend."

"He saved my life, Sarah. And so did you."

The woman smiled. "We'll talk about all that when you're feeling better."

"I'll be feeling better tomorrow," Cantwell said.

"We'll hear what the doctor has to say about that," Sarah said.

The TV news said only that there had been what appeared to be a terrorist attack on a group of off-duty firefighters in downtown Portland and that the attacker was dead and one of the firefighters wounded. There were no names or any other details.

They're covering it up, Mike Norris decided. Probably fearful of causing a panic.

He lay back on his cot, smiled, and yelled at the top of his lungs, "Hey, Azar! Was one of your boys involved in this?"

There was no answer.

Norris wondered if this incident had anything to do with the deaths of the two hunters in the Willamette. The media said anti-hunting extremists had killed the men. There was no mention of terrorists or a possible rehearsal for an arson attack. Yet another coverup. He was ninety-nine percent sure that Azar was behind the attack on the firefighters in the Hilton parking lot. What was the damned Arab up to? He planned to find out.

* * *

Nasim Azar watched the same TV news as Mike Norris. He had not authorized the attack on the firefighters, but he was sure that Cory Cantwell had been among them. The news said the gunman had been Middle Eastern, so it had not been the Ukrainian, who was sulking in his hotel room, promising much but delivering little. Then who?

Azar felt an immediate spike of panic. Where was Salman Assad?

His bodyguard's apartment was on the same floor as his own, and Azar rushed there and hammered on the door. "Salman, are you in there?" he called.

There was no answer.

The door was unlocked, and Azar pushed it open and stepped inside. "Salman?"

The answering silence mocked him.

He rushed to the bedroom. The top dresser drawer and been opened and not fully closed afterward. Azar pulled it wider . . . and his worst fears were confirmed. Assad carried a Smith & Wesson revolver, but he kept two backup firearms in the drawer, a Glock 48 and a SIG Sauer P232 .380. The Smith & Wesson was there and the Sig, but the Glock, his most effective weapon, was gone.

Azar felt the room spin round him, and he sat heavily on the bed, made up and squared away, as Assad always left it. In his heart, Nasim Azar knew what had happened. Assad had hoped to please him, and he'd no doubt that his faithful servant had tried to kill Cory Cantwell in the Hilton parking lot and had died a holy martyr. According to Islamic law, a martyr must be buried in the same clothes he wore when his martyrdom took place. Assad would probably be denied that honor . . . and Azar's heart felt that it must surely break.

But *Inshallah* . . . God willing . . . the noble Salman was even now enjoying his reward in heaven.

Azar's grief gave way to rage, a savage desire to lash out at the godless infidels and kill every last one of them. And there was an unbeliever close . . . under his own roof. He picked up the Smith & Wesson .38 and swung out the cylinder, checking the loads. Satisfied, he snapped the revolver shut and then left Assad's apartment and made his way toward the room where Mike Norris was held.

The time for a reckoning had arrived.

CHAPTER 35

The news of Cory Cantwell's wounding upset Jacob Sensor considerably. The newly appointed head of the Regulators could be out of commission for weeks, maybe months. Damn careless of him to allow himself to get shot.

The President was having second thoughts about the whole Regulator business and wanted to know why the National Guard could not be mobilized to fight pyro-terrorist attacks, thus displaying her lack of understanding of the terrorist threat and their methods. Whole forests could burn before the national guard was even mobilized.

But something had fallen into his lap that could change the President's opinion and prove that the Regulators were a force to be reckoned with.

"Jones, tell me about that Mount Shasta terrorist cell again," Sensor said, talking to the back of the man's head.

"If you could call it that," Caleb Jones said. "It's small potatoes."

"Tell me anyway."

His assistant swung his chair around. He and Sensor shared a tiny, cramped office in the Capitol Building, a crucial part of the low profile Sensor kept in the corridors of power.

"They're a homegrown bunch, college kids and wannabe hippies," Jones said. "The CIA watches them, but all they seem to do is talk to one another about the unfairness of white privilege and what an evil empire the United States is." Jones smiled and shook his head. "The CIA doesn't take them very seriously."

"I do," Sensor said. "I take any terrorist infestation very seriously. There are two national forests near Mount Shasta, Klamath to the west, Modoc to the east. Are the members of this cell of Middle Eastern descent?"

"Yes, I believe so," Jones said.

"Then they're Muslims," Sensor said.

Jones seemed doubtful. "I don't know, Mr. Sensor. They could be."

"And they also could be pyroterrorists."

Jones laughed out loud. "Mr. Sensor, I don't think those knuckleheads even know how to light a fire. By all accounts they're a bunch of losers. They're harmless."

"I consider any terrorist cell in California a danger," Sensor said. "How many of them are active?"

"Less than a dozen, about eight or nine They meet every Friday night at an abandoned fishing camp where one of their fathers keeps a cabin. The CIA report says they sit around and drink cheap beer and when they're not discussing girls, they talk about the great jihad to come."

"Then they are condemned out of their own mouths," Sensor said. "Innocent Muslims don't talk about jihad."

"Do you want me to have them closed down?" Jones said. "I can talk to the people who now own the property."

"No, I'll think about it," Sensor said. Then, "I could use a cup of coffee."

"I'm on it, boss," Jones said.

While the man was gone, Sensor placed a call to a contact in the CIA. The agent he spoke with said he'd call him back at home that evening.

Jacob Sensor sat in his library, his feet to the fire, a brandy in one hand, a cell phone in the other. "John, I know it's a lot to ask, but my future is riding on this operation. You know I'll make it up to you."

Sensor listened and then said, "As far as I'm concerned, they're terrorists. Yes, all of them. There must be no survivors. And don't forget you'll need a truck to transport the bodies to the Modoc. John, use your imagination . . . set fire to some underbrush or something. Just make it look good."

Another listening pause, then Sensor said, "The stakes are high, John, as high as they can be. The future of our nation depends on you. We must defeat pyroterrorism or see our forests go up in flames and with them our entire civilization. Damn it, John, we need the Regulators in the field, and this is a step in the right direction."

The man called John talked for a while, and then Sensor said, "Draw the SWAT team from as many agencies as you need, just make sure they know that they're killing dangerous terrorists. And, John, that's all they need to know. Yes, yes, I take full responsibility. When it comes to choosing between my country and the deaths of a few thugs, my country must always come first."

Sensor listened again, then said, "I agree. I'm ruthless,

but we're in a war, and ruthless men win wars. We live in a ruthless time, John, and one must be ruthless to cope with it."

After another stop, Sensor said, "Excellent. I have every confidence in you, John, and your loyalty will not go unrewarded. Good night, and God bless you."

CHAPTER 36

"You going to kill me, Azar?" Mike Norris said. "Well, go right ahead, damn you, and get it over with."

Nasim Azar white-knuckled the .38. "My good and faithful servant, Salam Assad, is dead, killed by the crusader Cory Cantwell."

"Cantwell killed him?" Norris said. "I doubt that. He's not the killing type."

"Then it was he or some other infidel," Azar said.

"Then why execute me? Hell, I didn't do it."

"An eye for an eye, a tooth for a tooth," Azar said.

Fear tied Norris's belly in a knot, but he pretended indifference. "Pity it ends this way, Azar. Just when I was about to throw in with you."

Azar hesitated, then said, "The prospect of a bullet in his skull can make any man have a sudden change of heart."

"Yeah, but I mean it." Norris smiled. "Hell, man, you're the only friend I've got. You're the one human being who even listens to me."

Azar thought that through, then said, "Have you reconsidered your part in the Scorching and the new Caliphate to be established in the Middle East? Be warned, Norris, I'll know if you lie to me."

"You have my word."

"The word of an infidel counts for little."

"Then how can I prove myself?"

"I will think on this," Azar said. He gestured behind him. "The next time I open that door I will do one of two things . . . welcome you to the brotherhood or shoot you between the eyes. I have not yet decided."

Norris decided to play humble. "I await your decision."

"Let me just say that right now, I'm inclined to my latter choice," Azar said. "Norris, you are a vile person, the scum of the earth."

The Ukrainian was used to following detailed orders, but after his failed attempt to kill Cantwell at the airport, he had heard nothing from Nasim Azar, and that troubled him. Had the man given up on the hit? If so, it was time he was paid what he was owed, and then he and Azar could part ways with no hard feelings.

He picked up his cell phone and punched in Azar's number and when the man answered, he said, "The Ukrainian."

"Ah," Azar said, "good to hear from you." Then, in reply to the Ukrainian's question, "Yes, yes, the contract is still in effect, and I want you to complete your end of it as soon as possible. I have additional information for you concerning the man Cantwell's whereabouts, but I don't want to impart such data over the phone. No, don't come here, it's not safe. I will send someone to you with all the details. Yes, with the money you've earned so far. Shall we say your hotel in an hour? Where is it located? Good. The next time we meet I hope you have welcome news for me."

Nasim Azar put down his phone, his face hardened by a veneer of hate. The Ukrainian's clumsy bungling was the direct cause of the beloved Salam's death, and the man must now pay the blood price for his failure. He picked up his phone again and called Adila Bukhari, a Palestinian assassin not as famed as the Ukrainian, but a true believer who had killed a number, one more than her age, of Zionists in Israel, Europe, and the United States. It was a measure of Azar's loathing that he would risk using a woman for the task, especially one on the Interpol and FBI's most wanted lists. But Adila, who'd lived quietly under the radar in Portland for the past two years, was beautiful, intelligent, and deadly, and she could be counted on to use her feminine wiles on the Ukrainian and then slide the knife blade between his ribs. She also knew how to keep her mouth shut.

Before she hung up the phone, the woman assured Azar that that the infidel was already as good as dead.

When the Ukrainian opened his hotel room door and saw the lovely young woman standing there smiling at him, he was convinced this was his lucky day. The visitor held up a bottle of champagne and two plastic glasses and said, "A little gift from Nasim Azar."

"Come in, and welcome," the Ukrainian said. Like Adila Bukhari he used English, the world's lingua franca.

Then, as the woman laid the champagne and glasses on top of the dresser, the Ukrainian said, "Did you bring the money?"

"Of course, but that's for later. Let's have a drink first." She smiled as she opened the champagne. "My name is Fatima Campbell, half–Saudi Arabian, half-American. Yours?"

"Just call me Ukrainian."

The woman was fairly tall, perhaps six pounds overweight, around twenty-four or five, her buttercup-yellow dress very short, revealing perfect legs. No pantyhose. But the tanned skin of her thighs and calves possessed their own amber glow. She wore her glossy black hair long, falling over her shoulders, and her face was fashion-model pretty, skin almost flawless, marred only by teenage acne scars on both cheeks that her makeup didn't quite cover. Her breasts were large, made even larger by the foam padding of her bra, straps pulled tight, showing a narrow and deep V of cleavage. Her eyes were moonlight black, shining with good health. She was the kind of woman who would give any man dirty daydreams.

Adila poured champagne into the glasses and handed one to the Ukrainian. "Mr. Azar sends his best wishes," she said. "I forgot to say that."

"Nice of him," the Ukrainian said. "I guess I'm forgiven." His eyes were fixed on the woman's breasts.

Adila sat on the end of the bed, the hem of the buttercup-yellow dress slipping halfway up her thigh. "Mr. Azar knows that things happen. How is the champagne?" she said.

"Krug Brut, 2004," the Ukrainian said, sitting beside her. "It's passable."

"And what about me?" Adila said, smiling. "Am I passable?"

The man placed his hand on her warm, smooth thigh and grinned. "More than passable. Desirable."

"I'm so glad to hear that," Adila said. "Mr. Azar would be very cross with me if I did not please you."

"You please me just fine," the Ukrainian said. "Why don't you take your dress off? We don't want to spill on it."

"Naughty boy. More champagne first," Adila said.

She walked to the dresser, her back turned to the man, and picked up the rare, 1920s vintage Maniago switchblade knife she'd left there earlier, covered with her purse. The Ukrainian stepped behind her and ran his hands over her hips and then up to her breasts, squeezing, as he nuzzled her neck.

Adila giggled, and then in one swift, practiced movement, she thumbed the Maniago open, turned, and expertly shoved the blade into the man's chest. The Ukrainian's cheeks drained of blood instantly as he staggered back and stared stupidly at the knife hilt protruding from his rib cage. An expression of disbelief replaced the shocked expression on the Ukrainian's face.

"You . . ." he said. "You . . ."

"Me," Adila smiled. "Now die quickly, you infidel pig. I need my knife back."

But the woman had seriously underestimated the Ukrainian. He was a hard man to kill.

He staggered to the bedside table, pushed aside the Gideon Bible, and lifted out the Russian-made 9X18mm

Makarov and turned, bringing the pistol up to eye level. He was a dead man, and he knew it, but he was determined to take his attacker with him.

Adila Bukhari realized her mistake. The Ukrainian was a lot tougher than she'd expected. She kept a Browning .25 in her purse and dove for the gun. She never made it. The Ukrainian pumped three bullets into her back, and the woman fell on top of the dresser and then slid to the floor, the buttercup-yellow dress scarlet with blood.

As voices sounded in the hallway, the Ukrainian sank to his knees, his face ashen, and all the life that was in him left. He fell on his front, the knife twisting under him.

Later the police would classify the incident as a hit made by the wanted terrorist and paid assassin Adila Bukhari. The victim was a foreign visitor, possibly another hit man. Since both parties were now deceased, the authorities did not see the need to investigate any further. Lead Homicide Detective Jay McIntyre's only comment, made off the record to an *Oregonian* reporter, was: "Good riddance."

CHAPTER 37

For the next two days Mike Norris had no contact with Nasim Azar. Adelia Palmer, who was afraid of him, silently brought his food and silently left again. She also supplied him with whiskey and cigarettes, and Norris took that as a good sign . . . unless he was a fatted calf being readied for the slaughter.

Across town, Cory Cantwell discharged himself from the hospital and returned to the Hilton, where Sarah Milano propped him up in bed with pillows and warned him that he needed follow-up visits to check on the progress of his wounds.

Jacob Sensor called to give Cantwell his best wishes and then almost instantly had to hang up to accept a phone call from the President.

"Jacob, I think congratulations are in order," the President said. "I'm told by Homeland Security that the timely actions of your Regulators averted what could have been a disastrous fire in the Modoc National Forest. I don't have all the details, but I hope none of your men were hurt."

"We came through unscathed, Madam President," Sensor said. "We destroyed a very dangerous pyroterrorist cell, and our fellow Americans can sleep safer in their beds tonight."

The President said, "As I said, I don't yet have all the details, but how many terrorists were eradicated?"

"Nine, Madam President, all of them armed," Sensor said. "They put up quite a struggle, but the Regulators dealt with them in short order, I can assure you of that."

"God is on our side, Jacob," the President said.

"Indeed. He is, ma'am," Sensor said.

The President lowered her voice and said, "As you know, I was seriously thinking of canceling the Regulators program as being so much pie in the sky, but this incident has convinced me otherwise. I want you to carry on, Jacob, and we'll find the funding from somewhere."

"Thank you, Madam President," Sensor said. "The taxpayers' money will be well spent,"

"Yes, that is now my considered opinion," the President said. "And once again, congratulations on a job well done."

Jacob Sensor made another call. "John, it's Sensor. I just had a call from the President, and she's extremely pleased with last night's action. Oh yes, yes, of course, it was the night before. Did everything go as planned? Good, good. The SWAT teams know that killing teenaged terrorists is part of their job. Because of the youth of the targets, were any objections raised? None? Excellent. Transferring the bodies to the Modoc forest was not a problem? Oh, your own agency did that. Well done, John, I'm in your debt. Now, to the other matter we discussed a while back, the possibility of a traitor in our midst. How did the Secret Service investigation in Los Angeles go? What did you say? She can either resign from the National Wildfire Service without a pension or face ten years in prison. I think she'll be happy to cooperate. Anything else? Ah, I already heard that the search of Mike Norris's apartment came up with nothing, Well, keep me posted. I want to keep an eye on this one. By the way, John, thanks to you the Regulators are a go! I know, wonderful news. Yes, I'll talk with you later."

Sensor looked out his office window at the people passing back and forth in the hallway. He shook his head and smiled. A woman willing to betray her country for a face-lift. What in God's name was the world coming to?

CHAPTER 38

An event more than four thousand miles away gave Jacob Sensor an unexpected boost that, as far as the President of the United States was concerned, sealed the deal for the Regulators.

The good news was passed to Sensor by Sir Anthony Bickford-Scott, who told him about the action in considerable detail . . .

Glen Affric National Nature Reserve in Inverness-shire, Scotland, is a classic landscape of lakes and mountains, and its vast forests of pine, birch, and oak are important havens for wildlife including red deer, pine martens, and golden eagles.

Located on Scotland's northeast coast, its remoteness made it a prime target for the Scorching, not because of nearby towns that could be endangered but as a fearful demonstration of the long reach of Islamic pyroterrorism.

The pilot of a light aircraft overflying the reserve spotted smoke rising from the edge of a pine forest near the Plodda Falls tourist attraction. He flew lower and saw five men who seemed to be starting a fire. They didn't look like firefighters, and he radioed his concern to controllers at the Inverness International Airport. As luck would have it, a team of smoke jumpers who'd been training in the area were at the airport sitting in an idling Shorts SD 360 aircraft and were immediately dispatched to the forest. Three of them were armed former SAS men.

As Bickford-Scott told Sensor, "It was a lucky convergence of excellent circumstances. The pilot reported the arson attempt while the terrorists were still active in the forest, and the SAS men were right there at the airport. Dash it all, Jacob, the . . ."

"Regulators," Sensor supplied.

"Yes, Regulators, if you want to call them that. Well, anyway, they were at the scene in record time and were still drifting down in parachutes when the firefight erupted."

Sensor said, "Surely your men were caught at a terrible disadvantage?"

"Not a bit of it," Bickford-Scott said. "The SAS men were armed with the excellent MAC-10 submachine gun, and they know how to use it."

Sensor said, "I'm not familiar with the weapon."

"As far as I was told, it's a fully automatic 9mm machine pistol with a 32-round detachable magazine, and the SAS version is fitted with a suppressor that cuts back on noise and recoil. In the right hands it's a deadly weapon, as the encounter with the Affric terrorists demonstrated. Our boys opened up as they were dropping and continued the fight even as they hit the ground. It was all over in seconds, Jacob. All five of the terrorists were killed, either right there at the scene or shortly afterward."

"How were the pyroterrorists armed?" Sensor said.

Bickford-Scott said, "Let me see, it's in the report somewhere . . . ah yes, here it is . . . each had a Russian MP-443 Grach Yarygin 9mm pistol. And somebody's written here that it is the standard sidearm for all branches of the Russian armed forces."

Sensor said, "That does not indicate Russian involvement in pyroterrorism. They have their own forests to worry about."

"No, indeed, it does not. But the Middle East is awash in Russian weapons . . . and American ones."

"I wonder if the MAC-10 would be good arm for my Regulators," Sensor said.

"Sorry, Jacob, but it's been banned in your country since 1994, and that was the semiautomatic version. It seems that Americans are not to be trusted with such a weapon."

"I could get around that, but it might be more trouble than it's worth," Sensor said. "And the gun would scare the hell out of the politicians. For now, Anthony, I'll settle for a copy of the report that I can send on to the President."

"I'll dispatch it right over," Bickford-Scott said. "It makes for some very satisfying reading. Five dead terrorists is not to be sneezed at. By the way, I'll also send you some Cuban coffee directly arrived from Havana and some Iranian saffron powder. I know how your cook loves to use it."

"That's very kind of you, Anthony," Sensor said. "And please give my congratulations to your SAS men. They did very well."

"I will, and please tell your Regulators about the action," Bickford-Scott said.

"Yes, I intend to," Sensor said. "Depend on it."

The message from the President left on Jacob Sensor's cell phone was short and to the point. "I read the British report, and I'm thrilled. Keep up the good work."

CHAPTER 39

Despite a terrible civil war that raged between 1975 and 1990, Beirut, the capital of Lebanon, has become increasingly popular as a tourist destination, slowly reclaiming its historic image as the "Paris of the Middle East." The bars and restaurants in the swinging districts of Achrafieh and Gemayzeh have a liveliness and sophistication you might expect in New York, London, Paris, and Rome. The busy district of Hamra swirls with Arabic coffee shops and colorful vibrancy, and Ramlet al-Baida is a beach that reminds the sun-browned tourist that just like Cannes, Barcelona, and Valencia, Beirut is a city on the edge of the Mediterranean.

But there are dangerous areas in the city where tourists dare not go, especially several districts south of the airport. One of these is Dahieh, a run-down Shia Muslim suburb that hosts a Palestinian refugee camp that has twenty thousand inhabitants.

Near the camp, in one of the poorest neighborhoods, on one of the grimmest streets, stood a bleak, featureless concrete block building that housed the headquarters of the Brothers of the Islamic Jihad, a vicious group that had footholds in the United States, Europe, and the Far East.

Four men in Arab dress sat around a table drinking coffee. The oldest of them and their leader, the sixty-eight-year-old, oil-rich Sheik Jamari Qadir, had just asked a question of one of the younger men, and now the youth, Kadar Muhammed, answered.

"I spoke on the telephone with Nasim Azar. He says the Scorching is on schedule, and the attack on the Willamette forest will go as planned. His own men will be assisted by the Jacks of All Trades, a group of Muslim patriots in Los Angeles."

"Aaaiii," Qadir wailed. "There will be many holy martyrs ere that day is done."

"Inshallah," the younger man said.

Qadir nodded. "Yes, yes, indeed. God willing."

Another man spoke, fifty-six-year-old Ahmed Sultan, chided by the others for being worn out by his fifteen-year-old bride. As was his habit, a Browning Hi-Power lay on the table in front of him. "And what of Jacob Sensor?" he said. "What of the infidel? When we give him the time and date of the Willamette attack, we betray our brethren. Can we trust Sensor to pay us?"

"We can trust him," Qadir said. "A hundred million dollars buys a lot of trust."

"He is no friend of Islam and the Caliphate," Sultan said.

"No, but Sensor badly wants to be President of the United States. Ambition like his makes for strange bed-fellows." Qadir shrugged. "We do him a favor, he does us a favor. As long as the money goes to establishing the Caliphate, I'd do business with the devil."

"Does Sensor have that much money?" Sultan said.

"He can get it," Qadir said. "In Washington he consorts with billionaires, and the American government's money is a bottomless pit. Their President Obama gave our brothers in Iran $50 billion without a second thought. Pah, what is a hundred million to a man like Jacob Sensor? Chickenfeed, as the Americans say."

Sultan shook his head. He looked haggard. "We will make so many martyrs, Jamari. So many young warriors lost."

"All in a good cause, Ahmed," Qadir said. "The reason a mujahideen is born is to die for the Caliphate. And the Scorching is postponed only for a while. When the time comes, American forests will be set ablaze, and Sensor's money will help us drive the Yankee devils from the Middle East. Fear not, my brother, the jihad will go on until the Caliphate is established and our Islamic world returns to the glories of the seventh century."

"Jamari, you will be a poor man by then," Sultan said, smiling. "Day by day you spend more and more of your great fortune on the jihad."

"If it is Allah's will to see the Caliphate come to pass, I'll beg for my bread in the streets and sleep in horse dung," Qadir said.

Sultan bowed in his chair. "Great sheikh, you are indeed a mighty river to your people."

"A word of warning. Nasim Azar must never know of our dealings with Sensor," Kadar Muhammed said. "This meeting should be kept secret."

"Of course, Azar must never know," Qadir said. "Who would tell him? Not anyone here."

The three other men muttered their agreement and in turn each swore an oath of secrecy.

"Azar knows of Sensor, but he fears him," Qadir said. "Since we first met in Washington a year ago at an Arab-US business roundtable, Sensor speaks directly to me. And no one else but me should ever speak to him. Jacob Sensor is as clever as a fox and as savage as a wolf. He is a dangerous man."

"Yet you trust him, Sheikh Qadir?" Sultan said.

"Yes, but only in this one instance. In no other," Qadir said. "I will war with him at a later date, but I will choose the time and the field of battle."

Muhammed said, "Perhaps I speak out of turn, Sheik Qadir, but there's a question that needs answering."

"Then ask it, Kadar, and I'll do my best to answer it," Qadir said.

"Then my question is this . . . what happens if Nasim Azar escapes from the burning forest? Could he do us harm?"

"Why would he escape?" Qadir said, answering the young man's questions with one of his own. "Will he not seek holy martyrdom with the rest?"

Muhammad shook his head and sounded hesitant when he said, "I speak often with Azar, and he is a slippery one. He spends our money and promises much but delivers very little in return. Who knows what a man like that will do or will not do?"

"He showed much skill in the making of bombs," Qadir said. "His martyrs killed hundreds of unbelievers, and for that he has my gratitude." The sheikh smiled. "But if it is the case that he refuses martyrdom, we will hunt him down and kill him like a mad dog. Does that answer your question?"

Sultan said, "It seems that the young man has doubts about this enterprise as I do, Sheikh Qadir. You put too much trust in the man Sensor to uphold his end of the bargain. It could be that you're making a grave mistake."

"Ahmed Sultan, perhaps your ardent young bride has addled your brain," Qadir said. "I have Sensor's word on the matter, and he has mine. Everything will come to pass as I have said it will. There is no doubt about that. Sensor is my bitter enemy, and I am his, but in this one instance we can work together for our mutual benefit."

There was a flintiness in Qadir's eyes that scared Sultan. The man's body bore the scars of seven great wounds sustained during the wars with Israel, and he was said to have killed a score of men with his own hands. "Then I bow to your greater knowledge of Sensor and his infidel ways," Sultan said. "You have my unqualified support, Sheikh Qadir."

"Then all is well," Qadir said. "But it would be better for you if you do not question my actions again, Ahmed."

"Ana asf," Sultan said.

"Your apology is accepted," Qadir said.

Sultan pushed the Browning across the table. "For you, Sheikh Qadir. It is loaded."

Qadir picked up the Hi-Power and said, "A fine gift indeed, Ahmed." He thumbed off the safety . . . and shot Sultan in the middle of his forehead.

The man jerked back in his chair and then slid sideways onto the floor.

In the stunned silence that followed, Qadir said, "Does anyone else present question my judgment?"

No one said a word, and Qadir said, "Then all is well." He nodded in the direction of the dead man and said, "Take that dog out of here. Tonight his young bride will grieve for what she has lost."

CHAPTER 40

Brigadier General Henry "Hank" Stuart accepted a scotch from Jacob Sensor and said, "What kind of military assets were we talking about here? I can only do so much."

"Enough to get the job done quickly and efficiently," Sensor said. "Your people will be up against small arms, pistols and rifles, nothing heavier.'"

"How many terrorists are we talking about?" Stuart said.

"Less than a hundred at a guess, maybe much less."

Sensor studied the soldier carefully. Despite the gray in the man's close-cropped hair, he looked too young for his rank. But the scar across his left cheekbone suggested he'd seen action. "Until the details are released to the media, this operation is to be conducted in the utmost secrecy," Sensor said. "And it goes without saying that it must look good to the President."

"Half a dozen Bell Venom helicopters armed with machine guns and a couple of Chinooks to carry a reinforced company of light infantry should be enough," Stuart said. "I can organize a force like that without too many questions being asked. But it will take time."

"You will be informed of the date of the terrorist attack on the Willamette very soon, General," Sensor said. "You'll have reasonable notice to start assembling your forces." He smiled. "Needless to say, you'll earn a second star for this."

"I'm a patriot, Mr. Sensor," Stuart said. "I'd undertake this mission without a promotion."

"And that is commendable of you, general," Sensor said. "But such patriotism will not go unrewarded. It's a rare commodity these days in an era of Open Borders Open Arms."

"Whoever came up with that should be stood against a wall and shot for a damned traitor," the soldier said.

"Indeed," Sensor said. "Another scotch?"

"Yes, one more and then I have to be on my way. I have a meeting at the Pentagon later today with Lieutenant General Baxter."

"Yes, I know him," Sensor said."

"Then you know he thinks the same way we do," Stuart said. "He has no time for those liberal fools in Congress."

Sensor smiled. "A wise man." Then, "General, I hesitate to bring this up, but I would like my Regulators in on the attack."

"Regulators?"

"A force of armed forest fire smoke jumpers I set up to dispose of pyroterrorists at the scene of the crime, as it were. I hope you don't mind them coming along."

"How many?" Stuart said.

"About half a dozen," Sensor said. "You could use them as paratroopers."

"I don't like including civilians in any operation."

"As a favor to me, General?"

Stuart nodded. "I suppose it can be arranged. Your men can ride along with the infantry."

"I'm forever in your debt," Sensor said. Then, smiling again, "How did Mrs. Stuart like the little birthday gift I sent her?"

General Stuart grinned. "She was delighted. Anne has wanted a Ford Mustang convertible since she was a teenager. And how did you know silver was her favorite color?"

"A lucky guess," Sensor said. "I'm so glad she likes it."

After the general left to attend his meeting, Jacob Sensor made a long-distance call to Sheikh Jamari Qadir of the Brothers of the Islamic Jihad. Qadir, because of his insomnia known to his contemporaries as Wahid Bila Nawn, the Sleepless One, answered the phone.

After identifying himself, Sensor said, "I've begun to make preparations for the attack. Now I need a date for the event and the plan to be used. Don't fail me, Sheikh Qadir."

"I won't fail you, Sensor," the man said, using the cool tone of voice he reserved for infidels. "And you must not fail me and my brothers."

"You will have the money I promised, Sheikh Qadir. A hundred million pending a successful outcome for the operation."

"I trust you, Sensor," Qadir said. "Earlier today I executed a man who did not."

"And that is a measure of your sincerity," Sensor said. "I am impressed."

"Soon I will be in touch with the man Azar, and when he tells me what I wish to know, you will be immediately informed," Qadir said. "Sensor, I do not expect Azar to survive the action."

"He will not. You have my assurance on that," Sensor said.

"There's one more thing I have to say. A favor to ask."

"Ask it, Sheikh," Sensor said. "And I will do my best to grant it."

"Because of our agreement, many Islamic warriors will die, and their martyrdom will be celebrated here in Lebanon," Qadir said. "Those men must be buried in the clothes they wore when they died. Do you understand?"

Sensor, thinking mass grave, said, "Of course I understand. And your wish will be carried out."

"I will be eternally grateful," Qadir said.

"Then I look forward to hearing from you, Sheikh Qadir," Sensor said.

"You will. Very soon."

Qadir abruptly ended the call.

Sensor laid his phone on his desk and smiled. *A hundred million bucks to a flea-bitten camel jockey like you? It will be a cold day in hell . . .*

CHAPTER 41

"It will be a cold day in hell before I let you out of that bed, Cory Cantwell," Sarah Milano said, frowning. "The doctors say you have to rest."

"Have you heard from Sensor this afternoon?" Cantwell said.

"Yes, he said to tell you that you and the other Regulators are on standby."

"Standby for what?"

"He didn't say."

"Where are Pete Kennedy and the Brits?"

"In the bar, running up a liquor bill."

The room telephone rang and Sarah said, "And that's probably the desk clerk to tell me that the Brits are cut off until their bar tab is paid." She picked up the phone and Cantwell heard her say, "Really? Yes, I'll come down and move it right away."

"What was all that about?" Cantwell said.

"Apparently the hotel wants to check on a water line, and several cars are in the way. One of them is ours." She picked up the keys from the top of the dresser and said,

"I'll be right back. And while I'm gone, don't even think about getting out of that bed."

"I am thinking about it," Cantwell said, but Sarah was already out the door.

Sarah crossed the parking lot and saw two men standing beside one of the cars that flanked her rental. She smiled as she approached them and said, "I'll move mine after you back out."

It happened very fast.

One of the men turned on her and delivered a straight right to her chin. As Sarah fell, the other man caught her, and then they both bundled her into the back of their car. A moment later they sped out of the lot, Sarah Milano still unconscious in the back seat.

"Ah, Miss Milano, you're coming around," Nasim Azar said. As her eyes fluttered open, he held Sarah's chin and studied it closely. "Yes . . . a rather nasty bruise, but no broken bones. That's good news, is it not?"

"Who are you?" Sarah said. She tried to move and found herself tied to an upright chair.

"As to who I am, my name is Nasim Azar. As to what I am, I'm your bitterest enemy."

Sarah looked around at a sparsely furnished apartment with a large window where she saw only an expanse of blue sky. "Where am I?" she said.

"You're in my home as my guest," Azar said. "Or, if you like, you are now the prisoner of the Islamic jihad."

Sarah fought against her bonds but to no avail. "They're tight," Azar said. "Only I can loosen them for you."

"Then do it," Sarah said.

"Not yet, Miss Milano. You and I have much to talk about."

"We have nothing to talk about. Those men in the parking lot . . ."

"Were mine, obviously," Azar said.

"What do you want from me?" Sarah said.

"I haven't yet quite decided," Azar said. "I have several options and at least one of them will not be pleasant . . . for you, I mean."

For the first time since she regained consciousness, Sarah felt fear. The man Azar had a smile like a cobra, and his black eyes held no light, like the blank eyes of a dead man.

"You want me to talk. Is that it?" Sarah said.

Azar grinned. "'The time has come, the Walrus said. To talk of many things . . . of shoes and ships . . . and sealing wax . . . of cabbages and kings.' Is that the kind of talk you had in mind, Miss Milano?"

"You're insane," Sarah said. "The Mad Hatter."

"Perhaps I am. But please, don't put my sanity to the test. Have you any idea, any concept at all, of what aqua regia, a combination of nitric and hydrochloric acid, can do to a beautiful face like yours? It will dissolve your skin, dear lady, and make the flesh fall off the bone."

Now Sarah was thoroughly scared, but she was determined not to let it show . . . at least for as long as she could. "You had me kidnapped and brought here," she said. "Tell me why."

"For the moment, you're my ace in the hole, Miss Milano," Azar said. "Soon I will let Cory Cantwell know that you're my hostage and that any move against my brotherhood will be answered with your, shall we say, painful death. You will also tell me all you know about the man Jacob Sensor, the mortal enemy of Islam."

Azar read the surprise on Sarah's face and said, "Oh yes, I know you work for Sensor. There is little that happens in Washington that is not picked up by my intelligence network. Loyal Islamic warriors are spread throughout the United States, right under your stupid infidel noses."

"I'll tell you nothing," Sarah said.

"Oh, but you will, my dear. That is one thing you can depend on."

Azar clapped his hands, and the two men who'd kidnapped Sarah came from the other room. "Untie her and then take her to the carpet storage," he said. "She will remain there until I send for her."

Azar watched Sarah as she was freed from her ropes and dragged to her feet. "Something to think about, Miss Milano," he said. "I now have a dozen loyal Islamic soldiers in Portland, and each and every one of them would delight in killing you as slowly as possible. I only have to nod my head and the terrifying acid will burn. Ponder on that while you await my summons."

Ten minutes after Sarah Milano was locked up in the carpet storeroom, one of Azar's men used a burner phone to call Cory Cantwell's hotel room. The man's words were brief and to the point. "The warriors of Islam have Sarah Milano in custody. You will be contacted later."

CHAPTER 42

"You let her be taken by Islamic terrorists? How in the name of God did you manage that, Cantwell?" Jacob Sensor said.

"A momentary lapse in judgment on my part," Cantwell said. "I should never have allowed Sarah to go to the parking lot alone."

"Damn right you shouldn't," Sensor said, yelling into the phone. "Cantwell, this could be a disaster." Then, "Did the terrorists make any demands?"

"No. They said they'd be in touch later. Mr. Sensor, I don't know what to say. . . . I'm devastated."

"You're wounded, Cantwell," Sensor said. "I told you to take time off. Damn it, man, you're not thinking straight."

"I think I should call the police," Cantwell said.

"No, no police," Sensor said. "I don't want any publicity, no media interest in this affair whatsoever. Do you understand?"

Reluctantly, Cantwell said, "Yes. I understand."

"Damn it, no matter how well I organize a plan, something I didn't anticipate comes along to screw it up.

Cantwell, I have another plan, and this time I don't want anything to screw it up. Not now. I'm too close."

Cantwell's anger flared. "I don't care about your plans. I want Sarah back."

"Then use your Regulators. Go find her. And for God's sake put Pete Kennedy in charge. You're not capable of rational thought at the moment."

"Doesn't it trouble you that Sarah's life could be in terrible danger?" Cantwell said.

"Of course, it troubles me. She works for me, after all."

"That's it? Just, 'she works for me'?"

"Sarah Milano is in a tough business," Sensor said. "She knew when she signed up that a day like this might come." He paused for a moment, collecting his thoughts, and said, "Find her, Cantwell. She's probably still in Portland."

"I'll try. But if we can't track her down, I'll call the police," Cantwell said.

"Cantwell, you're a part of the plan I've set in motion," Sensor said. "It's big, so big that it could help me land in the White House. Don't turn your back on me now."

"What are you saying, Sensor?" Cantwell said.

"Only this . . . if I have to, I'll sacrifice Sarah Milano."

Cantwell was stunned into speechlessness, and Sensor took the opportunity to say, "Keep me posted," before he thumbed his phone into silence.

"No cops, so where do we begin, Cory?" Pete Kennedy said.

Cantwell was out of bed and sitting in a chair. The

bullet wound had weakened him, and he heard feebleness in his own voice. "I don't know, Pete. I wish to hell I did."

"Have you any lead on the whereabouts of Mike Norris?" Kennedy said.

"He's gone, vanished," Cantwell said. "Anyway, I don't think he would be of much help."

Frank West said, "Boss, why don't we wait and hear what Sarah's kidnappers say? Maybe we can go from there."

Cantwell looked at the other Brits. "Any other suggestions?"

The only answer was an uncomfortable silence, and the SAS men tried their best not to look at him.

"Then we'll wait for a phone call," Cantwell said.

"What about Jacob Sensor?" Kennedy said. "Any help from that direction?"

Cantwell shook his head. "We're on our own. Sensor has bigger fish to fry."

The phone call came fifteen minutes later. It was from Nasim Azar, and Cantwell answered it.

"Listen to me," Azar said.

Cantwell said, "Where is . . ."

"I said listen," Azar said. "Don't talk, listen."

"I'm listening," Cantwell said.

"You will not go to the police or Sarah Milano dies. Is that clear?"

"Yeah, it's clear," Cantwell said.

"You will send your crusaders away from Portland or the woman dies. Is that clear?"

"Damn you, it's clear."

"You will make no aggressive moves against the

Muslim brotherhood in Portland or Sarah Milano dies. Is that clear?"

"Clear," Cantwell said, hating the man on the other phone.

"Last, but not least, you have three days to pay a ten-million-dollar ransom or the woman dies. You will be instructed on where to drop off the money. Is that clear?"

"I can't raise that kind of money," Cantwell said.

"You have three days."

The phone went silent.

Sarah Milano had been shoved into a windowless room where a couple hundred rolled-up, paper-wrapped rugs were stored. The space was air-conditioned, but there was no furniture of any kind, and there was a strong smell of mothballs.

After the door slammed shut behind her and a key turned in the lock, Sarah tested the walls. They were composed of panels of Sheetrock designed to repel moisture and were hard and unyielding. The ceiling was made from the same material. There was no give in the heavy wooden door, and the floor was laid with engineered hardwood.

Her prison was escape proof.

CHAPTER 43

His shackles clanking, Mike Norris threw himself on his cot and stared at the ceiling. He had no doubt that Nasim Azar would kill him or keep him locked up forever, if that's what it took. There was a time to fight and a time to surrender . . . and the time to surrender was now.

When Mrs. Palmer brought him his lunch, Norris said, "Tell Azar I want to speak with him." The black woman looked at him with frightened eyes, and Norris said, "Tell him that, damn you."

The woman scurried out of the room and an hour later Nasim Azar unlocked the door and stepped inside. "Well?" he said.

"I've thought it over and I want to join you," Norris said. "You're a stronger man than I first took you for."

"And to what do I owe this sudden conversion to the ways of the Prophet?" Azar said.

"I owe America and Americans nothing," Norris said. "Why should I allow myself to suffer on their behalf?"

Azar took the .25 Beretta from his pocket and said, "Maybe I'll just shoot you. That will end your misery."

"Then you'll lose a loyal ally," Norris said. "And a friend."

"Mr. Norris, we both know you're no friend of mine. Methinks thou doth protest too much."

"I'm sincere, Azar. I've never been more sincere in my life."

"You foolish man, sincerity does not substitute for truth."

"And I'm telling you the truth . . . I want to join you."

"Join in the jihad?"

"Yes, exactly that."

"Then I'll put you to the test, Mr. Norris."

"Any test, any time," Norris said. "I'm ready."

"I'll return in one hour," Azar said. "Think over what you've just told me, and if you still feel the same way, I'll seek the proof of your resolve."

"Come back in an hour and I'll still feel the same way."

"We'll see," Azar said.

Norris lay on his cot again, lecturing himself. Say anything. Lie. Deceive. Kiss Islamic ass . . . but save your life. Once you're free you can escape this place. And kill Nasim Azar on your way out the door. Norris smiled. He had a plan.

Nasim Azar returned within the hour and said, "Your decision?"

"I still feel the same way," Mike Norris said. "I haven't changed my mind."

Azar palmed the Beretta again. "Try any funny business, and I'll shoot you," he said.

"I won't try anything," Norris said. "You can trust me."

"I trust you as I'd trust a wounded wild beast," Azar said. "Your test awaits you."

He unlocked the shackles from Norris's wrists and then used the Beretta to wave the man in the direction of the door. "I'll tell you where to go," he said. "It isn't far."

It seemed to Norris that the warehouse was a warren of rooms, some large, others the size of a closet. Azar directed him to a room on the ground floor where two young men waited outside the door. Azar nodded to one of them, and the man took a key from a hook on the wall, unlocked the door, and opened it wide. Norris caught a glimpse of a woman as he was prodded inside. Azar joined him and then the door closed behind him.

The woman was beautiful and seemed frightened. Her chin was bruised, and Norris reckoned she'd suffered some rough handling.

"This is the woman of the crusader Cory Cantwell," Azar said. "Her name is Sarah Milano."

Norris was stunned. Cantwell's woman? What deviltry was this?

"Kneel," Azar said to Sarah.

"You go to hell," she said.

"Then die standing."

Azar passed the Beretta to Norris. "Shoot her," he said. "It's a small caliber, so go for the back of the neck."

"This isn't a test," Norris said. "Killing the woman proves nothing."

"Oh, but it does, Mr. Norris. It does to me," Azar said. "Now kill her."

"And if I don't?" Norris said.

"Then you'll never leave this place alive, and neither will she."

"Norris, get it over with," Sarah said. "I'm not going to beg a damned terrorist for my life."

"There you are, Mr. Norris," Azar said. "Words of advice."

"The woman has sand," Norris said.

"Yes, she's very brave. Now, for the last time, shoot her."

For long moments, Norris looked down at the little pistol in his hand. The room was very quiet, soundless as a tomb. Sarah stared at the man with frightened eyes, but her stance was still and defiant.

Norris shook his head. "You Arab asshole, Azar," he said. He raised the Beretta, shoved the muzzle against his temple, and pulled the trigger.

Click!

Norris smiled. "I figured out pretty quick that you wouldn't hand me a loaded gun that I could use to shoot you. My ma didn't raise a pretty boy, but she didn't raise a dumb one either." He threw the pistol at Azar's head. The man ducked out of the way and then pulled his dead bodyguard's .38 from a shoulder holster. The two young men burst through the door and stood there confused, waiting.

"You failed your test, Mr. Norris," Azar said. "You fool, if you knew the gun wasn't loaded, you should have pretended to shoot the woman."

"I was sure, but not a hundred percent sure," Norris said.

"Then you might have blown your own brains out," Azar said.

Norris shrugged. "No big deal. Who the hell would grieve for me?"

"No one, Mr. Norris," Azar said. "No one at all." He turned to the two young men. "Take him back to his room and chain him." He stared at Norris. "My promise. I'll kill you very soon."

After the Norris was taken away, Azar said to Sarah, "I have laid out my demands to the devil Cantwell for your safe return. Your fate depends on what he does next. He has three days to respond, so in the meantime I'll move you to more comfortable quarters."

"What kind of demands?" Sarah said. "The government of the United States doesn't pay ransoms to terrorists."

"The government? My dear, not the government. Cory Cantwell must pay your ransom and meet my other demands. If he doesn't"—Azar sighed—"your death will be most unpleasant."

CHAPTER 44

"I can guarantee that we're being watched day and night," Pete Kennedy said.

"I know, and that's why you and the others will have to leave," Cory Cantwell said. "Or at least be seen to be leaving."

"What's your plan, boss?" Nigel Brown said. "Let us in on it."

"Take the rental and head out of town," Cantwell said. "Sarah didn't pick up her purse, so her credit card will pay your expenses. Find a motel in the sticks and stay there until I call you. Just put some distance between you and Portland."

"Boss, you're still feeling poorly," Brown said. "Maybe one of us should stay behind with you. Lie low, so nobody knows we're here."

"Whoever the terrorists are, I'm sure they'll know how many Regulators are in this hotel," Cantwell said. "I can't take a chance with Sarah's life." He smiled. "And I feel fine."

"You don't look fine, Cory," Kennedy said. "You need more bed rest."

"I won't get any kind of rest until I find Sarah," Cantwell said.

"You're sweet on that girl, boss, aren't you?" Frank West's scarred, fist-pummeled face breaking into a smile.

"Yeah, I guess I am," Cantwell said. "I hadn't realized it until now."

"What will you do, Cory, after we leave?" Kennedy said.

"All I can do is wait here and hope something breaks my way."

Kennedy shook his head, looking doubtful. "That's a lot of hope."

"I know it is, but right now hope is all I've got," Cantwell said. "All right, get packed, all of you, and make a show of leaving."

"Cory, I don't feel right about doing this, stranding you in this hotel on your own," Kennedy said.

"And I don't feel right about it either," Cantwell said. "But we have no other choice. The terrorists want you gone, so let's do it. And remember, put a lot of git between you and Portland."

Kennedy nodded. "We'll head out of town and then go to ground."

"Like gophers," Cantwell said.

"Yeah, just like gophers," Kennedy said. "Except that we'll surface again right quick the minute you need us."

Pete Kennedy and the Brits did some noisy horsing around in the parking lot, drawing attention to themselves, before they piled into the Toyota and left for parts unknown.

Cory Cantwell was now alone in the hotel. He didn't feel good, his shoulder wound punishing him, and he was seized by a feeling of utter helplessness. Somewhere, probably just across town, Sarah Milano was a prisoner and her life was in terrible danger and there was nothing he could do about it. And he had three days to raise ten million dollars . . . an impossible task. The thought tormented him that even if the ransom was paid, Sarah would still die. It was in those dark moments that he realized he loved her, and it came to him as a shock. He liked women and had enjoyed many affairs, but he'd never felt like this before . . . head over heels in love with a woman he might now lose forever.

The hotel phone didn't ring that day, but in the evening, Cantwell got a call from Pete Kennedy on his cell. They'd booked into a motel off Interstate 84, fifty miles east of Portland in the middle of nowhere.

"But there's a general store nearby that sells beer, so my British friends are quite happy," Kennedy said. Then, "How are things on your end?"

"Nothing happening," Cantwell said. "I'm still waiting for . . . whatever."

"Keep us in the loop," Kennedy said.

"There is no loop, Pete. Just me," Cantwell said. "But if there are any developments, I'll let you know right away."

"Good luck, Cory," Kennedy said.

"Yeah, you too, Pete, good luck," Cantwell said.

Cantwell put down the phone. Restless now, he had to do something.

Despite Sarah's objections, he'd insisted on wearing clothes and not the pajamas she'd wanted to buy him. He wore jeans and a T-shirt and boots and planned to walk around the neighborhood and make himself a target. He'd see if he could force the terrorists' hand and maybe even capture one for questioning. Cantwell knew it was a forlorn hope, but he had to try something . . . anything. He pulled the shirt over his holstered Glock, aware of the swell of the fat bandage over his left shoulder. At least his arthritis was gone, either that or the greater pain of the bullet wound masked it.

The day was slowly shading into evening when Cantwell left the hotel. He strolled around the parking lot and then walked out into the street. Around him lay a quiet, residential and business area with fallen leaves in the gutters and windows lit behind drawn blinds. A single star burned in the darkening sky, but there was as yet no sign of the moon. Cantwell walked for thirty minutes around and then around the block again. Once a police cruiser passed him, its headlights dimmed, and then a middle-aged woman in high heels clacked along the opposite sidewalk before turning into a lane. He gave it up and returned to the hotel. The front desk told him he had no messages, and he made his way back to his room, exhausted.

It seemed that there were no terrorists about that night.

Not hungry but feeling that he should eat something to boost his flagging energy, Cantwell ordered a burger and fries from the room service children's menu, ate without appetite, and then got ready for bed.

The hotel phone rang at two in the morning and woke him from a troubled sleep.

"How are you, Mr. Cantwell?" Nasim Azar said.

"Who is this?" Cantwell said.

Azar ignored that and said, "I just wanted to congratulate you on sending your crusaders away. Oh, and to let you know that Miss Milano is still alive and well. For now, that is."

"I swear, harm Sarah and I'll . . ."

"You'll do what exactly? There is nothing you can do but pay her ransom. How much have you raised so far?" Cantwell said nothing, and Azar said, "As I thought, not a penny. Ah well, you still have another two days."

"Where is she?" Cantwell said. "Where are you keeping her?"

Azar laughed. "Wouldn't you like to know. Tell me, Mr. Cantwell, do you love Miss Milano?"

"That's none of your business," Cantwell said.

"It is my business, and I think you're in love with her. Oh, good. That means we can play a little game, you and I."

"I don't play games with terrorists."

"You'll play this one . . . that is if you really love the woman. She's very beautiful, isn't she?"

Cantwell said nothing. He was aware of his breath coming in short gasps, and his stomach felt like it was tied in knots.

"Suppose I tell you that you can forget the ransom and free Miss Milano? Huh? Do you like that? All that is required is one little action on your part."

"What kind of action?" Cantwell said.

"Do you have a gun, Mr. Cantwell? I'm sure that a great hero like you has one."

"Yes, I have a gun," Cantwell said.

"Then here's all it will take to set Miss Milano free as a bird. You place the muzzle of your gun against your temple and blow your brains out. Just as soon as the media reports the story, I will let the woman go."

"Go to hell," Cantwell said.

"If you really love Miss Milano, won't you do this one little thing to save her life? After all, real sacrifice should only be done for love. You make no answer, Mr. Cantwell. That means you're thinking about it, the ultimate sacrifice. Now bear in mind, that shooting yourself causes only a moment's pain, but Miss Milano's death will be long drawn out, perhaps for days, and be very painful. Spare her, Mr. Cantwell, spare the woman you love so much agony. Ah . . . I can't even bear to think about it."

Cantwell knew that making empty threats was useless, and he remained silent.

"I'll call you again very soon, Mr. Cantwell," Azar said. His voice had dropped to silken purr. "If you're still alive I'll be very disappointed."

The phone went dead.

Cantwell understood that the terrorist, whoever he was, was playing cat and mouse with him, tormenting him, making him pay for the crimes he'd committed against the Muslim brotherhood, the killing of so many holy warriors. He knew that nothing he did or said would ever set Sarah free. She was caught in a spiral of death, and there was no escape.

Utter despair clawing at him, Cantwell dropped his head onto the pillow. Would his suicide really free Sarah?

No, that was unthinkable. Such a suggestion was the raving of a madman. God almighty, how could hatred run that deep? He'd read somewhere that hatred is a weak emotion, a sign of failure. But he, Cory Cantwell, was the failure.

It was the haters who had the upper hand.

CHAPTER 45

Sarah Milano sat on the corner of the bed and looked around at the sparse furnishings of the room that until recently had housed Salman Assad. The dresser drawers and closet had been stripped bare, and the door was locked from the outside. An earlier check of the windows facing the Willamette River had revealed a sheer, two-story drop to the ground. There was no escape in that direction.

Sarah rose and crossed to the window again. There was a small parking lot in front of the warehouse, the spaces for a dozen cars marked with faded white lines, and beyond that a street. During the ten minutes she stood there, she didn't see a single pedestrian and only a handful of cars. The warehouse was obviously located in a business district, well off the beaten track.

Sarah realized then that the chances of Cory Cantwell finding her were slim to none, and slim was already saddling up to leave town. She found that thought vaguely amusing, and despite her fears, she managed a smile.

Would the man called Azar really kill her? Sarah's answer was a resounding yes. The man was a fanatic, and

Muslim terrorists didn't hold women in high regard in the first place. He'd kill her all right . . . and probably enjoy doing it.

The warehouse was deathly quiet, so the sudden and distant clanking of a chain and the man's muffled voice yelling, "Azar, you Arab asshole!" surprised Sarah. It seemed that the other prisoner was angry. Azar had called him Mr. Norris, so he could only be Mike Norris, the famous firefighter that Cory had been looking for. But why was he there? Why was he a chained prisoner? She had no time to contemplate that question, because a key turned in the lock, and the door opened.

A black woman bearing a tray stepped inside while a man stood outside the door, watching her every move.

"I'm Adelia Palmer," the woman said, smiling. "I've brought you some lunch, dear."

"Just a few seconds ago I heard a man call out," Sarah said. "His name is Mike Norris. Why is he here?"

Suddenly, the woman looked frightened. "I didn't hear a man call out. There is no man by that name here."

"But I . . ."

"No man here," Mrs. Palmer said. She laid the tray on top of the dresser and beat a hasty retreat through the open door that the guard slammed shut and then locked behind her.

Sarah felt a twinge of disappointment. There would be no help coming from that quarter. For all her motherly looks, Mrs. Palmer was probably a terrorist herself.

All at once realizing how hungry she was, Sarah checked the tray. Egg salad sandwiches on whole-grain bread, a couple of chocolate chip cookies and a glass of milk. Sarah smiled to herself. And the condemned ate a hearty last meal . . .

"Are you here to shoot me?" Mike Norris said, sitting up in his cot.

"Not quite yet," Nasim Azar said. "But I brought you good news."

"You're letting me out of here," Norris said.

"No, sorry to disappoint, but you will never leave here alive," Azar said. "No, my tidings are of far greater importance. Many mujahideen, all brave warriors of Islam, will arrive from Los Angeles tomorrow, and the attack on the Willamette forest will take place in three days hence. The infidels will die in their hundreds from the scorching and the bullet." Azar raised his hands above his head and did a strange little dance. *"Allahu Akbar!"*

"You damned heathen, what do you hope to gain by that?" Norris said. "All that will happen is that the United States will take its revenge and bomb the crap out of every damned dung-heap country in the Middle East."

"No, my friend, the Americans don't have the belly for that," Azar said. "Fearing repeat attacks on their forests all across the nation, they will seek peace with us and leave the Gulf states to the new Caliphate."

"In your dreams, Azar," Norris said. "That's not going to happen. We'll bomb you sand monkeys back to the Stone Age."

Azar said, "Norris, your infidel mind cannot comprehend this, but the great Sheikh Jamari Qadir, may Allah bless him, saw it all in a vision. He has told the faithful that he saw the Americans in the Willamette fall like stalks of wheat before a reaper, the bodies of men, women and children stacked up like cordwood beside three pools of water that had turned red with their blood. The great sheikh says that the Caliphate is now only weeks away from fulfillment, and before that time the American eagle will fly for home with its tail feathers smoking. This, Sheikh Qadir also saw in his vision."

It was a forlorn hope, but Norris tried it. "Azar, unchain me. Let me be a part of it."

Azar smiled. "You will never fool me again, Norris. But, since I am in such a joyful state of mind, I will grant you a boon. I give you three more days of life. You will not die until the day of the attack on the Willamette."

"Then let the woman go," Norris said.

"Miss Milano? No, she must also die, but sooner than you, I think. I will loose her to the Los Angeles mujahideen for their amusement before they dispose of her, and I will let the crusader Cory Cantwell know exactly what happened to his ladylove." Azar smiled. "What an exquisite revenge that will be."

"The woman really is connected with Cantwell?" Norris said.

"Connected? Not a word I'd use. I believe he's in love with her and she with him. So touching, isn't it, Norris?"

"You're a damned black-hearted devil, Azar," Norris said.

"Perhaps. But I am a soldier of Islam, and I pray to Allah that he allow me to die a martyr's death in the Willamette. Now I must leave. Mrs. Palmer will bring you food and yet another bottle of whiskey. Drink yourself into oblivion, Norris. It might be a better death than the one I plan for you."

"I hope I see you again in hell," Norris said.

"No, that will not happen. But I will look down on your terrible suffering from paradise," Azar said.

CHAPTER 46

"Brigadier Stuart, it's a go for August 8 at 0800 hours," Jacob Sensor said, his cell phone to his ear. "Can your troops be ready by then? The main terrorist attack will be in the Willamette Three Pools area. I'll make sure you get a map."

"We'll be ready," Brigadier General Hank Stuart said. "I've got five Venom helicopters armed with machine guns and a reinforced company of infantry in Chinooks. That's enough assets to get the job done, and we'll go in right on time."

"Try to minimize civilian casualties," Sensor said. "A few dead I can accept, but I don't want a huge butcher's bill."

"If it's carrying a weapon of any kind, we'll kill it," Stuart said. "If it's carrying a Pepsi and a hotdog, we'll be extra careful."

"I'll ride in one of the choppers with my Regulators and couple of hand-picked reporters," Sensor said. "Do you still plan to use the Portland airport Air National Guard Base as a staging area?"

"Yes. Be at the airport by 0700 hours, and I'll get you and your men on one of the Chinooks."

"That's perfect. You've done well, General," Sensor said. "You have my thanks."

"Helping to get rid of terrorist scum is all the thanks I need, Mr. Sensor."

"Then there's nothing more to be said, General," Sensor said. "I'll see you at the airport."

Sensor hung up and then made a call to Cory Cantwell.

"Anything to report on Miss Milano?" he said.

The man's voice was flat, emotionless, and that angered Cantwell. "You mean Sarah?"

"Anything to report?" Sensor said again.

"Yes, I have. The terrorists want ten million dollars to set her free. Apart from that, I've heard nothing else. Have you?"

"I've put the wheels in motion," Sensor said. "At the moment that's all I can do. And paying a ransom to terrorists is out of the question. The FBI has been informed."

"Well, hell, that makes me feel much better," Cantwell said.

"I drank a gallon of coffee last night just sitting up and worrying," Sensor said. "I'm doing all I can."

"I'm sure you are."

"Now, on to other matters," Sensor said. "The pyro-terrorist attack on the Willamette National Forest is set for the eighth of this month. I want the Regulators in on it."

"All five of us?" Cantwell said.

"Four of you, Superintendent Cantwell. You're wounded. You won't be a part of this operation. I tried to get the woman Merinda Barker to join you, but she's still undergoing jump training. A pity, because I would've liked a Native American woman on the team."

Cantwell knew it would be useless to argue that he wasn't disabled and said nothing.

"Order your men to be at the Portland airport at 0700 hours," Sensor said. "They'll report to Brigadier General Stuart at the Air National Guard Base. This is a big anti-terrorist operation, and the Regulators will be a part of it. They'll fly with the infantry in a Chinook and answer only to me."

"You'll be there?" Cantwell said.

"Yes. I'll be with the Regulators. I told you this was big. At the end of the day, we'll have killed a lot of terrorists."

"And you'll be famous," Cantwell said.

"And I will have served my country," Sensor said. "Superintendent Cantwell, your worry about Miss Milano has clouded your judgment. Please keep a civil tongue in your head. After all, I am your superior."

"I'll bear that in mind," Cantwell said.

Then, on a conciliatory note, Sensor said, "Superintendent Cantwell, you're a wounded warrior. I'll make sure you get part of the credit for the success of the coming operation."

"What about Sarah, Mr. Sensor? What does she get?" Cantwell said.

"We'll find her, and I'll leave no stone unturned until we do."

The phone went silent. Jacob Sensor was all through talking.

CHAPTER 47

I pursued my enemies and overtook them;
I did not turn back until they were destroyed.
—PSALMS 18.37 (motto of Israel's
Yamam counterterrorist squad)

Yamam, Israel's special police force, is the most feared and fearsome anti-terrorism unit in the world. Its expertise is in high demand around the world by intelligence agencies and police chiefs, and Jacob Sensor was one of its most ardent admirers. But even he, an acknowledged mover and shaker who stalked the corridors of power within the government of the mightiest nation on earth, had a difficult time penetrating the barrier of secrecy that surrounds Yamam.

But when Sensor finally did, his information was well received and, as is the way of Yamam, famed for its rapid deployment time, acted on immediately.

Sheikh Jamari Qadir and his Brothers of the Islamic Jihad were high on Israel's most-wanted list. The Brotherhood's "heroic soldiers of the Caliphate" and its ally ISIS had been responsible for terror bombings and other attacks in Israel and across the Middle East. In Pakistan the Brotherhood's suicide bombers had killed hundreds.

American intelligence believed that over the past five years, Sheikh Jamari Qadir had authorized nine out of every ten terrorist attacks around the globe.

Now, thanks to Jacob Sensor, Yamam knew Qadir, a hunted man, had gone to ground in a Lebanese slum and that the terrorist could be killed.

Five operatives, dressed like young Lebanese men in jeans, T-shirts and sneakers, but affecting the flashy watches and designer sunglasses the youngsters loved, surrounded the house near the Palestinian refugee camp, blasted in the door with a grenade, and then, armed with Glock 17 pistols and a single Uzi, rushed inside and killed seven men, one of them positively identified as Qadir. The action was over in seconds, and the five Israelis expertly lost themselves in the crowd that had gathered to gawk at the bullet-torn bodies.

The news of Sheikh Jamari Qadir's death delighted Jacob Sensor so much that he had to share the news with his friend, Sir Anthony Bickford-Scott at the British Embassy.

"We haven't been able to touch him, but I tipped off the Israelis, and they did the job," Sensor said.

"And saved yourself . . . how much was it?" Bickford-Scott said.

"A hundred million, but I'd no intention of paying it of course. Once he gave me the information I needed, I had other plans for Sheikh Qadir."

"Jolly good show," Bickford-Scott said. "Do you know what I admire about you, Jacob? You're a man completely without a conscience."

"Sir Anthony, let me tell you something, a guilty conscience is so tedious. All it does is slow a man down. When I first entered politics, I left my conscience outside the front door of the Capitol, and I've never felt an urgent need to pick it up again."

Bickford-Scott's voice was veneered by a smile. "The United States is in safe hands when you are around, Jacob. And talking about national security, I hear through the grapevine that some big anti-terrorist operation is planned, either in this country or the Middle East. Do you know anything about that?"

"Not a thing," Sensor lied smoothly. "How these wild rumors get started I do not know. I really do think that they originate in the Kremlin."

"It wouldn't surprise me. Russia gets up to all kinds of mischief. How was the Beluga caviar, by the way?"

"Excellent. Send me more if you get some."

"I'll speak to my contact at the Russian embassy," Bickford-Scott said. "Beluga is very hard to find, even for an *apparatchik*. But I'll see what I can do. Anything else I can help you with, Jacob? How are our SAS men doing?"

"Learning the ropes. They're coming along just fine."

"Glad to hear it. Jacob, if you find out any whispers about the big operation, let me know," Bickford-Scott said. "Whitehall expects me to keep abreast of these things."

"If I'm told anything, I'll call you immediately, Anthony," Sensor said. "But don't expect too much. I think it's just another Russian rumor."

Later that day Jacob Sensor learned from the CIA that a jihad had been declared against him and that there was a price on his head.

The threat didn't trouble him in the least.

CHAPTER 48

"Mrs. Palmer, are you a terrorist?" Sarah Milano said.

The black woman smiled. "Bless your heart, no. I'm a Baptist. Look, I've brought you some nice fried chicken and potato salad for dinner. And a piece of my own homemade chocolate cake."

The guard at the door didn't seem to be listening, but Sarah knew her time was short. Her words tumbling out rapidly, she whispered, "Mrs. Palmer, I'm being held prisoner here against my will. You have to help me."

"And a nice cold bottle of Pepsi to drink," the woman said, as though she hadn't heard.

"Mrs. Palmer, the men here are terrorists," Sarah said,

"Enjoy your dinner, dear," Mrs. Palmer said. She stepped to the door that the guard opened wide for her and left.

Defeated, Sarah sat on the bed. If Mrs. Palmer was a Baptist, she'd obviously been brainwashed by Azar. Even if she could, which was unlikely, she wouldn't help.

Sarah Milano chided herself.

What did you expect, Sarah? That she'd smuggle in a file like they do in the movies?

She began to eat. She must keep her strength up because there was always a chance she could overpower the guard. With a plastic knife? What were her odds of success?

Sarah felt a pang of utter hopelessness. She didn't have a hope in hell.

Scrambled eggs and toast and a bottle of water.

Mike Norris stared at his tray in disgust. Was that all the black woman could cook?

Still, the whiskey was welcome.

Norris poured himself a glass and stared at the TV. A pileup on I-84 had killed three people, meantime in overseas news an Arab sheikh had been blown away in Lebanon, and the Lebanese authorities blamed the Israelis and threatened to fire off scores of vengeance rockets. The Israelis denied the accusation and blamed the Saudis, who quickly denied the charge and blamed the Palestinians, who. . .

Norris thumbed the TV into darkness. Same old, same old.

The key turned in the lock, the door opened, and Nasim Azar stepped inside. His right arm hung at his side, the Beretta .25 in his hand.

"Azar, you snake, have you come to finish it?" Norris said.

The man shook his head. "I promised you a few more days of life, and I keep my word."

"Then why are you here?"

"Only to tell you that I won't visit you tomorrow," Azar said.

"Oh, no, that's a real disappointment," Norris said. "I so look forward to your visits."

"I have to attend a meeting that may interest you. It's with an Islamic brotherhood who call themselves the Jacks of All Trades. They've been arriving from Los Angeles for the past twenty-four hours."

"So they're plumbers or something, huh?"

"No, fifty holy warriors, Norris, the brave mujahidin I told you about. They will attack the Willamette tourist areas with guns and grenades and slay the nonbelievers as the Scorching set by my own *ghazi* begins."

"Azar, you idiot, where are young going to stash fifty damn terrorists in Portland?" Norris said.

"I have safe houses all over the city," Azar said. "These are the homes of true believers in the coming Caliphate. And I have already heard something from the mujahidin that fills my heart with joy and pride. Not one of them expects to live past the day of the attack. They will all seek martyrdom in this, the most sacred of all causes. You fool, Norris, you could have been a part of it. But instead, you'll die chained to the wall like a frightened cur."

"I'd rather die that miserable death than die with you and your gang of murderous thugs," Norris said.

"We have come a long way, you and I, Norris," Azar said. "What a pity it all has to end this way."

"There was no other way it could've ended, Azar. I just regret that I didn't put my hands around your scrawny neck when I had the chance."

"Yes, my friend, it all ends in regret, but for you, not

me. I will seek martyrdom with the rest and die a hero for Islam and the Caliphate."

Norris grimaced in imitation of a grin. "Azar, when your time comes, you'll squeal like a pig for mercy. I've met your kind before, all talk, no action."

Azar shook his head. "You foolish man, how little you know me."

Norris tried a different tack. "Then let the woman go before you meet your martyrdom."

"No, Norris, a thousand times no. The woman, like you, is already dead. Because I hate her so much, the whore of the devil Cantwell, her death will be infinitely more terrible than your own. Think yourself lucky."

Azar backed toward the door. "I will not see you tomorrow, but perhaps the day after that I will put you out of your misery. Pray that I do, Norris. Pray that I do."

CHAPTER 49

Cory Cantwell called Pete Kennedy at the motel and told him what Jacob Sensor had said about the terrorists' planned attack on the Willamette and the countermeasures he'd put in place.

"The Air National Guard base at 0700 hours on the eighth," Kennedy said. "We'll be there."

"We mention Sensor's name and they'll let us through," Cantwell said. "Pete, you'll make a detour and pick me up at the hotel."

"You're going with us?"

"Sensor ordered me to stay put," Cantwell said. "But he can go fly a kite. I want to be in the Willamette with the rest of you."

"Cory, do you think that's wise? You still haven't recovered from your wound."

"I've recovered enough. The pain isn't any worse than a bad toothache."

"Then it's bad," Kennedy said. "From what Sensor says, this is a major operation, and it could get rough. We could end up in a firefight."

"I'll take my chances," Cantwell said. "My mind is made up. It's what I want to do."

"Then I won't even try to talk you out of it. Any news of Sarah?" Kennedy said.

"Nothing new. Sensor says he's instituted a search, but I don't believe him."

"Hell, she works for him," Kennedy said.

"Pete, she's expendable. As far as Sensor is concerned, we're all expendable. He wants to be President, and his campaign will piggyback on his glorious defense of the Willamette against the terrorist hordes."

"Cory, if you need us to find Sarah, then to hell with Sensor's grab for glory. We'll skip the Willamette and come to your help."

"No, Pete, we'll do as Sensor ordered. If I can't find Sarah, four more people searching the city for her won't help. And she's a brave, smart woman. She might save herself."

"I hope so," Kennedy said. "Cory, maybe it's best you not stay in the Hilton. I doubt that the terrorists will return now they have Sarah, but it might be better if you hole up somewhere else for the next couple of days."

"Her kidnappers know they can contact me here," Cantwell said. "I'd better remain where I am."

"The cops?" Kennedy said.

"Sensor wants no police involvement. He says Sarah's abduction is entirely our baby. Anyway, I don't think the Portland police would have any better luck than I've had."

Kennedy said, "Cory, if there's anything I can do . . . anything at all . . ."

"Just be at the airport as scheduled, Pete." He managed a slight smile. "With me in the back seat."

"You can depend on me," Kennedy said. Then, "Cory, I hope you find Sarah."

"Me too," Cantwell said. "Me too."

Cory Cantwell stared at the hotel phone, willing it to ring. He'd settle for any news of Sarah, even if it was only another terrorist demand. He had to know if she was still alive and well.

"Where are you, Sarah?" he whispered aloud. "Where the hell are you?"

The phone didn't ring, and there was no answer to his question. Outside the wind tossed a scattering of raindrops against the window, and in the hallway, a cart rattled softly, a room service dinner on its way to someone . . . maybe a couple.

The walls closed in on Cantwell, compressing his worry and loneliness to a tight ball in his stomach. His shoulder ached, and he tried to work it in a circular motion. He found no relief, only an intensifying of the pain, and quickly stopped.

Cantwell stepped to the window and pulled back the curtain. Out there in the brightly lit city, Sarah might be held in a dark room. Maybe hurt. Maybe abused. Maybe scared. Maybe calling out for him to come to her. Maybe dead.

That last thought was too much to bear. Cantwell's head bowed and his shoulders slumped. A man at the end of his tether. Defeated, lost in a gloomy tunnel of despair with nowhere to turn and no end in sight.

CHAPTER 50

Mrs. Palmer brought Sarah Milano breakfast, but hardly said a word and left in a hurry.

Sarah wondered at the woman's curtness, not even a smile. *Does she know something I don't? Bacon, eggs, sausage links, and toast. Am I eating my last meal?*

Sarah didn't dwell on those questions. The possible answers could be very bad for her morale.

She took a shower, dried off with a couple of clean towels, and dressed again in her jeans and T-shirt. Then, once she'd figured how the remote worked, she watched a PBS show on the secret life of emus and then the local news. There had been a gang shooting, a child was missing from home, and there was no more rain in the forecast.

At midday, very early Sarah thought, Mrs. Palmer returned with her lunch tray. The woman laid the tray on top of the dresser and then whispered, "They've all gone with Mr. Azar."

Sarah caught on quickly. "Where is the guard?" she said.

"He stopped off at the bathroom and told me to wait.

But I had the key and brought the tray anyway." Her voice dropped to an urgent whisper again. "If you want to escape from here, now is the time to do it."

Was this a diabolical trap? A new form of torture thought up by Azar?

"Why are you doing this?" Sarah said.

"I heard the guard laugh and tell another man that you were a prisoner, not a guest," Mrs. Palmer said. "He said terrible things about what would happen to you that for shame I dare not repeat." She darted a fearful glance at the door, then added, "I'm a good Christian woman, and I will not see a young lady like you held against her will . . . and . . . and raped."

"Bless you, Mrs. Palmer," Sarah said.

"Look under the napkin," the woman said. "I found that ugly thing here a long time ago and hid it so it would never be used. But God forgive me, maybe you can use it."

Sarah lifted the napkin and revealed a heavy brass knuckle duster, four rings and a rounded palm grip, designed to damage tissue and fracture bones on impact. Used correctly, it was a fearsome weapon, and Sarah overcame her initial revulsion and realized that it was her only hope. She picked up the brass knuckles and slipped her fingers through the rings, aware of the fact that she'd never punched another human being in her entire life. Could she do it now, when her own life was at stake? Butterflies fluttering in her belly, she hoped she could.

"He's coming," Mrs. Palmer said. "Oh, be careful, Miss Milano. I'm so scared."

"That makes two of us," Sarah said.

The guard stopped at the door, looked inside, and then

stepped into the room. "Mrs. Palmer, what's going on here?" he said. "Do you have the key?"

Mrs. Palmer handed over the door key. "This one is a picky eater," she said.

Sarah pretended to be angry. "I don't eat bacon and sausage," she said.

"Then leave it," the guard said. "Mrs. Palmer, take the tray away."

The guard was a young man of medium height and build with a vague accent, Middle Eastern Sarah supposed. There was black stubble on the man's chin, her target area. What she was about to do should never happen to a fellow human being. Then, a quick, angry thought . . . the man had talked about her being raped and raped again, and he'd laughed about it. He didn't deserve any consideration or pity. The guard turned his head slightly to watch Mrs. Palmer pick up the tray and, putting her shoulder into it, Sarah swung at him. She was not a small woman, and she was strong, and the blow from the brass knuckles was devastating. She was sure she heard bones break as the metal rings smashed into the left side of the guard's chin. The man groaned and dropped to his knees. Sarah swung again, this time crashing into his head behind his ear. It was enough. The guard fell on his belly and lay still.

"Is he . . . is he . . ." the black woman said.

"Probably," Sarah said. "I hit him pretty hard." She threw the brass knuckles into a corner.

"Oh, God help us," Mrs. Palmer wailed.

Sarah rolled the man onto his back. Strands of drool trickled from his lips, and she could find no signs of life. Quickly, Sarah searched the guard's pockets and found a set of keys. He had a Ruger LCP .380 in a shoulder holster, and she removed the pistol and stuck it into the waistband of her jeans.

"Mrs. Palmer, we have to rescue Mike Norris," she said. "Do you have the key to his room?"

"It's with the guard's keys," the woman said. "But the man is chained to the wall and only Mr. Azar has the key to his wrist shackles."

"We have to free him somehow," Sarah said. She jangled the keys. "Lead the way, Mrs. Palmer. God help us, we have it to do."

The woman looked at the man on the floor. "What about him?"

"He's dead," Sarah said. "There's nothing we can do for him."

"Oh, sweet Jesus," Mrs. Palmer said, horrified, her hand to her mouth.

CHAPTER 51

Mike Norris sat up in his cot when the door opened and Sarah Milano and Mrs. Palmer stepped inside. "To what do I owe this honor?" he said.

"We're getting you out of here." Sarah said.

"What happened? How come you're here?" Norris said.

Using as few words as possible, Sarah told him about using the brass knuckles to overpower the guard and finding the keys.

"Cory Cantwell taught you well, Miss Milano," Norris said.

"Cory didn't teach me how to kill a man with a knuckleduster," Sarah said. "It's just something you know or you don't."

She tried the chains attached to the steel staple on the timber support beam and then the staple itself. "Maybe I can find a crowbar to loosen this," she said.

"No, it will take too long," Norris said. "Azar and his boys could return at any time. Get out of here while you still can and then call the cops."

"No, not without you," Sarah said. "If Azar gets back before the police arrive, he'll kill you."

"There's a quicker way." Norris said. "We fight fire with fire."

"What do you mean?" Sarah said.

He looked at the black woman. "You, what's your name?"

"I'm Mrs. Palmer." And then with a touch of defiance in her voice, "A good Christian lady."

"Are there cans of gasoline stored in this place, Mrs. Palmer, good Christian lady?"

"Yes, down in the garage. Two or three full cans, I think."

"Sarah, you and Mrs. Palmer bring a couple of those gas cans," Norris said.

"What are you going to do?" Sarah said.

"I'm going to set this support beam alight and when it's good and charred, I'll pull the staple free," Norris said. "That there is bone-dry wood, it will burn really fast."

Sarah shook her head. "No, it's too dangerous. I'll look for a crowbar or a metal rod or something."

"Damn it, woman, I'm a firefighter, remember." Norris said. "I can start a controlled fire in the beam and be out of here before the rest of the place burns down. It's a terrorist nest and needs to be burned to the ground."

"I don't think . . ." Sarah began.

"Do it, woman!" Norris yelled. "The more we talk about it, the greater the likelihood of Azar and his men returning to catch us here. Then we'll both die and probably Mrs. Palmer as well."

"Lord help us," the black woman said. "We'll bring the gas cans."

* * *

The cans of gasoline were in the garage area as Mrs. Palmer said. She and Sarah each grabbed a can, and Sarah found a hacksaw lying on a workbench and took that as well. Maybe Norris could saw through his chains.

"Look at these shackles," Mike Norris said, holding up his arms. "Each link a half inch of stainless steel. I'd be sawing all day and into the night. Fire is better and faster. Watch this."

Norris doused the support beam in gas to about half its height and picked up a red Bic lighter from the table by his cot. He thumbed the lighter into flame and said, "This is all it takes. I'll be out of here in no time." He waved a clanking hand. "Now you two leave and don't look back."

Sarah said, "Mr. Norris . . ."

"Mike."

"Mike. Don't do this. Try the hacksaw," Sarah said.

"I told you, I don't have the time. Azar could arrive at any minute. Now get out of here, both of you." Norris seemed remarkably cheerful. "At first it will be a controlled burn, and I'll be just fine."

Still Sarah was hesitant. "Mike, just stay where you are. When we get out of here, we'll call the police."

"I don't have a cell phone," Mrs. Palmer said. "My pastor doesn't hold with them."

"Then we'll stop the first police car we see," Sarah said. "Mike, it won't be long until you get help."

"Go, both of you," Norris said. "If the fire doesn't work, I'll wait for the law to rescue me." He smiled. "Or Azar to kill me, whatever comes first."

"Mike . . ." Sarah said.

"I'm about to light up this beam, so get the hell out of here," Norris said. "Get as far away from the warehouse as you can."

Mrs. Palmer grabbed Sarah's hand and dragged her from the room. "He means it!"

Sarah turned her head and yelled, "We'll send the police!"

"Yes, do that," Mike Norris said. "Tell them to hurry."

Norris waited until the women were gone and then doused the entire room and his bedding with gasoline, emptying both cans. Then he lit a paper napkin from his breakfast tray and dropped it into the spilled gas. Flames flared immediately. Because of the use of synthetic materials, it can take as little as thirty seconds for a small blaze to become a major fire. Forty years ago, people had fourteen to seventeen minutes to escape a house fire. Today that time has been cut to two to three.

After less than two minutes, the flames intensified, and the temperature in the room rose to 190 degrees. A hot cloud of gray and black smoke deepened below the ceiling and then reached open doorways and stairwells.

Mike Norris's skin began to blister, and he choked on cyanide and carbon monoxide fumes that had now reached 3,400 parts per million. He was beginning to die.

The warehouse had a brick façade and a stone floor, but above that two wood floors separated the levels and helped spread the inferno by two paths . . . direct flame contact and auto-ignition when furnishings and other objects spontaneously burst into flame without being touched by fire. At three minutes and thirty seconds, a flashover occurred in Norris's room. The temperature reached 1,400 degrees and everything in the room burst into flames, including the walls, ceiling . . . and Mike Norris.

He had time to cry out, "Azar! I've won!" before he turned into a blazing human torch and his voice was stilled forever.

Six minutes after Norris had first flicked his Bic, the entire warehouse was engulfed in flames, and all that remained of him was a cinder.

Nasim Azar still an unseen threat, Sarah and Mrs. Palmer ran into the parking lot and drove away. They saw no police cruisers.

CHAPTER 52

Adelia Palmer drove Sarah Milano to her home, a small ranch house in the poorer part of town with a well-kept front lawn surrounding a magnolia tree. While she made tea for them both, Sarah used the woman's landline phone to call the police and then Cory Cantwell.

"My God, Sarah," Cantwell said. "Are you all right?"

"Yes, I'm fine."

"What happened?"

And Sarah told him. Then, "I called the police. I hope they were in time to save Mike Norris."

There was a pause before Cantwell spoke. "Sarah, Mike is dead. He was a firefighter, and he knew that by the time the support beam was charred through enough to pull the chain free, the entire room would be blazing and him with it."

"Cory, but why?" Sarah said.

"He'd sold his soul to the devil, and he realized there was no going back from that. Burning down the warehouse, he got his revenge on Nasim Azar. I'm sure the place is just a pile of blackened timbers by now."

"Then he was a hero," Sarah said. "I mean, in the end."

"Yeah, maybe he was." Cantwell said. "Where are you?" And when Sarah told him Mrs. Palmer's address, he said, "I'll grab a cab and pick you up."

"I'm not going anywhere," Sarah said.

While they drank tea and waited for Cantwell, Sarah said, "Now you're out of a job, Mrs. Palmer."

"I didn't like that job anyway," the woman said. "Well, I did at first when all Mr. Azar did was sell his rugs. But after a while he changed and a lot of strange people used to visit. Not nice people. And he hired a bodyguard, that horrible Salman Assad, and then came Mr. Norris, who scared me." Mrs. Palmer shook her head. "Miss Milano, I think murders were committed in that warehouse, but I was afraid to quit my job, because I'd seen too much and could've been next."

"What will you do now?" Sarah said, helping herself to a chocolate chip cookie.

"There's plenty of jobs in Portland for cleaning and cooking ladies," Mrs. Palmer said. "I won't starve."

"Before I leave, I'll give you my phone number," Sarah said. "Call me if you ever need help." She read reluctance on the black woman's face and said, "Mrs. Palmer, you saved my life. I'll never forget that, or you."

"Then I will, Miss Milano. But I think you and I move in very different circles, so I won't call often." She smiled. "Do you know what you are? You're a Bond girl, like that lovely Diana Rigg lady and all those others."

Sarah laughed and it felt good. "No one's ever called me a Bond girl before."

"Well, you are," Mrs. Palmer said. "And every bit as beautiful as any of them."

* * *

Cory Cantwell asked the cabdriver to go past Azar's warehouse. But the police had closed the road outside because of the fire engines and other emergency vehicles, and they were forced to take a detour.

"From what I could see, looks like there's not much of that place left," the driver said.

"Yeah, looks that way," Cantwell said.

Sarah Milano said nothing, but she seemed troubled, her killing of the guard and the terrible death of Mike Norris weighing on her, as though the shock of what had happened only now hit her.

"I was really worried about you, Sarah," Cantwell said as the cab threaded through the busy streets of downtown Portland.

"I'm so glad you care," Sarah said. Her hand sought his and she clasped it tightly. "Over the past forty-eight hours I thought about you, a lot . . . how I missed you."

Cantwell leaned over and kissed her. "We'll never be separated again," he said.

Sarah smiled. "I hope not. Not ever."

When they returned to the Hilton, Sarah said she should call Jacob Sensor and tell him she was still alive.

"Sarah, I don't want to rain on your parade, but the great man doesn't give a damn," Cantwell said. "He more or less told me you were expendable."

Sarah smiled. "I've always known that. When I first accepted his job offer, I was fully aware of his reputation in government circles. Jacob Sensor would sacrifice his own mother to secure an extra twenty votes in the Senate for one of his projects."

"He wants to be President," Cantwell said.

"And he probably will," Sarah said.

Cantwell then told her about the coming counter-terrorism operation in the Willamette forest, and when he'd finished, he said, "He told me to sit this one out, but it's the day after tomorrow, and I'll be there."

"Sensor is leading the operation, of course?" Sarah said.

"Of course. It's all on him. We're at the height of the tourist season before the fall weather sets in, and the man who saved hundreds of innocent people from fanatical Islamic terrorists . . . well, it's a pretty solid credential for a politician running for the highest office in the land."

"So, should I call him or not?" Sarah said.

"Yeah, call him," Cantwell said. "If nothing else, you'll take a load off his mind, a life-or-death decision he doesn't have to make."

"My life or death," Sarah said.

"Exactly."

Jacob Sensor was overjoyed to hear that Sarah was alive and well, or so he said.

"I'm sure Superintendent Cantwell has told you about the big anti-terrorist operation I'm launching on the eighth. I call it Operation Guts and Glory." Then, a smile in his voice, "Do you like that?"

"Very original, sir," Sarah said.

"Yes, I thought so," Sensor said. "Now, Miss Milano, you make sure Superintendent Cantwell stays put in the hotel. Use all your feminine wiles to keep him there. He's not yet fit for a combat assignment. But I'll make sure a share of the glory is his."

"That's very generous of you, sir," Sarah said.

"I think Cantwell deserves it for what he's done in the past. Oh, I'm being called away. So glad you're back with us safe and sound, Miss Milano."

"Well, what did Sensor say?" Cory Cantwell said.

"He says he's glad to have me back. And he says his attack on the terrorists is called Operation Guts and Glory, and that some of the glory will be yours. Oh, and he told me to use my feminine wiles to keep you here."

"And will you?"

"No. Because I'm going with you."

"Suppose I said you can't?"

"Suppose I said, just try and stop me."

"Then I'd suppose wrong and you'd suppose right."

"I suppose," Sarah said. And she and Cantwell smiled.

CHAPTER 53

Nasim Azar was beside himself with rage.

His warehouse was burned to the ground, a quarter of a million dollars' worth of rare Persian rugs had gone up in smoke, an Islamic brother was missing, and his prisoners . . . he'd no idea if they were alive or dead.

Azar sat in the living room of a safe house in the Lloyd district of downtown Portland with Ibrahim Rahman, the twenty-seven-year-old leader of the Jacks of All Trades terrorist cell. The Jacks were no mere collection of psychopaths, but a group with the clear ideology that they were an important part of the coming apocalypse that would destroy Western civilization, bring about the Caliphate, and return the Islamic world to the seventh century.

"You suffered a grievous loss, my brother," Rahman said. "Let us hope that the infidels died in the flames."

"That is my wish," Azar said. "I've lost everything, all that I held dear."

"You will get your revenge in the Willamette forest," Rahman said. "If Allah blesses you, you will die a martyr with the rest of the mujahideen."

"How many of your brothers are now here in Portland?" Azar said. A stained pizza box with a single piece of gnawed crust lay on the coffee table in front of him.

"Fifty armed warriors. All are devout Islamic brethren who are willing to die to destroy the American devil."

"Allahu Akbar!" Azar said. Then, "You have made your plan, Ibrahim?"

"Yes. I'll show you," Rahman said.

He rose and took something from a desk drawer, swept the pizza box off the table, and spread out a hand-drawn map. "This plan was approved by the great Sheikh Jamari Qadir and his learned council. He said it needs no improvement because it was inspired by Allah. See here, Nasim. This is the Three Pools area of the forest where the infidel families gather." Rahman pointed to an adjoining green patch. "My brothers will start infiltrating the Willamette tonight and tomorrow, and this forest is where we'll gather. We will then attack through the trees and be on the infidels before they know what is happening to them."

"And my men?" Azar said. "Those who will add fire to your sword."

"How many will you bring?"

"Eight, plus myself."

"Then you will set a diversionary fire to attract the forest rangers and keep them away from the three pools. Hopefully the flames will spread quickly and burn fleeing unbelievers."

"The Scorching will kill many, my brother," Azar said. *"Inshallah!"*

"And now, we will have coffee," Rahman said, smiling.

"Your hospitality knows no limits, Ibrahim," Azar said.

"But I must leave you for a while, and I will drink coffee with you and we'll talk more on my return."

"Where will you go?" Rahman said.

"To inspect the ruin of my warehouse," Azar said.

Rahman shook his head. "Nasim, my brother, your words bewilder me. You must put earthly concerns behind you and, as I am doing, prepare yourself for martyrdom. Come, we will pray together."

"When I return, brother," Azar said. "I will pray with you then."

"So, I will await you," Rahman said. "But Nasim, remember this . . . martyrdom is not an end . . . it is a beginning."

"Wise words, Ibrahim," Azar said, as he made for the door.

Nasim Azar drove to the warehouse, a vast heap of ash and charred timbers behind the stone façade that still stood. Red and white-striped barricades and ribbons of yellow plastic with POLICE written on them at intervals had cordoned off the sidewalk and parking lot, probably because the firefighters feared the stonework might collapse. Azar parked at a distance, walked to the ruin, and stood outside the police barrier.

Behind him a car passed and then silence. The air still smelled acrid of smoke.

There was nothing to see except the complete destruction the fire had caused. Had any bodies been recovered? He had no way of knowing. If there had been, the firefighters would have swept up piles of gray ashes and shoveled them into cardboard boxes.

Now Azar felt a deep sorrow. He had so many doubts. So many unanswered questions. But when he returned to his car, his anger flared again. Did the devil Cantwell rescue his woman and then set fire to the place? He dismissed the thought. He could never have found her. She probably died in the fire along with Norris and the guard he'd left in charge. Mrs. Palmer had no doubt already gone home and missed the whole thing. Well, now she was out of a job.

Azar hated uncertainty, and he cursed Sarah Milano. Had the whore died? He wished Allah could lean down from paradise and tell him.

His heart as heavy as an anvil, he had one more stop to make. He drove to the Hilton hotel on Southwest 6th Avenue and parked in the lot, facing the door. He had no intention of attacking the man, but he had a glimmering hope that he might catch a glimpse of Cantwell grieving for his kidnapped woman. Then an amusing thought. He could yell, "Hey, your whore burned to death!" And then drive away. The devil Cantwell would be left to grieve for the rest of his life without ever learning the truth.

But Cory Cantwell did not appear, and after an hour Azar drove away. He had more important matters that needed his attention.

CHAPTER 54

"I didn't authorize an attack on the Willamette National Forest in Oregon," the President said. She was nearly fifty years old, but her fingernails were long and pointed and colored bright red, as though she'd just clawed a small animal to death. She was dumpy and angry, like the Queen of Hearts in *Alice in Wonderland,* and Jacob Sensor feared that she wanted his head.

"An oversight, Madam President," Sensor said.

"An oversight? How can you overlook an attack on a national forest with helicopter gunships and a battalion of troops?"

"Helicopters armed with machine guns, not gunships per se, and a reinforced company of troops, not a battalion."

"Jacob, don't bandy words with me," the President said. "When you masterminded this affair, you overstepped your authority."

"The operation will be led by myself and my Regulators," Sensor said. "That's why I considered it was in my bailiwick."

"The Pentagon is furious, and there's a possibility that

Brigadier General Stuart will be court-martialed. My God, man, Guts and Glory. Did you really think you could keep it a secret?"

Sensor sounded bitter. "Someone blabbed. Who was it?"

"I don't know," the President said. "It could've been anybody from a guy who services the helicopters to the general himself. A major attack on terrorists on American soil is a hard thing to keep a secret."

"If you call off the operation now, can you live with the consequences?" Sensor said.

"No, I could not. You're sure of your intelligence in this matter?"

"One hundred percent. The terrorist attack is scheduled for the eighth."

"The day after tomorrow."

Sensor nodded. "Exactly. We don't have much time."

For greater secrecy, he and the President sat in his poky little office in the Capitol, so close that Sensor, who was something of an expert on how alpha women smelled, identified her perfume as Bond No 9.

"I'll smooth things over with the army brass, most of them are Republicans anyway," the President said. "As their commander in chief, I will take full responsibility for Operation Guts and Glory."

There was a triumphant gleam in the President's eyes that Sensor did not like. "And reap all the credit, if it is a success," the President said

"And if it fails, and hundreds of civilians die?" Sensor asked.

The President was silent, but her wide mouth stretched in a smile as she stared fixedly at Sensor. He thought she looked like a dragoness.

"No, not me," he said.

"I think you'd better start planning your exit strategy, Jacob."

"Oh, please, this is foolish talk. Guts and Glory is aimed at destroying the terrorist enemy. It's not a political football to kick around. In any case, it won't fail. Our attack force is too strong."

"Then pray that it doesn't fail, or you will fail with it, Jacob," the President said. "The day after the attack, I'll address the nation on TV and tell the people of the United States what happened and how I saved the day. I think it will be a great boost for my reelection chances, don't you?"

Ambitions popping like bubbles in his head, Sensor said, "Yes, I'm sure it will."

"I'm so glad you agree," the President said.

Sensor tried to salvage something, anything, from this disaster. "I want my Regulators to lead the attack," he said.

"Then talk to General Stuart about it," the President said. "That is, if I can save his job."

"I'll be with them," Sensor said. "The Regulators, I mean."

"Then good for you, Jacob. You're very brave. In the cannon's mouth. That's the kind of dedication that draws my warmest gratitude. I'm sure you'll do very well." The President rose to her feet. "No, don't get up. I have to go and get into some cussin' and discussin' with the army brass."

The President left, and the sultry scent of Bond No. 9 lingered in the room.

* * *

Jacob Sensor sat back in his leather office chair and lit a cigar, thinking.

The President's decision to take credit for Guts and Glory was a setback, but one he could overcome. He'd think of something, something big. The trouble was that big ideas were hard to come by. But he'd set his sights on the presidency, and by God he was going to get there by fair means or foul. He smiled. He could always organize a coup. Maybe use the Ukrainian again, if the man hadn't gone to ground somewhere.

Well, it was a drastic plan, maybe a little too ambitious but one worth thinking about.

CHAPTER 55

Adnan Malouf, born in Syria, raised in the United States, radicalized in Iran, was in command of the first twenty Jacks of All Trades to penetrate the Willamette National Forest using moonlight and a map to find their way in almost total darkness. Two black Ford panel vans had come as close as they could to the Three Pools area, and they'd walked the rest of the distance.

All the mujahideen wore dark T-shirts, jeans, and desert boots, and each carried an AK-47 and a bandolier of extra magazines. All believed that martyrdom was a necessary and essential part of any terrorist act, and they were ready to embrace death like a long-lost brother. *Shahadat*, martyrdom, would also bear witness to their faith in Allah and Islam and assure their place in paradise.

Malouf told them, "The death of each martyr brings new, vigorous life to the jihad. Martyrdom, my brothers, is the most powerful weapon in our armory."

And as the President said later in a TV interview, "There's no reasoning with people like that. All you can do is kill them."

Malouf had sent fourteen of his men into the trees, the

other six to the parking lot behind the Three Pools. He said, "The infidel mob will flee from our gunfire and seek refuge in their cars. But you six men will be ready for them and cut them to pieces."

One of the mujahideen, a teenager, years younger than the rest, said, "Will there be fire?"

"Yes, the forests will be set ablaze as a distraction," Malouf said. "We will pray that the flames devour many infidels as they run hither and thither in panic."

No sacrifice was too great for his warriors of Islam. Malouf warned them they'd have to remain hidden among the trees for the rest of that night and all of the next day. Each carried a canteen of water, and that's all they would have. On no account were they to stand up or even crawl. "You must remain still, unmoving as statues," Malouf said. "If you need to relieve yourself, do it where you lie." He held his rifle aloft and said, "Allahu Akbar!"

The others joined in the Allahu Akbar shout, overjoyed that they had such a strong leader and that more mujahideen were on the way and ecstatic that they would soon enter the gates of paradise.

Throughout the night, the remaining Jacks arrived, led by Ibrahim Rahman. Nasim Azar had elected to enter the forest on the morning of the eighth with his men, bringing with them gasoline and drip torches

"After tonight it is unlikely that we'll meet again except in paradise," Azar said before Rahman departed the safe house. "May Allah protect you."

"I have just recited the ninety-nine beautiful names of Allah, may he be exalted, so the path to paradise lies open before me," Rahman said. "You should do the same, brother Nasim."

"I will," Azar said. "It will bring me strength."

Rahman wore a T-shirt and jeans and a ball cap. His AK-47 lay on the table along with a bandolier of ammunition. He had a triangular scar on his right cheekbone that made him look sinister. In fact, he'd acquired it after a clash of heads during a high school soccer game. He was thirty-five years old and came from a wealthy family. The gold and diamond Rolex on his left wrist was real.

"I must go now," Rahman said. "Perhaps you will hear that I died well. Do not fail to light the fires that will burn the unbelievers."

"Depend on it," Azar said. "I will not let you down."

Rahman picked up his rifle and bandolier and stepped to the door. "Farewell, my friend," he said. "We'll meet soon in paradise."

After the man left, Azar sat in the chair just vacated by Rahman and buried his face in his hands. His resolve was wavering. Many times in the past, without a second thought, he'd sent young men, suicide bombers, to their deaths with his blessing. But the eagerness for martyrdom from Ibrahim Rahman and his mujahideen . . . and from his own men . . . scared him.

Nasim Azar realized that he didn't wish to die a martyr for Allah. He wanted to live to a ripe old age when all his enemies were dead.

He stood and looked around him at the rental apartment. It was a seedy place with worn furniture, ragged carpets, and a constant smell of boiled onions. His own comfortable apartment was now ashes, but he had money in the bank, and his sponsors in the Middle East would send him more. He could buy another apartment. One thing was certain, the way his fellow Islamists lived . . . and died . . . did not interest him.

He would still take an active part in the jihad. Death to America! But he no longer wanted to die for it. Perhaps when he was much older, he'd think about martyrdom again. He recalled Corky Jackson . . . but not now when he was in the prime of life with too many enemies still alive. The devil Cory Cantwell for one.

CHAPTER 56

The late-summer sun filtering through the trees was hot, and the mujahideen were suffering. It was still only two in the afternoon but their bodies cramped from their enforced stillness, and fat blue flies and mosquitoes tormented them constantly. Pain brought symptoms of stress, headaches, or light-headedness, and mutters of complaint began to be heard among the younger men. They had to endure the remainder of the day and another night of this torture.

Ibrahim Rahman slowly and carefully rolled onto his back, and he stared at the blue sky beyond the tree canopy. The birds had shunned this part of the forest, but the buzzing, biting insects had made it their own.

"My brothers," Rahman said, in a hoarse whisper loud enough to be heard by the others. "Soon you will embrace the martyrdom you seek. The infidels will send police by the hundreds against you, and you will rejoice when you receive the final bullet." He paused, then said. "Your mothers and fathers will be enraptured when they hear of your sacrifice. Oh, how they will dance in the streets and glorify you."

Whispers of *"Allahu Akbar"* sounded among the pines.

"Not tonight, but the next night, you will be in paradise, and seventy-two virgin maidens will cater to your every need," Rahman said. He tried a little joke. "And I mean your *every* need."

This brought a round of subdued laughter.

"Now rest, my brothers," Rahman said. "Spend your time in prayer, and ask Allah to bless all your endeavors come the morrow."

A silence fell on the forest again, and the mujahideen suffered still.

"The coffee is to your liking?" Nasim Azar said.

The eight young men around the table nodded in unison.

Azar looked at the earnest faces, eight American-born youths who'd taken different paths to radicalization but ended at the same destination . . . jihad and the rise of the Caliphate. "Tonight you will purchase gas cans and fill them with fuel," Azar said. "As you know our other equipment burned in the warehouse fire and, alas, we must be content with what we can buy."

"Our sympathies to you, master," one of the young men said. Like the others he looked of Middle Eastern descent, but there were millions of Muslims in the United States, and his appearance did not draw much attention from unbelievers.

"My loss is of no account," Azar said. "My mind is no

longer on material things but on the jihad and my own coming martyrdom tomorrow."

"Allahu Akbar," the youths said, grinning, slapping one another on the back. This was a cause for celebration. The master thought the same way as they did.

Parroting Ibrahim Rahman, Azar said, "Remember, all of you, that martyrdom is not an end, it's a beginning. That's how we must think of it."

"The master is wise," one of the young men said, and Azar smiled and bowed his head in acknowledgment.

"Now, who has the map of the Willamette forest?" he said.

Azar spread the map on the table. "You have all studied this?" he said.

All the young men said that they had.

"Good." He pointed with his manicured finger. "There is the Three Pools recreation area that will be attacked by the brave soldiers of the Jacks of All Trades. But here, to the west, is heavy forest. As you can see, the tree line borders an open patch of ground. It is along that line"—Azar stabbed his finger into the trees—"that you will start the fire."

"Are we a part of the great Scorching that will soon set ablaze every forest in this country?" a young man with serious black eyes said. "I have heard of such a thing."

"Yes, it is real, and we are a part of it," Azar said. "And the faithful will praise your martyrdom for a thousand years."

"Allahu Akbar!" the man yelled.

"When does our attack on the forest begin tomorrow?" the serious man said.

"Tonight you will enter the forest under the cover of darkness and be ready to start the fires at ten in the morning when there will be plenty of people in the Willamette's Three Pools area," Azar said. "Use a good quantity of gasoline and make sure the trees are blazing. You have guns to engage the infidel police when they come?"

The eight terrorists drew handguns from various parts of their bodies, small, concealable .380s and 9mm pistols mostly. Only one of the young men carried a .38 revolver.

"This is well," Azar said smiling. "Truly, you are warriors of Islam."

"Master, you talk to us and give us orders as though you won't be in the forest with us," one of the men said, frowning.

"I'll be there, but a little later," Azar said. "I have some things that need my attention early tomorrow." He smiled. "Never fear, when it's time to do battle with the infidel, I'll be standing shoulder to shoulder with you."

That seemed to be enough for the young mujahideen, and no further mention was made concerning Azar's early-morning absence. He was relieved. Since he had no intention to be anywhere near the Willamette tomorrow, further explanation could have been awkward, and an accusation of traitor would be followed closely by a bullet.

"I see no need to talk longer," Azar said. He smiled. "I'm older than you young warriors, and I grow weary."

The men rose as one and file out the door and one stopped and said, "Until tomorrow."

"Yes," Azar said. "Until tomorrow. A great day for all of us."

Three criteria define the hypocrite: Whenever he

speaks, he lies. Whenever he promises, he breaks his promise. Whenever he is trusted, he breaks that trust.

Nasim Azar was guilty of all three, and he knew it. But he would do or say whatever it took to stay alive. Unlike the young mujahideen, his life was too important to be thrown away like yesterday's garbage.

CHAPTER 57

At 7 A.M. sharp, the six people packed into the Toyota rental were waved into the Air National Guard base at Portland International Airport, but only after Sarah Milano invoked the name Jacob Sensor and the airman at the gate made a call to someone higher up in the 142nd Fighter Wing command chain.

Sarah was directed to a narrow road that led to an open, grassy area half a mile to the west of the F-15 fighter complex. The arching sky was blue, cloudless, and there was no wind. The cool morning promised to become a warm and bright day, and as she drove Sarah fancied that the tourists would already be heading into the Willamette. She had butterflies doing somersaults in her stomach again.

"There's Sensor talking to a soldier," Cory Cantwell said. "Sarah, park beside the other cars."

Sarah pulled into a space beside Sensor's rented limo, silver in color and about a block long, and she and the others got out of the Toyota and waited until the five men buckled on their pistols. The Wildfire Service had provided the Glocks, but no ammunition or gun leather.

Sarah had remedied that by buying ammo, belts, and Kydex holsters for Pete Kennedy and the three Brits. The SAS men, used to air bases, showed little interest as they walked with Cantwell and the others toward three Bell Venom helicopters, each armed with a pair of M60D 7.62 mm machine guns, and two Chinook personnel carriers.

Cantwell and the others wore the olive green of the National Wildfire Service, but Sarah was in T-shirt and jeans and a pair of flats from the seemingly bottomless depths of her small suitcase. She carried her briefcase with the Colt Python inside.

Sensor frowned when he saw Cory Cantwell, but he smiled as he introduced Brigadier General Stuart. He said to Sarah, "Come to see us off, Miss Milano?"

"No. I'm going with you," Sarah said.

"I think not," Sensor said. "I don't want to risk you getting hurt."

"I'm a Regulator in everything but name," Sarah said. "I'll take my chances."

"You've already gone through a terrible ordeal, Sarah," Sensor said, using her first name for the first time ever. "I don't want to put you through another. This could be a nasty fight."

Sarah met Sensor's eyes and held her stare as though it was a weapon. "I've already been in a couple of nasty fights," she said. "I plan on going with Superintendent Cantwell and the others. I'll stow away on a Chinook if I have to."

Sensor was the first to look away. "Suit yourself." He looked a question at General Stuart, who said, "Captain

Buck Miller is in command of the Chinooks. You'd best talk to him about joining his soldiers."

"I'll be in one of the Chinooks," Sensor said. "It would be good if we all flew in the same helicopter." He turned to Stuart. "Excuse me, General," he said. "I'll talk to Captain Miller."

The soldier nodded and then said, "We move out at 0930 hours."

"We'll be ready," Sensor said. He stepped away from Stuart and spoke to Cantwell. "I've already lost a battle to Miss Milano and don't want to start another. I suppose there's no point in me ordering you to stay out of this one."

"Not at all. I'm going with my Regulators."

"I thought so," Sensor said. "Well, introduce me to your merry men."

Cantwell did, starting with Pete Kennedy, who seemed genuinely excited to be a part of the attack. The three Brits were old hands at this kind of operation, used to addressing senior officers, and they said all the right things. *A piece of cake, sir. Eager to get to grips with the enemy, sir. We will do our duty, sir.*

And this pleased Jacob Sensor enormously, and he was grinning like a Cheshire cat as he led the others toward Captain Miller and the Chinooks. Sensor was still smarting at the President's intention to take credit for Guts and Glory, if it was an unqualified success. But even at this late date, Sensor hoped he could deflect some of the glory onto himself. Maybe he'd lead a charge or something. No, not that. Leading charges was hardly his style. But a way might show itself during the battle. He could only hope and pray.

Captain Buck Miller was in full combat gear, including a helmet with the new Operational Camouflage Pattern cover. He carried an M4 carbine and a SIG Sauer M18 pistol and he looked capable, able to handle anything thrown his way. He had blue, analytic eyes that could and did unsettle civilians and a clipped, direct way of talking.

Used to women soldiers, Miller raised no objection to Sarah Milano's presence.

"You Regulators will ride in a Chinook and deploy with the infantry," the officer said. He called out, "Sergeant Baker!" A tall, well-built black soldier stepped to Miller's side and saluted. "This is Sergeant Cameron Baker," Miller said. "When we land you will stay close to him at all times. Is that clear?"

"Sergeant Baker is taking us under his wing," Pete Kennedy said, smiling.

"Yes, he is," Miller said. "Sergeant Baker, you will take good care of them."

"I will, sir," Baker said. "Any of you gentlemen been in combat before?"

Kennedy and the former SAS men said they had.

"Then you know the drill," Baker said. "Stay close to me, do as I say, and we'll all come out of this alive. We move out at 0930."

Jacob Sensor had listened to Sergeant Baker and when the soldier left, he said, "Attention everybody. A couple of reporters, war correspondents really, will be in the other Chinook, and I've decided to fly with them. If I don't see you until this is all over, I wish you the best of luck."

His smile had all the warmth of a Florida alligator's grin. "Don't let the Regulators down, gentlemen and lady."

Cory Cantwell watched tough, highly trained, and fully equipped troops file into the Chinooks and told himself that six people armed with handguns were hardly going to get a chance to cover themselves in glory. Especially with the slightly intimidating Sergeant Baker acting as mother hen.

But he said what Sensor wanted to hear. "We won't let you down, sir."

"Good, good," Sensor said. Then, slapping his hands together, "This is going to be a great day."

The wind blew his white hair over his forehead, and Sarah Milano thought he looked like Julius Caesar about to cross the Rubicon.

CHAPTER 58

The morning was warm, pleasant, no wind to speak of, clouds floating in the baby blue sky like lilies in a pond. The air smelled of pine and slightly of the dust kicked up by the wheels of Forest Service vehicles on the back roads. The silence was profound, almost sacred, birdsong from the trees the only incursion.

Visitors were already flocking to the park, escaping the heat of nearby urban localities, and the Three Pools area was filling up fast with young families determined to enjoy a mix of sun and water the whole long day.

West of the pools, eight young men stood at the edge of a mixed pine and fir forest. Behind them, honeysuckle, cranberry, and cat's ear bloomed in a grassy meadow about a hundred acres in extent, crossed by a stream that meandered among rocks and gravel banks.

It was after nine-thirty, and the young men were concerned. Where was Nasim Azar, their mentor and leader? The drip torches were ready and several cans of gasoline had been stashed in the trees. All was prepared for the great conflagration that would destroy the infidels fleeing the slaughter at the Three Pools.

"Perhaps he will not come," one of the young men said.

"He may be ill," said another.

"He will come," said a third. "He seeks a glorious martyrdom as fervently as we do."

The others nodded and said this indeed must be the case.

Nasim Azar will appear very soon, they said.

But that would not be the case . . .

Ten minutes passed and then came the slow realization . . . Nasim Azar was not coming. The traitor had chosen life over martyrdom. He'd disdained Paradise and embraced *Jahannam* . . . an eternity of fire in in the Seventh Level of Hell.

The young men talked among themselves and made the decision to cleanse themselves of the betrayer's demons. They would set the forest afire and perish in the flames as glorious martyrs.

Using gasoline and drip torches, they set blazes along the tree line. Pines quickly became columns of fire, and plumes of black smoke rose skyward. The young men exalted to see the destruction they'd wrought. Surely Allah looked down on the flames and smiled.

Then disaster. The devilish infidel hordes descended upon them.

The unmistakable rattling racket of helicopters drawing nearer sent the eight young men running from the trees into the meadow where they could get a better look at the sky. A Venom swooped in and turned broadside to give the man standing behind its machine gun a clear field of fire. The gun cut loose with a sound of a squealing hog in a slaughterhouse. A stream of 7.62 mm rounds tore into the men on the ground like a buzz saw and chopped five of them down in the first pass. The other three ran deeper into the meadow in headlong flight, away from the Venom and its terrifying gun. One of the terrorists stopped, pointed his pistol at the Venom, fired, and earned his martyrdom. The machine gunner was good, well-trained, his skill honed by five tours in Afghanistan, and as the other Venoms and the Chinooks flew over his helicopter, he dropped the shooter where he stood.

The other two saw their brother fall and decided to stop running and make their fight as befitted Muslim warriors. Both drew their weapons and fired on the hovering chopper. Several .380 rounds ticked through the thin aluminum skin of the Venom, and one of their bullets nicked the pilot's right arm, drawing blood. But then the machine gun shrieked again and cut down both terrorists in a hail of bullets.

One of the young men, a twenty-two-year-old from an upscale Portland suburb, his body all but cut in half by a dozen bullets, lived long enough to realize that he and the others had been betrayed by Nasim Azar. That realization didn't make his agonized dying any easier.

Ibrahim Rahman heard the approaching helicopters, but he didn't realize he was under attack until a hailstorm of lead rattled through the tree canopy and hammered some of the young mujahideen into the ground where they lay. Others cried out in fright and ran around like terrified chickens fleeing a fox, trying to escape the lethal hail of bullets and the resulting carnage of blood and brains.

Bullets kicking up dirt around him, showering him with twigs and pine needles, Rahman rose to his feet. He caught fleeting glances at the two Venom helicopters circling the stand of trees and yelled at the surviving Jacks to stand fast and fire at the helicopters.

"Use your rifles. Kill the pilots," he yelled.

Rahman's voice steadied the surviving mujahideen, and at least a dozen shouldered their AK-47s and returned the chopper's fire. A man close to Rahman let out a terrible gurgling scream as he took a round to the face, smashing it to a red pulp like a strawberry pie dropped on a bakehouse floor.

The young terrorist fell, and Rahman's voice took on an edge as he yelled louder, "The pilots. Aim for the pilots."

The Venoms flitted above the tree canopy like giant dragonflies, their machine guns still shrieking death. Then someone, probably Rahman, scored a hit.

The cockpit of one of the helicopters rose and suddenly greasy black smoke belched from its engine compartment. The rotors still turned but with a rough, chattering sound as the Venom pulled away, out of the fight, a dead soldier slumped behind his machine gun.

"Allahu Akbar!" Rahman screamed as the stricken chopper fluttered away like a bird with a broken wing.

He looked around him, quickly counting heads. Eighteen men still standing. No, now just sixteen as two fell under the surviving Venom's raking fire. He had to act fast while there were still enough of the faithful left to kill people at the Three Pools.

Rahman held his rifle aloft and called out, "Brothers! Follow me!"

He and the others ran from the forest that had become a charnel house of bloody bodies torn apart by machine-gun fire. Rahman's grim face was splashed with other men's blood. Now it was time to make the infidels pay. As fire engines wailed in the distance, he led the muja-hideen toward the Three Pools. They would gun the un-believers, men, women and children, down like sheep and the bright waters would soon turn red with infidel blood.

But then Ibrahim Rahman's heart sank. A line of sol-diers blocked his path to the pools area, and they fired steadily as they advanced though the trees.

As men dropped around him, Rahman got off a few shots with his AK-47 before it ran dry. He threw the rifle aside and pulled a Beretta from the holster at his waist and fired at a crusader he took to be an officer. The 9mm bullet hit the man in the chest, but the round was stopped by the ceramic plates of the bulletproof tactical vest, and the solder staggered a little but then kept on coming. It was that officer, a second lieutenant named Dave Monroe, who gunned Rahman. He hit him hard. Three bullets slammed into the terrorist's body and dropped him to his knees. Blood salty in his mouth, Rahman looked around him and saw that all of his men were martyred, but for a few wounded crawling across the sun-dappled forest floor. But a few of the solders also lay on the ground, dead or wounded.

"Allahu Akbar!" Rahman yelled.

More American bullets smashed into him, and he fell dead, his face in the dirt.

* * *

The remaining Chinook disembarked its contingent of soldiers on open ground near the parking lot behind the Three Pools. It was here that the only civilian casualties occurred as dozens of panicked visitors fled the shooting in the forest and dashed for their vehicles. They ran headlong into the six terrorists who were there waiting for them.

As the visitors appeared, the Jacks cut loose with their AK-47s and the ambushed civilians took heavy casualties. Terrified people sought refuge behind cars or fled back to the forest. A twenty-eight-year-old woman was killed as she tried to get into her car, and her six-year-old son was wounded in both legs. An elderly couple, confused about what was happening, stopped in the middle of the lot, looking around, unsure of what to do next. They both died in a hail of terrorist bullets, as did ten other people—three men, five women and two children.

The timely arrival of soldiers from the 40th Infantry Division prevented any further civilian slaughter in the parking lot. The troops charged out of their Chinook and deployed quickly, advancing in line as they swept the lot with fire. Five of the six terrorists were hunted down like rats, rousted from their hiding places and shot down. Surrender was not an option, especially after a soldier was killed by a sniper. The last of them, a Syrian national allowed into Los Angeles as a refugee, chose a suicide attack and charged the troops, his AK-47 blasting lead. It was later determined that the man had a total of twenty-six bullets in his body when he fell. As one sergeant said, "In the space of about ten seconds we killed him twenty-six times."

CNN TV News later reported that Al-Qaeda and the

Brothers of the Islamic Jihad took credit for the attack on the Willamette National Forest.

Cory Cantwell, Sarah Milano, and the others were aboard the Chinook that launched the infantry attack on Ibrahim Rahman's men in the pine forest. But they took no part in the action. Obviously following orders, Sergeant Cameron Baker kept them in the helicopter until the firing stopped.

"Sorry you couldn't go in with the infantry, but you were deemed to be a liability," Baker said. His smile was apologetic. "That was not my opinion, but the opinion of others."

Pete Kennedy looked a little put out, but the SAS took the news in stride. "Sergeant, don't you worry about all that," Frank West said. "If the attack had gone all to hell, we were prepared to go in and save the day."

"Truer words were never spoke," Nigel Brown said.

"Save the day SAS, that's us," Daniel Grant said.

"I'm sure General Stuart will be relieved to hear that," Sergeant Baker said.

CHAPTER 59

Cory Cantwell asked Sarah Milano if she felt up to looking for Nasim Azar among the bodies of eight dead pyroterrorists. "Of course," she said. "It would be good to know that murderer is dead."

But Azar was not one of them. Nor did any of the other dead terrorists match the description Sarah gave of the man.

"He chickened out on his own men," Sarah said. "I guess he didn't want to die a martyr for Islam after all."

"We'll find him," Cantwell said. "It may take time, but we'll find him. We found Osama bin Laden, we'll find Nasim Azar." Then, "Look, here comes our boss looking down in the dumps."

Jacob Sensor walked past the Chinook parked in the middle of the meadow, its helmeted aircrew standing around talking, waiting for orders now that the action was over and the gunsmoke had cleared.

He spoke to Cantwell. "Glad to see you are all alive and well."

Cantwell smiled. "We never left the helicopter."

"Nor did I," Sensor said. "Me and the two reporters

were kept inside until the shooting stopped." He moodily kicked at a wildflower bloom with the polished toe of his Berluti oxford and said, "Well, at least we got Sarah back in one piece. That's always something, huh?"

"Yeah," Cantwell said. "That's always something."

"Sixty pyroterrorists dead, three killed and five wounded on our side and a few civilians, and only twenty acres of forest burned, and I imagine the President is already taking the credit," Sensor shook his head. "There's no justice, is there?"

Cantwell made no answer, and Sensor said, "Well, the Regulators were here."

"The army classified us as a liability," Cantwell said.

"I don't care what the army classifies. We were here. Today. That's what matters," Sensor said.

"Here today, gone tomorrow," Cantwell said.

"No, Superintendent Cantwell, the Regulators are here to stay," Sensor said. "This action today is not the end of the war on pyroterrorism, it's only the beginning. The opening salvo in what's destined to be a long battle." He read the hesitation in Cantwell's face and said, "I still want you to be a part of it."

Police and emergency vehicles wailed in the distance, come to preside over the hurting dead, and the morning slowly began to mature into a warm, golden day.

"Where do we go from here?" Cantwell said.

"You and Miss Milano will stay here in Portland and recruit your Regulators from here," Sensor said. "After today's success, I can get the President to release the funds to build an office block with living quarters and a helipad and firing range attached. It's time to get very serious about this Regulator thing. I want a hundred trained people within the next twelve months. Can you do it, Superintendent Cantwell?"

"You mean can Sarah and I do it?" Cantwell said.

"Yes, you are a team," Sensor said.

"And we intend to stay that way," Sarah said. "We won't be apart again."

Sensor smiled. "Do I sense love in the air?"

"Yes, you do," Sarah said. "It came as a big surprise to both of us."

"Damn right it did," Cantwell said. "And it was the best thing that ever happened to me."

"Good. I'm very happy for you both. You're wonderful young people. Now, can you give me my hundred Regulators?"

"Yes, we can," Sarah said.

"Mr. Cantwell?" Sensor said.

"Yes, we can do it," Cantwell said. "There's something I've come to believe in very strongly, and it was Sarah's kidnapping that drove the lesson home. Evil exists in this world, and evil people can't be reasoned with. They can only be destroyed. I feel no sympathy for terrorists. We have to rid the world of them, and the Regulators can do their part and end the real threat of attacks on our nation's forests. And now I'm all though speechifying."

"Bravo!" Sensor said. "Well said. I have the feeling that the safety of forests like the Willamette will be in good hands. How is the shoulder, Superintendent?"

"It's all right," Cantwell said. "I think the bullet cured my arthritis."

"Glad to hear you're recovering," Sensor said. "Ah, there is General Stuart. I must congratulate him." He smiled. "Well, so long for a while, you two lovebirds. I'll stay in touch."

Pete Kennedy and the three Brits waited until Sensor left before they approached Sarah and Cantwell. In the distance voices were raised as the dead were carried out from among the trees and taken to ambulances. The Three Pools area was almost deserted, most people deciding that they'd had enough excitement for one day.

"Jacob Sensor talked to us," Pete Kennedy said. "He says he'll talk to the British authorities about having our three SAS men on permanent loan."

"Suits us," Frank West said. "We like it here." He was chewing on a stem of grass. "Of course, the United States immigration people might have something to say about that."

"I hope we can clear it with them," Cantwell said. "I really need you three hoodlums."

"We haven't done much," Dan Grant said.

"Except sit around and drink your booze," Nigel Brown said.

"Once the Regulators are fully operational, you'll have plenty to do," Cantwell said.

"I have a feeling Jacob Sensor will see to that," Kennedy said.

Cantwell nodded. "He will. If he isn't in jail."

"He won't be," Sarah said. "Put Sensor in jail and he'll sing like a canary. By the time he finished talking you'd have to lock up most of the government and half the intelligence departments."

Pete Kennedy seemed puzzled by this talk. "Do you two know something about Sensor I don't?" he said.

"Yeah, and we'll tell you about it sometime, that is if you don't find out for yourself," Cantwell said.

The Venom helicopters chattered westward, heading for the airport, and troops were filing into the Chinook, leaving it to the Portland police and fire department to do the cleanup.

"I have an idea," Sarah said. "We take the helicopter back to the Air National Guard base and pick up our car."

"And then?" Kennedy said.

"And then we drive to the Hilton and prop up the bar for an hour or maybe three," Sarah said.

Frank West's face broke into a wide grin. "Miss Milano, you're a lady after my own heart," he said.

"And mine," Cory Cantwell said.

CHAPTER 60

Jacob Sensor sat in front of his fire, drinking single-malt whisky and remembering what had happened. The anti-terrorist action had gone to plan, and only the ending was screwed up. Instead of the glory and fame that was rightfully his, the President had claimed it all. Her plan. Her determination to end the pyroterrorism menace. Her presence at the airport, wishing the troops *bonne chance* as she watched them leave. Her raw power bid for another term.

And for Jacob Sensor. Nada. Not even a mention. Not so much as a crumb.

It was unfair. So damned unfair.

Firelight cast a crimson glow on the walls of his darkened library and the *tick-tock-tick* of the grandfather clock in the hallway was loud in the silence. His phone rang.

"How are you, my old friend?" Sir Anthony Bickford-Scott said.

"Are you here to commiserate?" Sensor said. "My fortunes are at a low ebb."

"Yes, I watched the President on TV," Bickford-Scott

said. "She took all the credit for Guts and Glory. Didn't she, old chap?"

"Bitch," Sensor said. "Two-timing bitch. Sir Anthony, there's no honesty and plain dealing left in this world."

"A very unfortunate turn of events," the Englishman said. "My staff at the British Embassy are appalled."

"And with good reason," Sensor said. "I laid my life on the line in the Willamette, and what do I get in return? Nothing. The cold shoulder. Jacob who?"

"Oh, my dear friend, how awful for you," Bickford-Scott said.

"I don't need sympathy to make me feel better, Anthony," Sensor said. "I need revenge."

After a long pause, Bickford-Scott said, "There is something . . ."

"What is it?" Sensor said.

"I hesitate to mention it," the Englishman said.

"Mention it," Sensor said. "Don't keep me in suspense."

"It involves the Russians."

"Damn, I hate the Russians. Always meddling in my affairs," Sensor said.

"This comes down from Vladimir Putin himself," Bickford-Scott said. "The stakes are high, Jacob. Very high."

"I don't trust Putin," Sensor said. "He's a snake in the grass."

"It's an insertion, Jacob," Bickford-Scott said.

"Where?"

"Haiti."

"What kind of insertion?" Sensor said.

"No troops, no ships, no planes. Only advisers."

"Advising on what?" Sensor said. A log fell in the fireplace and sent up a scarlet shower of sparks.

"A deepwater port at Le Mole St. Nicolas," Bickford-Scott said.

"How deep?" Sensor said.

"Deep enough for an aircraft carrier task force."

"Hell, Tony, that's on the west coast about . . ."

"Fifty-five nautical miles from Cuba, give or take."

"So, Russian carriers on our doorstep, you mean," Sensor said.

"Eventually," Bickford-Scott said. "Of course, with the port goes the usual nonsense about bringing food and medical aid to the Haitian people."

"What's Putin's deal?" Sensor said.

"A ten percent reduction in nuclear warheads in time for the next presidential election."

"She'll never go for it. Congress won't go for it, and there will be saber-rattling."

"You have to smooth it over, Jacob," Bickford-Scott said. "As far as the United States government is concerned, all the Russians want is to build a deepwater port to help alleviate the suffering of the poor Haitians. A port for trade purposes only, Jacob. Make it clear that Putin has no warlike intentions."

"But he does, obviously," Sensor said.

"You know that, I know that, but no one else needs to know it," the Englishman said. "It will be years before the Mole St. Nicolas port is ready to accept carriers." Bickford-Scott laughed. "Jacob, we could all be dead by then."

"In the meantime, if I can swing this for the Russians without starting a war, what's in it for me?" Sensor said.

"A recently built, million-dollar dacha fifteen miles from downtown Moscow in the posh Rublevka district, a stone's throw away from Putin's own dwelling," Bickford-Scott said. "You will also get the credit for bringing Vlad to the nuclear disarmament negotiating table and that can only help your future presidential aspirations."

Sensor took time to light a cigar and then said, "The port thing can be done, Anthony. Yes, and by God, I'll do it."

"Jolly good show," Bickford-Scott said. "And there's icing on the cake, old boy. Haiti exports more than half the world's vetiver oil, used to make very expensive perfumes. The Russians will pressure the Haitian government to make sure that you get a substantial cut of those profits as a retainer while you work for their interests."

"The deal gets better and better," Sensor said.

"Of course, you'll be taking bread out of the mouths of Haitian children, Jacob," the Englishman said. "Will that hamper your efforts on Russia's behalf?"

"Whether or not Haitian children eat is hardly my problem," Sensor said. "Getting a deepwater port for Russia is."

"Jacob, you're such a wonderfully remorseless man," Bickford-Scott said. "If you weren't there already, I'd say you'll go far. Oh, hold on a moment, Jacob. My cat wants up on my lap. Come on, Bonnie. There you go. Comfy? Now, where was I?"

"You were telling me what a wonderfully remorseless man I am," Sensor said.

"Ah yes, now you tell me this . . . how is your Regulator project going now the Willamette action is over?"

"Splendidly," Sensor said. "I'm sure I can get the funding for a headquarters complex in Portland. Superintendent Cory Cantwell will be in charge, at least for the time being."

"You don't think he's the right man for the job?"

"I'm not sure. He's a little laid back. I'd like someone more aggressive. And I have a feeling that he and my former assistant Sarah Milano will marry soon, and that might distract him from his duties. Time will tell, I suppose."

"Indeed, it will," Bickford-Scott said. "On a happy note, I have a new supply of the Beluga caviar, and I'll send you over some, along with some Cuban cigars."

"That's decent of you, Anthony," Sensor said. "I'm running low on both items."

"Good, then I'm just in time. I think Bonnie wants her din-dins, so I'll leave it here for the time being, Jacob. Ta-ta for now. I'll be in touch."

"Yes, goodnight, Tony," Sensor said.

Sensor poked a burning log into place and smiled.

Once again, things were looking up. Damn it all, there was nothing he couldn't do.

CHAPTER 61

The great sheikh Jamari Qadir was dead, assassinated by Zionists, and for Nasim Azar that was a terrible blow. The main source of his income was gone. Azar still had a few thousand dollars in the bank, nowhere enough to keep him in any style. He was forced to rent a mean little house in a mean street in the meanest part of town and had been forced to go begging, cap in hand, to the decimated Jacks of All Trades in Los Angeles.

They told him someone would be in touch to discuss the matter of his poverty.

The man they sent two weeks later was a blind man, the eighty-four-year-old scholar Zaman Al-Mufti, who'd lost his sight when a suicide belt accidentally exploded in his home in Palestine. The Jacks had brought him to California, eager to share in his wisdom. With the old man was the imposing Daud Harbi, a six-foot-four Saudi Arabian executioner, famed in the Arab world for his skill with the *sulthan,* the beheading sword. It was said that Harbi had executed five hundred people, sometimes as many as ten a day. He was a devout Muslim, well versed in the Qur'an, and a cold-hearted killer. He had flown into LAX the day before at the invitation of the Jacks.

The two men Azar had allowed into his home refused coffee, and he took that as a slight. But more disturbing was that the tall man carried something long and curved wrapped in a blanket.

Al-Mufti was dressed in the Western fashion in slacks and a polo shirt, mirrored glasses concealing his empty, burned-out eye sockets. Harbi also wore tan pants and a shirt, but his glittering black eyes were not hidden. The old man took a small leather pouch closed with a drawstring from his pocket. He said, "Nasim Azar, for every back there is a knife. You chose to wield that knife."

Suddenly Azar was frightened. But his voice was steady when he said, "I do not understand."

"A fatwa has been issued by the Jacks of All Trades, calling for your death," Al-Mufti said. "That much do you understand?"

Azar was shocked. Numb. His own voice sounded hollow to him. "Why? What have I done?"

"The saddest thing about betrayal is that it comes from friends, never enemies," the old man said.

"Whom have I betrayed?" Azar said. "Am I not a loyal soldier of Islam?"

Outside in the street a car skidded, a horn honked, and a man yelled.

Al-Mufti said, "Perhaps you once were, Nasim Azar, but no longer. How many pieces of silver did you receive for betraying the mujahideen in the Willamette forest? The tears of the widows bear witness to your terrible crime."

"I betrayed no one," Azar said. "Who dare say I betrayed the mujahideen?"

"Perhaps the holy martyr Ibrahim Rahman for one," the old man said. "I heard his voice in a vision, calling out for vengeance."

"I am wrongly accused," Azar said. "Blind man, you bring a giant to punish me. This is not justice. It is the work of the devil."

Daud Harbi spoke for the first time. "Son of a dog, only you knew the martyred Ibrahim Rahman's plan of attack. Only you could have betrayed him."

Azar was now on the verge of hysteria. "My only sin was not dying with the rest of the brothers that day. There was no betrayal."

"I am deaf," Al-Mufti said. "I do not hear your lies. Show me your hands, Nasim Azar."

Azar stretched out his hands.

"Turn them over. Show me the palms," the old man said.

When Azar did, Al-Mufti untied the leather bag and poured sand into his open hands. "This is the sand of your native land, and you can hold it as you die. Nasim Azar, it is a small mercy I extend to you, and you can but hope that Allah will also be merciful." He pointed to the floor. "Now, kneel you and take the blade."

But Azar was not ready to die. The Smith & Wesson .38 was in the drawer of the side table beside his chair by the window. He made a play for the gun . . . but forgot, or didn't know, that not all victims of the headsman meekly bow their heads and quietly await the sword.

As Azar dashed for the table, Daud Harbi expertly swung the *sulthan*, its razor-sharp, curved edge catching him on the run. The blade hit Azar in the front of his throat, sliced though flesh and bone, and neatly lopped off his head. The head sprang from Azar's shoulders, hit the floor with a dull thud, and rolled into Al-Mufti's feet. The old man kicked it away. It was the head of a traitor and an unholy thing.

Harbi raised the sword high, and blood from the blade ran down his muscular forearm in scarlet rivulets.

"Allahu Akbar!" the executioner yelled.

And Zaman Al-Mufti said, "Praise be to God."

Keep reading for a special excerpt . . .

KNOCKDOWN
by WILLIAM W. JOHNSTONE *and* J. A. JOHNSTONE

*They call him "The Rig Warrior." Name: Barry Rivers.
Occupation: Long-haul trucker. Special skills: Defender
of freedom. Patriot. Government-sanctioned killer.*

A NATION OFF THE RAILS
No one saw the first attack coming. A perfectly
orchestrated assault on a mass-transit railroad line that
left countless Americans dead. Then came more attacks.
More rail systems sabotaged. More civilian lives lost.
Intelligence experts are convinced this is no ordinary
terrorist attack. To pull off something like this, it
would take a deep-state traitor with dark foreign
connections. And to stop them, it will take someone
who isn't afraid to shed blood.

A HERO OFF THE GRID
Enter Barry Rivers, the Rig Warrior. An urban legend
in the intelligence community, Rivers has been living off
the radar for years. But when he sees his country under
attack, he reaches out to his son in the FBI to track down
the enemies in our own government. To these high-
ranking traitors, Rivers is a threat to their global agenda.
But when Rivers revs up his tricked-out 18-wheeler—
and goes after a runaway train on a collision course
with disaster—all bets are off. The war is on. And with
Barry Rivers at the wheel, it's going to be the ultimate
knockdown, drag-out fight for America's future . . .

Look for **KNOCKDOWN,** *on sale now.*

CHAPTER 1

The fat man ran the keen edge of the blade across the ball of his thumb, studied the bead of dark red blood that was the result, and then licked it off.

"You see, my machete is very sharp, *gringo*. You will barely feel a thing when I cut your head off with it."

"Yeah, well, I guarantee you'll feel it when I shove that pigsticker up your *culo* and start twisting it, Pancho."

The man sitting at the table in the corner of the little cantina slurred his words. The mostly empty bottle of tequila in front of him explained why. The fiery liquor he had guzzled down also explained the boldness of his response.

The fat man scowled and stepped closer to the table.

The three men who had been at the bar with him started in that direction as well, as if they sensed that the situation had just become more serious. They couldn't have actually heard the words—not with *Tejano* music blaring in the cantina, mixing with the breathless drone of the announcer calling the soccer game on the TV mounted above the bar and trying to make it more exciting than it really was. No, it was far too loud.

Maybe they smelled the blood.

A big man sitting at the bar turned his head to watch the three *amigos* headed for the table in the corner. He swiveled on the chair and stood up. He towered over everybody else in here, and his shoulders were as wide as an axe handle. Thick slabs of muscle on his arms and shoulders bulged in the fabric of his black T-shirt.

"*Señor*," the bartender said behind him. The big man looked around. The bartender shook his head worriedly and went on in English, "You should not interfere, *señor*. Those men, they are . . . Zaragosa."

The big man frowned.

The bartender lowered his voice even more. The big man could barely hear him as he half-whispered, "Cartel. *Comprende?* Look around."

The big man looked and got what the bartender was talking about. Everybody else in the cantina was doing their best not to even glance in the direction of the looming confrontation in the corner. Nobody wanted to get involved and risk offending the cartel.

"That guy's an American," the big man said. "I'm not gonna just stand by and let him get hurt."

An eloquent shrug from the bartender. He had tried to prevent trouble. No one could blame him now for what might happen.

Over in the corner, the fat man with the machete said, "What did you call me?"

"Are you deaf as well as stupid, Pancho?"

The man at the table reached for the bottle. He had lean, weathered features under close-cropped gray hair. It was difficult to tell how old he was. Anywhere from fifty to seventy would be a good guess.

His hand trembled a little as it closed around the neck of the bottle. Whether the tremor was from age, a neurological condition, or too much to drink was also impossible to say.

The fat man spat a few curses in Spanish, lifted the machete, and slammed it down on the table in front of the *gringo*. The blade bit deeply into the old, scarred wood. The fat man's lips drew back from his teeth in a snarl as he leaned forward.

"I will not cut off your head," he said. "The next time, my blade will cleave your skull down to your shoulders, *viejo*!"

"Ain't gonna be no next time. You really are stupid. Your little knife's stuck, *gordo*!"

At the same time, the big man moved up behind the fat man's three *compadres* and said in a loud voice, "Hey! What're you doing to that old geezer?"

The fat man wrenched at the machete. The old man was right. The blade had embedded itself so deeply in the tabletop that it was stuck.

The old man came up out of his chair like a rattlesnake uncoiling and swung the tequila bottle he held by the neck.

The fat man tried to jerk back out of the way. The old man was too fast. The bottle smacked hard against the side of the fat man's head but didn't break. The impact made the fat man take a quick step to his right, but he caught himself and grinned.

"I'm gonna mess you up, *viejo*."

The old man said, "Oh, crap."

The fat man's three buddies turned toward the big *hombre* who had challenged them. He didn't give them a chance to set themselves. Throwing his arms out wide, he charged them, grabbing the two on the flanks and bulling his shoulder right into the one in the middle. That bull rush swept them all backward into the fat man, who was trying to wrench the machete loose from the table.

It was like a tidal wave of flesh washing over the fat man and knocking him forward into the table. The old man hopped out of the way with a nimbleness that belied his age.

The weight of all four men came down on the table. Its spindly legs snapped, and the whole thing crashed to the floor. The fat man and his *amigos* sprawled on the wreckage. One of the men howled in pain as he got pushed against the edge of the machete and the blade sliced into his leg.

With an athletic grace uncommon in a man of his size, the big *hombre* had caught his balance before he could fall on top of the others. He took a step back and looked at the old man. "We'd better get out of here."

"Not yet," the old man said with a gleam in his eyes. "Pancho and me still got to settle up."

CHAPTER 2

The big man rolled his eyes and then swung around to face the rest of the customers in the dim, smoke-hazed cantina. They were watching with a mixture of keen interest and trepidation, but none of them seemed eager to mix in.

According to the bartender, the fat man and his friends worked for the Zaragosa drug cartel, and nobody wanted to mess in cartel business.

The old man leaned over, caught hold of the fat man's dirty shirtfront with his left hand, pulled him up a little, and used his right hand to slap him hard, back and forth. Before that, the fat man had appeared a little stunned from being knocked down, but the sharp blows knocked his wits back into him.

He roared in anger and used a foot to hook one of the old man's legs out from under him. The two of them grappled together and rolled across the filthy floor.

Two of the other three tried to get up and rejoin the fight. The third man was still yelling as he clamped both hands around his leg, which was bleeding heavily from the machete wound. It looked like he might have nicked an artery.

As the two cartel members scrambled to their feet, the big *hombre* caught them by the neck from behind. The muscles in his arms and shoulders bunched as he slammed the two men together. Their heads *clunked* loudly. Both men came unhinged at the knees and crumpled to the floor again.

The big man gestured toward the bleeder and addressed the room at large in decent Spanish: "Somebody better help him before he bleeds to death."

When he turned his head, he saw that the old man somehow was getting the best of his overweight opponent. The wiry old codger knelt on the fat man's chest and punched him in the face again and again. Blood blurred the fat man's features. The big *hombre* stepped up behind the old man and hooked his hands under his arms.

"Come on," he said. "He's out of it. And we need to be out of here."

The old man was breathing hard. He glared down at the fat man. But after a few seconds, he said, "Yeah, you're right." He shook free of the big man's grip. "Let's go."

With the four cartel members out of action, no one else in the cantina made a move to stop the two *gringos* as they headed for the door. They stepped out into the hot night air. Gravel crunched under their feet as they crossed the parking lot.

The door of the squalid cinder-block building slammed open behind them. The big *hombre* looked back and muttered, "Oh, crap."

The fat man stumbled out of the cantina and waved his

hand, which was holding a pistol. It spurted flame and thundered in the night. The big man sprinted toward the pickup he had driven across the international bridge from Texas earlier in the evening. The old man followed him.

"Where's your car?" the big *hombre* flung over his shoulder.

"Don't have one! I walked across the bridge!"

That could actually be smarter than driving in Mexico, but wandering around a border town at night wasn't a very bright thing to do these days. Such places had always been hotbeds of crime, but now, with the so-called authorities virtually powerless when compared to the cartels, *norteamericanos* risked their lives being anywhere near the border, let alone across it.

At the moment, however, the big *hombre* was glad he had transportation out of here. The fat man was shooting wild, but there was no telling when he might get the range.

"Come with me!" the big man yelled to his newfound companion. He hoped nobody had stolen or slashed his tires while he was in the cantina, or damaged the engine in some way.

The big man unlocked both doors of the pickup with the remote key as they ran toward it. The old man yanked the passenger door open and piled in while the big *hombre* threw himself behind the wheel.

Gravel kicked up not far from the pickup as the bullets came closer. The engine cranked, caught. The big man slammed the truck into gear and peeled out, spraying gravel behind him. A wild turn onto the potholed highway, and he was speeding toward the cluster of high-intensity lights that marked the international bridge a quarter of a mile away.

The big man watched the rearview mirror. No headlights popped into view. That was good. Even if the bridge wasn't busy, crossing would take long enough that the fat man and his friends could catch up if they wanted to. Maybe they were back there attending to the guy who'd sliced his leg open.

"Well, that was a mite exciting," the old man said. He didn't sound drunk anymore.

The big man just glanced over at him and didn't say anything. At the bridge, he guided the pickup into the Ready Lane line behind two other vehicles. The American border guards passed those through fairly quickly. Still no headlights coming up behind the pickup. The old man handed the big *hombre* his driver's license. He put it with his own and handed them to the guard as he pulled up to the now-lowered barrier.

The guard scanned the RFID chips on the licenses and then nodded at the results that came up on his scanner. He asked the usual customs questions about regulated goods they might have with them.

The big man said, "Nope, not a thing."

The guard handed the licenses back, then nodded at his cohort in the control booth, who pushed buttons and started the barrier lifting. The big man waited for it to clear and drove through at an unhurried pace, back onto Texas soil.

He drove through the border city, a garish oasis of lights in the vast darkness of the border country, and pulled into the parking lot of a nondescript motel on the north side of town, away from the border.

He brought the pickup to a stop beside an eighteen-wheeler parked at the edge of the lot, a Kenworth long-hood conventional with an extra-large sleeper behind the cab.

The big *hombre* killed the lights and engine, then sat there in the darkness for a long moment before he turned to the old man and said, "All right, Barry, what the hell was all *that* about?"

Connect with Us

Visit us online at
KensingtonBooks.com
to read more from your favorite authors, see books
by series, view reading group guides, and more.

 Join us on social media

for sneak peeks, chances to win books and prize packs,
and to share your thoughts with other readers.

facebook.com/kensingtonpublishing
twitter.com/kensingtonbooks

Tell us what you think!

To share your thoughts, submit a review,
or sign up for our eNewsletters, please visit:
KensingtonBooks.com/TellUs.